THE WHITE TOWER

Other Books by
James Ramsey Ullman

HIGH CONQUEST
THE STORY OF MOUNTAINEERING

THE OTHER SIDE OF THE MOUNTAIN
AN ESCAPE TO THE AMAZON

MAD SHELLEY

River of the Sun.

Windom's Way.

THE WHITE TOWER

JAMES RAMSEY ULLMAN

J. B. Lippincott Company
Philadelphia & New York

To the memory of
A. F. U.
and
W. I. F.

Chapter 1

Now *they were there again. . . .*

They were in the seventh and last flight, and the city, as they came over it, was no longer a city but a lake of orange fire. There were the bright beams of the searchlights and the tracers rising in a flowing dome against the darkness. There were the swift, scudding shapes of the other planes. In the sudden glare that filled the cockpit Martin Ordway could see the face of his co-pilot, Riggs, bent tensely over the instrument panel. He saw the yellow down on the cheekbones, the blue boy's eyes, the tiny pulse throbbing in the tight line of the jaw.

The orange lake rushed up at them, reached out for them. Then it tilted suddenly away and streamed past below. The chimneys of a factory appeared ahead, rising through the flame like the fingers of a charred hand.

The next moment came Bixler's voice:

"Bombs away!"

. . . and now it was over again.

Ordway pulled toward him. His body thrust hard against the back of his seat as the plane climbed and banked. The ravaged city wheeled away beneath them, throwing up flames and beams and tracers in a fountain of bright fire. Around them the flak exploded, hung suspended for an instant in dark, wreathing puffs against the white shafts of the searchlights, and disappeared. In another few moments they would be above them. Beyond the propellers now there were the stars.

A sword of light cut through the sky. There was a white flash behind Ordway's head, followed by a shattering roar, and he was hurled forward against the bindings of his seat. The plane bucked and lurched. Its two engines coughed and slackened. It seemed to hang motionless in the darkness—disemboweled, trembling, poised to plunge. Ordway braced himself back into his seat. His gloved hands moved from wheel to throttle to controls and his feet worked swiftly among the pedals. The engines caught for an instant, stuttered again, and the nose of the plane went down. Then the engines took hold again. The propellers bit the air.

They levelled off. Ordway pulled the wheel back gently and they began to climb. The flak was beneath them now, and the bright thin scrawl of the tracers; the fires of the burning city were only a faint red glow beneath the pall of smoke that filled the night below. The phosphorescent glow of the instrument dials had gone out, and it was black in the plane. There was no sound except the deep humming of the engines. They sped westward above the dark earth, under the stars.

Martin Ordway removed a glove and passed his hand slowly over his eyes. Then he flicked the key of the interphone jackbox. "Everyone all right?" he asked.

The interphone was dead.

"Ted?" he said, turning.

Riggs, the co-pilot, stirred and mumbled a few words. Ordway could scarcely see him in the darkness, but it seemed to him there was something wrong about the outlines of the boy's neck and shoulders.

"Ted—you've been hit."

"I guess I have." Riggs' voice was low and hoarse.

"Where, do you know?"

"In the back, I think. Sort of high up on the side."

"Does it seem bad?"

Riggs did not answer at once. Ordway tried the interphone again, then removed his throat-mike. "Bix!" he called. "Harry!"

There was no reply. Ordway unfastened his safety belt and leaned over toward Riggs. "Ted," he said.

"Yes?"

8

"Think you can hold your wheel a minute?"

"Sure." The voice was a little stronger. "Sure I can, Marty."

"I'll be right back. Then I'll fix you up."

"I'm okay. It's nothing, really."

Riggs shifted his shoulders slowly, seeming to square himself. His hands moved out and took the wheel before him.

"Just hold her steady," Ordway said.

"Sure, Marty."

Ordway got up and half clambered, half crept between the wheels and down through the entrance to the bombardier's compartment.

"Bix," he said.

There was a faint gleam of shattered glass, the scudding night beyond, and, on the floorplates of the nose before him, a dark, sprawling shape. Taking his flashlight from his overalls, he let its beam fall on the face of Lieutenant Bixler, the bombardier-navigator. For a moment he crouched motionless, peering down at the face. Then he snapped off the beam.

Crawling back between the wheels and the pilots' seats, he stood up and groped his way back into the body of the plane. He was unsteady on his feet after the long hours of sitting and had to brace himself with his hands as he came down the two steps from the cockpit to the radio compartment. Ahead of him he could see dimly two jagged rents in the left wall of the fuselage, through which the wind poured with a low moaning sound.

"Harry," he said.

Sergeant Wasniewicz, the radio-gunner, was seated at his control panel, his head resting on the bench among the coils and dials. Ordway raised it and looked into his face.

"Harry," he said. "Harry."

He jerked down the zipper of the man's overalls and fumbled at the sweatshirt beneath. He had just removed his hand when the nose of the plane lurched violently downward and he, Wasniewicz and the radio apparatus went crashing forward along the floor. He brought up against the steps to the cockpit and lay there a moment, half-stunned and sick with the sensation of falling. Then he pulled himself to a kneeling position, partly climbed and partly slid up the steps and over the back of the pilot's seat, and got a hand on the wheel. He pulled back on it, but it did not budge. He got both hands on it, hooked his knees around the edge of the seat and pulled with all his strength. The wheel moved slowly backward. He felt the angle of their fall lessen, and kept pulling. In a few moments the plane was flying level. Then slowly it began to climb.

He got himself set in his seat and tested the throttles, wheel and pedals. They were all working. But the instrument panel was a dark expanse of shattered glass and plastic and the right-hand engine was misfiring. He worked the gun and fuel-mixture controls, but it still missed. The plane, he suddenly noticed, had developed a slight tilt to the right, and the steel floorboard was trembling violently. Nevertheless, they continued to climb. Their speed seemed only a little below normal.

"Jesus, Marty, I'm sorry."

The sound of Riggs' voice startled him. In the darkness he could see that the boy was sitting motionless in his seat, looking straight ahead. His back was erect, but his head seemed to be awkwardly pulled down between his shoulders.

"Don't worry about it," Ordway said.

"I must have blacked out for a minute."

"How do you feel now?"

"Okay."

"I'm going to fix you up." Ordway took his first-aid kit from the pouch in his parachute harness. "Do you think you can hold the wheel while I put on a dressing?"

Riggs did not answer.

"Ted—"

It was a long moment before the boy spoke, and when he did it was not in answer to Ordway's question.

"How're Harry and Bix?" he asked suddenly.

"They're all right, Ted."

"No they're not. They're washed up."

Ordway took his own wheel between his knees, pulled off his gloves and began opening the dressing-packet.

"I'm washed up too, Marty," Riggs said.

"The hell you are."

The boy was silent. Still holding the wheel with his legs, Ordway leaned over toward him, the dressing in one hand, his flashlight in the other. He turned on the beam.

10

Riggs' helmeted head was sunk down deeply between his shoulders. From under the helmet a few strands of tow-colored hair straggled down over the paper-white skin of his forehead. His eyes were open and very blue. His mouth was open too, and from it a gleaming crimson stain spread downward, over his chin, across the front of his overalls, into his lap. A cluster of minute pinkish bubbles rose and fell between his lips as the breath sucked in and out.

Ordway snapped off the beam and shifted back into his seat. "We'll be home soon, Ted," he said.

He levelled off the plane and advanced the throttles a little. The left engine responded, but the right one sputtered and stalled. After a few moments he got it going again, but it was missing badly now. The plane's list to the right was more pronounced.

He snapped on the flashlight again and moved the beam slowly over the instrument panel. Some of the fuel and electrical gages were still working, but the navigational instruments had been knocked out. The altimeter was locked immobilely at eleven thousand feet, and the needle of the compass swung in long idle arcs from its pivot pin. Leaning forward over the wheel, Ordway peered into the night ahead. There was no other plane in sight. He swung the bomber's nose to right and left, so that he could see to the sides and the rear; but there were no planes. There was not even a vapor trail streaking the darkness.

He judged that they were at about nine thousand feet and heading in a southwesterly direction. The earth slipped past below—black, still and lightless. The last orange glow of the burning city had faded from the sky behind them, and the night towered vast and umblemished from the horizons. Ahead of them was darkness, above them the stars.

Perhaps five minutes had passed when Riggs spoke again.

"Marty—" he murmured.

"Yes, Ted?"

"You'll write Frances, won't you?"

"You'll write her yourself."

The boy was silent awhile.

"She's some girl, Frances," he said at last. "You know something, Marty: I never slept with her." There was another pause. "I never slept with any real girl. Only a few whores."

His voice was very low but clear. Presently he shifted his shoulders a little, so that his head seemed to sink even more deeply between them. The two men sat silently as the plane droned on.

"Marty—"

"Better not talk," Ordway said.

"You know, this isn't too lousy a way to go, Marty. Up in a crate. Stars and bombs and all that crap. Guys like us aren't good for anything else anyhow."

"Try to go to sleep, Ted," Ordway said.

"Guys like us after the war—what the hell are we good for? Just so many more jerks looking for jobs. Flying, that's all we know. Flying and dropping eggs and killing a few Krauts. That's us, Marty. That's all there is, there isn't any more. Just us and Old Man Percentage, sitting up there on a cirro-stratus, working on his double entry." Riggs coughed gently and shifted again in his seat. "My pop had it all figured out: when I got home I was going to go to business school and learn to be a certified public accountant. A C.P.A. Sure . . ."

He coughed again and was quiet. Another five minutes passed; perhaps ten. At intervals Ordway looked across at him through the darkness, but the boy sat hunched and still.

Suddenly he spoke again:

"First thing I'm going to do when I get home, though, is marry that girl, Marty. . . . Know what I always call her? Biscuit. Her name's Frances, of course, but I call her Biscuit. . . . Isn't that the goddamndest name for a girl? . . . Biscuit. . . ."

Riggs, Theodore L., 1 Lt., C-P, 21, Burbank, Calif.
Bixler, John R., 2 Lt., B-N, 23, Murfreesboro, Tenn.
Wasniewicz, Harry, T/Sgt., RO-MG, 24, Waban, Mass.

The staff sergeant in S-1 would make the prescribed notations and turn the page.

Ordway, Martin F., Capt., P, 31, Larchmont, N.Y. . . .

Ordway peered into the blackness off to the left. He had seen a whitish, faintly luminous streak that might be the vapor trail of another plane. He banked toward it, passed through it, and swung back on his course. It was mist. Other shreds and wisps of mist were drifting past him now, undulating like slender gray scarves in the darkness.

The plane droned on. The left engine maintained a steady hum; the right one rose, stuttered, fell and rose again. Behind him Ordway could hear the air pouring through the rents in the fuselage and the gentle creaking of the bomb-bay doors that Riggs had not had time to close. The long scarves of mist came up out of black nothingness, streaked past the plane in sudden wild gray tumult and disappeared in black nothingness behind. Peering down between them, he searched for a familiar landmark: the Black Forest, the Lake of Constance, the lights to the south that would mean the Swiss frontier. But he could distinguish nothing. The distant earth flowed by, dark and featureless, under the lean, trembling oblongs of the wings.

Riggs, Theodore L. KIA.

Bixler, John R. KIA.

Wasniewicz, Harry. KIA.

And the prescribed notations.

He was not thinking of the dead men. He was not thinking at all. He sat staring, unseeing, at his shapeless gloved hands on the wheel, and the roar of wind and engines seemed to be flowing through him in an immense dark tide. He felt tired and very old.

He was old. He was old and spent and thirty-one. There were places in the world on that October night—well, a few places anyhow—where men of thirty-one were still young men; where they were laughing and drinking, dancing to swing bands, falling in love for the first time, hopefully beginning the practice of their professions; but those places were not the cockpit of a shattered bomber over ravaged Europe, and there were no ME-109's prowling the dark skies and no dead friends dripping their lifeblood out upon the steel floorplates around them. Years are not the only auditors of a life. If age is a brown, creased face, hard eyes and a nerveless hand, this man was old. If it is a torpor of the body and a slow strangulation of the mind, he was old. And if it is tiredness, he was old. For he was utterly tired. He had been tired for so long that he could scarcely remember the days when he had not been tired; when he had still possessed the will to do, to act, to achieve; when a bombing plane had been more to him than a trembling, roaring prison of steel and sound, and war more than an endlessly and meaninglessly repeated pattern of engine-drone, bomb-burst, death.

Martin Ordway was tired in his bones. And he was tired in his soul.

Until a few minutes ago the night had been the same as any other night. You walked out to the airstrip in the cool darkness. You wisecracked with the ground crew, waited for the signal, stepped up the R.P.M.'s until the roaring filled the wide sky and the crannies of your brain. You took off. You flew, hour after hour, through a roaring emptiness. And then at last, suddenly, it was no longer emptiness but roaring, shattering brightness, and you banked and dove and went over. You dropped your eggs. You dropped them, thinking about wind velocity and flak and directional equations and the delicate shifting hairlines of Bix's bombsight. You dropped them, not thinking of the toppling stone, the scream, the legless man, the breastless woman, the faceless child; not thinking of the one that went astray through the roof of the maternity hospital. You dropped them, and tried to believe you were without blackness and horror in your heart, because you lived in a certain kind of a world in which dropping them was necessary, and therefore right. You dropped them for the Four Freedoms and the United Nations and the Dignity of Man and the column of check-marks under your name in the H.Q. log-book. You dropped them in the bright orange lake and raced for the emptiness and the darkness.

In the darkness it was safe again. It was almost safe, almost quiet again. Planes around you were hit, buckled, exploded, went down in quick thin streaks of fire; but you were not hit. It was not yet your turn. It would never be your turn. . . . And then it was your turn. The turn of Riggs, Theodore L., Lt., C-P, 21, Burbank, Calif.; of Bixler, John R., 2 Lt., B-N, 23, Murfreesboro, Tenn.; of Wasniewicz, Harry, T/Sgt., RO-MG, 24, Waban, Mass. They had met the Great Imponderable of war, committed the one ineradicable and irremediable error of being in the wrong place at the wrong time. . . . Or was it the right place at the wrong time? Or the wrong place at the right time? . . . In any case, a certain number of smallish, jagged fragments of metal, moving at high velocity, had passed through their pelvises, their small intestines, the membranes of their throats and the sockets of their eyes. They lay in a variety of strange positions that their mothers would not have liked to see them in. Their blood dribbled away across the steel and aluminum floorplates of the plane and out into the dark roar of the slipstream. And they died.

Ordway, Martin F., Capt., P, 31, Larchmont, N.Y., on the other hand, had not died. The young men were gone, but the old man, the old tired young man of thirty-one, was still there. The Great Imponderable had come and gone; it had passed, swiftly and invisibly, in smallish, jagged fragments of metal; it had whispered, "No, not here. No, not yet." He was spared (perhaps) to return once more. He was spared to feel the smooth hard earth of the airstrip under the wheels and hear the roar of the engines die at last and clamber stiffly out and walk slowly away in the cool darkness; to smoke a cigarette and taste hot coffee and empty his bladder; to listen to Bob Hope and Gracie Allen on the radio and inspect the latest Grable and Hayworth pinups on the board walls of the mechanics' hut; to stand against a long, dim, man-swarming bar and drink and drink; to fall, clothes and all, shoes and all, nausea and D.F.C. ribbon and all, across a cot and sleep and sleep. And dream . . .

A sudden sharp tremor passed through the plane and entered his body. He opened his eyes. The shattered dials of the instrument panel were gleaming faintly in the darkness. Above them, the glass of the windscreen was opaque with moisture.

The automatic wipers were jammed. He fumbled at the mechanism with a clumsy gloved hand, and presently they began to move slowly and jerkily across the glass. The stars were gone. The earth was gone. The plane was boring through a weaving ocean of gray mist.

He pulled back on the wheel and felt the nose go up. The engines held for a moment; then the right one missed and sputtered, and the plane jerked around and began to tilt. He forced it back sharply, opening and closing the throttles and manipulating the ailerons. The plane swung back level, dipped again, swung back again. Its righthand motor thumping and faltering, it plunged on into the clouds.

Ordway sat perfectly still. It was his hands, his feet, the blind pilot's instinct, that had caught and righted the plane. There had been no mind or will in it; no fear, no hope, no resolve. He was lost. He was lost, and he was sitting quietly, almost peacefully,

15

waiting, and what he was waiting for he did not know. Speed, altitude, direction, the three dimensions of a flyer's world, were no more than the lettering on the faintly gleaming faces of the shattered dials. He glanced at his watch. More than an hour had passed since they pulled out of the bomb run. The plane might still be over Bavaria or Wurttemberg, cutting great aimless arcs through a hostile sky. It might be over France, Switzerland, the Rhine valley, the Rhone, or even winging swiftly southward toward Italy and the sea. He did not know, nor did it seem to him greatly to matter. Certainly it did not matter to First Lieutenant Theodore Riggs, Second Lieutenant John Bixler or Technical Sergeant Harry Wasniewicz.

He reached forward and opened the emergency panel of the windscreen, and a torrent of mist poured in a cold tide through the cockpit. He felt it against his face, in his nose and mouth and eyes, in the folds and crevices of his clothing. He drew in a deep breath against its onslaught and moved his tongue slowly around the circumference of his lips. It did not smell or taste of the sea. And yet . . . body and senses were tense now, waiting. Somewhere, he had known that smell and that taste before; somewhere he had felt that same curious fusion of wind and mist pouring in a cold, pure tide against his face, pouring through his hair, his clothing, his skin, his very bones and blood. Somewhere, sometime, very long ago . . .

Martin Ordway raised his eyes.

Through the filmed windscreen and the blurred whirl of the propellers he could see only great banks of vapor streaming toward him through the darkness. They extended away before him, wave upon wave, depth beyond depth, into the miles of night. Beyond them were space and emptiness. . . . And then, in the next instant, his eyes straining and his heart suddenly wildly pounding, he knew that it was not emptiness. For an imperceptible moment the mist seemed to thin; for a fraction of time so brief that it was scarcely a part of time at all, the encompassing gray ocean parted, revealing the night beyond. . . . Something was there. Something was there, behind the miles and the darkness, filling the sky and the night. It was a thing without form or substance, the merest white evanescent gleam in the emptiness and nothingness of space. His eyes could not actually see it; his mind could not en-

16

compass it. But it existed. *It was there.* Unlighted by sun or stars, it rose like a monstrous beacon into the sky, burning through the darkness with an inner incandescent power of its own. . . .

The mist closed in again. Gray night and emptiness closed in again. Ordway sat motionless, listening to the new sound that filled the plane and staring at the blade of the righthand propeller that stood up in the darkness beyond the windscreen, rigid and still. The plane lurched sharply to the right again and began to fall.

It did not seem to him that he was making a decision. What he did was without physical effort, without plan, without conscious direction of his will. He picked himself up from the floor of the cockpit, where he had been thrown. He half clambered, half crept past the dark, still figure in the other seat and the dark, still figure on the floorplates behind. He reached the open bomb-bay, crouched over it and felt the great waves of air battering up at his face and clothing.

He jumped.

There were the torn fuselage, the retracted wheels and the black swinging doors of the bomb-bay. There were the great gray wings in the gray mist. Then there was only the mist. His entrails contracted in the nausea of falling, and his head and shoulders revolved gently downward past his legs with the liquid rhythm of a high diver in a slow-motion film. There was no earth, no sky. He plunged downward through gray space.

Then the nausea passed. The sensation of falling passed. He closed his eyes and felt the tides of air sweeping across his face and body. He spread his arms wide and held them trembling against the battering flood that sought to pinion them back to his sides. . . . The ring, his airman's instinct told him; it's time to pull the ring. . . . But he did not pull it. Behind his closed eyes he was falling again through the clean blue sky above a little Connecticut airfield. It was his first jump, and he had bailed out quick and neat, and he was falling and he was not afraid. Until it came time to pull the ring. Then fear had gripped him; air and earth had gone black and swimming before his eyes and his muscles had locked. He couldn't find the ring! He couldn't reach it! He gave a mighty cry, alone in the blue air. He reached it. He pulled it.

How many times had he pulled it since? Twice. No, three times.

Over the patterned rectangles of Kelly Field; over the slate-green Channel; over the brown Tunisian hills. You jumped, you fell, you pulled. You were jumping again, and falling and pulling again— each time the same. Until the last time. Until the time when you were not even falling any more, but only skimming gently through gray space; with no earth and no sky; with your eyes closed and your arms flung wide and the roar of the night a soft, far-off whisper in your ears; with no strength to pull and no will to pull. Until this time . . .

There was the violent, familiar jerk and the sharp stab of pain in his genitals. He heard the creak of canvas webbing and saw the great ghostly flower curving above him in the darkness. He looked down incuriously at the gloved finger in the steel ring at his waist. . . . No, not this time, he thought. Not yet. . . . He closed his eyes again.

When he reopened them he was no longer in the mist. A great ceiling of gray stratus clouds filled the sky above him, but the air through which he was falling was clear and black and he could see the dark earth below. It seemed to be a deep valley into which he was descending. Its level floor extended for perhaps three miles in one direction, a mile in the other, and he could faintly discern the contours of forests, fields and a winding road. Beyond them, on every side, the earth appeared to curl abruptly upward like the sides of a cup, climbing in dark forests and scree-slopes to the gray ceiling of the clouds. Above the cloudline there was nothing. The mountains—if they had been mountains—that he had seen before from the plane were invisible in fog and night.

He floated softly downward. A faint stirring of the air set him gently revolving and made a whispering sound in the silk shroud lines. Then the moving air passed on and it was utterly still. He hung motionless in his harness.

He seemed to be falling faster now. The ground was coming up to meet him, and he could see trees and rocks and fences and the black glint of a stream. The rutted earth of the road stretched away before him. First it passed between open fields; then it threaded a stand of timber and crossed the stream on a tiny bridge; then it curved suddenly back upon itself and wound up the side of a gently sloping knoll. On the top of the knoll there was a building. It was a big building, low and rambling, with many

18

white, pointed gables raised against the dark mountainside beyond. A single yellow prick of light gleamed from one of its windows. A feather of gray smoke rose from its chimney and hung motionless in the night.

Martin Ordway's eyes moved slowly from the building to the road to the bridge across the stream, then back to the building again. . . . Yes, of course, he thought. You have known all along where you were going. It is the same, and you have come back. It is the valley, and you have come back at last. . . .

The pounding of his heart swelled until it seemed to fill the darkness between the earth and sky.

Then he hit the ground. It was, it seemed to him, the lightest landing he had ever made. He was conscious of no sharp concussion, no dragging and scraping and wild tugging of the chute, but merely of a gentle, almost imperceptible transition from the element of air to the element of earth. He was lying on cool, grassy turf, and the silk shroud of the chute piled up into a still white billow beside him. But when he tried to get to his feet he did not seem to be able to. He lay motionless where he had fallen, watching the clouds. He listened to the sound of the footsteps approaching along the packed earth of the road. He looked up at the seamed brown face with the blue eyes that seemed to be bending over him.

"Hello, Andreas," he murmured.

Then there was darkness.

Chapter 2

. . . But still, behind the darkness, there was Andreas Benner. There were Peter Zurneisen and Christian Mehrwalder and Anton and Matthias Kronig and all the rest of them with their wonderful Valasian and Oberland names standing on the station platform as the little rack-rail train rounded the last steep tree-banked curve and clanked to a halt. Behind them were the prim square, the single shop-lined street, the dormered roofs and brown church steeple of Kandermatt. Still farther behind, tiering up like an immense painted cyclorama in the summer sunlight, were the meadows and the forests, the glaciers and the peaks.

Benner had come forward diffidently, his nailed boots scraping on the wooden platform; but his smile was warm and his grip tight as he shook hands.

"Willkommen, Herr Martin. It is good to see you back."

"Thanks, Andreas. It's good to be back."

"Your father is not with you this summer?"

"No, he's in America."

"But you will be climbing again?"

"Oh, yes."

"Good. Then perhaps I shall come to see you tomorrow at the Gasthof?"

"Fine," Martin said.

There was a bus from the station to the inn, but he had merely thrown his two bags into it and then set out on foot. First he stopped at Frau Rushli's tiny confection shop and bought a thick brown slab of chocolate; then he walked slowly down the narrow, cobbled street, looking at the boots and ropes and cuckoo clocks and carved wooden figures that filled the windows. Then, almost before he knew it, the stores were gone. There were no longer cobbles under his feet, but packed earth; he was passing between prim farmhouses and fenced barnyards, and ahead of him lay meadows and forests. The village, the railroad, Europe, the whole world dropped away behind him as he walked along the winding road into the valley of Kandermatt.

It had been hot in Paris in that early summer of 1932. Hot as he had thought only New York could be hot. The lawns of the Bois and the Luxembourg spread brittle and gray under the baking sun, pedestrians' heels sank inch-deep into the soft asphalt of the boulevards, and the lecture halls and classrooms of the Beaux Arts reeked of damp chalk and perspiration. To make things still worse, the examinations had been the hardest ever. Hour after hour, day after day, he had sat hunched over his problem sheets and drawing board, while the fat, languid flies droned around his head and the sweat oozed out from his wrists and smudged his designs; and when at last it was all over he was limp and stale. He had not even waited for his marks or for the Saturday night parties that were to celebrate the end of the semester. The next morning at eight o'clock he was sitting in a second-class compartment of a southbound P.L.M. express.

He had scarcely noticed the dusty-green countryside flowing past—the fields and villages, the vineyards and cathedrals, the Seine, the Aube, the Saône. He read the *Paris Herald* for a while. (The Republicans had renominated Hoover at Chicago; Hindenburg had given his legal O.K. to the Nazi party's brown uniforms; the Washington Senators were two games ahead of the Yankees.) Then he turned the pages of a Tauschnitz mystery. (This time it was a munitions magnate and prussic acid.) Then he let the book fall to his lap and slept. When he awakened a Swiss customs official was tapping him lightly on the shoulder, and a distant range of mountains hung like a great white comber against the darkening evening sky.

You changed trains at Basle, and again at Berne, and again at Interlaken. Each time the train was smaller, the grades steeper and the locomotive whistle shriller and lonelier in the mountain night. And then at last it was morning, and the sun was shining again, but gently and sparklingly now, from a cool, deep-blue sky; and there were the station platform and the village sliding silently around the curve ahead. And then the train was gone, the station and the village were gone, and there were only the meadows and the forests and the peaks, and all the rest of the world was gone —remote, forgotten and improbable beyond the valley walls.

He had been in Kandermatt for only three weeks the previous summer, before his father had left for Cherbourg and home and he had begun his architectural studies at the Beaux Arts. But as he walked alone now along the winding road he remembered each curve and straightaway, each field and fence and tree as clearly as if it were home to which he was returning. For perhaps three-quarters of a mile the road followed a small stream between open pastures; then it crossed the stream on a wooden bridge, curved through a dark stand of timber and emerged into the open again on the other side. Ahead of him, on the summit of a low green knoll, he saw the sprawling wings and sharp white gables of the inn.

Voices came from the tennis court at the foot of the slope, and he cut over across the grass to the wire backstop. A young man and a girl were alone on the court, playing singles—running hard, hitting hard and shouting taunts at each other between shots. The young man, on the far side of the net, was of about his own age. He was dressed only in sneakers and shorts and had a power-fully muscled, deeply sunbrowned body, pleasant, regular features and curling yellowish hair. The girl was three or four years younger —tall and straight, with long tanned arms and legs, a mass of cop-per-colored curls and a slender body that was almost, but not quite, ready to turn into the body of a woman. Martin watched silently for a few moments while they volleyed. Then a hard-hit ball shot past the girl and skidded into the backstop.

"Out," she called.

"In," said Martin.

The girl looked around in annoyed surprise. But in almost the same instant the frown faded and her gray-green eyes went wide.

"Binks!" she cried.

"Hello, Carla."

22

He came around the backstop, and she ran to him and took his hands. The young man in the far court leaped the net and came running too.

"Martin—du alter Lausbube!"

"How are you, Stefan?"

They shook hands. They all talked at once. They sat in the grass on the edge of the court and talked and talked.

Then Carla broke off suddenly. "What are you staring at?" she asked.

"You," Martin said.

"What's the matter with me?"

"Your pigtails. They're gone."

"Of course they're gone, silly. You don't expect a grown woman of fifteen to go around wearing pigtails?"

"Certainly not, gnädiges Fräulein."

"Perhaps I should explain, Martin," said Stefan Raudiger, "that since you have last seen her Fräulein Dehn has become the femme fatale of Vienna."

"Very funny, I'm sure," Carla snapped at him. Then she turned back to Martin. "No, really, Martin—I am grown up now. I am a woman. Of course Stefan here cannot understand such things, but you will treat me with a little respect, won't you?"

"Aber natürlich, gnädiges Fräulein."

Stefan laughed. For a moment Carla looked sternly from one to the other, and then she laughed too. "Oh Binks, Binks, it's so good to see you!" She put out both hands and pulled him to his feet. "Come on—we'll go up to the inn."

"How about your game?"

"Piffle with the game. I had him five-two anyhow."

"I don't wonder, the way you call his shots."

"How dare you say such a thing! . . . And besides, how could I know someone was looking?"

The three of them laughed again. And arm and arm they went up to the inn.

There were the meadows and the peaks and the summer sunlight. There were Martin Ordway and Stefan Raudiger and Carla Dehn. . . .

They followed the cool forest paths beside the Aarn, and the sound of the stream was a deep silver rumbling in their ears. They sat on a smooth-topped boulder just above the spray, munching cheese and bologna sandwiches and drinking cold tea from Carla's thermos. Through the narrow gash that the Aarn cut between the treetops they could see the towering gray and white shapes of the surrounding mountains: the Karlsberg, the Rotalp, the Wunderhorn, the Graf and Gräfin, the Dornelberg, the Himmelshorn, and behind and above all the rest, like an immense white cloud rising from the ridges, the still, gleaming summit of the Weissturm.

"You go up the Dürren Glacier," Stefan said, pointing. "Then you cross a half-mile scree-slope and climb straight up, and you come out on the south ridge of the Karlsberg. . . ."

Martin nodded. For a long while he remained motionless, his hands clasped about his long legs, his dark eyes squinting upward. But it was not the Karlsberg at which he was staring.

Then they were in the dining room of the inn, and the sun streamed in long shafts through the great plate-glass window and struck sparklingly on the chartreuse carpet and pewter-laden shelves. The two stuffed ibex heads eyed each other malevolently from their opposite walls. A clattering of chinaware filled the room, and the waitresses, in flowered shirtwaists and dirndls, darted between the tables and in and out the swinging kitchen doors.

The Bauers, with their five blond, saucer-eyed children, were at the table in the corner; then came the Wilsons, Carla with her mother and father, the Jacquimots, and Major Austen-Fellowes of the British Alpine Club, with his beagle and special bottle of Amontillado. Martin and Stefan, who was also alone, shared the first table in the next row, followed by Herr Doktor Justitzrat Naffziger and his wife, Miss Snapes, the elderly schoolteacher from Manchester, and the three well-nourished couples from Rotterdam. Beyond them were the "transient" tables, for the use of guests of a week or less, and in the far corner that of Herr and Frau Knubel, owners and proprietors of the Gasthof zum Blauen Himmel.

On Fridays lunch was served a half-hour later than usual, because the second morning train, which arrived at twelve-forty, usually brought a large delegation of weekenders. The "regulars," however, were always in the dining room before their arrival. They could hear the bus stop on the terrace and the sound of scraping feet and thudding baggage in the foyer; then everyone looked up as Herr Knubel appeared in the doorway, shepherding the newcomers. A few of them would start for the empty tables, but Herr Knubel invariably held up a polite hand and unobtrusively blocked their way until they were all assembled and quiet. Suddenly, with a restrained yet commanding gesture, he turned and extended his arm toward the plate-glass window and the valley and mountains beyond.

"*Panoram!*" he announced succinctly.

Then the weekenders sat down to their *Heringsalat* and eggs with noodles.

Then the three of them were sitting on the carpeted stairs, looking down across the foyer into the crowded lounge. The four-piece orchestra, brought up from Interlaken especially for the evening, ended *Wienerblut* with an off-key flourish and scraped disconsolately through *Night and Day.*

"I wish there was someone to dance with," Stefan said.

Martin nodded sadly. "They're all either children or grandmothers."

Carla rattled the folds of her long taffeta skirt and drummed lightly on the bannister in time to the music. "I wonder if either of you gentlemen would get me a drink?" she inquired.

"Sure," Martin said. "What do you want? Lemonade? Perrier?"

"I think I'll have a whisky, please."

"What?"

"A whisky, please."

"Oh yes, of course. Does madame prefer it with siphon or plain water?"

"Neat, thank you."

Martin crossed the foyer and lounge to the bar and ordered a dubonnet. Returning to the stairs he presented the glass with a bow.

"Thank you," said Carla. She raised her glass and looked from one to the other of them with cool gray-green eyes. "May you both find charming dancing partners, *messieurs.*"

She sipped the drink appreciatively.

"Good whisky?" asked Martin.

"Very nice. A trifle sharp, though. What brand is it?"

"Rotgut."

"Rotgut? . . . Oh, that is an American brand perhaps?"

"One of our finest. Don't you like it?"

"Yes, it's very nice; but a wee bit sharp. I think I prefer Haig and Haig."

"Yes, the Haig is very nice too."

The orchestra had switched to *Parlez Moi d'Amour*, and they sat for a while, listening. Martin fished a package of Camels from his pocket and offered one to Stefan.

"Thanks," said Stefan.

"Thank you," said Carla.

She took one and tapped it neatly on her thumbnail, and after a moment's hesitation Martin grinned and gave her a light. She drew in a deep breath, blew it out quickly and coughed. Simultaneously there was another, more authoritative cough behind them and Herr Doktor Justitzrat Naffziger came thumping down the stairs.

Martin and Stefan got to their feet to let him pass. Carla jumped up too and swung around quickly to get the cigarette behind her back. The hem of her skirt sent the half-filled dubonnet glass tinkling down the steps; then she backed into the bannister railing and dropped the cigarette with a quick cry. There was a sudden smell of burning varnish and taffeta.

"Good evening, Herr Doktor," Martin and Stefan said together.

Herr Doktor Justitzrat Naffziger stopped and looked at them. Then he looked at the cigarette butt and the broken liquor glass. Then he looked at Carla.

"Unverschämt!" he said.

They walked up through the sun-flecked forests to the long slopes of gorse and juniper above. They threaded their way cautiously among the crevasses of the glaciers, floundered across the scree and boulder heaps, followed, roped and panting, after Andreas Benner, up the steep pitches of cliffs and ridges. They lay stretched at full length on the warm rock of sunlit ledges, squinting at the toy world of the valley below and the white wilderness of the peaks above.

"Andreas—"

26

"Ja?"

"Let's try it sometime?"

"Try what?"

"The White Tower."

The guide relighted his stub of a pipe and shook his head slowly. "The Weissturm, it is not like the other mountains, Herr Martin."

"I know it's not. That's why we want to try it."

"One must be a very strong and experienced climber for such a thing. I had been up every peak in the Oberland many times before I even thought of trying the Weissturm."

"And even then you couldn't make it?"

Benner shook his head again. "No one has ever made it from the Kandermatt side."

"But there always has to be a first time, doesn't there?" asked Carla.

"Perhaps."

They sat for a long while, watching the afternoon shadows gather in the valley and creep slowly up the mountainsides. At last they too were in shadow, and it grew suddenly cold. But the sun still struck fire on the white summit behind them as they tramped the long route down to the inn.

Sunday afternoons—occasionally on other days as well, but always on Sunday afternoons—they walked up the shady Aarntal Path and had tea with Nicholas Radcliffe. Radcliffe was an English geologist who lived in an isolated chalet halfway up the side of the valley, with an enormous library, an even more enormous collection of rock specimens and a foursquare and formidable old Derbyshire housekeeper called Mrs. Meach. Although only in his middle forties, he was already bald, except for a shaggy, sandy-gray fringe above the ears. His face was weathered and thin as an ax blade, with keen, inquiring blue eyes and a great bold beak of a nose. . . . "Like a vegetarian vulture's," Carla had once described it. . . . In that summer of 1932 he had already lived in Kandermatt for five years, and he knew the valley and the mountains above it as well as the oldest and most experienced of the guides.

They sat in the disordered book-choked study, drinking the sweet weak English tea and munching the hot buttered scones that Mrs. Meach kept ferrying in from the kitchen. Then they went out to the verandah steps and sat looking at the great mountains beyond the valley.

"Climb anything this week?" Radcliffe asked.

"Nothing much," said Carla. "The Rotalp again. And Tuesday Andreas took us halfway up the Gräfin by the east ridge."

"I'd call that a pretty fair climb myself."

Carla shrugged. "It's all right for beginners, I suppose."

"There's only one mountain we really care about," Martin said quietly.

"And which is that?"

"The White Tower."

The older man seemed about to smile. But he didn't smile. "Of course it is," he said.

"Have you ever tried to climb it?"

Radcliffe seemed to hesitate a moment. "No," he said quietly, "I never have."

"Why not? It seems strange, after all the climbing you've done—"

"Yes, it is strange in a way, I suppose."

"Don't you want to try it?"

There was another short pause before the Englishman answered. "Once in a great while I almost think I do," he said. Then he smiled. "But we pre-Paleolithic fossils have to leave something for the next generation, you know. And besides, I'm afraid Mrs. Meach would take a very dim view of the proceedings."

Presently he went inside, brought out his binoculars and showed them the various routes that had been attempted on the mountain and how high each attempt had carried. Then Carla, Stefan and Martin passed the binoculars around. Each of them had a route which he favored, and they described them in detail and argued.

"That's the way old Mummery wanted to go," Radcliffe nodded, as Martin carefully detailed his proposed line of ascent. "But he was killed out in India before he ever got a whack at it."

Nicholas Radcliffe had been an accomplished mountaineer in his younger years and had climbed with two of the famous British Himalayan expeditions of the early twenties. More recently his activity had been largely confined to long foothill explorations of rock formations and glaciers; but he still contributed frequent articles to alpine as well as geological journals, and his knowledge of the technique and history of mountaineering was encyclopedic. On those quiet, sunlit afternoons on the verandah of his chalet he would talk to his three young visitors about the great climbs and climbers of the past. About Edward Whymper and his titanic, tragic battle with the Matterhorn. About Alfred Mummery inching up the "impossible" marble-smooth precipices of the Chamonix Needles. About De Saussure on Mont Blanc, Hudson Stuck on McKinley, Fitzgerald on Aconcagua, the Duke of the Abruzzi on the Mountains of the Moon.

But most of all he talked of Everest—and George Leigh Mallory. He had known Mallory well; had himself, in fact, been a member of the celebrated 1924 Everest expedition and with his own eyes seen the great climber, with his young companion, Andrew Irvine, creep upward along a skyline ridge, a scant eight hundred feet beneath the summit of the world, and disappear forever into the mist. Again and again he and the other climbers had tried to struggle up after them to the summit pyramid of the mountain. Each time they had gone upward through cold and snow and bitter winds of space, to the very limits of their endurance; and each time they had failed. After eight years, the fate of the two men remained as complete a mystery as on the day they vanished.

"Do you think they made the top?" Carla asked.

Radcliffe shrugged. "I don't know, of course. I like to think so. If any human being ever deserved to make it, it was George Mallory."

"He must have been a great mountaineer."

"He was more than a great mountaineer, my dear. He was a great man. A consecrated man." Nicholas Radcliffe paused a moment, remembering. "He was thirty-eight that last summer, which is no longer so very young for high climbing. But in his heart and spirit he was younger than any of us. When we were pinned down in the lower camps he used to pace up and down hour after hour like some sort of caged animal, burning with the desire to do, to act, to conquer. And then at other times he would sit quietly and apart, staring up at the mountain like—well—almost as the three of you are staring up at the White Tower right now. When you came near him his eyes were like deep blue ice, but you knew that inside he was on fire."

"Why do you think he wanted to climb it so terribly?" Martin asked.

"Why do you three want to climb the White Tower?"

Martin was silent for a while, his dark eyes squinting upward. "I don't know," he said.

"Mallory knew. And I've always believed it was his knowing, more than anything else, that made him a great man. I was with him once when he gave the answer. It was in Albert Hall, in London, when he was giving a lecture about the 1922 expedition, from which he had just returned, and when he had finished speaking the floor was thrown open for questions. Most of the questions were the usual sort—about routes and equipment and weather and the use of oxygen and so on. And then someone stood up in the back of the audience—it was a young girl, as I remember it, not much older than Carla here—and she said: 'I think I understand *how* you try to climb Everest, Mr. Mallory, but I still don't see *why* you want to climb it.'

"Most of the crowd laughed. But Mallory didn't laugh. He stood there on the platform for a little while, thinking out his answer. And then he told them.

" 'I want to climb it,' he said, 'because it is there.' "

As the sun sloped away toward the western ridges Radcliffe would bring out his flute and sit on the steps playing Mozart, Schubert and Debussy. And still later, Carla, Stefan and Martin would march singing down the cool forest aisles to the valley and the inn. At first the only German songs of which Martin knew the words were *Die Guten Kamaraden* and *Heidenröslein*, and Stefan's and Carla's English repertory consisted exclusively of *Swanee River*; but as the summer passed they learned each other's songs. And they learned many other things as well.

They knew the pastures and the forests, the paths and the streams. But best of all they knew and loved the still, empty world above the tree line. In a tiny green pocket among the rocks near the terminal moraine of the Dürren Glacier was a squat stone shelter known as the Heilweg Hut, which had been built by the Swiss Alpine Club for the convenience of climbers of the near-by peaks. This they made their headquarters for their forays onto the surrounding ridges and glaciers, planning their routes there, eating

30

their lunches and teas, sprawling relaxed on the springy, sweet-smelling moss when they returned in the late afternoons from their explorations and ascents.

And once it happened that they spent the night there.

They had been exploring all day along the tumbled south ridge of the Himmelshorn, but lost their route on the way down, and when at last they reached the hut it was already after seven and the sun had set.

"We had better keep right on going," Carla said.

Stefan shook his head. "It would be night before we could get down off the boulders, and we haven't even a flashlight. One of us would be sure to break a leg."

"But Father and Mother—"

"A daughter one day late is better than no daughter at all."

"But—"

She had argued, but not very hard, and they had stayed at the hut. First they turned their pockets inside out and assembled a meal consisting of two chocolate bars, a stale wedge of cheese and assorted cracker crumbs. They nibbled the frugal fare slowly, filling up the continuing emptiness with long swallows of achingly cold water from the little stream that flowed close by the hut. When they had finished, they sat out on the soft bank of moss, singing and listening to the echoes come eerily back to them from the great rock-walls above. Then Carla and Martin lay quietly with their eyes closed, while Stefan dug deep into his bottomless repertory of stories. Horrendous Gothic stories they always were—of dark doings in Bohemian forests, witches' sabbaths on the Brocken, and pale heroines dangling from forlorn precipices while wolf-faced little mountain men gnawed furtively at the ropes—and as Stefan's low voice droned on Carla shivered slightly and moved a little closer to Martin and took his hand in hers.

When the stories ended it was almost dark. They sat silently for a while, watching the lights come on like tiny pinpricks in the valley far below and the mountains thrusting skyward, like great promontories into a dark unfathomable sea.

The Blue Hour, Carla called it. . . .

Presently Stefan arose and stretched himself. "Well, let's turn in," he said.

Carla looked at the hut, then back at him, then suddenly away. "Oh no—I couldn't," she murmured.

"What do you mean, you couldn't."

"Sleep in the hut—with two men."

Martin and Stefan laughed. "Stop flattering yourself, Fräulein Lorelei," Martin said.

Her eyes flashed with sudden anger. "Don't you dare talk to me that way!"

"Then stop acting like an idiot."

"Who's acting like an idiot?"

"All right, have it your own way."

The boys went into the hut, lighted a candle, took two straw-filled mattresses from the stack in the corner and laid them out on the floor. As they were taking off their boots Carla appeared in the doorway and looked around suspiciously.

"Enter, O Irresistible One!" Stefan invited.

Ignoring them, she crossed to the pile of mattresses, selected one, and spread it in a far corner of the room. She removed her boots and dropped them to the stone floor with a thud. Then Stefan blew out the candle.

For perhaps five minutes there was silence. Then her voice came suddenly through the darkness. "Stefan—"

There was no answer.

"Martin—"

"Well?"

"There are rats."

"Of course there are rats."

"I think they're getting ready to run over my face."

"That's what rats do."

Silence again.

"Martin—"

"What is it now?"

"Do you think—that is—couldn't you or Stefan stand guard?"

"Stand guard? What for?"

"The rats."

"Of course," Stefan murmured. "Where's the machine gun, Herr Leutnant?"

"If you're scared of the rats you'd better come over here between us," Martin said.

There was still another silence, longer than before. Then Carla got slowly to her feet, dragged her mattress across the room and lay down between them.

"I am a bad woman," she said.

"Okay, you're a bad woman."

When he awakened, later, he found that she had shifted in her sleep so that one outstretched arm was flung lightly across his shoulder. He raised his hand to move it, changed his mind, and left it there. For a while he lay quietly staring into the darkness and listening to the low, distant rumbling of the glaciers.

And presently it was morning.

The golden summer days filed past; then the weeks. And then at last, it was the end of August. . . .

Time after time they had begged Andreas Benner to go with them to the Weissturm, but on each occasion he had merely pulled a little more thoughtfully on his stub of pipe and shaken his head. They had tried the other guides—Peter Zurneisen, Christian Mehrwalder, the Kronig brothers—with no better luck. And in the end, after endless planning and with an almost desperate defiance, Martin and Stefan had determined to try it on their own.

Not the least of their problems was Carla. Although as skilled and experienced a climber as either of them, she was nevertheless still only a girl of fifteen; and besides, it was obvious that her parents would never dream of sanctioning any such hare-brained exploit. Reluctantly they decided that she would have to be excluded. Inventing a variety of explanations of their whereabouts, they spent a day packing supplies and equipment up to the Heilweg Hut and a second carrying them to a still higher hut near the snout of the Dornel Glacier.

Here they spent the second night, and at dawn of the third morning they were on their way. Moving slowly under the weight of their packs and ropes, they ascended the great slag-heap of the Dornel moraine, emerged onto the glacier, and plodded upward, hour after hour, over the rugged highway of ancient blue ice. At nine and again at eleven they stopped briefly for rest and a bit of food, and it was at the second halt that Martin paused suddenly, his canteen halfway to his mouth, and pointed to the minute dot moving toward them up the glacier below. As they watched and waited the dot became a human figure and the figure became Carla. "Good morning," she said coolly, sitting down on an ice-hummock beside them.

"How did you know where we were?" Martin asked.

"Where did you think I thought you were?"

"Well, now that you're here you can turn right around and go back."

"Oh, but I couldn't!"

"What do you mean, you couldn't?"

"I could never get down the glacier—with all those terrible crevasses."

"You got up it all right."

"But it is much more dangerous going down."

There was a few moments' silence.

"But your father and mother," said Stefan. "They'll be—"

"They'll be very glad to see me when we get back."

The two boys looked at each other. Then they looked at Carla. Suddenly Martin swung his pack onto his shoulder and grinned.

"Come on," he said. "Let's get going."

For the rest of the morning and all through the afternoon they followed the Dornel and its tributary glaciers upward into the heart of the range. And at last, just as the sun was setting behind the Burggen Ridges to the west, they came off the ice and scrambled up a short boulder-slope to the deep notch between the Wunderhorn and the Weissturm. There was a third hut here, but much smaller than the Heilweg or the Dornel—scarcely more than a lean-to. They made tea and heated a can of beans over Stefan's tiny kerosene stove and sat discussing their plans for the next day while the cold purple shadows closed in around them. Then they crawled into the hut, spread their two blankets over the three of them and went to sleep.

It grew bitterly cold during the night, and at five o'clock, when they got up, their joints were stiff and their fingers and toes almost numb. The air was clear and black around them, but the stars had disappeared and the mountain walls above were swathed in drifting mist.

"It will clear later," Stefan said, sniffing professionally.

They ate a hasty cold breakfast, stowed a few things in the lighter of their two packs and started off. For perhaps half an hour they moved diagonally upward over boulders and loose rocks; then they came to the foot of a long snow-slope, which they had decided from earlier reconnaissance offered the most likely means of access to the great east ridge of the mountain. Pausing to rope up, they began the ascent. At first they climbed rapidly, moving all at the same time and each kicking his own footholds in the firm snow. Presently, however, the slope began to steepen and the surface became covered with a thick glaze of ice. Here it became necessary to cut steps with their axes, and they moved only one at a time, with the other two belaying the rope from such points of vantage as they could find. Martin had estimated that the ascent of the whole slope would take about two hours, but almost twice that time had elapsed before they topped the last slippery pitch and came out, panting but triumphant, on to the bare rock of the ridge.

Here they rested a few minutes, looking down at the route up which they had come and up at the possible routes that lay ahead. It had grown light as they climbed, the mist had cleared, and they could see the east ridge towering away above them, gray and desolate, into the blue morning sky. They were on the White Tower at last. The muscles of their legs were throbbing, and their shoulders and backs were wet with sweat. But as they sat now quietly staring upward it was not physical exertion that caused the wild and sudden pounding of their hearts.

For almost two hours they followed the ridge. Then it tapered off into an unclimbable knife-edge, and they traversed to the left across a belt of ledges. They ascended a dark, curving couloir, worked slowly around a perpendicular cliff-face, inched up a pitch of steep, smooth slabs, regained the ridge, followed it for an hour, traversed again. Since they had left the snow-slope, hours before, the summit of the mountain had been hidden from them by intervening ridges and shoulders, but now suddenly it swung into view again, and they stopped dead in their tracks. Martin could not have said what it was that he had expected to see, but in any case it was not what he saw now. The final snowcap of the Weissturm hung, blindingly white in the sky, an unimaginable distance above them. Rather than appearing appreciably closer than it had in the early morning, it actually seemed farther away—farther away, even, than it had seemed from the valley of Kandermatt, thousands of feet below.

He looked at his wristwatch. It was half-past three.

"At this rate—" he began. Then he stopped. There was no use saying it. They sat for a while on a sunny ledge, not looking at each other, not speaking. Then they got up stiffly and prepared to descend.

Stefan went first, turning his face in toward the mountain and letting himself down from the ledge onto the steep slabs up which they had come. Suddenly he slipped. There was a sharp scraping of boot nails on the rock, and the rope went taut around Martin's waist. He braced and held, and the scraping stopped. After another moment Stefan's face appeared, white and sweat-streaked, over the rim of the ledge.

"It's trickier going down," he said.

He waited briefly and tried again. Several minutes passed, and Martin and Carla could hear him moving cautiously around on the slabs. Then he came up again and pulled himself onto the ledge beside them.

"*Es geht nicht*," he said, shaking his head.

Martin tried it, while the others manipulated the rope from above, but with no more success. The minute horizontal crevices which had provided adequate holds on the way up seemed to vanish into smooth rock beneath his groping feet, and after the first few yards he was clinging to the mountainside merely by the precarious friction of his palms and thighs.

"It may be better over to the left," he said, when he had re-gained the ledge.

They tried it to the left. Then they tried it to the right. They kept trying it along the whole length of the ledge until their knees showed through their thick woolen trousers and their fingertips dripped blood. They struggled to boost one another up the over-hanging cliff-face above them. They inched out to the far corners of the ledge and looked down at the gray slabs curving into space.

"We mustn't lose our heads," Martin said quietly.

"No," the others agreed. "We must not lose our heads."

They rested awhile. Then they tried the slabs again. Then they opened the rucksack and divided one of their three remaining sandwiches among them. By the time they finished eating, the sun had set. They tried the slabs once more. Then it was dark.

They found a partly sheltered spot on the inside of the ledge, under the overhang of the cliffs above, and sat huddled together for warmth.

"All right?" Martin asked Carla.

"Yes—all right," she said.

"Sure?"

"Sure, Binks."

After a while he opened the pack again, took out their flashlight

36

and began beaming it down toward the valley. He flashed it three times in quick succession, waited a few moments and flashed it another three times. He kept on flashing until the batteries gave out. Then he lay down close beside Carla and Stefan and closed his eyes.

He dozed and awoke several times in the darkness. Then he awoke for the fifth or sixth time, and the darkness was thinning. They were so cold and stiff they could at first scarcely stand up, but they moved about the ledge for fifteen or twenty minutes, stamping their feet and beating their hands against their bodies, and at last a semblance of circulation began to return. They divided one of their two remaining sandwiches and waited for the sun to rise.

With the warmth of full day, they tried the slabs again; but on the third attempt Martin slipped and was saved from falling only by the rope.

"If anyone saw the flashlight they should be coming up by now," Stefan said.

They sat silently on the rim of the ledge staring down toward the glaciers and the valley. Then they began to shout. They shouted all together and then one after another and then all together again, until their voices cracked. Then they were silent again, watching and waiting.

And suddenly, wonderfully, miraculously, there was a faint answering shout. Leaning far out from the ledge and peering downward, they could see three tiny specks far below them, moving slowly up the long snow-slope which they had ascended the day before.

A half-hour passed, then an hour, while they shouted and waved. At last the three figures reached the top of the snow and began the ascent of the ridge. At intervals they disappeared, sometimes for as long as ten or fifteen minutes, but each time they reappeared, and each time they were a little larger, a little nearer. By late morning, they had reached the foot of the slabs, directly below the ledge, and were working their way cautiously up a steep chimney that bounded the slabs on the right.

There was no need to shout any more, and Martin sat down wearily on a rock between Stefan and Carla. Presently he put his hand over Carla's and smiled.

"Good girl," he said.

37

But the girl did not smile back. She did not even look at him. She was looking up past his shoulder, past the cliff-face above them, past the ridges and ice walls and precipices and pinnacles that tiered endlessly above them, to where the summit of the White Tower curved shining and remote against the noonday sky. And he saw suddenly that her eyes were filled with tears.

A moment later Andreas Benner pulled himself up over the rim of the ledge and stood looking grimly down at them and shaking his head.

"*Verdammtes Kinderspiel*," he muttered.

. . . There was Andreas Benner, behind the darkness, shaking his brown, weather-beaten head. There was Nicholas Radcliffe sitting on the steps of his verandah, his flute lying across his bony knees. There were the bright crowded dining room and the green meadows and pastures and the dark slanting forests and plunging streams and the long clean slopes of furze and blue-budded juniper, and above them—always huge and still and changeless far above them—the white peaks rising to the Weissturm and the Weissturm to the sky. There were two young men squinting solemnly upward, and a girl between them holding their hands and smiling.

From the high hilltop on which he seemed to be sitting Martin Ordway looked down into the deep, gleaming valley of the past.

Or was it a hill on which he sat? It was suddenly too high for a hill, too high for a mountain, even. It seemed to have no sides, no base, and the earth below no longer spread green and still in the sunlight, but was flowing past, distant and blurred, as if under a great curtain of whitish mist. The wind seemed to have risen too. It was pouring in a vast tide against his face and clothing, crumbling the last fragments of the hilltop away from beneath him, swelling and intensifying moment by moment until it was a monstrous pervading roar in his ears.

Now he was leaning far over and peering downward; but the earth was gone. Carla, Stefan, Andreas, the inn, the valley—everything was gone. There was only the black, tapering outline of a wing, and beyond it mist. Far away, against the dark horizon, there was a faint reddish glow, as if from a burning city. Around him were the sprawled bodies and quiet gray faces of the dead.

38

Chapter 3

The roar diminished to a drone, the drone to a faint, distant humming. He was descending again, revolving slowly through gray space; the dark earth rose gently to receive him; he was lying upon the soft earth, arms outspread, and the parachute was drifting down in soft white folds upon his face and body. He opened his eyes.

For a few minutes he remained perfectly still. Then he pushed aside the sheet that covered his face and lay staring up at a ceiling. The ceiling was not made of beaverboard and corrugated tin, but of whitewashed plaster. Running from the center to one corner was a long, wavering crack that rather resembled the outline of the channel coast of France. He raised himself slightly on his elbows and looked around. He looked at the iron bedstead that rose beyond his feet, at the yellow-flowered wallpaper, the table and chairs, the porcelain bowl and pitcher on the washstand, the window with its tied-back white net curtains.

Beyond the window was mist, and the room was filled with a flat, watery light. Martin Ordway brought up his left arm and looked at his watch. It had stopped at twenty minutes of ten.

He pushed the bedclothes aside, swung his feet slowly to the floor and stood up. He was lightheaded and his legs felt rubbery, but he seemed to be neither injured nor ill. He looked down at the unfamiliar blue cotton pajamas he was wearing. Then he crossed to the small mirror that hung on the wall above the washstand and stared at the old young-man's face that stared back at him from the glass.

It was a strong face, well-boned and deeply tanned, but the fine lines at the corners of eyes and mouth were too many and too deep and the flesh over the cheekbones was drawn tight and thin. At the moment, he thought wryly, it was a face a good deal the worse for time and sleep; a day's growth of stubble bristled on the long line of his jaw, and his black hair rose in a ruffled crest on his head. His dark eyes seemed, somehow, a little darker and larger than they should be. They gazed back at him steadily—almost too steadily—like the eyes of a man who has had the right number of drinks and then one more.

Leaving the mirror, he went to the window and looked out. The air was filled with thick gray fog. He could see the faint outline of a near-by tree and, below him, a few yards of close-cropped lawn. Beyond these there was nothing.

He turned and stood looking again, one by one, at the objects in the room. Then his eyes fell on a chair in the corner. There was a pile of clothing on the chair, but it was not his flying clothing. There was a pair of heavy brown worsted trousers, a maroon woolen sport shirt, a belt, a pair of clean underdrawers and a light-tan pullover sweater. On the floor in front of the chair were a pair of walking shoes, with gray woolen socks tucked into them.

His eyes searched the room again, and he opened the door of a cupboard behind the bed. His own things were not there. After a moment's hesitation, he removed his pajamas and began putting on the strange clothing. The shirt was tight around his chest and shoulders, and the worsted trousers were too short; but the shoes fitted him almost perfectly, and once the pullover sweater was on he felt moderately well clothed and comfortable. He poured some water from the pitcher into the bowl on the washstand, splashed his face and head, and smoothed back his hair. Then he crossed to the door and opened it.

A long, dimly lighted hall stretched away before him. He walked down it slowly, between two rows of closed doors, his shoes tapping loudly on the uncarpeted hardwood floor. Presently the hall turned and widened, and he was descending a flight of stairs. Halfway down, he stopped suddenly and stood staring at the small discolored gouge which his hand had touched on the smooth bannister railing. Then he continued down the stairs and crossed an empty foyer into an empty, oak-panelled lounge. Here he stopped again and looked slowly around him, as he had done upstairs in the room in which he had awakened. His eyes fell on the wide French windows that formed one of the walls of the lounge. He went over to them, opened them and stepped outside.

Instantly the fog closed in around him in a weaving, gray veil. There were ten yards of damp lawn before him; then a clump of bushes and a low fieldstone wall; and beyond them nothing. A woman, or perhaps it was a girl, was sitting on the wall. She held some sort of pot or vessel in her lap, over which she was bending, but she put it aside as she heard the sound of the door closing and raised her head. Ordway took a few steps toward her and stopped. She watched him silently for a moment; then she arose and approached him.

"Hello, Martin," she said.

Ordway stood motionlessly, looking at her. He stood looking at the straight, slender figure in tweed skirt and white shirtwaist; at the soft, oval face; at the short, coppery hair bound back in a green ribbon; at the full mouth, the small uptilted nose, the wide-spaced gray-green eyes. He put out his hands and took hers and held them, standing silent and motionless again.

"Hello, Carla," he said at last.

They stood beside the wall, and his eyes moved slowly over the terrace and the façade of the inn and the white gables piercing the mist above.

"I'm here," he said.

"Yes, Martin. You're in Kandermatt."

"And you're here."

"Yes."

They were silent again.

"Did you know it last night?" she asked.

"No." He paused, shutting his eyes. "That is—I'm not sure. It seems to me now that I did. There was a moment in the plane, just before I jumped, when I imagined I was. . . . And then later, coming down. . . . I thought my mind was playing tricks on me. I guess I thought I was dying." He paused again and opened his eyes. "What happened?" he asked.

41

"You came down in the pasture on the other side of the road. Andreas was out, looking after one of his goats that was sick—"

"Then it was Andreas?"

"Yes. He saw you, and then he came and woke Herr Knubel, and the two of them managed to carry you up here. They did not know who you were until they got you inside."

Ordway passed a hand over his eyelids. "I—I don't remember—"

"They said you were barely conscious. You were talking about parts of planes and calling for people. At first they thought you were badly hurt, but when we got you upstairs and undressed we saw you were just exhausted. Frau Knubel kept wanting to wake you up and make you eat and drink something, but you just lay there breathing long and slowly, and slept and slept."

"What time is it now?"

"About four in the afternoon."

"Then I've been sleeping—"

"Almost fourteen hours. It was just after two when they brought you in."

Ordway stared out across the wall into the gray banks of mist. "When I first looked out the window I thought the sun hadn't risen yet. It could have been dawn—evening—any time."

"The clouds closed down early this morning. Usually when it's like this it clears by evening."

"For the Blue Hour."

"The Blue—?" She stopped suddenly, her eyes full on his face. Then she looked away. "Yes," she said presently, "it should clear later."

There was a silence between them, and Ordway again passed a hand slowly over his closed lids. When I open them, he thought, she will be gone. When I look at her again all that will be there will be the mist.

"Do you feel ill, Martin?" she asked.

He opened his eyes. She was there.

"No," he said. "I'm just a little tired, I guess. A little—well—lost."

"But you are all right?"

"Yes. I'm all right."

There was another silence.

"Andreas," he said quietly. "And Herr Knubel and Frau Knubel. They're still here."

"Yes."

"And the others?"

"Most of the villagers and guides are still here. Mr. Radcliffe still lives in his bungalow up on the Aarntal Path."

"Old Nick and his rocks. . . . And Mrs. Meach?"

"Yes, Mrs. Meach too."

"How about the others?"

"The others are gone."

"The Bauers, the Wilsons, Major Austen-Fellowes, the Jacquimots?"

"All gone."

"And Stefan?"

She averted her eyes again. "No, Stefan is not here either."

He stood quietly for a moment, looking down at her.

"But you are here," he said.

She did not answer.

"And your father and mother?"

She shook her head. "I am not here as a guest any more. I work here now."

"Work?"

"Around the inn. For Frau Knubel."

"But—"

"Oh, it's just dull woman's work—housekeeping, marketing. There's nothing to tell about it." She looked up at him again and her voice suddenly changed. "Tell me about yourself, Martin? You are a soldier now? A flyer?"

"Yes."

"You have been in Europe long?"

"Almost two years. Counting England and Africa."

"And you are—"

"A bomber pilot. With the American Army Air Corps—in France." Ordway stopped suddenly, his hands tight and motionless against his sides. In the stillness beyond the terrace it seemed to him that he could hear the deep droning of an engine. The gray mist seemed to be flowing, cold and gentle, into his bones and blood. "I—I'd almost forgotten," he murmured.

Instinctively his eyes went outward, upward. "Did it—?"

43

The girl shook her head. "No, it did not come down. Not in the valley."

"Ted," he said quietly. "Bix—Harry—"

"Those were your friends in the plane?"

He nodded.

"They will be all right. If they come down in Switzerland they will be all right."

"Yes," he said. "They'll be all right." For a long moment he was silent, staring out again into the mist. Then with a sudden gesture he reached out and took her hands again. "Carla," he said, "today—here, now, this very minute—is the first time in two years that the war has been far away. Don't let's talk about it. Not quite yet. Just let me stand here quietly and look at you. Let's just talk about—"

"What, Martin?"

"About Kandermatt. About you."

"But there's nothing to tell. Truly. There's—"

She looked away from him again, seeming almost visibly to withdraw into herself. He was suddenly aware that her hands, in his, were cold and trembling slightly.

"Carla," he said, "what's happened? What is it? Tell me—"

There was a sound of footsteps on a gravel path, and two figures approached them across the terrace, through the mist. "Also," a voice said. "Unser Patient ist schon genesen."

A baldish, wispy little man with bright chipmunk's eyes and a long pointed nose was shaking Ordway's hand in both of his. "Herr Ordway," he murmured, over and over again. "Herr Ordway, yes, Herr Ordway—"

"Hello, Herr Knubel."

"And you remember Andreas? Yes? Of course." The innkeeper indicated his companion. "Old Andreas Benner."

Ordway stared at the oaken stump of a man who stood before him; at the massive shoulders, the square, weathered face, the clipped, gingery moustache, the sky-blue eyes. He felt his hand compressing in a long-forgotten granite clasp.

"Your old guide Andreas," Knubel was saying.

"My old friend Andreas," Ordway said.

Benner's lips parted in a slow, leathery smile, but he did not speak.

"It was you who found me, Andreas," Ordway said.

"And lucky for you it was," Herr Knubel put in. "There is not another person in the valley could have got you up here from the pasture." He paused and chuckled. "He came up here first and called me down, but why I still do not know. I held one foot and the parachute while he carried the rest of you."

"Andreas was always lugging somebody around like a pile of cordwood."

The three men laughed. Then suddenly there was a silence. Ordway looked from the two men to the girl, who was standing quietly by, to the stone wall and the gray fog beyond.

"I don't know where to begin, Herr Knubel," he said at last. "All I can say is—" he paused and smiled slightly, "—well, that here I am."

"And here you are welcome."

"Thank you." Ordway looked around him again, uncertainly. "Only I don't know what I can—"

Herr Knubel raised a small, important hand. "You are a guest of the Gasthof zum Blauen Himmel, Herr Ordway."

"But—"

"You are our guest. Just as you were in the old days. The only differences are that your name will not be on the register and you will not find a bill under your door on Saturday mornings."

"But you'll get in trouble, won't you?"

"Trouble? How?"

"I'm a uniformed combatant in a neutral country."

"I see no uniform."

Ordway stared down at his tan sweater and worsted trousers. "But even so, I'm subject to arrest. The authorities will be after me."

"To my certain knowledge, Herr Ordway, the authorities have not the remotest notion that you are here."

"No one saw me come down, then?"

"In Kandermatt, at two in the morning? I am afraid you would have been lying there in the pasture a long time if Andreas had not been lucky enough to have a croupy goat."

"You mean—"

"That you are safe here. That you can remain with us, unmolested, until you decide what you wish to do."

45

Ordway was silent a moment.

"I only woke up a short while ago," he murmured. "I haven't—" he hesitated—"I'm afraid I'm not thinking quite straight yet."

"There is no hurry." Herr Knubel coughed discreetly and tugged at his long nose. "Andreas and I have this morning been discussing some of the possibilities. We shall go into them when you are rested."

"Possibilities?"

"For your escape, Herr Ordway."

"Oh."

"It is not out of the question, you know."

"But—" Ordway's glance moved from Herr Knubel to Benner. He noticed for the first time that the guide was wearing a belted forest-green tunic and that there was a metal emblem on the band of his hat.

"Andreas is a member of the Mountain Patrol Corps," Herr Knubel said.

"And you think there may be some way—" Ordway began.

Benner nodded and spoke for the first time. "It is not out of the question," he said.

"But all that is for later," Herr Knubel put in. "Meanwhile you will rest here and be safe. It will be better, I think, if you do not go down to the village. They are good people there, but they will talk. Here at the *Gasthof*," he counted off on his fingers, "there are only myself, Frau Knubel and Fräulein Dehn, all of whom you know, and a half-witted kitchen girl, who would not know the difference between an American aviator and the ghost of Wilhelm Tell. As guests, there are Monsieur and Madame Delambre—they are French and very well-to-do; no trouble there—and the Herren Hein and Mohler."

"Swiss?"

"No, they are Germans. They are nothing to concern yourself about, though. They are convalescents of some sort—here for the quiet and mountain air—and they keep almost always to themselves." The innkeeper pulled at his nose reflectively. "However, simply to take no chances whatever: for them you shall be Mr. Ordway of the International Red Cross in Geneva."

Ordway nodded. "And the other guests?"

"There are no others."

"You have only—?"

"Four, yes. With you, five." Herr Knubel shook his head sadly. "I am afraid you will not find Kandermatt as you remember it, Herr Ordway."

"I've found the important things as I remember them. You, Andreas, Carla—"

He looked around suddenly. The girl was gone.

Simultaneously, a peremptory feminine voice was calling them from a window. "*Also, willst du dass Herr Ordway da draussen in diesem Sauwetter verhungert?*"

"Come," said Herr Knubel.

The three men went through the French windows into the lounge.

"Grüss Gott, Herr Ordway," the woman said.

"Grüss Gott, Frau Knubel."

She had aged too, he thought, but not so much as her husband. Her skin had yellowed and was furrowed with wrinkles, but her features were sharp and mobile, her bright black eyes were brighter and blacker than ever, and her dark, coarse hair, still pulled relentlessly back into a tight bun, showed scarcely a trace of gray. He held her dry, bony hand in his and smiled down at her.

"It is almost like the old days," she said. "And now come along. It must be more than a full day that you have not eaten."

She led the way across the lounge, through the empty foyer into the dining room. It was empty too. Along one wall, near the swinging door to the kitchen, three tables were set with faded red-and-white-checked cloths and heavy chipped chinaware. The other tables stretched away down the room in lonely files, their tops bare, the chairs stacked neatly on them with their legs upward. The chartreuse carpet and pewter-laden shelves were gone, but the two ibex heads still stared at each other from their opposite walls with baleful yellow eyes. The great expanse of plate-glass window that composed the south wall was intact. Instead of Herr Knubel's prided *Panoram*, however, it disclosed only a gulf of gray, weaving fog.

They sat down at the largest of the set tables, and a shuffling girl with pink cheeks and a goitre brought in lentil soup and pork shanks, cheese and goat's milk. Ordway had not realized before that he was hungry, but once the food was set before him he fell to it ravenously. The others watched him as he ate.

"It is not a meal that would have come out of my kitchen in

47

the old days," Frau Knubel said. Ordway murmured something appreciative, but she shook her head. "No, no. It is not like it used to be."

"What is there anywhere that is like it used to be?" asked Herr Knubel.

"Things are hard here too?" Ordway asked.

"In the big cities, no. There things—how do you Americans call it?—boom. With the war, of course. And the diplomats and spies and refugees. In the mountains—though—" Knubel shook his head sombrely.

"No tourists, I suppose."

"Tourists! Switzerland has almost forgotten what that is—a tourist. All the great resorts are shut down—empty. St. Moritz, Montreux, Grindelwald, all of them. What do you expect for a tiny hidden-away place like Kandermatt?"

"Not even your own people come?"

"The Swiss?" Herr Knubel gave a bitter little laugh. "Fine chance you would have finding a Schweizer spending his money to go to a resort."

There was a short silence. Ordway was gazing across the room at the wide plate-glass window and the mist beyond.

"And the mountains?" he asked. "No one climbs the mountains any more?"

Herr Knubel shook his head.

"It's hard to believe. But then how—" Ordway looked from Herr Knubel to Benner.

"I am not a guide any more, Herr Martin," Benner said. "I am a member of the Mountain Patrol Corps."

"Do you climb much with them?"

"Our duties take us up to the glaciers and passes."

"But not to the peaks?"

"No," said Benner. "It is four years now since I have climbed one of the big peaks."

There was another silence. Ordway finished his meal, and they got up and went back into the empty lounge.

"Where's Fräulein Dehn?" he asked.

"Somewhere about the inn," said Frau Knubel. "She is—well —she is no longer exactly a guest, as in the old days. She helps me with many things."

"Yes, she told me."

"You have already seen her then? Do you not think she has grown into a lovely woman?"

"Yes. I do." Ordway hesitated a moment. "How long has she been here, Frau Knubel?" he asked.

"Since she came back it is—let me see—almost two years."

"Two years she's been here? Without going away?"

Frau Knubel nodded. Then she looked past his shoulder at the man and woman who had just entered the lounge.

They were scarcely a couple that Ordway would have expected to find in a lonely, almost deserted inn, in a mountain valley. The woman was tall, young, full-breasted and beautifully dressed in casual sports clothes. Her face was broad, but not to heaviness, with exquisitely regular features and deep violet eyes, and her hair was wound in a mass of shining gold braids about her head. She walked into the room with the easy languor of a great tawny cat and nodded to Herr and Frau Knubel with a slow, almost indolent smile. The man was as tall as she, with narrow, slightly hunched shoulders. He had a thin, fine-drawn, aristocratic face, prominent nose and high forehead, and wore shell-rimmed glasses with thick lenses, that made his eyes seem very large and dark. Like the woman's, his clothes—gray slacks, a sports jacket and foulard scarf—were in perfect taste and of the finest quality.

"Monsieur and Madame Delambre—Mr. Ordway," Herr Knubel said.

Madame Delambre added a gracious nod to her fixed, pearly smile, and her husband extended his hand. "Welcome to our castle in the clouds, Monsieur Ordway," he said in almost unaccented English.

"Thank you."

"You are, Herr Knubel tells me, an old guest of the inn. This is almost, in a way, a sort of homecoming for you."

"In a way, yes." Ordway's glance went back to the woman. "You are old visitors here, Madame Delambre?"

"My wife, unfortunately, speaks neither English nor German," Delambre explained. "You speak French perhaps, Monsieur Ordway?"

"I used to once, fairly well, when I went to school in France. But I've grown rusty, I'm afraid."

"My wife will be glad to give you a chance to practice." The two men smiled. "To answer your question, though: no, we have never been here before. In Switzerland, many times. In St. Moritz, Mürren, Lausanne, Vevey, the whole list of them. But never here. Kandermatt is our wartime discovery—our, shall we say, ivory tower above the storm."

"I see," said Ordway.

There was a momentary lapse in the conversation. "I have omitted to tell you, Herr Ordway," Herr Knubel put in, "that it was Monsieur here who was kind enough to supply the clothes you are wearing."

"It's very good of you, Monsieur Delambre. Right at the moment I seem to be the orphan child of Kandermatt, but I promise you I'll—"

"A pleasure, sir." Delambre waved a deprecatory hand. "The trousers, I see, are a little on the brief side."

"Not nearly as brief as what I'd be wandering around in without them."

The three men laughed. Benner, who had been standing in the background, advanced and cleared his throat. "At five o'clock I must report at Patrol Headquarters," he said. "I will come back tomorrow at the same time. Perhaps then I will have some information."

Herr Knubel nodded, and the guide turned to go.

"Andreas," Ordway said.

"Herr Martin?"

"What are you planning to do?"

"Only to collect some information, that is all."

"You're sure you won't be getting yourself into trouble?"

"Do not worry, Herr Martin." A slow smile creased the broad mahogany face. "By this time old Andreas knows how to find his way around a few other things besides mountains."

He waved a hand and went out. Frau Knubel departed toward the kitchen, and Madame Delambre murmured "Pardon, messieurs" and went upstairs. For a few moments Ordway, Herr Knubel and Delambre could hear her heels tapping on the bare floor of the hallway above. Then the sound faded away.

Ordway walked to the French windows and stood with his hands in his pockets looking out at the mist.

"It is peaceful in our ivory tower, is it not?" said the Frenchman.

For half an hour Ordway lay with closed eyes in the tepid water of the tub, listening to the gentle, remote gurgling of the ancient pipes. Then he shaved with the razor and soap that Herr Knubel had brought him, re-dressed himself in Delambre's clothes and went downstairs again.

The foyer, lounge and dining room were empty. He looked into the kitchen, but there was no one there except the pink-cheeked waitress with the goitre. Returning to the foyer he stood for a few moments, undecided, then crossed to the front door, opened it and went out. Fog still filled the air with opaque grayness, obscuring everything beyond a radius of a few yards. Following the low stone wall, he circled the terrace around the inn, stopping briefly at the side and back doors and in front of the boarded-up frame bungalow that once had been the servants' sleeping quarters. Presently he came to a break in the wall where a dirt road started down from the terrace, and stopped again for a moment. Then he followed the road down.

He walked slowly, his hands in his pockets, his shoulders hunched against the mist. The road twisted and dipped down the slope of a knoll, rounded a weed-grown tennis court, and debouched into another slightly wider road. He crossed a small wooden bridge over a stream, passed through a stand of tall timber and then, for perhaps half a mile, between open pastures. Then there were trees again, and, presently, a footpath forking off to the left. Leaving the road, he followed it into the forest.

Now he was walking along a winding gray-green tunnel, and the earth was springy and root-veined beneath his feet. Long-forgotten —yet strangely unforgotten—shapes swam up at him out of the mist: a weathered brown rock with the vague outline of a turreted castle; an oak-root that writhed across the path like a thick black snake; a thin silver birch rising suddenly among the dark evergreens and larches. He stopped, went around to the other side of the birch and stood looking at the carved letters—S.R., C.D., M.O.—that showed faintly on the trunk. Then he walked on again. Ahead of him, behind the forest and the mist, he could hear the deep rumbling of the Aarn.

Suddenly, for the second time since he had awakened, his

51

thoughts went back to the day before—the night before. It was no longer a river that was dinning in his ears, but the engines of a stricken bomber. He felt Wasniewicz's heavy body slithering across the aluminum floorplates as the plane lurched; he saw the tiny pulse flickering in Riggs' white jaw-line and the blood spreading down from his mouth across the front of his flying suit like a great crimson napkin.

Bixler, John R.

Wasniewicz, Harry

Riggs, Theodore L.

With the prescribed notations. And a letter to a girl called Biscuit. . . .

The forest walls slipped past on either side. Then they thinned and fell away behind him, and he was picking his way slowly through a labyrinth of tumbled boulders. The river seemed suddenly to spring out of the earth to meet him. It came down over a steep, rocky pitch to his right in a wild cascade of foam and plunged into a deep basin below. Here, for a brief instant, it became a still, green pool; then it moved forward again, at first very slowly and gently, then faster and faster, as if sucked onward by some immense hidden pump, until it was a smooth, racing torrent. Then it struck the rocks again, split into a hundred gleaming ribbons, circled and crisscrossed in a fifty-yard frenzy of white water, and finally drew together again and plunged out of sight among the trees below. Along its entire visible length rose a great fringe of spray, merging into the gray, windless mist above. Its sound, as Ordway approached it from the bordering forest, swelled quietly from a rumble to a pervading roar.

He followed the path upstream among the boulders, climbed a steep wooded spur and crossed the river on a high cable-strung footbridge. On the far side was another spur, climbing still higher, and as he ascended the path along its edge the Aarn slowly dropped away beneath him into a deep gorge of spray and shadow. Presently the trees were beneath him too, and he came out on an open, scrubby slope surmounted by a bald knob of rock. He clambered to the top of the knob and sat down. He sat listening to the again-remote rumbling of the river and watching the mist drift in slow gray billows across the treetops below.

Dear Biscuit.—No. Dear Frances . . . Dear Mrs. Riggs, Was-

niewicz, Bixler . . . Dear Mrs. Smith, Madame Duval, Frau Schulz, Comrade Ivanova . . . I am so sorry, madam, believe me. So regretfully, respectfully sorry. So officially, quintuplicately, adjutant-general-departmentally sorry. . . .

He closed his eyes and held his hands to his face, pressing the lids gently with his fingers.

There was the report to be written. (*Reports on all missions will be written out as soon as possible, so that details will not be forgotten.*) That was if you got back. It was a strange thing that he had not once thought about getting back, until Andreas and Herr Knubel had hinted at it on the terrace. And he had not thought about it since. . . . Well, Andreas would be returning the next afternoon with his "information." In the meantime there was nothing he could do. *Ordway, Martin F., Capt., Plt., 31, Larchmont, N.Y.*, was a line in a book at *S-1*, with a tentative MIA pencilled opposite. The Martin Ordway who really existed was a tired, solitary man in sweater, sport shirt and too-short worsted trousers sitting with his hands over his eyes on a knob of rock in a forest in the remote Alpine valley of Kandermatt.

Kandermatt . . .

He folded his arms across his knees and looked out over the tree-tops into fog-filled space. . . . That was another thing he had not thought about. How had he come to Kandermatt? How, flying blind and crippled in the night over Europe, over the fields and forests, lakes and rivers, ruined cities and ravaged countryside of half a continent, had he come to the Alps, to that region of the Alps, to that very range, river, village, dropping slowly, gently out of darkness and roaring death into the still, lost valley of the past? . . . It was chance, of course. Chance only. The chance of ten thousand vagrant air currents; of a hundred thousand off-beat whirrings of a faulty propeller; of the dip of a punctured wing, the angle of a warped aileron, the light touch of a finger on a stick. The chance that, instant by instant throughout the universe, in the spinning of a coin, a sperm cell, a stellar nebula, simultaneously creates its unimaginable millions of alternatives and blindly and irrevocably ordains one.

Yes, it was chance. It was only chance. He knew that.

And yet . . .

For several minutes he sat motionless, his eyes on the gray rock around him. Then he looked at his watch. It was almost seven; it would be getting dark soon. But it was not getting darker. Looking around him with sudden awareness, he had the curious impression that, on the contrary, it was growing lighter. The rock under his hand seemed to have taken on a pale gleam, and the leaves and branches of the trees below were becoming clearer in outline, like images in a twisted lens shifting slowly into focus. He watched silently and waited.

The mist was lifting.

Dense billows rose languidly from the forest, like the smoke of a thousand fires. For a few moments they hung motionless above the treetops, then broke into long streaming tatters and dissolved. Depth after depth, the gray veil thinned, and the earth beneath it emerged slowly, as if from beneath a vast withdrawing sea. Presently the whole forest was revealed; then fragments and patches of green fields beyond; finally the whole sweep of the fields, the road, the river, the white roof of the inn, the church steeple of the distant village. There was no wind. The mist did not blow away. It merely seeped upward, impelled by some invisible, silent chemistry of the air, and in its place was the valley of Kandermatt, spread peacefully in the evening light.

Now the mist was no longer mist at all, but a vast sea of low-lying clouds. And the clouds too were receding. Moment by moment, mile by mile, the valley walls emerged: the tilted pastures, the dark tiers of forest, the desolate scree-slopes, the silver threads of streams. For an instant the clouds seemed to hang motionless against their upper reaches in an opaque, motionless ceiling. Then there was a sudden white glint behind them. The glint brightened, expanded, boring and burning its way through, and the cloud-mass slowly dissipated into fragments, like a great crumbling wall. Glaciers and snowfields came into view, gorges and precipices, ridges and peaks, tiering one beyond the other, one above the other, into immeasurable depths of space. Where a few moments before there had been nothing, a new world had sprung into being—a silent, soaring, gleaming world, transfixed like a huge white wave against the sky.

Ordway's gaze travelled slowly along the jagged arc of the horizon. The mighty, unforgotten shapes rose up for him again out of the distance and the years. His eyes moved up the bouldered slopes of the Rotalp, across the precipices of the Karlsberg, the icefields of the Wunderhorn, the high tessellated rampart between the Graf and the Gräfin. They followed the twisting rock-spine of the Dornelberg to its wedge-like summit, descended to the deep blue shadow of its gorges, climbed again over glacier and buttress and up the mile-high granite faces of the Himmelshorn.

Then presently he was no longer staring at the mountains but at the sky above them—at a single white cloud that still hung suspended in space beyond the ridges and domes and pinnacles of the range. The sun had already set behind the summits of the Burggen Peaks, to the northwest, and valley, foothills and the range itself lay spread in a deep sea of twilight. But the cloud, high above them, was still shining in the rays of day that streamed up from below the horizon. As he watched, its whiteness turned gradually to pink, and from pink to flaming fire. Then the glow faded, all color faded, and it was white again—a cold, radiant white shape unmoving and immutable in the sky.

And in that instant he knew it was no cloud.

For a long while he remained staring upward through the fading light. From where he sat the vast base and trunk of the White Tower were hidden by the intervening masses of the Dornelberg and the Himmelshorn; all that was visible above them were the great curving domes of the precipice-tops and, resting lightly upon them, the snowy crown of the summit dome. The sky behind it had faded now to a deep gun-metal gray. Above its eastern ridge a single star had appeared, brightening slowly.

The dome was not jagged or tapering, like the crests of the nearer, lesser mountains that ringed it. Immeasurably larger than all the others, it was still not sheer mass that set it apart; immeasurably higher, it was still not mere height. Alone and unchallenged, it needed no ultimate thrust of turret or spire to assert its supremacy. Innocent of struggle, or aspiration, of conquest or defeat, it rose in austere and gentle certitude to its appointed place in the sky—and stopped. It was a fact. It existed. . . .

It was there.

Martin Ordway sat for another few minutes watching the stars come out and the blue shadows flow in a slow wave up the mountainsides. Then he looked at his watch again, arose, and walked slowly back through the dark forest to the inn.

Chapter 4

≈≈≈≈≈≈≈≈≈≈≈≈≈≈≈≈≈≈≈≈≈≈≈≈≈≈≈≈≈≈

Nicholas Radcliffe's chalet had not changed. You swung around a wide bend in the path, passed through the lop-sided, never-closed gate, and there it was, rust-colored and prim, clinging to its hillside.

Ordway crossed the minute terraced garden, climbed the veran-dah steps and tapped with the wooden knocker. Presently the door was opened by a square-faced, square-bodied woman with white hair and placid brown eyes.

"Hello, Mrs. Meach," he said.

The woman looked at him blankly. Then she took a half-step forward and squinted her eyes against the bright morning sun. Then she took a half-step back.

"No," she murmured. "No!"

"Yes," Ordway smiled.

"Mr. Martin—" She raised her hands, as if to put them on his shoulders, dropped them and burst into tears.

"It's not that bad, is it?" he asked.

"It's that good, Mr. Martin—" She was crying, holding his hand and trying to dry her eyes on her apron, all at the same time. "But the Doctor he'll be killing me," she exclaimed suddenly, "stand-ing here gabbing with you like this."

She turned quickly to go inside, but at the same moment Rad-cliffe appeared in the door. He was even taller and thinner than Ordway remembered him: a sunbrowned cadaver of a man with

—yes, he thought, Carla had had it right—the face of a vegetarian vulture. The bald dome of his head was a little balder than before, the fringe of sandy-gray hair a little grayer and shaggier; but the bold line of the predatory nose was unblurred by the years, and his eyes, peering out into the full sunlight, were still a keen, metallic blue.

"Well?" he asked, looking from Mrs. Meach to Ordway. And then suddenly, "Well! Well!"

Ordway grinned as they shook hands. "That will cost me exactly fifty francs," he said.

"Fifty francs? What will?"

"I made a small bet with myself on the way up that the first words you'd say would be: " 'Mrs. Meach, bring our guest a cup of tea.' "

"Wrong. But they're the second words." Radcliffe waved his housekeeper toward the kitchen. "And the Huntley and Palmers, Mrs. Meach," he added. "This is a very special tea."

He led Ordway through a dark hallway and into a large, disordered room that was half library and half laboratory. Books lined three of the walls from floor to ceiling and overflowed in assorted stacks on the floor. The desk, table and several chairs were piled high with pamphlets, typescripts and dog-eared copies of various scientific journals. Along the fourth wall, in front of the windows, was an unpainted workbench littered with more books, more pamphlets, bottles, test tubes, chemical apparatus, two Bunsen burners and a conglomeration of stones and rock fragments of all shapes, sizes and colors. Radcliffe swept a pile of *Geological Reviews* from an armchair and made his guest sit down. Then he walked to the workbench, leaned back against it and peered at him silently. "Well!" he said again, "now let's have it."

"I got here night before last," Ordway said.

"How?"

Ordway told him. The Englishman listened quietly, his long arms folded across his chest, his head cocked forward and a little to one side. "I shall leave it to that undisputed mistress of the cliché, Mrs. Meach, to observe that it's a small world," he said, when Ordway had finished. "Apparently, however, it is."

There was a rattling of chinaware in the doorway, and the housekeeper came in with the tea and crackers.

"Two lumps, no milk. Right?" said Radcliffe.

"Right." Ordway looked admiringly at the bowl of cut sugar.

"Hoardings," Radcliffe explained.

"It's a small world," Mrs. Meach said, shaking her head in wonder.

She retired to the kitchen again, and the two men sat sipping their tea.

"A bomber pilot," the Englishman said meditatively. "Tell me about it."

"There's not much to tell. You fly. You drop bombs. If you're lucky you fly back."

"I remember you always wanted to be a flyer. Years ago." Ordway nodded.

"But there was something else, too," Radcliffe narrowed his eyes and rubbed his hand slowly along the sharp ridge of his jaw. "Let me see. . . . An architect, that's it! You were studying at the Beaux Arts in Paris and you were going to become an architect."

"I did. In a way."

"In a way?"

"Architects weren't eating very well in New York in the middle thirties. Meanwhile I'd learned to fly on the side, as a sort of hobby, and when the war came that was that." A thin smile touched Ordway's lips. "I'm afraid I was a bit of a flop at building houses, but they seem satisfied with the way I knock them down."

Radcliffe was silent a moment. "And now what?" he asked presently.

"If the authorities catch up with me, they'll intern me, of course. They haven't yet. Andreas and Herr Knubel have some idea about—"

"Smuggling you out?"

"I think so. I don't know anything about it yet, though."

"You want to get back, naturally?"

"Yes. That is—" Ordway passed a hand over his eyes. Then he got suddenly to his feet, crossed to one of the windows and stood looking out across the valley at the frozen stillness of the peaks. "I don't know," he said.

Radcliffe watched him a few moments without speaking. "Just a few miles beyond those mountains," he said, "there are armies marching, cities burning, a whole world clutching at its own throat. It seems incredible from here, doesn't it?"

Ordway nodded.

"Sometimes weeks go by," the Englishman went on, "when I almost forget there is such a thing as a war. I sit cooped here in my study, writing and fiddling with my rocks; or I tramp over the scree-slopes and glaciers, collecting my specimens. When every so often the newspapers come up from Berne or Zurich I sit down and look at them and it's like reading Wells or Jules Verne."

Ordway turned back from the window. "You haven't been out then?" he asked.

"Out?"

"Home."

"This is home." Radcliffe paused, rubbing his jaw again. "Do you know how long I've lived here in Kandermatt? Seventeen years. In all that time I've been back to England exactly twice. The first time was in 1929, when my mother died. The second was for two weeks in 1936, to buy some books and give a lecture at Brasenose. I'm still an Englishman—yes—of course I am. But what use would I be in England now? Another mouth to feed. Another ration book to issue. Another superannuated fuddy-duddy with an ARP button and a bucket running around throwing sand in the wrong places and telling anybody who'll listen what it was like at Passchendaele and Vimy Ridge.

"No, Ordway—there was a very wise old bird who once said that every man should cultivate his own garden. That is what I've tried to do with my life: cultivate my little garden of rocks. I suppose that by now I know more about the rock structure and glaciation of the central Alps than any geologist since Agassiz. I collect my specimens, work out my theories, write my books. And I like to think that by doing so I'm better fulfilling my function—better serving mankind, if you will—than by fatuously trying to turn myself into something I am not and chasing off in all directions like Leacock's horseman."

Radcliffe refilled Ordway's teacup and paced slowly about the cluttered room with his hands thrust deep into his pockets. "Well, now you know the reason I'm still here," he said at last.

"It sounds like a good one," Ordway said.

"Yes, doesn't it?" The Englishman smiled a little at the corners

59

of his mouth; then he stopped near his workbench and stood stroking his chin. "It would be so satisfactory if it were the real one."

Ordway stared. "The real one?" he repeated.

"Oh, it is partly, I suppose." Radcliffe's voice had become low and almost toneless. "Or at least was, in the early days. But then came Dunkerque, and France went under, and suddenly I knew I had to go back. I hadn't felt that way about anything in years. Not since—well—Everest. It didn't matter what the difficulties were. Nothing mattered. I had to go—that was all there was to it."

He paused and let out a long, slow breath. "Well, I started off. One day in July, I threw a few things into an overnight bag, went into Interlaken and took the train to Geneva. Geneva was a madhouse that summer—you can imagine. I went to the British minister and consul, but they were helpless. I went to the Swiss foreign office, and they could do nothing. Then after several days, through some friends at the university, I was put in touch with a group of refugee Frenchmen. They were already forming the rudiments of an underground, and after a lot of palaver they said they thought they could get me through. A few nights later a man I'd never seen before came to my hotel room and handed me an Alsatian peasant's outfit and a revolver. I was to stand in front of a certain number on the Rue du Rhone at six the next morning and a furniture van would pick me up. As we neared the French border I was to crawl into a hidden compartment between the cab and the body of the van, which the driver would show me. When—or perhaps it was if—we got to Lyons, I was to leave the truck and look up a certain produce dealer in the Place de L'Hôpital, who would give me further instructions.

"The man left, and I sat there in that hotel room all night. I looked at that bundle of peasant's clothes. I looked at the revolver. I began thinking of all my books standing on the shelves back here, and of Mrs. Meach and the sound of the Aarn and the monograph I was writing on the foliation of strata. And suddenly I knew the jig was up. I didn't have what it took, that was all. No more than I had had it up there on the northeast ridge of Everest sixteen years before. I was still no adventuring hero, but just a timid middle-aged duffer with a head full of Pleistocene fossil deposits and a temperamental digestion. . . . Well, old boy, I told myself—here you are again. It's retreat in good order again. . . . Before it got light I went out and threw the clothes and revolver in the lake. Then I went to the station and waited for the first train to leave for Interlaken."

Radcliffe had half-turned and stood looking absorbedly at the litter on his workbench. Ordway finished his tea and put down the cup and saucer.

"The first reason's better," he said.

"Better, perhaps. But truer?"

"Yes, truer too. You're being a fool if you're still blaming yourself."

The Englishman turned back to him and seemed about to speak; then he stopped himself and shrugged his hollow shoulders. "Come on," he said suddenly in a different voice. "It always stinks of my damned acetates in here. Let's go out to the verandah."

They sat on the rough-hewn verandah steps, and he set about the elaborate business of filling and lighting a pipe. Ordway sat with his chin in his hands, his eyes moving slowly across the panorama that spread before them. Radcliffe's house was situated on the eastern slope of the valley, at the point where the upper reaches of open pasture met the lower fringes of forest, and directly in front of it the earth tilted away in a thousand-foot incline of shimmering grass. At the foot of the slope spread the valley floor, its jigsaw fields bright in the sunlight, the road and the river, the village and the white inn tiny but jewel-clear beneath the cloudless gulfs of air. Above it, the west wall of the valley climbed steeply in pasture, forest and scree-slope to the cold tumbled wilderness of the peaks.

The ridges and summits rose, one behind the other, one above the other, in solemn stillness. From their center, springing up from its satellites like a mountain resting on mountaintops, the Weissturm struck with blazing fire into the sky. Ordway sat silently squinting at it through the blue miles.

"*It* doesn't change," Radcliffe said.

"No."

"From day to day it's different. From hour to hour; even minute to minute. Day and night come; sun and rain and snow and fog and wind come; and with each of them it's different. It's different, and yet it doesn't change. The years and the centuries come, and it doesn't change."

He fell silent again, drawing slowly on his pipe.

"Do you go up often?" Ordway asked.

"To the glaciers? Every few weeks."

"To the Tower, I mean?"

"Only as far as the hut."

"You've still never tried—?"

"Climbing it?" The Englishman shook his head. "No, that's another of those notions a man has when he's—well—younger." He paused, blowing out a thin cloud of smoke, and chuckled softly. "Remember how you and Miss Dehn and that blond Viennese boy used to walk up here in the late afternoons, and old Meach would fill you full of tea and those horrifying scones of hers? And then you'd sit out here on the steps and look at the Tower through the binoculars, and each time one of you was sure he'd figured out a route?"

"Yes," Ordway said. "I remember." For another few moments he continued gazing at the mountain. Then he turned and looked at Radcliffe. "Do you see her often?" he asked.

"Who?"

"Carla."

"Oh, occasionally in the village, or when I stop by at the inn."

"She works there now?"

"So I understand."

"Has she—talked to you?"

"Talked? Of course. We're still very friendly."

"I mean about why she's here. Why she came back."

"No, she hasn't said anything about that." Radcliffe shook his head slowly and pulled at his pipe. Then he shrugged. "After all, old boy, there's no accounting for where much of anyone is these days. You—myself: why are we where we are? Or half the people in the world? . . . I came back. Miss Dehn came back. Now you're back. 'Sufficient unto the day . . .' "

He sat for a few moments gently stroking his jaw. Then he slapped Ordway vigorously on the knee and got to his feet. "And now, my boy, steel yourself. You are about to hear Debussy's *Mandoline* played on a flute as, I give you my personal guarantee, it has never been played before."

62

Ordway walked slowly down the winding path through the bright patterns of shade and sunlight. He traversed a steep slope of pasture, passed a belt of pine and larch and crossed a quick little stream on a chain of worn stepping stones. Emerging into pasture again, he continued for a short distance, then stopped and sat down on a bank of grass beside the path. A flock of sheep, a small boy and a shaggy dog were moving about on the slope, far below. He watched them for a few minutes and then lay back on the soft turf. Closing his eyes, he listened to the chirping of the pipits in the near-by trees and felt the autumn sunshine pouring, warm and gentle, through his body.

Perhaps ten minutes had passed when he heard the sound of footsteps. He sat up, rubbed the drowse from his eyes and saw that two young men were approaching, one behind the other, up the narrow path. They were dressed in white sport shirts and khaki shorts and wore heavy, nailed climbing boots. The one in the lead carried a coil of rope over his shoulder, and the second a light rucksack. They plodded steadily upward until they came abreast of Ordway, then stopped and looked down at him.

"Grüss Gott," said the first one.

"Grüss Gott," Ordway said.

He looked from one to the other. The one who had spoken was a man of about his own age, of medium height and compact frame, with smooth dark-brown hair, gray eyes and handsome, almost Grecian, features. The other was short, yellow-haired, and appeared slightly younger. Both had clear, light skin, and their bare legs and forearms were hairless and strongly muscled.

"Es ist ziemlich warm heute, nicht wahr?" the second one said.

"Ja, sehr warm," Ordway answered.

"Sie sprechen Deutsch, also?" said the taller one.

"Nur ein—" Ordway searched for the word—"ein wenig."

"So? Was sprechen Sie denn besser? Französisch? Englisch?"

Ordway hesitated an instant. "Englisch," he said.

"Good," the young man said. "I can speak English too. Not like an echter Engländer, to be sure—but enough." He studied Ordway briefly with cool gray eyes. "You are the new guest at the Gasthof, I imagine?"

"Yes."

"We are at the Gasthof too. My name is Hein and my friend

63

here is Herr Mohler. Perhaps Herr Knubel has mentioned our names to you."

"Yes, he has." The two men stood looking at him, waiting. "My name is Ordway," he said after a moment. "Martin Ordway."

Hein repeated the name and bowed slightly. "*Es freut mich sehr*," said his companion.

"Herr Mohler, unfortunately, does not speak English," Hein explained. He removed the rope from his shoulder, threw it on the grass and sat down beside it. "You do not mind if we rest here with you a moment? It is warm climbing today."

"Of course not," said Ordway.

The one called Mohler sat down too, unslung his rucksack and took out a heavy felt-covered canteen. Unscrewing the cap, he offered it to Ordway.

"Thank you, no," Ordway said.

"*Es ist frisch.*"

"I'm not thirsty, thanks."

Mohler drank, passed the canteen to Hein and then put it back in the rucksack. There was a few moments' silence, and Ordway looked at the yellow rope lying coiled in the grass.

"You're going up for some climbing?" he asked.

"Just for a bit of exercise," said Hein. "On the rocks above the Blausee. . . . You know the Blausee, Herr Ordway?"

"Oh, yes."

"You have been in Kandermatt before, then?"

"Many years ago."

"It is a beautiful place, is it not? The valley and the mountains. Others may talk all they want about Mont Blanc and the Matterhorn and the rest. But for those who know mountains there is just one peak in the Alps that stands out incomparably above all the others, and that is the Weissturm."

"You know the Alps well, then?"

"Oh yes. Herr Mohler here and I have climbed in almost every district from Chamonix to the Dolomites. In past years, of course. More recently—well—one has been busy elsewhere, has one not?"

Ordway nodded, and there was another pause.

"You have done much climbing yourself?" Hein asked.

"Some. Also before the war."

"You are planning to do any while you are here?"

"I don't know. Perhaps. I haven't thought about it."

"You will be in Kandermatt for a while, I suppose?"

"No, not long."

"Ah, that is too bad." Hein smiled slightly, his gray eyes steady on Ordway's face. "Holidays are always too short, are they not? . . . Well, in any case, perhaps we could arrange a day's climbing before you go."

"Yes, perhaps we could."

Ordway glanced at his watch, and simultaneously Hein picked up his rope and got to his feet. "*Also, Hans,*" he said, "*lass uns weitergehen.*"

He swung the rope onto his shoulders, and Mohler adjusted his rucksack.

"*Heil—*"

Hein broke off. The gray eyes seemed to be smiling again.

"*Auf wiedersehen, Herr Ordway,*" he said.

"*Auf wiedersehen,*" said Ordway.

He sat watching them plodding up the path until they disappeared into the timber. Then he got up and slowly continued his descent through the quiet pastures.

It was late afternoon when he reached the inn. The terrace was deserted, as usual, and there was no one in the foyer. Going through the dining room, he opened the kitchen door and looked in, but the only person there was Annamarie, the waitress.

"*Haben Sie Fräulein Dehn gesehen?*" he asked.

She shook her head.

"*Wissen Sie wo sie ist?*"

She shook her head again, then suddenly burst into a giggle. Ordway closed the door, returned to the foyer and stood for a moment, undecided, at the foot of the stairs. Then he went into the lounge.

The Frenchman, Delambre, was seated in an armchair near the windows, reading a book. "Oh, hello," Ordway said.

"Good afternoon."

Delambre nodded pleasantly. Ordway crossed to the table against the far wall and stood thumbing the pages of a six-months'-old *Illustrierte Zeitung.*

"Glorious weather today," the Frenchman said.

65

"Perfect."

"You have been for a bit of a walk, perhaps?"

"Yes."

"You have had a good view of the mountains, then?"

Ordway nodded.

"*Formidable*, eh?"

"Oh yes."

There was a short silence. Then Delambre closed his book and smiled. "Having succinctly disposed of the climate and terrain," he said, "may I suggest that we have a drink together, Monsieur Ordway?"

Ordway abandoned the *Illustrierte Zeitung*. "Nothing I'd like better. But there's no longer a bar, is there?"

"No, but fortunately I am in a position to offset Herr Knubel's error of omission. I can offer—let me see now—cinzano, anise, cognac Courvoisier four-star, Holland gin and a fair-to-middling Merseault '28."

Ordway smiled. "The cognac sounds fine. That is, if you—"

"It is my choice too." The Frenchman got to his feet. "If you will excuse me a moment, I shall bring it down."

He bowed slightly and went out. Ordway paced slowly about the lounge until he returned carrying a bottle and two brandy inhalers.

"I think you may find this rather pleasant," Delambre said. He set the glasses down, filled them and handed one to Ordway. "*Alors—aux survivants—*"

Ordway looked at him questioningly.

"To—the survivors."

They drank, and Ordway felt the liquid spreading, rich and warm, through the avenues and crannies of his body. When he had finished he held the inhaler up and looked at the crest and initial D that were delicately etched on the crystal curve of its side. "You've managed well, for a place like Kandermatt," he said.

Delambre shrugged his thin shoulders. "One does what one can. Fortunately I was able to salvage a little when the barbarian came." He paused, refilling the glasses. "You are interested in the arts and literature, Monsieur Ordway?"

"I was once."

"Perhaps then you would be interested sometimes in seeing

66

some of the things in my room. There is a Van Gogh—his early period—a Toulouse-Lautrec, a few of the moderns, several oriental and Majorcan ceramic pieces, and some rather choice books."

"You really *did* manage, didn't you?"

"It was not easy, I assure you. No transport, no facilities, no anything. And the *Boche* everywhere, hunting for loot. But I plotted and bribed and connived, as only a Frenchman can, and in the end succeeded in getting a handful of possessions out with me." Delambre sighed gently and sipped at his brandy. "It is a desolate world in which we live, Monsieur. I am afraid life would have long since become intolerable for me if I could not at least be surrounded by a few civilized and lovely things."

"Madame Delambre—I hope you won't mind my saying so—is very lovely too."

"My wife—yes. She is a beautiful woman," Delambre took off his shell-rimmed glasses and swung them slowly in his fingers. "She is not French, you know."

"I'd thought perhaps—"

"She is half Dutch and half Swedish. Her name is Astrid." Delambre seemed about to continue and then paused. He took a handkerchief from his sleeve, wiped his glasses carefully and put them back on. "Yes," he said, "she is very lovely."

He picked up his glass and sipped the brandy slowly. Ordway glanced at the book that lay on the table beside his chair.

"*L'Immoraliste*," the Frenchman said. "Do you know Gide?"

"I once read *The Counterfeiters*. Years ago."

"And did you like him?"

"No, not a great deal, as I remember. His point of view seemed to me—well—decadent."

"Decadent?" Delambre pursed his lips and pulled at them gently with his long fingers. "Perhaps. But is not that perhaps the most intrinsic quality of the world we live in—decadence?"

"Speaking generally, I wouldn't know. The most intrinsic quality of the world I've been living in the past few years is death."

"Ah, but exactly. Death—decadence. Decadence—death. The one is the becoming, the other the accomplished fact. Whether it is of the body or the spirit is immaterial; it is all one; and it is the enzyme and zygote of our civilization, no matter how fondly or fiercely we would wish it otherwise." Delambre tapped the book beside him. "That is why Gide is great, monsieur. He sees, he knows, and he is not afraid to tell. More than any other writer—alone with a few men like Modigliani in painting and perhaps Schönberg in music—he truly understands the sickness of our times; this tragic and ever-widening gulf between the world of the mind and the world of fact, between our thinking and feeling and our doing. His very homosexuality is—again to use the word—intrinsic. It is modern man, impotent to cope with the confusions and monstrosities he has created, turning inward on himself; self-devouring, self-consuming . . . ."

Delambre paused and sipped his brandy. "You are a bomber pilot, Monsieur Ordway?"

"Yes."

"But you have not always been a bomber pilot?"

"Of course not."

"No. There was a time when you were something else. An engineer, perhaps; a lawyer, a student, a journalist—it does not matter. You were young, hopeful, ambitious, your energies directed toward the things of the spirit and the mind. Then the war came—another war—the endless war. The world said to you suddenly, 'No, you are none of these things you imagine yourself to be. You are a bomber pilot.' And it made you a bomber pilot. I asked you before if you were interested in literature and the arts, and you answered that once you were. That implies that you are no longer; or, rather, that the world no longer permits you to be. It has taken you and changed you from a thinker into a doer, from a force into an agent; it has made you into a tiny cog in its monstrous machinery. Oh, a very remarkable cog, I grant you—a very precise, ingenious, effective bit of mechanism. But a cog none the less. And in the process what has happened? What has happened, if you will allow me to be presumptuous, is that you are probably no longer a thinking, feeling man in the sense you once were. Your mind, perceptions and sensibilities have grown decadent and in danger of atrophy."

Delambre drained his glass and reached for the bottle. "Monsieur?" he asked.

Ordway shook his head. "I'm still working on this, thanks."

The Frenchman poured the brandy into his own glass, inhaled

68

its bouquet and sipped. "At the other extreme," he went on, "take the case of one like myself, who is a writer."

"I didn't know—" Ordway began.

"Oh yes, I am a writer." Delambre smiled deprecatingly. "I shall not hold it against you, however, that you are not acquainted with my name. Most of my work is of a—well—somewhat special critical and philosophic nature and is, thus far, known only to a rather intimate circle. . . . As I was about to say, however: this world-decadence, this frustration of which we were speaking manifests itself in an opposite, and yet parallel, way in men who are not doers in the outward sense but are attempting to live the sentient, contemplative life. A man like Gide, for example. Or Modigliani or Schönberg or any true artist. The machine rejects them, and they reject it. They strive to rise above it, to ignore it, fight it, change it—what you will; but they cannot. They are in it and yet not part of it, and it crushes them to death. They can still think and feel—yes; but they can no longer do. They still write their books and paint their pictures and compose their symphonies; but the vitality, the bone and blood, the integration with life is gone. They too, like the doers, the machine-men and war-men, have become sterile and atrophied."

Delambre smiled gently. "Forgive me, Monsieur—I am talking too much, as I am afraid I always do with the third cognac. But you should read a bit more of Gide—you really should. You will find he will tell you as much about the nature of things as aerial photographs, tachometers and high frequency radio receivers."

He arose, holding his brandy glass, walked to the window and stood silently looking out.

"There is a world at war," he said suddenly, "and there is also a world of peace. There is the miracle of a six-ton bomb and there is the miracle of a snowflake. There is the field of rotting corpses and there is the White Tower. Ah yes, there is still enough of the good, the true, the beautiful left in the world, Monsieur Ordway, if one has but the wit to find them. Come, I propose another toast." He raised his glass and smiled again. "To all good and true and beautiful things. To warm, glowing cognac in crystal inhalers; to Monsieur Gide and Monsieur Van Gogh; to a gardenia on dark hair and a ruby on a white finger; to lovely women and the cold, beautiful mountains—and atrophy. . . ."

Andreas Benner was sitting on the terrace wall as Ordway came down the verandah steps. His booted feet were planted firmly on the ground and his gnarled hands rested on his knees. He looked as if he had not so much as moved a muscle since he had been there.

"How long have you been waiting?" Ordway asked as he crossed to him.

The guide got up and shook hands with a quick, formal jerk. "Only a little while, Herr Ordway."

"The name's Martin."

"Only a little while, Herr Martin."

"You should have let me know you were here."

"There was no hurry."

Ordway laughed. "Still the same old Andreas, eh? '*Komm ich heute nicht, komm ich morgen ja.*'"

The corners of Benner's eyes crinkled into the hundred tiny lines that meant he was smiling. "You still remember well your *Deutsch*," he said.

"I still remember you, you mean." Ordway took a pack of cigarettes from his pocket and held them out. "*Amerikanische*," he said. "You used to like them."

"*Jawohl.*" Benner took one and held it tightly between thumb and forefinger while Ordway gave him a light. He smoked silently for a few moments, exhaling the smoke from his mouth in long blue jets and shredding the cigarette-end between his teeth.

"I have made already a few inquiries," he said.

"Yes?"

"There is not, of course, much that can be done in a small village like Kandermatt. But I have got a little information, and it seems there are possibilities."

"What happens now?"

"There is a certain man I should see down in Interlaken. I shall go there tomorrow."

"But—"

"That part is easy. I go to Interlaken every few weeks anyhow, for other things. What this man will tell me, though, of course I do not know. Perhaps he will say it is impossible. Perhaps there will be a long delay."

There was a moment's silence, and Ordway put his hand on

the guide's arm. "Look, Andreas," he said. "This is wonderful of you, and I appreciate it more than I can tell you. But I won't have you getting yourself into trouble, understand?"

"I shall not get into trouble, Herr Martin."

"After all, it's not a matter of life and death for me. Switzerland is neutral. Hundreds of American and British flyers have come down here over the past two years, and all that happens to them is that they're interned."

Benner nodded. "Yes, there have been many."

"And how many of them get out?"

"A few."

"Have you been—?"

"Helping to get them out? No."

"But then why—?"

"I have never helped pull them down off the Weissturm, either."

They were silent again, smoking.

"They have found your plane," Benner said suddenly.

Ordway swung around. "When? Where?"

"Late yesterday, I think it was. Over on a mountainside above Lauterbrunnen. They found two bodies in it."

"Only two?"

"There were more?"

"There were four of us. Three after I jumped." Ordway paused briefly. "They were dead then, of course."

"It is not necessary that you tell me that, Herr Martin."

"One of them must have been thrown clear somehow."

Benner nodded. "There are many ways a man can disappear on a mountain. Into a crevasse; down a slope—"

"Yes, of course." Ordway turned away, looking at the road and the timber and the bright meadows below.

Dear Mrs. Bixler. Dear Mrs. Wasniewicz. Dear Biscuit . . .

His eyes moved over the valley floor, then slowly up the steep pastures and forests to the gray world of rock above. "You can almost see the Heilweg Hut, Andreas," he said presently.

"Yes. It is there—see—by that outcropping of red rock, straight down from the Karlsberg." The guide pointed.

"But I can't see the lake."

"No, the lake is down behind."

71

Benner dropped his remaining half-inch of cigarette to the grass and stepped on it carefully with a heavy boot.

"Have you been to the hut lately?" Ordway asked.

"I was there last about three weeks ago, with the Patrol."

"It's gone to pot, I suppose?"

"*Bitte?*"

"Is it run down?"

"Yes, it is run down. The *Alpenverein* closed it officially almost three years ago."

"And no one goes there except the Patrol?"

"Herr Radcliffe uses it sometimes when he is collecting his stones. The French gentleman, I think, has been there once or twice."

"I met the two Germans while I was walking this afternoon," Ordway said. "They seem to be climbers."

"Yes, they have made some ascents."

"Have you gone with them at all?"

Benner shook his head. "Even in the good times the Germans do not often use guides. They think they are better than the guides."

"These two seemed to know their way around."

"*Bitte?*"

"They sounded like—well—experts."

"Yes, I have heard that they are. The one called Hein—the older one—before the war he is supposed to have made some terrible climbs."

"Terrible?"

"The Matterhorn faces; the Eigerwand; that sort of thing, like so many of the young Germans were doing." Benner shook his head again. "That I have never understood. We Swiss—yes, and the English and French and Americans too—we climb mountains for sport. But the Germans, no. What it is they climb for I do not know. Only it is not for sport."

The two men were silent again. The sun had begun to slope away toward the west, and the first pink tinge of evening touched the snow-peaks high above.

"And Carla?" Ordway asked suddenly.

The guide looked at him questioningly.

"Fräulein Dehn. Does she go up to the mountains sometimes?"

72

"No, I do not think so."

"You see her often?"

"Not often. Sometimes when I am here at the inn. She works now for Frau Knubel."

"Have you any idea why she's working here?"

"Why?"

"Or why she's in Kandermatt?"

"A person must live some place. Kandermatt is better than most, I suppose." Benner paused and shook his head. "No, she came back—let me see—it is two years ago now and has been here ever since. That is all I know."

A gong in the inn sounded three times. "There is your supper, Herr Martin," he said. "And I must report at Patrol Headquarters."

"When will I see you again, Andreas?"

"Tomorrow I go down to Interlaken, and it will be late before I am back. I will stop by the following morning and let you know how things are going."

"Good." Ordway hesitated. "Only—"

"Ja?"

"Only, remember what I said before. Don't get yourself in trouble. It's not that—well—important."

The guide looked at him curiously. "You want to go—do you not, Herr Martin?"

It was a moment before Ordway answered. "Yes," he said. "Yes, of course."

"Then do not worry, and we shall see what can be done."

They shook hands, and Ordway watched the stumpy, broadshouldered figure swing through the gate and down the dirt road into the timber. Then he entered the inn and went upstairs to his room to wash.

He did not wash immediately, however. Instead, he sat down on the edge of the bed and sat studying the interwoven squares and lozenges of the faded green carpet.

In his mind he went back, one by one, over the meetings and conversations of the day: Radcliffe; the two Germans on the pasture slope; Delambre; Benner. He recalled the afternoon before: awakening in the strange, familiar room in which he now sat; the girl sitting alone on the terrace wall; the bald knob of rock above the Aarn, and the valley and mountains emerging from the mist. Beyond that his mind would not go. He closed his eyes and struggled to face his thoughts back to the hours and days before, but they would not go. Everything before the moment of his awakening was blurred and remote to him, as if shrouded in fog and night.

What was it then that had been happening to him in those past thirty hours? What had happened that he had stood there on the terrace, not five minutes before, and not cared whether Benner came back from Interlaken with his "information" next day or next month? Why—to face right up to it—didn't he seem to care if he ever got out; if he ever got anywhere? . . . Was it fear, perhaps? Fear of himself and the gray, horizonless sterility in which his mind seemed trapped and transfixed. . . . Or of the world he lived in; of the dark, looming shapes that were arising everywhere from the world's corruption—drawing always closer —faceless, swarming, obscene. . . .

He got up and went to the washbasin and began slowly and carefully to soap his hands. I am a bomber pilot, he said to himself quietly. I am an American bomber pilot who had to bail out over Switzerland and by a rather fantastic coincidence came down in a place which I once knew. I am probably a little shaken and a little tired, and I am waiting to see if Andreas Benner can find a way to get me out. That is all there is to it. Those are the facts.

But it was not facts that he wanted. It was the truth.

Chapter 5

The rays of the setting sun streamed eastward over Europe. They slanted across the plains of Germany, the brown hills of Italy and the fields and vineyards of France. They moved gently over the gutted meadows, the torn forests, the blackened, smoking cities, the gun emplacements, the tank traps, the long brown and gray columns that crept endlessly along the roads. They flickered briefly on the wings of soaring planes and on the corroded steel of helmets lying half-buried in the mud. They shone rich and glowing on the spires of Cologne cathedral and on the still, huddled figures of the three pigtailed schoolgirls lying side by side on the cobbles of the marketplace of Arnhem. They struck shining fire on the still, white summits of the Alps.

The sun, huge and golden, hung impaled on the rugged rock-spine of the Burggen Ridge. Then it disappeared, and a deep purple shadow moved swiftly across the valley floor. It fell on the trim lawns and white gables of the *Gasthof*, on the meadows and vegetable patches, on the slanting forests and twisting paths and the cold silver ribbon of the Aarn. It raced up the mountainsides, past glacier and snowfield, precipice and ice-wall, to the skyline ridges. For a few moments the peaks stood aloof, white and blazing in the light from beyond the horizon. Then, one by one, the twilight climbed their summits: first the lower ones, then the greater, finally the greatest. On the very pinnacle of the White Tower there was a last tiny glint of fire. The next instant it was

75

gone, and the mountain rose gray and gleaming against the darkening sky.

In the valley the bells tinkled as the sheep descended from the upper pastures, and the Aarn still rumbled among its ancient stones. There was no other sound within the unbroken circle of the peaks.

Herr Knubel peered through the glass panel in the swinging door and waited until Annamarie had left the kitchen. Then he went in and for the next ten minutes moved methodically about, looking into the stove, the sinks, the icebox and the corners of the cupboard shelves. His inspection completed, he walked down the empty hall to the two-room wing which served him and Frau Knubel as living quarters.

His wife was at the table in the sitting room, making entries in the big red-and-black-bound ledger. Knubel sat down in an armchair and took off his shoes.

"*Das Dreckmädel,*" he said. "You would think it was the cockroaches we are paying her to feed."

Frau Knubel continued scratching in the ledger.

"Besides, I think she's smuggling food out to that no-good family of hers."

"Maybe you won't have to be fussing about it so much longer," his wife said.

"Why? What do you mean? She hasn't given notice, has she?"

"No. But people expect to get paid, you know. Even for feeding cockroaches."

Herr Knubel got up and looked over his wife's shoulder at the long columns of figures. She had taken a six-weeks' bookkeeping course at a business school in Basle twenty years before, and he had never been able to understand their finances since. He sighed, returned to his chair and sat tugging meditatively at his long nose.

"A chef we once had," he said. "A chef, two assistant chefs, one baker, eight waitresses, two busboys, three kitchenmaids. Now we cannot pay for one cretin with kleptomania and a goitre."

His wife ran her pen down a line of figures, counting half-aloud. "Eight mouths we were feeding, with four paying. Now it is nine mouths, and still four paying."

"He will pay in time, don't worry."

76

"In time. To be sure. Along with the peace treaties and other reparations. I'm sure that will make Münz the grocer very happy." Frau Knubel pushed back the ledger, removed the pince-nez she was wearing and looked at her husband with sharp black eyes. "What does Andreas say, eh?"

"About Herr Ordway?"

"Yes."

"He thinks he can get him out all right."

"How soon?"

Knubel shrugged. "In a few days perhaps. A week. Two weeks."

"And he will stay here until then?"

"Where else is there for him to go?"

Frau Knubel was silent a moment, biting her thin lip. "We could get in trouble with this, of course," she said.

"We could. It is not likely though."

"Why not?"

"It is not likely anyone will find out about him."

"But if they do?"

Knubel shrugged again. "We go to jail, I suppose. Or pay a fine."

"Pay a fine!" His wife laughed harshly. "With what, may I inquire? I thought already things were so bad they could not get worse. Now we pick up someone to eat us out of house and home without paying a counterfeit sou, and if the authorities find out he is here we go to jail."

"It is not easy," Knubel agreed. "But what is there to do? Would you have me report him?"

Again his wife did not answer at once. She put her pince-nez back on, pulled the ledger toward her and began running the pen down a new column. "No," she said at last in a scarcely audible voice. "I would not have you report him."

Her pen scratched on, and Knubel sat quietly pulling at his nose. Presently he got up, crossed in stockinged feet to the window and pushed back the faded net curtains. He stood for several minutes looking out into the purple dusk.

"This was the time they used to come back," he said softly. "From the picnics and the climbs. They used to come down out of the Aarntal Path over there and pile their boots and axes in the hall, and the old ones would go upstairs for their hot baths and the young ones would go into the bar. They always began to sing

77

in the bar, and you always got angry about it. Remember those three young couples who came down every July from Rotterdam? Every Saturday night they used to have one *kirsch* too many and sing their damn heads off."

He was silent again, peering into the distance. "Everyone was down by this time, except the high climbers. On a clear night like this you could sometimes see their torches way up there, coming down one after the other over the glaciers. Even without the telescope you could see them."

He stood looking out for another few moments; then he let the curtains fall, pulled down the shade and returned to the armchair. Opening a carved pinewood box, he took out a long, thick cigar, removed it carefully from its wrapping, bit a small neat hole in the end and lighted it. Then he leaned back in his chair, watching the blue clouds of smoke curl toward the ceiling.

"I thought you were trying to save your cigars," his wife said, looking up.

"Save them?" Herr Knubel shook his head and sighed a little. "And what is there to save them for?" he asked.

Nicholas Radcliffe arose from the table, a finger marking his page in Geikie's *Fossiliferous and Other Limestones*, which he was re-reading. As he was about to leave the dining room, however, Mrs. Meach appeared from the kitchen with a dish in her hand. "You've forgotten your dessert," she said reprovingly.

"I don't believe I'll have any tonight," Radcliffe said.

"But it's plum duff."

"I'm afraid I'm not quite up to it. Put it in the icebox and perhaps I'll eat it before I go to bed."

"And how about your tea, sir?"

"I may have that later too."

Shaking her square head disapprovingly, Mrs. Meach retreated into the kitchen, and Radcliffe went into the library and resumed his reading. He read for only a few minutes, however. Presently he got up, took his flute from its case in a corner cupboard and went with it out onto the small verandah of the chalet. He did not play it, but held it idly across his knees as he sat down on the verandah steps and looked out across the darkening valley.

It had been seventeen years since he first looked at the valley

78

from these steps, almost thirty since he had first seen it from the village below. Every form and feature of it was as familiar to him as his own body or the clothing he wore: the clustered gables and the brown steeple of the church; the white-roofed inn; the winding road (he knew every bend in it); the rumbling Aarn (he knew each pool and cataract); even the individual stones and trees and patches of tilted pasture. He knew them all. He could see them now, each and all of them, spread out beneath him in the fading light.

His eyes moved slowly upward. They moved past the forests and scrublands, the gorges and waterfalls, to the empty world of rock and ice above. But it was not an empty world to him, for, even more than the valley, it was his home. He knew each detail of that austere and intricate masonry: each pass, each ridge, each glacier; the black basaltic dyke on the south face of the Himmelshorn; the reddish sandstone of the Karlsberg; the moraines, the crevasses, the cornices, the tiny flakes of mica gleaming in the dusk of the sunless gullies.

Cultivate your garden. . . . That was Voltaire—canny, dyspeptic old Voltaire—and how wise and true the words came down the years from the bright, tight, vanished little world of the Eighteenth Century. He had tried to live his life by those words. Above all else, he had valued and sought the power of concentration, of husbanding and directing his mind and energies, of mastery in the one field of human knowledge that he had selected as his own. He had built his house, lonely, perhaps, but sound and strong, and cultivated his garden of rocks. He had shut out the weeds and jungle. He had shut out the night and the wind.

And yet—Radcliffe's blue eyes still travelled upward—and yet the wind still blew. Beyond the high encircling rampart of the peaks it blew in a wild dark tide across the ravaged face of the continents and oceans. Staring upward through the still twilight, he could see it raising a fine fringe of spume along the white ridges of the skyline. Closing his eyes, he could feel it stirring, cold and fitful, through every duct and adit of his body.

He was staring at the peaks again. His gaze moved over gorge and glacier, ridge and precipice, past the Rotalp, the Graf, the Gräfin, the Himmelshorn, down into the deep blue shadows of the icefields, then slowly upward along the pure and terrible

79

symmetry of the Weissturm. It moved up the gleaming snow-slopes, the monstrous buttresses, the ice-walls and rock-walls, the tiering ledges and thrusting ridges, until it rested at last on the gentle white dome of its summit. In all that vast sweep of space and silence only one thing moved. From the topmost pinnacle of the dome a thin thread of snow streamed eastward in the wind against the evening sky.

For a long time Radcliffe sat motionless, his eyes raised, his flute lying idly across his bony knees. And presently, as he still stared, it seemed to him that another shape was slowly taking form behind the soaring outline of the Tower. A greater shape. The greatest of all shapes. Through the gulfs of twilight he could almost see the two tiny figures creeping upward along that forlorn and timeless ridge.

Mallory . . . Mallory . . .

He had been dead twenty years. It was twenty years ago that June that the mist had closed in over the East Ridge of Everest and he and Irvine were gone. And all the rest were gone too. Not dead, perhaps, like George and Sandy, not lying forever dead in the unimaginable loneliness of the Himalayan night; but gone none the less. The young men that they all had been were gone. . . . Why did they return, then? Why did they keep coming back into his thoughts, into his garden—those lost, long-gone, forgotten young men, with their boots and their windburned faces and their laughter and their young eyes squinting upward at the peaks? Young men like Mallory, like Irvine . . .

Like Ordway.

Radcliffe closed his eyes again and shook his head a little, as if to clear it. Perhaps that was what it was, he thought. Perhaps it was the young aviator that had set his mind off on its bemused wanderings—the big dark-eyed young American in his too-small borrowed clothes, standing smiling in the doorway. Presently he raised his flute from his knees and began playing the serenade from Die Zauberflöte. He played slowly and softly, listening to how the sound seemed to travel down the slope before him, move across the still valley and flow back at him, from the slopes on the other side. It was dark when he finished playing. Going inside, he put the flute away, got the plum duff and a cup of tea from the kitchen and settled down to the next chapter of *Fossiliferous and Other Limestones*.

When Andreas Benner finished feeding the chickens he watered the leeks and radishes and prodded the sick goat into its shed. Then he went into the kitchen and sat down.

"I thought you were playing *jass* down at the Dyhrenfurths' tonight," his wife said.

"No," he said, "I do not feel like playing cards."

She looked at him curiously over her shoulder from the tub where she was cleaning a fowl, but he did not continue. For several minutes he sat motionless in his chair, staring at the knotted veins on the backs of his thick brown hands.

"You are on patrol tomorrow?" his wife asked without turning.

"No."

"I thought Tuesdays you were always on patrol."

"Usually I am. But for tomorrow I was relieved." He paused a moment. "Tomorrow I must go down to Interlaken."

Frau Benner turned and looked at him again. "To Interlaken? Why?"

"I have business there."

"What kind of business?" Benner did not answer. She waited a moment, then wiped her hands on a rag and came around and faced him. "It is business about that *Amerikaner*, isn't it?"

"Yes," Benner said.

"You are going to get yourself in trouble with that *Amerikaner*."

"I do not think so."

"You think you can get him out?"

"Yes."

"And if they catch you?"

Benner shrugged.

"If they catch you there will be the devil to pay. You are a member of the Patrol Corps."

"I am a guide."

"You used to be a guide. Now you are a member of the Patrol Corps, working for the canton."

"I am a guide," Benner repeated. "And this American was once a *Herr* of mine. We climbed together many times, years ago."

"You had hundreds of *Herren*. I suppose if they all fell from

81

the sky onto our doorstep—the Americans and English and Frenchmen and Germans and Swedes and all the rest of them—you would decide it was your duty to rent a special train and drop each of them off at his home?"

Benner did not seem to be listening. "He was a good *Bergsteiger*, that boy," he went on quietly. "A little wild, perhaps, but good. Once I pulled him out of a crevasse in the Dürrengletscher. Another time we got caught in a storm and spent all night out on the north ridge of the Wunderhorn. In the morning we took off our wet clothes and lay on a ledge in the sun, and the bread and cheese was all spoiled, but there was still a flask of wine, and he found in his pocket some American chocolate they call 'Ershibars,' and we ate them. It was for him I went the highest that any guide since my father has gone on the Weissturm. He and Fräulein Dehn and that *Wiener* boy—they were trying to climb it alone, *die Esel*, and I went up and pulled them down."

He fell silent and sat staring again at the backs of his hands. He heard his wife's voice rising and falling and saw her round red face grow rounder and redder, but he did not say anything. Then at last he saw that she was finished.

"Well?" she asked. "You do not agree with me?"

"You have all the right reasons, as usual," he said.

"And you will do as you please, as usual, I suppose?"

He shook his head slowly. "Not as I please, *Liebchen*. As I think right."

After a few minutes he got up and went out into the doorway. He filled his pipe and lighted it and sat on the stoop for a while, looking up through the dusk at the snow-peaks and listening to the deep, tireless rumbling of the Aarn. Then he arose and went inside again. Avoiding the kitchen, he climbed the stairs, opened a creaking door and entered a musty slope-ceilinged attic. A kerosene lamp hung from a crossbeam in the center of the room, and he went over and lighted it.

He stood looking about him in the flickering yellow glow. Against the wall, near the door, was a neat row of five pairs of shoes. Three of the pairs were boots, with oiled leather uppers and tricouni nails glinting dully around the edges of the thick soles; the other two were *Kletterschuhe* of rope and canvas. Beyond the shoes, in the corner, was a pile of sharp-spiked crampons and an open packing-box filled with pitons, karabiners, hammers and leather slings. Along the side wall, on a long row of nails, hung corduroy and dark woolen knickerbockers, faded flannel shirts, sweaters, a large and a small rucksack, a water-flask, a pair of smoked goggles, two battered brown felt hats and a green hat with a fragment of a hawk's feather in the band. In the far corner, on the floor, lay coil upon coil of carefully braided rope, ranging in color from brash, gleaming yellow to weathered coffee-brown. Above the rope, three ice axes hung from hooks in the wall.

Benner walked slowly across the room and took the axes, one by one, from their hooks. He unfastened the leather shields and stood for several moments running his thumb gently along the cold, lightly greased steel of the blades.

"Andreas!" his wife's voice came up from below.

He put the axes back in their sheaths, hung them on the hooks, blew out the kerosene lamp and started down the stairs.

"You might help me get rid of all these feathers and guts," his wife called irritably from the kitchen.

Paul Delambre turned the stem of the brandy glass in his long fingers and stared meditatively at the rich amber liquid. He and his wife were alone in the lounge of the inn, and there was no sound except the soft clicking of her knitting needles. He drank down the brandy and resumed reading *L'Immoraliste*.

. . . . *What frightens me, I admit, is that I am still very young. It seems to me sometimes that my real life has not begun. Take me away from here and give me some reason for living. I have none left. I have freed myself. That may be. But what does it signify? This objectless liberty is a burden to me. It is not, believe me, that I am tired of my crime—if you choose to call it that—but I must prove to myself that I have not overstepped my rights.*

Look! I have here a number of white pebbles. I let them soak in the shade, then hold them in the hollow of my hand and wait.

. . .

He reached for the bottle on the tabouret and refilled his glass. He sipped the brandy slowly as he continued reading.

After a few minutes his wife yawned and got up, pushing her knitting into a blue mesh bag. "Are you coming up?" she asked.

"No, not yet." Delambre closed the book. "I think I shall do some writing tonight."

"To whom?"

"Not to anyone. On my book."

"Oh."

"Why do you say 'oh' and look at me like that?"

"It is a long time now since you have worked on your book."

"And if it is? Is that any reason why I should not begin again? Perhaps you forget, ma chérie, that that is what I am—a writer."

"There is no need to get upset about it," she said placidly.

"Upset? Who is upset?"

He watched her as she crossed the lounge and ascended the stairs, her yellow hair glinting and her thighs smooth and full under the clinging fabric of her skirt. Then he got up and went to the writing table in the corner. Taking a vellum-bound notebook from his pocket, he laid it on the table and sat down. After a moment he arose again, went back to the tabouret and got the brandy bottle and glass. He sat down again, filled the glass and began turning the leaves of the notebook.

On the first page was written *L'Ame Qui Rie, par Paul Delambre*, and, at the bottom, *2me Juillet, 1940*. The next ten or twelve pages were filled with script, about half of it clean, the other half blackened with x's and deletion lines. The rest of the book was blank. Delambre read through two or three of the pages, tore them from the book and, crumpling them in his hand, dropped them in the wastebasket under the table. He took a sip from the glass and turned to the first blank page.

He was no longer so young, he wrote, and sometimes the thought filled him with fear. For his true life, he knew, his life of the spirit, had not even begun. He yearned to go away—to seek, to find—to win from the dark chaos of the world the secret of . . .

His pen stopped moving across the page, and for several minutes he sat staring at the scarred surface of the table. Then he drew a thick black line through what he had written, refilled his glass and began writing again.

It did not seem to go right, however. He wrote, crossed out, wrote, crossed out; then he tore out the page and threw it in the wastebasket and sat meditatively sipping his brandy and studying the complex paint-flake pattern of the table-top. It was not until he went out onto the terrace for a breath of air that his thoughts fell into a clear, cohesive pattern. Then, staring up through the darkness at the white silence of the peaks, he felt the strength and vitality returning to him—felt the vast, complex congeries of images and ideas that thronged his mind emerge again in pure and burning clarity. A thrill of exhilaration passed through his body like a cold, clean wind. He could think and feel again! He would write again! Not tonight, perhaps—no, not in the tired fag-end of a spent day, that would be simply a waste—but in the morning, when the sunlight was rich in the blue sky and his energies were fresh and keen. He would sit down then, serenely, strongly, and the things that he must say would pour from him as from a great geyser out of the earth. He would write and write. . . .

Going up the stairs, his foot slipped on the worn carpet and his knee came down heavily on the step. He only smiled, however, and he smiled again when he discovered that he had turned the wrong way in the second-floor hall and was opening the wrong door. He retraced his steps and went into his room.

The small silk-shaded bed lamp was the only light burning, and the hideous hotel furniture and vomitous green carpet were mercifully blurred in shadow. But the Van Gogh and the Toulouse-Lautrec gleamed at him from the wall; the Sung horses reared their delicate white outlines against the dark-blue and russet background of his bookshelves; the Tanagra dancers rose, slim and exquisite, from among the jars and bottles on the dressing table. For a passing instant it almost seemed to him that he was entering his old room in the house on the Rue Castellane.

His wife lay on the bed, filing her nails. She had undressed and was now wearing a sheer powder-blue night-garment that revealed her lush body almost as completely as if she had been nude. Delambre's eyes moved over the long, tapering legs, the rounded, full-fleshed thighs, the soft curve of her belly, the high, firm breasts pressing against their sheath of silk. The skin of her arms and shoulders was a gleaming pink in the soft light of the bed lamp, and her hair, thrown loosely behind her on the pillow, was a cascade of dull gold.

"You did not write long," she said, without looking up.

"No," he replied. "The light was bad."

He undressed in silence and when he had finished stood at the window in his pajamas and bathrobe, staring out at the night. His hands felt cold and moist, and he rubbed them slowly up and down against the rough wool of the robe.

"Have we no cognac in the room?" he asked.

"You had it downstairs," his wife said.

"That's finished. I mean the rest."

"It's in the closet. Only—"

"Only what?"

"Don't you think you have had enough?"

"No," he said. "Most definitely I have not had enough."

He got the bottle from the closet, opened it and poured himself a glass. When he had drunk it his hands felt warmer and he went back to the window.

"I think I may do a bit of a climb tomorrow," he said.

"A climb?"

"Oh nothing very strenuous. Up to the hut, perhaps. Just to get back the feel again." He paused, but the only sound from the bed was the thin scraping of the nail-file. "I used to do quite a bit of mountaineering, you know. Mont Blanc, the Jungfrau—"

Still his wife said nothing. Delambre's gaze moved up and outward through the night to where the immense silhouette of the White Tower rose gleaming against the stars. He felt again, as he had earlier on the terrace, a sudden cold, clean wind of exhilaration flowing through his blood and bones. "A man has need of many things," he said. "There are times when he needs the things of the body and times when he needs the things of the mind. And there are other times when he needs none of these, but only the great simplicities—the mountains, the sea, the sky. Men cannot live by intelligence and graciousness alone. Any more than nations can. Any more than France could. They must have in them not only tempered steel, but granite and iron. They must not only think and feel, but do.

"I have been thinking about this American," he continued after a pause. "This aviator. I shall put him in my book. Not precisely as he is, to be sure—not as an individual called Ordway or John Smith or whatever his name is—but as a symbol. He will be the airman-technician-soldier of the Twentieth Century; the doer; the *Tatmensch*. Over against him will be the man of thought and sensitivity, the artist-philosopher. Separately, each by himself, they

86

are sterile, impotent, lost—two aimless spinning neutrons in a void. But put them together, integrate them, and they become an atom, a force. The man who is these two men in one: he and he only is the complete man. Whatever may happen to him, whatever he is called upon to endure, he remains strong, unassailable, unvanquished."

For a few minutes Delambre stood motionless at the window, gazing upward; then he turned back to the room. His wife had stopped filing her nails and was lying back on the pillows with her eyes lightly closed and her arms twined in her hair above her head. The bodice of her nightdress had come loose and sloughed to the side, exposing the soft white mound of one breast. It was rising and falling gently with her breathing, and the pointed nipple was pink and gleaming in the faint light of the bed lamp.

A sudden blind anger shook him. "Mindless slut!" he shouted. "Kitchen maid!"

He stood looking aimlessly about him, his heart pounding, his hands opening and closing. His eyes fell on the brandy bottle, and he poured himself out a drink, spilling half of it down the front of his bathrobe. He drank what was left of it, poured out a second drink and drank it more slowly. When he had finished he set the glass down, walked over to the bed and stood looking down at his wife. She still lay without stirring—relaxed, voluptuous, a great golden animal.

Then she opened her eyes and looked up at him. With a low murmur that was almost a sob he sank down on the bed beside her. He passed his hands tenderly over her hair, her cheeks, her throat, her breasts.

"Astrid," he whispered. "Be kind to me. Be kind and sweet and loving to me, Astrid, my love."

She raised a hand and passed it lightly, almost perfunctorily, over his hair. Presently he reached out and switched off the bed lamp, so that he could no longer see the contempt in her cool violet eyes.

It was already dark when Siegfried Hein and Hans Mohler trudged up the twisting road to the inn and climbed the stairs to their room. They put their rope and axes in the closet, undressed and rubbed their bodies vigorously with alcohol.

"Stiff?" Mohler asked.

Hein shook his head.

"I'm as creaky as an old hinge."

"Nonsense," Hein said. "A little scramble like that just tones up the system." He flexed his arms and legs and watched with satisfaction how the firm, resilient muscles sprang to life under the pink-white flesh. "Another two or three days' exercise and I'll be ready for a real climb." He resumed rubbing himself, singing snatches of a Bavarian mountain song:

> *"Er geht an's Berg hinauf,*
> *Er steigt bis in die Höh,*
> *Gewinnt das blitzend' Ziel*
> *Für Deutschland . . ."*

He was interrupted by a knocking on the door, and a moment later Herr Knubel appeared, carrying two letters. "These came in the noon delivery," he explained. "They were in your box."

Hein took them and handed one to Mohler. They were in identical envelopes and postmarked Stuttgart.

"The *Herrschaften* have had their dinner?" Knubel inquired.

Hein nodded. "In the village."

"Do the *Herrschaften* wish for anything else?"

"Thank you, no."

The innkeeper left. Then the two men opened the letters and read them in silence. "Wednesday, the fifth," Mohler said. "That means leaving here tomorrow."

Hein stood motionless without speaking, his gray eyes narrowed and his lips compressed into a thin line. Suddenly he crumpled the letter in his hand and threw it on the bed. "The adjutant at the *Regierungsamt*," he said. "You know what that means, don't you?"

Mohler nodded.

"It means they're going to put us behind desks. It means they think we're not good enough to lead troops any more." Hein's hands were balled into tight fists at his sides. "*Gottverdammt*, they can't do it! I am a field officer. I have commanded men for four years—in Norway, Jugoslavia, Greece, Russia. They can't kick me around like that and shove me behind some counter in a supply-office!"

88

He began pacing up and down the room with quick, angry strides. Mohler watched him in silence.

"I don't like it either," he said at last. "But what can we do?"

"Plenty."

"Such as what?"

"I'll think of something."

Hein stopped pacing suddenly and stood staring out the window into the darkness.

"You have to report on the fifth too?" Mohler asked. Hein did not answer, and he repeated the question.

"No. The nineteenth. My inactive status didn't start until two weeks after yours." Hein gave a bitter little laugh. "And they obviously don't want to have me around any sooner than they have to."

"Will you come back to Stuttgart tomorrow, then?"

"I don't know." Hein turned from the window and sat down in one of the chairs. The violent anger that had seized him had passed, and his voice was again low and even. "I don't think so. I think perhaps I shall stay on another few days."

"You might as well."

"I can get in a bit more climbing, at least."

"If there's anyone to climb with."

"There's that broken-down Frenchman—he's always gabbing about what a mountaineer he is. Or there's the new one . . ." Hein fell silent a moment, musing. "What do you make of him, Hans?" he asked.

"The tall one on the Aarntal path?"

"Yes."

"I think he is an Englishman." Mohler waited briefly. "Don't you?"

"No."

"What is he then?"

"An American."

"What makes you think so?"

"I can tell. There is a difference."

"How do you think he got here?"

"There are many ways, I suppose. Some Americans live in Switzerland. Diplomats and that sort of thing. On the other hand—"

"He might be a spy. Or an escaped prisoner."

"Or almost anything." Hein shrugged. "After all, look at ourselves. Or at half the foreigners in Switzerland. Civilian clothes —papers in order—and no questions asked."

"Are you going to check up on him?"

"Later, perhaps." Hein passed a hand meditatively over his chin. "I think perhaps I shall get a little better acquainted first."

He got up, went to the window again and stood looking out into the night. Mohler brought out a suitcase from the closet and began packing his clothes. Neither spoke for a while.

"Do you know what I should like to do?" Hein said suddenly.

"What?"

"Before I leave here, I'd like to make one real climb."

"What do you mean, *real*?"

"The kind we used to do before the war, on the Matterhorn faces and the Eigerwand. A seventh-degree ascent. A great ascent. I'd like to arrive at the *Regierungsamt* in Stuttgart two weeks from tomorrow and salute smartly and say, 'Oberleutnant Hein reporting for duty, sir. I have served in the field in Norway, Jugoslavia, Greece, Russia. I have been twice wounded and awarded the Iron Cross and the Medal of Valor. I have just returned from a month on inactive status, sir, during which it was my good fortune and privilege to make the first ascent of the Weissturm from the Kandermatt Valley, for the greater glory of *Führer* and *Vaterland*. And now, *Herr Kommandant*, you may kick me behind my desk along with the rest of the worn-out, gutless old men.' "

Hein's voice had gradually risen as he spoke. Now he stopped abruptly and was silent again.

"You want to try the Weissturm?" Mohler said after a moment.

"Not try it. *Climb* it."

"They say it's impossible from this side."

"They said the Eigerwand and the north face of the Matterhorn were impossible."

"Yes, but—"

"But we climbed them."

Mohler continued packing. Hein remained for a while at the window, staring up at the white battlements of the distant mountaintops; then he turned away, crossed the room slowly and stretched himself out on his bed.

"Yes," he said presently. "I think I may try a bit of mountaineering with our tall, mysterious young American visitor. I think I might rather enjoy showing him what a broken-down, combat-fatigued, pen-pushing nincompoop of a German Wehrmachts-offizier can do."

Carla Dehn walked in the darkness along the winding road. She had been walking since mid-morning, stopping only at long intervals to rest in a green clearing or on a flat rock beside the Aarn; but she was still not tired. Her footsteps held to their slow, unbroken rhythm on the rutted earth, as she came around still another familiar curve and the white gables of the inn swung into view against the forests and the peaks.

Except for the rare times when she had been ill, this was the first day in nearly two years that she had not spent most of the morning and afternoon at her work around the inn. She had set about it as usual after breakfast, making beds, tidying the lounge and foyer and helping Frau Knubel with the daily marketing list. For almost three hours she had succeeded in focussing her eyes and mind on bedspreads, dusty corners and the outrageous price of mutton ribs. Then the moment came when she could do it no longer. Murmuring a meaningless excuse to Frau Knubel, she had walked from the house, across the terrace, down the slopes of the knoll and along the road. Hour after hour she had walked: up and down the familiar woodland paths, through the tall, slanting belts of larch and spruce, among the gray, weathered boulders of the rumbling Aarn.

Now, walking home again at last through the dark stillness, it seemed to her that the river's tumult was still dinning in her ears. The Aarn was already half a mile behind her, but she knew it did not matter. She could put it a mile, ten miles, the breadth of the Alps behind her; she could return to her work, eat, sew, walk, read; she could lie sleepless on her bed in the darkness and press the heels of her hands against her ears. And still it would make no difference. The flood was loose again, and its sound would follow her wherever she went, whatever she did—always louder, deeper, more imperious. A man had come to the quiet valley, and her peace was gone. A stranger—yes, yes, she thought bitterly, he is a stranger now—had come impossibly, fantastically down from the night under his silken shroud, and the peace she had struggled so hard for through the long years and won for herself at last was shattered into a thousand quivering fragments.

She stopped suddenly and stood at the roadside pressing the tips of her fingers against her closed eyelids. Then she dropped her hands to her sides and held them there until they no longer trembled.

"He is a stranger," she said.

Presently she began walking again. The road ran for a way between open fields, then through a stand of timber and over a tiny wooden bridge that crossed a stream. Just beyond the bridge was the beginning of the narrow side-road that wound up the knoll to the inn. Reaching it, she hesitated; then she began the ascent. Five minutes later she was walking quickly across the dark, seemingly deserted terrace.

But it was not deserted. As she neared the kitchen door a tall figure separated itself from the surrounding shadows and approached her. She felt she was going to run, but instead she stopped and stood quite still.

"You frightened me," she said.

"No, I didn't," said Martin Ordway. "You knew I'd be here." She did not answer.

"Why have you been avoiding me?" he asked.

"I haven't. Truly I haven't."

"Where have you been all day, then?"

"Down in the village."

"You're still a bad liar," he said, smiling.

It was a moment before she spoke again. "Look, Martin," she said suddenly. "You do not understand, but it is different now. I am not a guest here any more, as I once was. I work here now. There is always something to be done, and Frau Knubel sends me on errands—"

"Up the Aarntal?"

"How do you know?" She was staring up at him, and her voice was edged.

"A scout is alert. He is also trustworthy, loyal, brave, clean and tells the truth. You'd make a hell of a scout."

"Oh, you are impossible! You're—"

"Unverschämt?"

"Yes, unverschämt!"

He laughed. "Good. And now that we've finally agreed on something, will you please stop playing The Mysterious Veiled Lady and talk to me like a human being?"

"But, Martin, I don't—"

He had cupped her elbow in his hand and was leading her across the terrace. When they came to the low stone wall that ringed it he drew her gently down. "Now swing around," he told her. They swung and sat facing the steep slope of the knoll and valley and mountains beyond. "It's better when the feet dangle."

He took his cigarettes from his pocket and held them out to her.

"No, thank you," she said.

"They're Camels."

She hesitated.

"And I'm sure the Herr Doktor Justitzrat Naffziger is safely in his featherbed by now."

He took a cigarette from the pack, lighted it and handed it to her. Then he lighted one for himself.

"At least I can still make you smile," he said.

They were silent for a while, seated side by side on the big, smooth stones of the wall. The moving tips of their cigarettes made a tiny orange tracery in the darkness, and the gray smoke rose straight up into the windless night.

"Carla—" he said.

"Yes?"

"What is it, Carla?"

"What is what?"

"What is it that's the matter? Why are you here in Kandermatt? Why are you acting this way?"

The girl did not answer.

"Aren't you glad to see me again?"

"Oh, yes, Martin. Yes." For a moment he could feel her eyes on him; then she turned her head away. "It's only that—" She hesitated and stopped.

"Go on," he said.

"That things are different."

"The valley isn't different. The forests and the mountains and the stars—they aren't different."

"No," she said quietly. "They stay the same. But we don't stay

93

the same, Martin. We grow older. Things happen to us. We change."

"You haven't changed." She started to speak, but he did not let her. "That first instant yesterday afternoon, when I found you standing out here and you turned and saw me and came walking toward me through the mist—in that first instant I said to myself: No, she hasn't changed. She's a woman now, not a little girl any longer. But she's still Carla. She's still—" He stopped and looked at her in the darkness.

"Still what, Martin?"

"Lovely."

They fell silent again. Ordway flicked his cigarette away and watched the thin glowing streak disappear into the shadows below.

"I should be going in," the girl said suddenly.

"No. Not yet." He put his hand on her arm. "Tell me about yourself. About what you do here."

"I've told you. I work. I dust and make beds and help Frau Knubel with the marketing."

"And lie out on the pine needles at night, counting the stars above the Tower?"

It was a moment before she answered. "No," she said then, "I do not do that any more."

"Do you climb up to the meadows? And the glaciers? Do you lie on the straw mattresses in the Heilweg Hut and listen to the glaciers rumbling in the dark like tired old lions?" He paused and laughed softly. "Do you remember the night you wanted Stefan and me to stand guard because you were afraid of the rats? And we explained to you that you were squealing so loud the rats had already run for their lives?"

He paused again. The girl was sitting beside him, motionless, her head turned away.

"Tell me about Stefan," he said. "Where is he? Do you ever see him?"

"Please, Martin—"

The sound seemed to have been ripped out of her, half words and half a sob. With a quick, convulsive gesture she swung herself around and in another moment would have been running across the terrace. Ordway swung around after her and caught her by the arm.

"Don't! Don't!" She pleaded. She was looking up at him almost

94

with terror. "Oh Martin, Martin—what is it you want of me?"

He gripped her arm tightly in his hand and looked down at her. Gradually, almost imperceptibly, the pull against it lessened, and presently she was no longer pulling away at all. He let his hand slip gently down her forearm until it held hers.

"I want you to meet me at the top of the west pasture at nine tomorrow morning," he said. "We're going to walk up the path to the hut."

"I can't."

"Yes you can."

"But I mustn't. My work—"

"You can get out of it."

She started to speak again, but her voice trailed away inaudibly. Her breath was coming in short, sharp jerks and she held her head averted.

"You don't want to go?" he asked.

"Oh yes, yes I do. Only—"

He released her hand. "At nine," he said.

She turned a little and raised her head. For a moment he could see the faint glint of her eyes through the darkness.

"Goodnight, Carla," he said.

"Goodnight, Martin."

"Binks," he said.

"Goodnight—Binks."

Ordway lighted another cigarette and for several minutes walked slowly up and down across the terrace. Then he entered the inn, passed through the empty lounge, went up the stairs and into his room. When he had undressed he turned out the light and lay on the bed staring into the darkness.

A wisp of breeze touched the curtains at the open window and set them gently stirring. He watched them for a while, then got up again, went to the window and looked out. The valley of Kandermatt lay black and still before him. There was no sound. Nothing moved. In the distance the valley rose to the forests, the forests to the rocks, the rocks to the glaciers, the glaciers to the peaks. The peaks hung white and frozen against the darkness. High above the rest loomed the White Tower, withdrawn in space and silence, brooding over the night. It seemed to Ordway as far away as the stars that circled it. As far away as a world at war.

Chapter 6

He reached the head of the pasture, rounded a patch of wild gooseberry bushes and found her sitting on a low rock beside the path. She was wearing a short woolen skirt and green shetland sweater, white anklets and stout walking shoes. A brown paper bag lay on the grass beside her.

"You're early," he said.

"I was afraid if I didn't get away early I would not get away at all." She looked up at him and smiled. "Were you thinking that perhaps I would not come?"

"No, I wasn't thinking that."

He put out his hands, and she took them and got to her feet. Then he looked questioningly at the paper bag.

"Lunch," she said.

"Oh."

She laughed. "Somebody has to remember things like lunch. And I knew even twelve years couldn't change you *that* much."

Ordway said "Oh" again and compressed the grin from his lips. "I've decided to retain my dignity," he announced. He picked up the bag, tried unsuccessfully to squeeze it into two or three pockets, and finally stuffed it down the front of his sweater. "If the *gnädiges Fräulein* will excuse a temporary pot-belly until—"

"Until the cheese starts to melt. Of course, *mein Kapitän*."

She laughed again, and he laughed back, fished out the bag and held it in his hand. There was a moment's silence as he stood looking at her.

"Shall we start?" Carla asked.

They followed the twisting path through alternating patches of grass and berry-bushes, crossed a wire fence on a rickety stile and entered the lower fringes of the forest.

For perhaps half an hour they moved upward through a green tunnel of oaks, beeches and maples. Then these began to thin; they passed through a belt of mixed leaf-trees and conifers, and then presently the lighter greenery of the valley trees was gone altogether and they were climbing slowly through dark aisles of pine and balsam, larch and spruce. Every few hundred yards the path crossed a stream on a worn plank or chain of stepping-stones —quick, glinting freshets plunging noisily down the still forest slopes to the meadows and the Aarn. At intervals it emerged abruptly from the trees onto a bare rim of hillside, and they could see the valley floor spread out below, with its road and river, houses and fields. On the opposite slope, beyond, Radcliffe's chalet showed as a minute reddish smudge against the steep green of the upper pastures.

At the stream crossings they paused briefly, steadying each other across, and now and then they stopped at the open places, pointing out objects below. For the most part, however, they climbed uninterruptedly and without speaking. Carla went first, walking with a slow, easy rhythm, her motions light and seemingly effortless in spite of her heavy shoes. In the forest shade, her brown skirt and dark green sweater blended so harmoniously into the background that Ordway could scarcely see her from a few yards behind. Then suddenly a shaft of sunlight would strike down on her through the treetops, outlining her slender figure against the dark pine-boughs and touching her hair with bright copper fire.

Ordway trudged steadily behind, his smooth-soled shoes slipping occasionally on the roots that veined the path, his breath coming evenly enough, but a little faster than he would have preferred. Every few minutes he paused and drew in a deep draught of air. It was mountain air, scented with balsam, pine-resin and distant snow, and it sucked down into his body with the clean, sparkling freshness of dry wine. It was growing perceptibly cooler, too, as they ascended, but no breeze stirred in the forest, and when they passed through the open patches of sunlight he could feel his back and shoulders going damp beneath his shirt. He stopped, pulled off his sweater, tied the arms around his waist and plodded on.

It was shortly before eleven when they emerged from the trees onto a bold grass-covered promontory that hung out over the valley. They stood for a few minutes looking at the miniature world far below them, then sat down on the soft turf.

"Remember it?" Carla asked.

Ordway nodded. "The Drachenfels. 'Pleasant forest walk, suitable for timid ladies and older children. Time: two hours from upper pasture'—Baedeker."

"We made it in one hour and fifty-five minutes. Congratulations."

"It was nothing, *gnädiges Fräulein*." Ordway lay back in the grass and stretched his legs. "At least, practically nothing. A few weeks' rest and I'll be as good as new."

They laughed, and he lay looking up at her and smiling, until she turned her head away.

"You haven't climbed many hills lately, I suppose?" she asked.

"No, not many."

"Are you sorry you climbed this one?"

"What do you think?" She did not answer. "Are you sorry?"

"No, I'm not sorry. Yet."

"But you expect to be any minute?"

"I—I don't know."

They were silent for a little while. Ordway rolled over onto his stomach and lay plucking idly at the grass. "It hasn't been twelve years," he said.

Again she did not answer.

"It hasn't been five years or one year or six months or six weeks. Time hasn't anything to do with it. We were here before and now we're here again—that's all."

"Does it seem that way to you, Martin?"

"Doesn't it to you?"

She shook her head slowly. "No. To me it seems so very long ago."

"Have I changed that much?"

"You?" She studied him a moment. "I am not sure yet. But everything else—"

98

"Not you. Not Kandermatt." He stared down at the valley. "Last night after you left me I walked around out on the terrace trying to put my thoughts in order, and the more I tried the more I felt like one of those H. G. Wells professors who disappears into a time-machine and comes out the other end. The mountains, the valley, the road, the inn—all exactly as I remembered them. The Knubels, Andreas, Nick Radcliffe, yourself—"

"All the others are gone, though."

"The others don't matter. Except Stefan." He paused again and looked at her. "What about Stefan, Carla?"

It was a moment before she answerd. "What do you mean, what about him?"

"Why wouldn't you tell me about him last night? Why won't you now?"

"There's nothing to tell, Martin. He is all right, I suppose. He lives in Vienna. I—I haven't seen him for a long time."

"And that's all?"

"Yes, that is all."

They were silent again, and he lay watching her.

"Don't, Martin," she said. Her voice was barely audible.

"Don't what?"

"Don't look at me that way. Please."

He reached out and put his hand over hers, resting on the grass beside her. She averted her eyes from his, but did not withdraw it. And suddenly he realized that she was waiting—and that he was waiting too.

"Carla."

"Yes?"

"Carla, I—"

He paused, and they waited. They waited for him to speak, to smile, to laugh; to sit beside her closely as he had used to sit, one arm around her, the other pointing upward at the peaks; to sweep away, in one quick time-obliterating gesture, the veils and barriers that the years had set between them.

. . . Carla, I am afraid. That was what he wanted to say. I am afraid of those twelve years I was just now trying to pretend did not exist, and of what they have done to us. I am afraid, because now, with a sudden and terrible clarity, I am thinking of all the things I was going to do in the world and didn't, all the things

99

I once believed in and then forgot. We used to walk together along these mountain paths—remember? We used to sit together on the grass slopes and rock ledges—you and Stefan and I—and you would lean forward with your chin in your hands, looking down into the valley, while Stefan made up his bright, fantastic stories of mountain-gods and mountain-devils. And when he was finished we would laugh a little, but only a little, because in those days there were many bright, fantastic things we believed in. We believed in the fundamental goodness of men—do you remember? In laughter and contentment for their own sakes. In the future. In ourselves.

Carla—twelve years have passed and we are here again. The tide of war, of chance, or whatever you choose to call it, has washed us up again on these old familiar mountainsides, ebbed for a moment and left us here. The valley is the same, the mountains are the same, even you and I are the same—and yet everything is different. What are we trying to say to each other? And why is it that we cannot say it? I don't know. Perhaps there are no words for the things that have happened to us in those twelve years. . . . But this much I do know, Carla: we cannot let them go on happening to us any longer. Something has been lost and we must find it; something has gone and we must get it back.

These were the things he wanted to say. Getting stiffly to his feet and helping her up, he said: "It's half-past eleven already. We'd better be going if we want to get to the hut for lunch."

Beyond the Drachenfels the timber thinned rapidly. The path wound upward through a belt of dwarf pine, swarming with redstarts and quick, darting finches; then, in a series of sharp switchbacks, across a steeply tilted zone of moss and scraggly moss-hugging shrubs. The forest receded until its tree-tops were a slanting green carpet far below. The soil was no longer a dark, loamy brown, but weathered gray, shot through with great swathes of wildflowers. They crossed a slope on which a wave of pink and sky-blue primulas rose in an unbroken sweep to the skyline. In the gravelled earth beside the path were hundreds of gleaming green cushions of campion moss studded with their tiny violet blossoms —exquisitely delicate and incredibly tough.

Presently rocks began to appear among the grass and flowers:

at first merely small scattered stones; then tumbled heaps of boulders; finally massive, monolithic outcroppings of living rock, forcing their way through the thin skin of earth and sprawling gray and glinting in the sunlight. Suddenly a mountain hare skittered across the path before them. A little farther on a stone-marten perched on a boulder watched them motionlessly with unblinking eyes.

Then they came up over the rim of a long slope and stopped. In one instant, it seemed to Ordway, they had passed from one world into another. In the one step it had taken to surmount the final rocky crest of the slope everything about them had changed as startlingly as if they had passed in a single timeless second from equator to pole.

The valley had swung out of sight below. The neat little meadows and houses of Kandermatt were gone—the Aarn, the village, the green pastures and forests, the soft multicolored slopes of moss and flowers, all were gone—and in their place was the desolate gray-white world of the mountains. Ahead of them, for a distance of perhaps two miles, stretched a savage slanting wilderness of huge rocks—the great terminal moraine of the Dürren Glacier. Beyond and above it loomed the thick white snout of the glacier itself and the gleaming expanse of the ice-field, and, still higher and more distant, the gnarled battlements of the Karlsberg thrusting in a great irregular wedge into the sky. In that whole monstrous sweep of desolation only one thing moved and lived. Far away, from under the lip of the glacier, a milk-gray torrent of water plunged down over the rocks. Its spray flew upward and hung glittering in the still air. Other than this there was only silence and transfixion in the gray world above the forests.

For an hour or more they followed the path upward among the boulders. The Karlsberg did not seem to grow nearer as they advanced, but merely larger and taller—an immense, white-skirted pyramid swinging majestically upward from the horizon to the zenith. Simultaneously, from behind it and on both sides, the rest of the great range rose mile by mile into view: snow-peaks and rock-peaks, piled tier on tier behind each other into the distance; forlorn scree-slopes and glittering glaciers; gorges, buttresses, precipices, ridges; and between and beyond them all, framed in jagged notches and spreading upward to the summits in a broadening sea, the deep shining blue of the alpine sky.

Clambering slowly behind Carla, Ordway stared up at the gray, white-hooded host. The Rotalp, the Dornelberg, the Graf and Gräfin, the Wunderhorn and Himmelshorn and Wetteralp—they were all there, unchanged and unchanging, exactly as he remembered them. Only one was still missing. Only the greatest. For a brief moment as they topped one of the ridges of the boulder-slope it seemed to him that he had caught a glimpse of a pure white line climbing the sky behind the fanged ridge of the Dornelberg. But in the next instant it was gone. Like the storybook king among his courtiers, the Weissturm chose to remain hidden behind its encircling satellites until the time should come for it to reveal itself.

By one o'clock they were directly beneath the Dürren Glacier, and a few minutes later they crossed the stream that spouted out from under its lip.

"The hut is just beyond the next rise," said Carla, pointing.

The boulders were enormous now and the path the merest twisting thread among their tumbled gray confusion. Within another fifteen minutes, however, they had crossed the remainder of the slope and came out on the abrupt ridge that marked the end of the moraine. Beyond it the ground fell away in a gentle slope into a small V-shaped pocket in the mountainside. There was a thin silver stream flowing across its floor, a sparse carpet of moss and minute wildflowers between the rocks, and in its center the squat, weathered shape of the Heilweg Hut.

As they approached it there was a sudden scurrying sound and a fat brown marmot scampered off toward the boulders. Ordway ascended the three stone slabs to the door and tried it. It was locked.

"Andreas says the Patrol leaves a key," Carla said. She felt in a crevice beneath the steps and came up with one. Ordway opened the door and they stepped into the hut.

It was no different from any of a hundred such huts scattered through the Alps from the Dauphiné to the Ortler. There were rough stone walls, held together by great splotches of cement; a broad fireplace; smoke-darkened beams supporting the steep-sloping shingle roof; a pile of straw mattresses in one corner and a small pot-bellied stove in another. In the center were a deal table and two benches, their unpainted surfaces covered with carved initials. A broom, an ax and a tin bucket stood against the wall, but the cupboard above them, that had once held a few cooking utensils and emergency supplies, was bare.

Ordway walked slowly around the room. The fireplace was bare also and the stove pocked with rust. An Alpine Club bulletin on the inside of the door, dealing with climbing accidents and distress signals, had yellowed and curled with age.

"Let's eat outside," he said.

Carla nodded and they left the hut.

In the warm sunshine by the quick little stream the ghosts dissolved. Carla opened the paper bag and brought out a long loaf of fresh bread, two chicken legs and a great golden pat of Neufchâtel cheese. Sitting on a bank of soft moss, they ate hungrily but slowly, savoring each mouthful and pausing often to scoop up palmfuls of cold water from the stream. As they ate, the marmot they had frightened away returned cautiously from the boulder-slope and sat watching them from the top of a near-by rock.

Below the narrow green defile in which they sat the mountainside curved steeply away, and for the first time since they left the Drachenfels they could again see the valley of Kandermatt below. Incredibly tiny and remote it appeared now across the oceans of blue air—an insubstantial toy-world of brightly colored pasteboard spread on a green carpet far away. When he had finished eating, Ordway sat looking down on it for several minutes, his hands clasped about his knees. Then he lay back on the flowered moss, and the sun and sky and the great ragged wedge of the Karlsberg swam gently together before his half-closed eyes.

"Martin—"

"Yes?"

"Sing for me."

"I can't."

"You always used to sing. Right here. We would eat our lunch and lie out here on the moss and close our eyes in the sun, and then you would sing."

"I can't any more," he said. "I don't remember the old songs any more."

"Sing a new one then. One that you Americans sing in the war."
He shook his head. "This isn't the kind of war you do much singing in."

They were silent for a little while.

"You are tired of war, aren't you, Martin?" she asked.

"Who isn't?"

"I mean tired in your bones. In your soul."

"I wouldn't know about my soul, I'm afraid. Along with a few hundred million other people I seem to have misplaced it somewhere."

"Don't you believe in what you are fighting for?"

"Believe in it?" He was silent a moment, squinting up into the golden sun. "Yes, I suppose I do. I believe it's necessary that we fight. I believe that fascism and militarism and their governments and their way of life must be wiped off the earth, if it's to be any sort of an earth worth living on."

"Then—"

"Yes, I still believe those things," he said quietly. "At least I think I still believe them. . . . Only something seems to happen to you after a while. You fight for just so long. You fly out on so-and-so-many missions and drop so-and-so-many bombs. You destroy so-and-so-many cities, kill so-and-so-many people—at least in a plane you don't know how many—and watch so-and-so-many friends die. And you know it's necessary and that it's your job and that that's the kind of world you live in and all the rest of it. But something happens to you just the same. . . ."

"You have been fighting for two years now, you said?"

"I've been in Africa and Europe about that. I went into the army early in '42."

"As a volunteer?"

"Yes."

"And before then?"

"I was an architect."

"Oh, then you did—"

"Finish school? Yes. Those two years at the Beaux Arts and then two more at home. Then I got a job in a New York office."

"How wonderful, Martin!"

"There wasn't anything very wonderful about it, I'm afraid. I was just beginning, of course, and even the established men were having their troubles in those times. I managed to scrape along, though. The firm I was with seemed to have confidence in me, and finally, after about five years, gave me my first real job on my own—a development of workmen's houses in a Rhode Island factory town. I was about halfway through when Pearl Harbor came along. The army wanted flyers, of course, and I knew how to fly, and that was that."

"I remember, you always wanted to fly, Martin."

He nodded. "Ever since May 21st, 1927, to be exact. Do you remember that date?"

She thought for a moment and shook her head.

"I was—let's see—fourteen then and in my last year at Larchmont Junior High School. There'd been a baseball game that afternoon against another school, and I'd made a home run with three men on base, and I remember—"

"You made a what?" she interrupted.

"A home run in a baseball game. With the bases full."

"Oh. And that is good?"

"Well, it's nothing to be ashamed of. . . . Anyhow, when I got home later I could hardly wait for my father to come in, so I could tell him about it. When he showed up at last I went out to the garage to meet him; but I never told him about the home run, because there was the evening paper on the seat beside him, and there it was about Lindbergh."

"And from then on you knew you were going to be a flyer?"

"From then on every kid in the country knew he was going to be a flyer. Most of them grew up and forgot it, of course; but I didn't forget it. All through high school my mind was made up that I was going to be an airline pilot. Then when I went to college I began getting interested in architecture too, and my father had a few talks with me, and things didn't work out that way. But I knew I was going to fly too, even if it was only on the side—and I did."

"You used to talk about it that summer, sitting right here where we are now."

"Yes, I used to talk about it. I used to dream about it." Ordway paused a moment, squinting into the distance. "I still remember the first time I went up. It was the summer after I went back home, I think. The plane was just a pipsqueak two-seater training

105

crate at some suburban airfield—maybe it could have made seventy-five miles an hour with a hurricane behind it—but I still remember the hammering of that little motor and the sound the wind made pouring over the wings and the fuselage. I sat there in the front cockpit with my hands doubled into fists and kept saying to myself over and over again, 'This is what you're made for—this is what you're alive for,' and I wanted to yell it right out at the top of my voice, only I was afraid the instructor would think I was frightened or crazy and call the whole thing off."

"It is a wonderful thing, Martin, when a person wants something that much. And loves it that much."

"Yes—I loved flying. In a way, even, it was more than loving it. It was—well—*believing* in it." He lapsed into silence again for a few moments. "When you're a kid, Carla, believing comes easy. In flying. In Lindbergh. In lots of things."

"But now you no longer believe in them?"

"I don't know," he said. "I don't know."

They lay quietly again on the moss-cushioned bank. He moved his hand so that the cold bubbling water of the little stream passed over it and closed his eyes, watching the shifting play of sunlight beneath his lids. Then, presently, he opened his eyes again and turned his head and saw that she was watching him. He smiled a little.

"So we are both afraid, you see," he said.

"Afraid?"

"Yes. Afraid and tired and trying to escape. Trying hopelessly and blindly to get back to where we once were." He paused, but she did not speak. "Isn't that why you are here? Isn't that why I am?"

She started to speak, stopped herself and looked away from him. "You are here because your plane broke down," she said in a low, flat voice.

"And you?"

"You don't know anything about my reason."

"But that is what you're going to tell me now."

"No," she said. "No." And then suddenly she was looking full in his face again. Her gray-green eyes were wide and staring and her whole body was trembling gently with a silent sob. "Oh. Martin, Martin—why have you come back?" she cried.

Ordway put his hand lightly over hers, without speaking.

"I knew this was going to happen from the moment I heard you had come down in the meadow; from that first instant I saw you on the terrace." Her voice was low again, but the words came rapidly, almost wildly. "I have tried so hard to make a new life here—to work and find peace—to forget you and him and everything that had been."

"Him?"

"Stefan."

"Then you—"

She did not speak for a moment, but sat silently looking at him. The sound of her breathing became slower and more even and her eyes seemed gradually to grow grayer and colder.

"I married him, Martin," she said.

She paused briefly and looked away again. When she resumed speaking her voice was quiet and almost toneless. "We were married in Vienna in August, 1936, when Stefan was twenty-three and I was just nineteen. We stayed there a few months while he was working in his father's office; then he got a position as a reporter on a newspaper in Linz—you remember he always wanted to write—and we went there to live. For almost two years we were very happy. Stefan did well on the paper, and they promoted him first to a more important reporting assignment and then to be one of the assistant editors. He was still as gay and handsome as ever, and everyone in town liked him. He was always kind and sweet to me, and—well—we loved each other.

"Then in the spring of 1938 there was the *Anschluss*. There was no great excitement about it in Linz—much less than you would expect. One night everything was the way it had always been, and then the next morning the Germans were there. That's all there was to it. Some of the people were for Schuschnigg, of course, some were for the Nazis, and a lot didn't know who they were for. But it all happened so quickly no one could do anything in any case. Stefan had never had much use for the Nazis—he had always said they were primarily a Prussian militarist organization, even though Hitler himself was an Austrian—but like everyone else, all he could do now was wait and see what happened.

"The Germans closed the paper for a few days and began calling in the editors along with the other business and professional men of the town. A few of them they turned over to the Gestapo and sent away, and the rest they told to go back to work. Finally it was Stefan's turn, and he was gone for two days and a night, while I waited and waited and thought I would go out of my mind; and then at last, on the evening of the second day, he came home again. And the next morning he went back to work.

"For a few months things almost seemed the same as they had always been. And then suddenly—or at least it was suddenly to me—Stefan was offered a position as assistant editor on one of the big weekly magazines in Vienna. It was a wonderful job for such a young man, and he took it, of course, and we went back to Vienna, and I was happier and prouder of him than ever. I can hardly believe now that I didn't know what was going on by that time. But I didn't yet. I was very young, I suppose, and in love —and I was going to have a baby."

She paused, and Ordway gently pressed the hand that lay beneath his on the moss. "Carla," he said.

"Anyhow," she went on, her voice low and even, "several more months went by before I realized that Stefan had become a Nazi. Oh, I knew he worked for an officially approved publication, of course, and that he was going along with the current like everyone else; but that he was the real thing, an actual, active party member, I never could have dreamed. And then came one terrible night when we were invited to dinner at the home of Stefan's publisher. Do you know who the guest of honor was? . . . Goebbels. . . . And after dinner he came over and stood smiling at me with that sunken-in, death's-head face of his and told me what a splendid job my husband was doing and how important a man he was sure to become in the new Nazi Ostmark."

"I don't wonder that you couldn't believe it," Ordway said. "I can hardly believe it myself."

"It seemed impossible to me. Like some sort of wild nightmare."

"What did you do?"

"That is the terrible part of it, Martin: I didn't do anything. Days and weeks and finally months went by, and every day I kept telling myself that I was going to do something, but I didn't. I just went on being his wife as if nothing had happened: making a home for him, entertaining his friends, living with him, sleeping with him. Oh my God, don't you see how it was? I still loved him, and because I loved him I stayed with him, and soon I was no better than a Nazi myself."

"Nonsense! You couldn't be any more a Nazi than I could."

"No, no, that isn't true. That's what they all say: 'I am not a real Nazi. I don't cremate Jews or rape Polish women. I am innocent of evil. My hands are clean.' . . . But their hands are not clean. They are black and bloody—blacker and bloodier even than Hitler's and Himmler's and the rest, who in their perverted minds at least believe in what they are doing, while the rest of us are driven only by self-interest and fear. . . . This Nazi thing, Martin —you cannot know it as I do, you have not lived with it and felt it and been poisoned by it. It is not just a thing of politics and government, but of mind and spirit. It is not just what men say and do, but what they are. And those of us who stood by and watched this thing happen, because we were too weak and selfish and cowardly to do otherwise—we are the most to blame of all. . . ."

For the first time her voice had risen, and Ordway could feel her hand trembling beneath his own. Now, suddenly she stopped and sat silently for a few moments watching the bubbling current of the little stream. When she resumed speaking it was again quietly and evenly.

"At last I got to the point where I simply could not go on like that any longer. I began talking with Stefan, arguing with him, pleading with him. I tried every means I could think of to fight against this thing that had happened to him, to bring us back together again before it was too late. But it was no use. Sometimes he would ignore me and sometimes he would get angry. But most often he would just sit there quietly, blond and handsome and charming as ever, and when I was finished he would smile and say, 'Das kleine Mütterchen muss sich nicht über dieses politisches Zeug plagen.' And then he would put his arm around me and begin to make love to me. And that was the worst of all.

"Then suddenly I did the first thing. Stefan was a Nazi, and, yes, by being his wife I was a Nazi too; but at least I was not going to bring another damned little Nazi into the world. I was seven months' pregnant then—much too late for an ordinary abortion —but I found an old Hungarian midwife who agreed to what I wanted, and she brought on a premature delivery for me, and the baby was born dead."

Ordway sat staring at the stream. Carla paused another moment and then went on, her voice and face still expressionless.

"The baby was born dead and I went home. I went back to Stefan and went on living with him for almost another year. Don't ask me why, Martin. Don't ask me anything. I just did, that's all. I went back home to him, and for ten months I went on pretending that things were the same as always, that I was his wife, that I was still alive. The war began—first in Poland, then in Norway, Holland, Belgium, France. At first it looked as if Stefan would be called into the army, but then they decided he was too important on the paper and kept him there. It didn't seem to affect me one way or another. Nothing touched me. Nothing meant anything any more. I'd become like some sort of drug addict, with all the people and things around me blurred and remote and everything that happened to me seeming to be happening to someone else. Months went by like that. . . .

"And then at last I did the second thing.

"It was one night in the summer of 1940—a few weeks after France had surrendered—and there had been some sort of meeting of the staff of Stefan's magazine at our house. When the others left, Stefan went up to bed, but I stayed down in the living room, reading a book. It was almost two when I finished, and I was just getting ready to go upstairs, when I noticed Stefan's briefcase lying on his desk. I remember standing at the door for several minutes, with my hand on the light switch, looking at the briefcase. Then I went over and opened it.

"Inside were the papers they had been drawing up at the meeting. Mostly they consisted of a long list of names of local people whom the magazine was investigating in connection with a big drive on 'subversive elements' in the city. There was a paragraph under each name giving the history of the person and also pencilled notations like *Jewish grandparents—voted Socialist in 1934 —receives money from uncle in Milwaukee*. I read the list through and recognized many of the names. One or two of them, perhaps, had been politically active at one time or another, but most of them were—well—just people. There was one of the typesetters on the magazine, the old woman who owned the delicatessen down the block, a violinist at the *Staatsoper* who was an old friend of Stefan's and had been at our house many times.

"I stood looking at the papers for a long while. Then I walked over to the fireplace and lit a match and burned them. Even at the time I knew there was no sense to it—that there must be many copies of the list—but that did not seem to matter. I burned every sheet, one by one, and then I took all the other papers from the briefcase and burned them too. When I was finished I went upstairs and got a hat, coat and pocketbook. Stefan half woke up and said, 'Aren't you coming to bed yet?' and I said, 'Yes, in just a minute,' and then I went downstairs again and out of the house.

"I walked through the streets until it was almost daylight. Then I went to the station and took a train for Innsbruck, and at Innsbruck I got a bus to Feldkirch, on the frontier. I had my papers and an old passport in my pocketbook, and apparently there was no alarm out yet, because I managed to talk my way through. By ten o'clock of that next evening I was in Switzerland."

"And you came right to Kandermatt?" Ordway asked.

Carla shook her head. "Not for over two years. First I went to St. Gallen, where I had friends. Later I worked for several months as a waitress at a hotel in Zurich, and after that I was secretary to a lawyer in Berne. . . . But it was still no good, Martin. I could still find no peace. There were Germans everywhere, war everywhere. One evening in Zurich I was waiting on two men in the hotel dining room, and one of them dropped his wallet while he was paying me, and when I picked it up I saw the Gestapo card. Another time I was walking along the street in Berne, and there, not six feet away from me, looking into a shop-window, was a cousin of Stefan's who is with the consular service.

"Finally I could stand it no longer. I wrote a letter to Herr Knubel, asking him if he could give me some sort of work for old time's sake, and he wrote back telling me to come on, and I came.

"That was in the fall of 1942. I have been here ever since."

She was silent, sitting on the soft bank of moss with her hand beneath Ordway's, watching the quick silver currents that wove through the little stream. Ordway did not speak either. After a while he released her hand and moved over and put his arm around her and held her gently and close.

Chapter 7

It is like the movies, he thought. It is like being in one of those theatres where they never stop, and Greer Garson is smiling through the tears; and then Greer Garson is gone and there is the jailbreak or the longhorns stampeding, and then that is gone and there are the angry congressman and the decomposing Japs and the Yakima County Apple Queen and the wolf chasing the three-little-somethings and the little man coming up out of the floor with his organ; and then Greer Garson smiling through the tears again, and you reach for your hat. . . . It is like coming out of the theatre into the street and blinking in the daylight, with the movies remote behind you in the cool darkness and no longer real. But the street and the daylight are not quite real either, and any minute Greer Garson will come walking around the next corner with Walter Pidgeon and you will step on a decomposing Jap.

You have been to the movies and now you are back where you started. This is where I came in, you say. But it is not where you came in, and you are not back where you started. The street is different, and the people walking along it are different, and the sky is a different color, and the sun is in a different place. The hours of the afternoon that went with you into the theatre do not come out with you into the street. You have left them there in the cool, flickering darkness. And you walk a little faster because you are afraid you will be late for dinner.

Martin Ordway looked at the girl lying beside him. She lay

quietly with her eyes closed, breathing in long even breaths. Her head, turned toward him, was resting on her out-stretched arm, and her forearm and face were warm and golden-brown against the cool grayish green of the moss. If her eyes were open, he thought, they would be the same color as the moss.

"Carla," he said softly.

She did not move, and he sat for a few minutes watching her. Then he got up and went into the hut. They had left the door open, and as he entered there was a sudden scampering on the stone flagging and the fat marmot ran out past him. He walked slowly around the room again, peering into the cupboard, examining some of the carved initials on the table and benches and reading through the old Alpine Club notice on distress signals. Presently he went out again and stood for a while on the steps, looking around him. Carla was still asleep. On the far side of the stream he noticed a narrow path that moved up the mossy slope and disappeared among the boulders beyond. It leads up to the lake, he thought, remembering.

He crossed the stream and ascended the path slowly, his hands in his pockets, his shoes scuffing gently against the worn pebbles. He rounded an outcropping of gray rock, and the hut and the stream and the girl lying quietly beside the stream were gone. Twelve years were gone. If he turned now he would see a girl of fifteen walking behind him. And a boy with a strong sunbrowned body and curling yellow hair.

I can hardly believe it myself, he had said. . . .

It was what you said when there was nothing to say. When there was everything to say and nothing to say it with. . . . Stefan is a Nazi. . . . Your mother is a whore. . . . The crucifixion was a publicity stunt. . . . The purpose of life is death.

I can hardly believe it, you said.

It was hollow and fatuous. It was not even true. You could believe it. You could believe anything they told you now, because the field was wide open and everything started from scratch. Not to believe a thing meant that there must be something else, opposed and contradictory, that you did believe—and you had no something-else any more. There was the cool dark of the movie house and the dusty sun on Main Street. There was the little girl with taffy hair and a violin case hurrying to her music lesson, and there were the decomposing Japs. There was Stefan laughing in the mountains and Stefan composing lists of Jewish grandmothers. One was as believable as the next. As true and real, as untrue and unreal, as the next.

Ordway stood still on the path and did a thing that he had done many times in three years of war. He picked up a stone and held it in his hand, looking at it and feeling it. It was small and round and gray and hard and smooth and cold and made of stone; and that was all it was. It was there. You closed your eyes and opened them, you thought about it and stopped thinking about it, and it was still there. Thinking about it did not change it by so much as a molecule or an atom, because it was outside thought—truer and more real than thought. Because it was reality itself. Reality was things, and things happening; it was people and things happening to people; and thinking was what you did about it afterwards, and where the trouble started.

He dropped the stone back onto the path. He knew it would make a dull clunking sound as it hit, and it did, and that was real. The pebbles grinding under his shoes and the faint, pleasing tiredness of his legs and the cool air sucking in and out of his lungs were real. The sun, warm on his neck and shoulders, was real.

And nothing else, he told himself.

But as he began walking again, slowly, up the path, the girl and boy still walked behind him. And the world through which he moved was not merely a world of rock and sunlight, but a world of thoughts and images, memories and desires.

. . . . There was New York. New York on an October evening. In its own Blue Hour.

You were in a bathroom. It was a shining white-tile-and-nickel bathroom, with the hot water streaming down and fogging the glass partition, and then the cold water coming down, sharp and stunning, and then the big rough Turkish towel. Then you came out of the bathroom, and there were your evening clothes lying on the bed. The old Rogers Peet dinner jacket; the black silk socks and black batwing tie; the gleaming white shirt with the amethyst studs your mother had given you for your eighteenth birthday. One of the amethysts was gone—you'd lost it at one of those Christmas parties in thirty-five or six and never replaced it—but it didn't

114

matter, because you always put that stud in the bottom hole, and the vest hid it. You got dressed and went downstairs and got into a cab and called for Carla.

Carla would live on Central Park South, high up, so that you could see the yellow headlights curving endlessly through the blue darkness of the park below. She was wearing an evening dress, but it wasn't taffeta any more, and her arms and shoulders were soft and cool, but warm and glowing under the coolness, and her hair shone in the lamplight like dark copper fire. You sat in the window-seat together and had three martinis. Not two, not four—exactly three. Then you went to the Chambord and had oysters Rockefeller and Chateaubriand with sauce Bernaise and cherries Jubilee and sparkling burgundy. Then you went to the Persian Room and danced and to the Stork and danced and to all the other places and danced (all at no charge, of course), and at first everyone watched you dancing and stared admiringly at Carla and wondered who she was, and later everyone went away, and there were only the two of you dancing, and the colored lights in the darkness and an orchestra playing *Wienerblut* and *Night and Day*. And you looked down at Carla and smiled and whispered, "This is what we have been waiting for."

But it was not what you had been waiting for. Because even as you spoke, the lights above you in the darkness were changing from soft violet and amber to a glaring green. The muted strings of the orchestra swelled into a pounding, jerking dissonance of drums and brass. You could see the faces of the musicians now—the thick moist lips, the glazed eyes, the twitching shoulders; the sleek, sharp ferret-faces of the waiters; the puffy, painted rapacious faces of the other dancers. Moment by moment, the music grew louder, faster. You were pressed close together now in the crowd, and you could feel Carla's thighs grinding against your own and smell the thick, sweet scent that rose from her hair and breasts. Her slender jewelled hand was like a white bird's claw on your shoulder; and now suddenly she raised her face and looked up at you with eyes the color of the weaving spotlights and a red smile carved over her teeth.

And then the music stopped. The weaving lights, the weaving dancers, everything stopped. And there was Stefan. He shouldered his way toward you through the dancers, and the dancers were gone, and then the music and lights and darkness were gone, and there was only Carla and yourself and Stefan standing beside you, very cool and blond and blue-eyed, and saying to her gently: "*Bitte, kleines Mütterchen,* I shall take you home now." And then they were gone too—everyone and everything was gone—and you were walking slowly along an empty street in the windy dawnlight. Your legs felt like lead and there was the taste of lead in your mouth and throat, but you kept on walking and turned a corner into a second street and then another corner into a third street. This street stretched ahead of you, gray and still, as far as you could see. A block or two ahead an old woman in a black shawl was poking in an ash can, and yesterday's newspapers were swooping fitfully along the gutters in the wind.

. . . . There was New York, and then New Haven, and then Paris and the dusty, sun-splotched ateliers of the Beaux Arts. There was perspective and sciagraphy and 3B Wolff crayons and Professeur Ridabaud and the Boulevard Raspail and the Luxembourg and the Dingo and the Rotonde. There was the green countryside and the great gray cathedrals. Rheims, Chartres, Strasbourg, Cologne; Durham, Wells, Exeter, Salisbury.

You had visited almost all the famous cathedrals in those days, and you had thought a lot about cathedrals. Not that formal religion meant much to you; what you were interested in was the expression of the human spirit—of a time, a place, a society—in terms of stone and space. And when the time for the annual prize competitions came you had submitted a design for an industrial laboratory, because a laboratory, better than anything else, seemed to you to express both the pragmatic and spiritual values of the world in which you lived. It was an ambitious design, and you had worked hard on it and were rather proud of it, and Professeur Ridabaud, who inspected all the drawings before they went up to the judges, had been impressed also. Indeed, he had had but a single criticism to offer. "In a six-story building, Monsieur Ordway," he had pointed out gently, "it is often considered useful to have stairs."

You did not forget about stairs in the drafting room of Blake and Birdsall on East Forty-fifth Street. You forgot about cathedrals and Temples of Science and a good many other things; but stairs and storm doors and dumbwaiters and linen closets and rock-wool insulation were the very stuff of which your life was made. You worked on Plane Sections A, B and C, while Carrick, on your right, did Elevations F and G, and Matson, over in the corner, did Front Auxiliaries L and M. You finished your blueprints and brought them in to Mr. Birdsall and started them over again and argued with contractors about doorknobs and with carpenters about towel racks and waited and hoped and prayed for the day when you would be assigned a whole house to do on your own. And finally, after two years, you were assigned it. It was a two-car garage for a Mr. and Mrs. Grimback in Garden City, and you sweated and dreamed and fidgeted about it as much as if it had been the Lincoln Memorial. But at last it was finished, and there it was; and it was only another two-car garage, of course, but it was all yours and nobody else's (except the Grimbacks'), and you were proud and happy about being an architect for almost the first time since you had forgotten the stairs.

You did two or three more garages, a couple of summer cottages at the seashore and a branch office of the Corn Exchange Bank in the East Bronx. You helped Mr. Birdsall and the other senior members of the firm with the detail work of the important jobs. On weekends you flew rented Stinsons and Piper Cubs at a little airport in Westchester. And in between times you fell in love with Joan Nettleton. Afterwards, of course, you tried to convince yourself that it hadn't been the real thing—that it was only a matter of a delectable body, dark, laughing eyes and a few moonlit nights on the Sound. But it *had* been the real thing, and you knew it, and the first few months after she eloped with that bandleader from Chicago were not months you would greatly care to repeat.

And then, in the spring of 'forty-one came the assignment for the workmen's housing development in Pawtucket. It was no cathedral or Temple of Science, to be sure; it was just five rows of almost identical frame bungalows in a drained swamp behind a machine-tool factory. But it was the first job you'd been given that was something you could really get your teeth into, and you got a satisfaction from it that you had not had from any work you had ever done before. You planned and drew and re-drew and watched your plans and drawings become human dwellings. You learned that a six-by-four modern kitchen could hold almost as many knotty problems as a peristyle, and that a backyard play-pen for six Polish kids who had never before played anywhere except

117

on the city dump was perhaps as satisfying a contribution to the ultimate scheme of things as a well-turned flying buttress. As the months went by you became more and more absorbed in your work. Joan, flying, everything else you had ever done or cared about, did not matter very much any longer.

And then it was a sunny Sunday afternoon in early December, and you were half-dozing on the living-room sofa in the house in Larchmont, and your mother came in and tried to get the Philharmonic on the radio. And suddenly five rows of bungalows in Pawtucket did not matter very much either.

. . . . There was the radio. There were the newspapers and the speeches and the stunned surprise and *I-can-hardly-believe-it*. There was 90 Church Street and down to Washington and back to 90 Church Street and physical examinations and counting blocks and more physical examinations. There was Upton, Miami, March Field, Kelly Field. . . .

In the beginning it was wonderful. Partly, of course, it was the newness of everything—the learning, the doing, the excitement. But it was also much more than that. For years you had watched the world around you sicken and fester, seen it swell slowly, month by month and year by year, like a great balloon filled with the poison gas of savagery and corruption. You had looked on, with mingled apprehension and shame, while your own country ducked and teetered and sidestepped and danced its hit-parade jig of business-as-usual through the wards of the madhouse. You waited. . . . And waited. . . . And then at last the balloon burst. The sick, festering bladder split open—suddenly, utterly, irrevocably. And you were glad. You hated war, but you were glad. You did not want to kill or be killed, and still you were glad. For it seemed to you that you and your generation were being given an opportunity that had never before been granted to men; that all the evil of the world had at last been concentrated into tangible, combatable form, and that that form was the form of your enemies. If a man was born onto the earth to fight and die—and there was a formidable weight of historical evidence to show that this was exactly what he was born for—what better way could there be of fighting and dying than against the monstrous sickness of mind and soul for which Germany and Japan had come to stand before the world?

That had been the beginning, and it had had in it the potent magic of all beginnings. It was the magic Michelangelo had captured, once and forever, in his tremendous mural of *The Bathers*. *The Bathers* is a battle-scene; there is no battle in it—no blood, no agony, no death—and still it is perhaps the greatest battle scene that has ever been painted. "What is the supreme moment of any action?" Michelangelo had asked himself. "The beginning, of course." And so it was the beginning of a battle that he had painted—a company of Florentine soldiers surprised by the enemy while bathing in a stream. He had caught them in the very instant of their surprise—taut, startled, reaching for their arms; and he had caught, too, the tempest of the spirit that seizes all men when they know that they are about to fight for their lives. It was men and the spirit of men that mattered to Michelangelo. Not mere struggle and bloodshed; not mere killing and dying. . . .

Yes, the beginnings were the great times. But beginnings did not last. You picked up your arms and the fight was on. You went from airfield to airfield and learned your job. You went to England or Italy or New Guinea and did your job. You went out on your missions and came back from your missions and went out again. You dropped your eggs and more eggs and bigger, better, louder eggs. You killed and you died—or, if you went on living long enough, a great many things inside you died.

It wasn't that you didn't try to hold on to what you'd had at the beginning. You tried like hell. But the war was too big for you. It got away from you. Your world narrowed down to the wing, the group, the squadron; to the next cigarette, the next drink, the next leave, to the endlessly repeated details of your job. And it was the job, gradually and subtly, that became the most insidious thing of all. It was a necessary job, an important job; multiplied by a thousand and a million it was the one great job of the world. It was reality, and yet, when you came back to the individual—and always, always, always, in war as anywhere else, you came back to the individual—it was in a far truer, deeper sense an escape from reality. . . . *Flying and dropping eggs and killing a few Krauts— that's all there is, there isn't any more*. That was what Ted Riggs had said, and died. That was what a thousand and a million young men like him were saying or thinking, day after day, month after month, year after year, as they went out to die. It was what you said or thought yourself. The war became for you a matter of missions and reports, of R.P.M.'s and bombsight readings, of tiredness and Old Man Percentage and the smell of death; and the other thing—the thing you were fighting for and living for and were willing, if you had to, to die for—got lost.

Sometimes you thought it was because you were too old; because you were a tired old man among boys. For the others were boys—almost all of them. They were fighters, doers, heroes if you like; they carried the burden of a world at war; and still they were boys. Flying and fighting was their job, the same as it was yours, but in their case it was more than a job, because it was the only job they had ever had. It was their life. It was all that they knew. . . . You, on the other hand, knew other things; wanted other things. There were times when what you wanted most of all was never to fly or fight again, never even to see a plane again, as long as you lived.

Still, when you had flown your first fifty missions and had the choice of going home, you had not gone. Many of the others had gone—the younger men, the boys—but you had stayed. You did not know why—but you stayed. You called yourself a fool—but you stayed. You went on flying your missions, dropping your eggs, killing-and-not-being-killed. You flew your fifty-first mission, and your sixty-first, and your ninetieth, and your hundredth. And even now, when fate or luck or Old Man Percentage or whatever it was had knocked you out of it at last, and all you had to do—in fact, what you were supposed to do—was show your dog tags and spend the rest of the war as an internee-guest at a Swiss resort hotel—even now you were sure that in some way, for some reason, that was not what you wanted. Even now you were standing by, unresolved and acquiescent, while Andreas and Herr Knubel set in motion the wheels that would take you back to it again. To fly again; to fight again. . . .

You fight to win—period, someone had said.

You fight to stay alive. You fight to die. That's all there is, there isn't any more.

Period.

. . . There was the sunlight and the rock.

The path curved upward among the boulders, twisted back on itself, climbed again, passed between great shouldering shapes of granite and schist and entered a narrow gorge. For perhaps five minutes he threaded his way through a deep twilit corridor between perpendicular walls. Then the gorge bent, the walls flared out abruptly, and he came out on the crest of a low, open saddle between two ascending ridges.

Martin Ordway stopped and stood still.

Directly in front of him, in an irregular rocky bowl beneath the saddle, was a tiny lake the color of purest cobalt. On the far side of the bowl the ground rose again, levelled off and spread away into gray miles of desolation. It was a desolation so vast, so monstrous and absolute, that it seemed no part at all of the green and living earth, but rather the imagined landscape of a long-dead and frozen planet. Stone piled upon stone, slag upon slag, boulder upon boulder, into a gray monotony of distance—a still, petrified waste without color or form, without pattern or direction; a gigantic and ancient rubble-bin choked with the detritus of the centuries.

Along its central sweep the waste was almost flat. On either side it tilted suddenly and buckled upward into the bleak shale-slopes and towering cliff-faces of the mountainsides. The mountains, too, were desolate and ravaged—scarcely recognizable as the same shapes that rose so pure and gleaming into the sky above the valley of Kandermatt. There was no green of forests or pastures, no sparkling white of glaciers. Here, in the hidden inner core of the range, their flanks rose gaunt and skeletal to the precipices, the precipices to the ridges, the ridges to the gray and crumbling battlements of the peaks. Seen from this side, even the summits themselves did not stand out in clear and individual identity. They seemed pressed together, piled chaotically one against the other, in a twisted, warped confusion of aimless masonry.

Ordway's eyes moved slowly over the immense vista of ruin and decay. The waste before him narrowed gradually as it stretched into the distance. The mountain walls on either side slowly converged. It was as if the structure of the earth itself were slowly and inexorably converging, carrying the whole vast tattered fabric of peaks and wasteland with it into one distant ultimate node of sterility and nothingness.

And then . . .

The mountain walls fell away. The earth appeared almost to be gathering itself together. And leapt upward. What happened then seemed to Ordway to be not so much a phenomenon of form and substance, to be apprehended by the eye, as a single stupendous crash of music. Naked and gigantic, the White Tower rose out of the earth. Its core sprang up from depths of pressure and dark fire; its flanks ripped like swords through the brittle crust of the land. Range and valley, gorge, rock-slope and wasteland lay sprawled in tilted wreckage around its base. The mountain spilled them aside, steepening and tapering as it soared into the upper air. It climbed higher and still higher, in long, gleaming, sunlit arcs. It rose, ice-sheathed and granite-bowelled, from the dark recesses of the earth into a world of its own above it in the sky.

The mountain was made of rock and ice. It was made of glaciers, rock walls, ice walls, buttresses, dykes, precipices, slabs, crags, chimneys, ridges, cols, cornices, crests, spires, domes. It was made of unimaginable billions of whirling molecules of basalt and dunite, diorite and iron; of ancient, creeping rivers of ice; of avalanches of rock and snow; of the spindrift that streamed from its flanks and the lightning that blasted its ridges; of the cloud and mist that enveloped it and the sun and wind that beat down upon it; of black fire within the earth and the gray, patient erosion of time. The mountain was all these things, and all these things were the mountain. A substance, a process, a living organism, it built itself up, cell upon cell, detail upon detail, mass upon mass, into its ultimate gigantic whole.

But the mountain was more than the sum of its parts. As vast and intricate in structure as a thousand cathedrals piled one upon the other, its essence was not complexity, but simplicity; not profusion, but oneness. In a single sweeping gesture it climbed from the earth into the sky. As a single mass and form it brooded, still, white and secret, above the valleys and the ranges. Its glaciers rose to its buttresses, its buttresses to its trunk, its trunk to its ridges, its ridges up, up, up, past crag and shoulder, precipice and ice wall, to the last gleaming crown of summit snow. Each merged into the other, became the other, became the mountain; and in the end there was only the mountain. It was there. An entity. A finality. Rising from the very core of that dead world of rock and air, it seemed to Martin Ordway, as he stared up at it now through the blue miles of space, to possess the finality of death itself.

Of life itself. . . .

He sat on a low, flat boulder with his elbows resting on his knees, and the girl and the boy were there again, behind him. Then he turned and looked around, and the boy was gone, but Carla was coming toward him along the path that led down from the saddle. She came close and stopped and stood beside him.

"I shouldn't have gone off like that," he said.

"It is all right, Martin. I knew where you had gone." She was silent a moment, looking at him. "Do you still want to be alone?" she asked.

"No. I've been alone enough. We've both been alone enough."

He took her hand, and she sat down beside him on the boulder. They sat looking at the tiny blue lake and the waste beyond the lake and the mountain beyond the waste.

"What have you been thinking of?" she asked. "Stefan?"

"A little."

"And of what else?"

"Oh, about Norden bombsights and Michelangelo and 3B Wolff crayons. And oysters Rockefeller and you and myself."

"And about the White Tower, too?"

"Yes," he said. "About the White Tower too."

They were silent again. He was sitting motionlessly again, looking into the distance with dark, squinting eyes.

"Carla—" he said presently.

"Yes, Martin?"

"Do you remember those Sunday afternoons long ago at old Radcliffe's?"

She nodded.

"And the night at the hut?"

"Yes."

"And the night on the ledge?"

"Yes."

"And have you ever felt—" He hesitated. "After all these years do you still ever want to go—to try again . . ."

He stopped and turned his head and looked at her and was about to go on. But in the same instant he knew there was no need to go on. Her eyes were wide and burning on his face, and her hand, in his, was suddenly tight and warm and gently trembling.

"Yes, Martin," she whispered almost fiercely. "Oh yes—yes—yes."

Chapter 8

$\mathbf{A}$ndreas Benner came up the winding road and along the terrace with his slow, bow-legged stride. He crossed to where Ordway was sitting on the verandah steps, took off his green Patrol Corps cap with his right hand, shifted it to his left and shook hands.

"Let's go inside," Ordway suggested.

Benner looked dubious. "It is perhaps better we should stay out here," he said.

"There's no one in the lounge."

"It is not that, Herr Martin. It is that Frau Knubel becomes very angry about boot nails on the floors."

Ordway grinned. "Still keeping me out of trouble, aren't you?" He got up, and they crossed the terrace to the low stone wall, and as they walked he put his arm around the guide's broad shoulder and held him tight. "It's good to see you," he said. "Do you hear, Andreas? You don't know what it means to find something in the world that's still what it used to be."

"It is good to see you too, Herr Martin," said the guide.

They sat down on the wall, and he studied the backs of his hands for a moment while he selected the words he was about to speak. "I have made certain inquiries in Interlaken," he said.

"Well?"

"I have spoken yesterday with this certain man there whom I know, and he thinks perhaps something can be done."

124

"That they can get me out, you mean?"

Benner nodded.

"How? When?"

"How, he does not know yet. Sometimes, he says, it can be done by plane, and sometimes it is by other ways. With France free again it is of course much easier than before. Still, there are many difficulties."

"Did he have any idea how soon—"

"Such a thing takes time and planning. He thought in ten days perhaps. Or two weeks."

Ten days would give them time, Ordway thought. If Andreas would do it. If he would only do it. . . .

"You're to see him again then?" he asked.

The guide shook his head. "For reasons one can understand he does not like people to come to see him too often. There is another man with the railroad who goes every day back and forth between Interlaken and Kandermatt. When things are ready he will speak to Christian Mehrwalder, who is a relative of his, and Christian will speak to me, and we will then have our instructions."

"You're quite sure all these people can be trusted?"

"You trust me, Herr Martin?"

"I wont even answer that."

"Danke, Herr Martin. Then you can trust them too."

In the silence that followed Ordway studied the square leather-brown face of the guide. Suddenly he grinned again. "Andreas Benner," he said, "—Secret Operative No. 42X."

"Bitte?" said Benner.

"Just a joke, Andreas. It seems so strange to find you doing—well—this sort of thing."

The guide shrugged. "Most of us are doing strange sorts of things these days, are we not, Herr Martin?"

"Yes, I suppose we are."

"And the arrangements so far, they are satisfactory to you?"

"They sound fine. Except that—" Ordway hesitated.

"Except what?"

"That I'll never forgive myself if you get into trouble about this."

"That is not likely," Benner said.

"Still it's possible."

"There is an old saying in the Grisons that the best way not to fall into the crevasse is not to cross the glacier."

"Well?"

"We are already halfway across it, Herr Martin."

Ordway smiled. Then his smile slowly faded and he looked at Benner curiously. "You really want to do this, don't you?" he said.

The guide nodded.

"But why? Switzerland is neutral."

"One's country may be neutral. One cannot be neutral about one's friends."

"Then it's simply as a friend that you're doing this?"

"As a friend. Of course."

"I mean, it's not because of any—well—convictions about the war? You'd do the same if I were on the other side?"

Benner looked at him in momentary surprise. Then he considered the questions carefully. "No, I do not think I would," he said.

"Why not?"

"Because if you were a Nazi you would not be my friend."

Ordway smiled again. "I remember twelve years ago I used to think you were a pretty good diplomat. I've an idea I was right."

Benner shook his head slowly. "No, Herr Martin. I am a good Swiss, I hope, and a good Catholic. Once, perhaps, I was a good guide. And that is all I am."

It was a moment before Ordway spoke again. "You miss your old job, don't you, Andreas?" he said.

"Twenty-three years I was a guide in Kandermatt. When they take away what a man has been for twenty-three years there is— how should I say it—an emptiness."

Ordway nodded. "The war makes a lot of emptiness. It's not what you hear about so much. What you hear about are all the big, loud, angry things. But what you feel most is the emptiness." He paused again, looking out over the still, green valley. "At least Switzerland is luckier than most," he said. "Belgium, Holland, Czechoslovakia, all the rest . . ."

"Ja," said Benner. "It is luckier than most. And yet—"

"And yet what?"

"And yet sometimes, Herr Martin, I wonder if we are so lucky.

If it would not almost be better otherwise." He shook his head slowly and stared at the ground. "I am not a fighting man and I do not want to kill. No, I do not even want to kill Nazis. But to fight, that is at least a kind of life, and here there is no longer any kind of life at all. It is as if we were on some sort of white frozen island above Europe; we watch and wait and wait and go on living, but we do not live. The war is all around us, but we do not fight it. The mountains are all around us, but we do not climb them."

There was a short silence. Ordway's eyes moved slowly up the valley walls to the gray-white world above. "Fräulein Dehn and I were up in the mountains yesterday," he said. "We visited the Heilweg Hut."

"It is a pleasant walk to the hut," said Benner.

"It was as if it had been only a few months, or even a few weeks, since I'd last been there. We found your Patrol Corps key and went inside. Then we ate our lunch sitting on the moss by the stream. There was even a fat marmot to watch us. After we'd eaten Fräulein Dehn fell asleep, and I followed the path up to the lake."

"The lake is very blue this year," Benner said. "For a few years since you were last here it was slowly turning green. Herr Doktor Radcliffe said it was a kind of microbe that was living in it and making it green. But the microbe must have died or gone away, because now this year it is blue again."

"Yes, it was very blue. And the wasteland beyond it was gray. The mountains were gray too—very naked and old-looking, with hardly any snow. Only the Weissturm had any real snow on it, and it was shining in the sun. The Weissturm is beautiful from across the wasteland, Andreas."

"The Weissturm is beautiful from everywhere, Herr Martin."

"It was the first time I had really seen it—close up, all of it— since I've been back. I must have sat there for an hour watching it, alone. Then Fräulein Dehn came and we sat watching it together, and suddenly it was as if there hadn't been any twelve years at all. Any minute Stefan Raudiger would come walking around the boulders and sit down beside us. And the next minute you would come, and the four of us would sit there among the rocks, staring and pointing and arguing about routes."

He paused and looked at Benner, but the guide did not return his glance. His eyes remained fixed on the ground, and his motionless body seemed almost to be a part of the stone wall on which they sat.

"Do you remember all the times we asked you to try it with us?" Ordway asked.

"*Ja*, Herr Martin," said Benner. "I remember."

"And all the times you turned us down?"

"*Ja*."

Well, this is it, Martin Ordway thought. He drew in a long breath. . . .

"I'm going to ask you again, Andreas," he said quietly.

"I know you are, Herr Martin."

Ordway stared at him. "You know?" he repeated.

Benner was looking at the thick, stumpy fingers which he held spread out on his knees. "I know the kind of man you are," he said. "I know how much you have always wanted this thing. Also—" he hesitated a moment—"also you were talking about it the other night."

"The other night?"

"When Herr Knubel and I were carrying you up from the pasture. You had been talking about the war and planes and your friends that were killed, and then all at once you were fighting with us and trying to stand up and swearing."

"I must have been seeing Germans."

"No," said Benner, "it was not Germans."

"What did I say?"

"There is an American swear word, 'sonabeech'?"

"More or less."

"You said, 'Just wait, you big white sonabeech—we're going to get you yet.'"

Ordway continued staring at him for another moment. Suddenly he thought he was going to laugh. But he didn't laugh. Instead, he sat very quietly for a little while, looking out across the wall at the valley and the peaks and the deep blue October sky.

"You want this thing too, don't you?" he said.

Benner did not answer.

"Don't you, Andreas?"

The guide nodded. "*Ja*, Herr Martin. I want it too. Always since

128

I can remember I have wanted it more than anything else in my life."

"Then—"

Benner was still looking meditatively at his hands. "The Weissturm, it is not like other mountains," he said quietly. "It is a great and terrible thing."

Ordway nodded silently.

"Also it is late in the year. Storms and the snow will be coming soon."

Ordway said nothing.

"There is little equipment available these days. The huts are not stocked. The old routes and markers will be wiped out with the years."

The guide raised his head slowly and looked at Ordway. Behind the brown granite of his face doubt and caution and his inborn peasant conservatism were struggling with the dreams and desires of a lifetime. "It would be a hard and desperate venture," he said. "All the chances would be against us, and none for us. For more than a hundred years now, since there were first mountaineers in the Alps, men have been trying to climb the Weissturm from the valley of Kandermatt. Many of them have been killed. All of them have planned and worked and struggled and frozen and worn themselves out. And all of them have failed. It is almost certain that we would fail too. You know that, Herr Martin? Everything would be against our succeeding. Everything."

He stopped and was silent, wrapped deeply in his thoughts.

"Go on," said Ordway.

Benner's hands were opening and closing slowly against his knees, but he did not speak.

"Those aren't the real reasons you've kept away from the Weissturm all these years. Or the reasons you're afraid of it now. There's something else you haven't told me."

"Ja, Herr Martin, also there is something else." He hesitated still another moment, and Ordway, sitting beside him, could almost physically feel him drawing his body and mind together. "My father, Franz Benner, was a guide here in Kandermatt before me," he said at last. "He was a great guide, and alone of all the guides of that time in the Valais and the Oberland, he believed that the Weissturm could be climbed from this side. Many times he tried it, in the years when I was still a boy. Each time he got a little higher than he had been before—higher than any man had ever been on the south and east sides of the mountain—but never could he quite get to the top. And then, in the last summer before the first great war, he tried one last time with two English *Herren* who were famous climbers of that day, and this time he did not come back.

"One of the Englishmen they found later on the Dornelgletscher, beneath the south face. The other Englishman and my father they never found. Five, ten, twenty times they searched, but they found nothing on the glacier and lower ridges, and higher onto the Weissturm they could not and would not go. I was only fifteen then, Herr Martin, but I swore to the Lord and the Virgin, this I will do in my lifetime: I will climb to the top of this beautiful, terrible mountain that has killed my father."

Benner paused, gazing again at his gnarled hands. "*Ja*," he went on in a low, even voice, "to climb the Weissturm, that is a thing I have always known I must do before I die. And still I have not climbed it. Thirty years have passed, and I have not climbed it, or even really tried to climb it. Oh yes, I have been on it many times—more than any other guide in the Oberland. I have explored, reconnoitred, brought other climbers down, gone higher than any other man, except only my father. But never have I set out to reach the top. Every year for thirty years I have told myself, now, this year, you will do it. And every year I have found some excuse. The weather is not right. The season is not right. It is not yet the time.

"The other guides, they were afraid of the Weissturm. Perhaps I was afraid of it too, but I do not think so. At least it was not of its rock and ice and storms and precipices. And still—still I have not gone. It was a thing that I must do and yet could not do. It is not yet the time, I kept thinking, always not yet the time. And so the years went by, and after a while I was no longer so young any more. And then the bad years came, and the second war. And the emptiness . . ."

Benner was silent.

"And now at last it *is* the time, isn't it?" said Ordway.

The guide raised his head again and looked at him steadily.

The eyes, in the dark face, gleamed like blue sky behind ancient rock.

"*Ja*, Herr Martin," he said very quietly. "Now at last, with God's grace, it is the time."

Benner's thoughts moved as his body moved—slowly, deliberately, warily. Herr Knubel's exploded about his tiny office like so many snapping firecrackers.

"You will go up by the Aarntal, no? Or by the Blausee? . . . Yes, the Blausee is better. Provided it does not snow, the Heilweg and the Blausee are definitely better. . . . You have all the rope you need, Andreas? . . . And the axes and crampons? And tents? . . . The food will be a bit of a problem, of course. Bread, cheese, meat, tea. I think Rushli, down in the village, still has a few tins of Danish pemmican. . . . Food. What else? . . . Clothes. Ah yes, clothes for Herr Ordway here. We shall have to think about that. . . ." Herr Knubel pulled his nose vigorously, and his little chipmunk's eyes were sparkling as he looked from Ordway to Benner to Carla Dehn. "It is like the old days, *meine Kinder!*"

"There is much to be done," Benner said.

"*Gewiss, gewiss.* And it must be done quickly too. When is it you say you expect word from Interlaken?"

"In ten days. At most two weeks."

"*Also*, the time is short, no? One must make allowances for delays, difficulties, storms. Today is what? Wednesday. You should start up for the hut tomorrow morning."

"Friday morning," said Benner.

"Friday then. At the very latest," Herr Knubel was struck by a sudden thought. "You can get off all right from the Patrol?" he asked.

"I have two weeks' leave due. I was going to take them next month for the woodcutting and to bring the goats down from the upper pastures, but they will let me take them now, if I ask for it."

"There's Fräulein Dehn too," Ordway put in.

"What about Fräulein Dehn?" asked Herr Knubel.

"About her getting off."

The innkeeper waved a reassuring hand.

"I was thinking perhaps that Frau Knubel—" Carla began.

"Frau Knubel is a most admirable and efficient woman, *gnädiges*

Fräulein. But it so happens that *I* am the proprietor of the Gasthof zum Blauen Himmel." Herr Knubel permitted himself a glance into the hallway to make certain that his admirable and efficient spouse was not within hearing; then he slapped an open palm firmly on the desk top. "I say you may go, Fräulein. Therefore you may go."

Ordway bit the smile from his lips. "Thank you, Herr Knubel."

"Thank you," said Carla.

Herr Knubel nodded gallantly. "A pleasure," he said.

Benner had taken a sheet of paper from his pocket and was adding to the list on it in a slow, careful hand. Ordway studied it over his shoulder.

"That's going to be a hell of a lot to carry," he said.

The guide nodded. Then he checked back over the list and stared meditatively at the point of his pencil. "Too much, Herr Martin."

"You don't think we can manage it?"

Benner shook his head.

"And we can't eliminate any of it?"

"We must eat. We must have clothing, tents, equipment. For four years now there has been nothing stored at the huts." Benner paused and shook his head again. "No, Herr Martin, I have been thinking much about this. For such a mountain as the Weissturm three climbers are not enough."

Ordway was silent a moment. "How many do you think we should have?" he asked.

"Four at the very least. Six would give us the best chance."

"Could you get any of the other guides? Christian Mehrwalder, perhaps, or one of the Kronigs?"

"They would not do it. For twenty years there has not been another guide in Kandermatt who would go near the Weissturm. And even if they would, it would not be wise, I think, to let too many people know you are here."

There was another pause.

"There's Doctor Radcliffe," said Carla.

"I had thought of the Herr Doktor," Benner nodded. "He is no longer a young man, to be sure, but he was once a remarkable climber and he knows the mountains better than many guides." He turned to Ordway. "What do you think, Herr Martin?"

Ordway considered a moment. "I think yes," he said. "If he'll come."

"We can go up and see him this afternoon," said Carla.

Ordway nodded.

"There is also Monsieur Delambre," Herr Knubel suggested. "And the remaining German."

Ordway looked at him sharply. "One of the Germans has gone?"

"Since yesterday morning. You need not worry, though, that it has something to do with you. He was called straight back to Germany."

"Which one is still here?"

"Herr Hein."

"That's the older, dark-haired one?"

"Yes."

Benner was rubbing his square chin reflectively. "I have seen Monsieur Delambre on a few small climbs behind the Heilweg Hut, and he appeared to be not bad in his technique. Also he has told me that he has made various ascents from Chamonix and in the Engadine, but how good he is on a big mountain I do not know. Herr Hein was, of course, a famous mountaineer before the war; but I do not imagine, Herr Martin, that you wish very much to climb with a German?"

Ordway did not speak at once, and when he did it was not to answer the question. "You feel that six is the ideal number?" he asked.

"*Ja*, for a mountain like the Weissturm six is best. It gives both strength and *Biegsamkeit*—how do you say it?—pliability to a party. There can be two ropes of three or three ropes of two. Also it is best for trying various routes, for making bivouacs, for accidents or storms."

"And you think Delambre is all right?"

The guide shrugged. "One does not know for certain, of course."

"How about his drinking?" Ordway looked from Benner to Herr Knubel.

"His drinking?" The innkeeper looked surprised, then shook his head. "I do not know anything about that. Unfortunately, as you know, the *Gasthof* no longer has a bar."

"He seems to have a pretty impressive supply of his own, though."

133

"He has some brandy, wines, liqueurs—yes, of course. He is a very well-to-do man. But as for *drinking*—no. What gave you that impression, Herr Ordway?"

"I'm not sure. He doesn't exactly seem to dislike the taste of five-star cognac, but then who does?" Ordway paused, thinking back to the afternoon in the lounge. "It was something about his eyes, perhaps. Or his hands."

Herr Knubel shrugged. Ordway looked at Carla, but she shook her head.

"And you, Andreas—you're willing to take a chance on him?"

"From what I have seen of him, yes."

"All right," said Ordway. "We'll ask him."

"And the other, Herr Martin?"

"The German?"

"No," said Carla suddenly. Her voice was curiously hard and flat. "We do not want the German. . . . Do we, Martin?"

"I don't know," he said slowly.

"You don't know? You don't mean you would—"

"I'm not sure. I haven't thought enough about it yet." Ordway stared at the floor a moment; then he looked at Benner. "He's an expert climber, you say?"

The guide nodded. "Of the first rank."

"Meaning we'd have a good deal better chance if we had him along."

"That would probably be the case, Herr Martin."

"How do you feel about it?"

Benner examined the backs of his hands. "There is the Weissturm," he said. "There is also the war." He shrugged his broad shoulders. "It is for you to decide, Herr Martin."

Ordway was silent again, thinking. "We can talk more about it later," he said finally. "After we've seen Radcliffe." Suddenly he smiled a little. "After all, we don't even know yet if any of them will want to go."

"Want to go?" Herr Knubel exclaimed, throwing both hands ceilingward. "*Gott im Himmel*, who would *not* want to go on such a venture!"

Ordway's smile widened. "Would you?" he asked.

"I?" Herr Knubel looked astonished. Then he looked hurt. Then he sat tugging thoughtfully at his nose. "*Ja*, Herr Ordway," he said, "—most deeply and greatly would I want to go. For almost thirty years now have I lived in Kandermatt, in the shadow of the Weissturm, and all that time I have looked up to it where it stands there in the sky and said to myself, yes, to climb such a mountain would be enough achievement for any man's lifetime." He paused and sighed delicately. "But, alas, one's dreams and ambitions cannot always be fulfilled in this world. I am an aging man now. I cannot stand heights. I suffer from the arthritis, the diabetes and the insomnia. Also there is the *Gasthof*: the accounts, the marketing, the maintenance. There are the repairs and the servant problem. There is the wholesale grocer I must see next week and the Tuesday meeting of the town council. There is—"

Herr Knubel broke off and spread out his hands in a resigned gesture. "You see how it is, Herr Ordway. For some it is the heights and the glory, for others the sweat and toil in the vineyards." He sighed again; then abruptly his manner changed and he jumped to his feet. "But we have had enough of philosophy, no? There is work to be done! Come, we shall go now over to the storehouse and select the available provisions."

They went through the empty foyer, descended the verandah steps and came out on the terrace. The innkeeper drew in a deep breath of the keen air and gazed meditatively upwards at the glittering rim of the peaks. "*Die Alpen*," he murmured. "*Die wunderschönen, weissen Alpen!*"

A sudden idea struck him and he clapped his hands together briskly. "Do you know what I shall do? You remember the telescope that used to be here on the terrace, for watching the climbers? I shall take it out from the storehouse and set it up again and watch you through it. Across the glaciers and boulderslopes, up the ridges and precipices to the very summit I will follow you. I will be with you every step of the way. . . ."

As they walked across the terrace Herr Knubel's eyes were sparkling. "*Ach, ja, meine Kinder*," he murmured happily, "truly it is like the old days again!"

It was mid-afternoon when Ordway and Carla came down from Radcliffe's chalet into the bland sunshine of the pastures. Reaching the first stile, they sat side by side on the top step and looked idly out over the valley.

"You remember them now," Carla said.

He glanced at her questioningly.

"The old songs. You've been singing them all the way down."

He smiled. "They must have been hiding somewhere."

"Now sing me a new one."

"I don't know any new ones."

"Yes you do."

He considered a moment. "I'll sing a war song," he told her.

"No."

"This is a very special sort of war song. About the food shortage." He sang a verse softly and began a second; then he broke off suddenly and looked at her. "What's the matter?" he asked. "Don't you like it?"

"I don't understand the words."

He shook his head. "Your English must be very rusty."

"Start again," she said. "More slowly."

He began again.

"Mercy—is that the first word?"

"No, mairzy. M-a-i-r-z-y. It's very simple. . . . Mairzy doats."

She repeated it. "And then?"

"Dozy doats, obviously."

"And—"

"Little lambs—you know what lambs are?"

"*Kleine Lämmer—*"

"Idivy."

She stared at him, frowning.

"Clear now?" he asked.

The frown slowly faded, and she nodded. "Yes, now it is good clear English," she agreed.

"Of course."

"I know some more good clear English too."

"What?"

"Go to hell."

Then they were laughing. They sat on the stile and laughed, and looked into each other's eyes and laughed, and it suddenly occurred to Martin Ordway that he had not laughed that way in a long time, except after he had been drinking. We are not laughing at a silly song or joke, he thought. We are laughing because we want to laugh. Because there is laughter inside of us.

She was quiet again now, her head half-turned away toward the valley, and he sat looking at her.

"Carla," he said.

"Yes?"

"Nothing. I just like to hear myself saying your name again." She smiled a little, without turning.

"It's going to be all right, isn't it?"

She nodded.

"I'm glad old Nick's coming."

"So am I," she said. They were silent for a little while; then she turned and looked at him. "What are you going to do about the others, Martin?" she asked.

"Delambre and Hein?"

"Yes."

"I think Andreas would like to have them," he said.

"Did he say so?"

"Not in so many words. But it's pretty obvious that he would." Ordway smiled. "I don't think a middle-aged geologist, a girl and a half-shot bomber pilot exactly make up Andreas' idea of a championship climbing team."

"And you—do you want them?"

He waited again before answering. "Yes," he said slowly, "I think I do."

"Why?"

"Partly for the same reason. As long as we're going to try it, we may as well give ourselves as good a chance as we can. And then, also—" He hesitated.

"Also what, Martin?"

"I don't know exactly how to put it. It seems—well—to fit in somehow."

"To fit in?"

"With Kandermatt. With you and me and the mountains and everything that's happened in the last few days."

Carla looked at him intently and seemed about to speak. Then she looked away again at the valley.

"You don't like it, do you?" he said.

137

"I see no reason not to ask Monsieur Delambre—if you and Andreas think he will help."

"But not the German?"

"No."

"Why not?"

"Because he is a German."

Ordway was silent a moment, squinting into the distance. "I wonder," he said.

Carla was watching him again.

"I wonder if he *is* a German—here. Are you an Austrian here? Am I an American? Or a bomber pilot? Or an architect? Are any of us what we have always been, here in Kandermatt? . . . I don't know anything about this Hein. For all I know, he's a Storm Trooper, a Gestapo agent, a Luftwaffe pilot. Until a few days ago my job in the world was killing his kind, and his job was probably killing mine. In another couple of weeks it will probably be our job again. But here—now . . ." Ordway's eyes moved slowly up the valley walls to the world of rock and ice and sky. "Do you remember what Andreas said this morning? 'There is a war. And there is the White Tower.' . . . Do you understand what I am trying to say?"

"Yes, Martin—I understand."

"But you still don't agree?"

It was a moment before Carla answered. "It is for you to decide," she said quietly. "Without you there would be no climbing of the Tower. There would be—nothing. You must do what you think is right."

A slow smile came into his face. "That's what my father always used to tell me. But when I did it there was usually hell to pay."

Carla smiled back at him but did not answer; then she got up and descended the stile. "We had better get back to the inn," she said. "There are still a hundred things to take care of."

They swung down through the pasture, walking abreast now because the path was wider. The sun fell warm and golden on her arms and cheeks and danced in a hundred minute flickerings in the soft copper of her hair. . . . He had once known a girl in New York with hair like that, Martin Ordway thought. Her name had been May (or was it Kay?), and she had been a Powers Girl (or maybe it was a Conover Girl—anyway it was some kind of a

Girl), and they had always used her in full-color ads because of her hair. Hair almost exactly like Carla's, he thought. And yet not quite exactly—not at all like it, really, he realized suddenly—because the things that shone in May-or-Kay's hair had been kleigs and baby spots and the thing that shone in Carla's was the sun. He thought about Carla's hair in the weaving purple-orange of a New York night; under a Madison Avenue hat; against the cool, sweet whiteness of a pillow-slip. . . . This is a hell of a time to be thinking about pillow-slips, he told himself. Without even a sleeping bag or proper blanket roll in the whole damn valley. Well, at least it was lucky that Radcliffe had a supply of good Scotch-wool blankets. It was lucky that Radcliffe was around at all. . . . And then he was suddenly puzzled again, thinking about Radcliffe. About the way he had stood there in his little garden, listening, smiling . . .

"You are worrying about something," Carla said.

"Not worrying. Just thinking."

"About Herr Hein?"

"No. About old Nick."

"You are sorry we asked him to come?"

"No. I'm just curious—"

The Englishman had been squatting over his autumn vegetable patch as they came through the gate, and as he got to his feet to greet them it was like some sort of long, articulated yardstick unfolding joint by joint. He had stood silently leaning on a rake and listening while Ordway spoke, and presently, a slow, deep smile had come into his beaked face and sharp blue eyes. And when Ordway had finished he had shown neither surprise nor hesitation, nor even asked so much as a single question. He had merely nodded and said quietly, "Yes, old boy, I should like very much to come."

"It seemed almost that he knew in advance what I was going to ask him," Ordway said.

Carla nodded a little. "Yes," she said. "He knew."

"But how—"

"Andreas knew too, before you asked him. Didn't he?"

"Yes," he said.

"And I knew."

He was silent, watching her face.

139

"I don't know how to explain it, Martin," she said. "It was as if—well, almost as if all of us up here in the valley were waiting for something. Doctor Radcliffe, Andreas, Herr Knubel. Even the others—"

"You mean Delambre and Hein?"

"Yes, even they, I think."

"Did you ever talk about climbing the Tower?"

She shook her head. "No. You cannot live in Kandermatt, of course, without thinking about the Tower—without feeling the Tower. But no one ever talked about it. None of us were actually thinking about climbing it. Any more than we were thinking that one night you would come floating down into the valley out of the sky. And yet—"

"Go on," he said.

She hesitated a moment longer, and when she spoke again it was very slowly and quietly. "Shall I tell you a funny thing, Martin? That night you came down I was lying awake in my room, and suddenly I heard footsteps on the verandah and then Andreas calling Herr Knubel and telling him about a parachutist lying out in the pasture. After a few minutes they went out, and I lay there until I heard them coming back, and then I got up to see if there was anything I could do to help. I put on my bathrobe and slippers and was coming down the stairs when I heard them crossing the verandah and opening the door. I could not see you yet, but suddenly something had begun happening inside of me. My heart was pounding so hard I had to stop walking and stand quite still, holding the bannister."

"You mean you knew it was I?"

"No, I do not think I knew that. And yet I knew something. That something was happening. Or was about to happen. I had felt like that only once before in my life. The night of that meeting in our house in Vienna, after Stefan had gone up to bed, and I sat there alone in the living room staring at his briefcase on the desk."

She paused again and then continued. "I stood there on the steps, waiting, while they brought you in and laid you on the couch in the foyer; but I still could not see your face. My heart was pounding so hard I could scarcely breathe, and I wanted to run away, so that I would not have to see who it was. I was afraid to know, and still I had to know. And then, the next minute, I was walking downstairs again. I came over to the couch and looked at you, and suddenly the pounding was gone, and I was standing there, very calm and quiet, and thinking, Yes, of course—*it is he.*"

Ordway started to speak, stopped himself, and walked silently along with his eyes on the path.

"It was the same later," Carla said. "Those times on the terrace, and then yesterday, walking up to the hut. You were back, and I was happy that you were back, and at the same time I was afraid. That was why I was avoiding you."

"I'd imagined it was because of Stefan. Because you didn't want to tell me about him."

"Yes, it was Stefan too." She was looking up at him now, and her voice was suddenly very low. "Oh, don't you see, Martin? It is all the same thing. Stefan, the baby, the war, everything. For two years I have been hiding from them, shutting them out of my mind and my life. There is nothing beyond these mountains, I have said to myself—nothing but more mountains. There is no past, no future. There is only Kandermatt and the forests and the snowpeaks. There is only the *Gasthof* and beds to make and floors to sweep. And there is nothing else. Nothing. *Nothing.*

"And then you came. You were lying there so quiet on the couch in the foyer with your parachute on the floor beside you. We were standing together on the terrace, walking along the forest paths, sitting on the moss beside the stream at the Heilweg Hut. And I was happy that you were back again—oh so very happy, Martin, believe me—and at the same time I was afraid, because everything I had built for myself during these last years was slipping away from me. I had promised myself I would not go with you up to the hut. But I did. And then, lying there by the stream, when you got up and went into the hut—"

"I thought you were asleep," Ordway said.

"No, I was not asleep. I heard you going into the hut, and then coming out again and starting up the path, and without opening my eyes I knew where you were going. I just lay there for a while, with my heart pounding again the way it did that first night when they brought you in, and I knew that if I got up and followed you it would all be finished. Everything I had struggled and prayed for through those years—forgetfulness and peace of mind and sanctuary—all of it would be finished, gone forever. I will not go, I kept telling myself. I will not, *will not* go. And then I got up and I went. I came up through the gorge, and out on the other side, and there you were by the lake, where I knew you would be. You were looking across the wasteland at the Weissturm, as I knew you would be doing. And then, when I sat down beside you, you said what I knew you were going to say. And all at once it was again the same as on that first night; my heart had stopped pounding, and I felt very calm and quiet, and I sat there thinking: *Yes, of course, we are going to climb it.*"

Her voice, as they walked along, had remained low and even. But now abruptly, as she spoke the last words, it broke, and she stopped and stood quite still on the path. Her back was turned to Ordway and her hands were pressed to her face.

"Carla," he said.

She neither moved nor spoke, and he put his hands on her shoulders and turned her around. For a moment her shoulders were stiff and tense under his touch; then they began to tremble, and a low, broken sob rose from deep inside her. With her hands still covering her face, she leaned suddenly against him. "Hold me a minute," she whispered.

He folded his arms around her and held her gently and tenderly.

"Not like a little girl," she said. "Like a woman."

He drew her closer and held her tight. He felt her hair against his face and her head pressed against his shoulders; he felt her breasts and stomach and thighs and legs and all of her soft, slender body pressed trembling and sobbing against his own. Then her hands were no longer over her face, but around his neck, and her face was no longer hidden, but raised to his, and he was kissing it, tasting the bitter salt of her tears and the sweetness beneath the tears, and feeling her clinging to him, body and mouth and tears and sobs all clinging to him, sweet and close and fierce. And then, in the next instant, she was no longer clinging to him, but breaking away. She had broken away and was standing again with her back to him, her hands over her face and her shoulders tight with her sobs.

He waited silently and without moving until her sobbing began to subside; then he put his arms around her waist and held her lightly from behind. She neither responded to his touch nor moved

142

away, and they stood quietly while her crying lessened and at last stopped altogether.

"Turn around now," he said.

She shook her head.

He swung her gently about, so that she faced him, but she would not look at him.

"I am so sorry," she said.

"No."

"I am so ashamed."

"No."

She was silent for a few moments. Then she said, "Give me a handkerchief, please."

"That's better," he said.

He fished a handkerchief from his pocket, handed it to her and waited while she dabbed it at her nose and eyes.

"How do I look?" she asked when she had finished.

"Like hell."

"Everyone will know I have been crying."

"We'll explain that I've been beating you."

"But—"

"But nothing," he said.

They followed the path down through the meadows and into the forests beside the rumbling Aarn. Coming to one of the little streams that fed it, he steadied her across the stepping stones, and as they continued walking on the far side he still held her hand. Presently the path twisted up a steep timbered slope and they came out on the bald knob of rock where he had sat, alone in the mist, on his first evening in Kandermatt. But there was no mist now. Valley and valley-wall, forests, glaciers and mountains stood up clear and immaculate in the golden sunlight. Far above and beyond the other peaks the summit of the White Tower hung still and gleaming in the October sky.

"Afraid of it?" he asked.

"A little."

"But not sorry?"

She did not answer.

"Are you sorry I've come back, Carla?"

"No," she said quietly.

"And that we're going to climb the Tower?"

"No."

"And that we need each other?"

"No, Martin."

They descended the far side of the knob, and the valley-walls and mountains swung slowly out of view behind the interlacing treetops.

"Sing for me again," she said.

"We'll both sing."

"But we don't know the same songs."

"There's one we both know."

"Which is that?"

"*Mairzy Doats,*" he said.

And they sang.

Chapter 9

On the stone flagging of Herr Knubel's storeroom supplies and equipment accumulated in sprawling, serried piles. Martin Ordway prowled restlessly among them, checking and sorting.

"The crampons," he said suddenly. "There are only three pairs of crampons."

Carla rustled through her lists. "Andreas has only three pairs. He is borrowing the others from Anton Kronig."

"And the evaporated milk—"

"Frau Knubel keeps it in the kitchen cupboard. Annamarie is bringing it down."

"We hope."

There were the crampons, the ice axes, the pitons, pitonhammers and karabiners. There were the great yellow coils of rope. There were tents, groundcloths, rucksacks, packboards, boots, espadrilles, Balaclava helmets, mittens, flashlights, goggles, extra boot-laces. There were pots, pans, knives, eating utensils, canteens, a fireless cooker and two Primus stoves. There were tea, coffee, sugar, bread, sausage, cheese, chocolate, and tins of meat, margarine and fruit.

"Seems to me there's only one thing missing," Ordway said at last.

"What?" asked Carla.

"The three-ton truck to carry it."

145

Andreas Benner trudged back and forth along the road between the inn and his farm, transporting the contents of his attic to the stacks on the storeroom floor. Between trips he went down to the village to arrange his leave at Patrol Corps Headquarters and to borrow extra clothing and climbing equipment from his fellow-guides.

"Was gibt's?" they asked, their eyes narrowing curiously.

"Only a little trip to the glaciers," he explained.

"With whom?"

"With Herr Delambre. You know—the Franzose at the Gasthof."

"And you need all these things for a little glacier trip?"

"He is a wealthy man. He wishes the best of everything."

The others smiled wisely. "For a good payment, eh?"

"Jawohl," he agreed. "For an excellent payment."

At first he had tried to tell the same story to his wife, but with her it had not worked.

"It is that American, too, isn't it?" she said.

"Ja," he conceded, "the American too."

"I have told you—you will get in trouble with that American."

"No, I shall not get in trouble."

"How much are they paying you?"

Benner hesitated.

"They are paying the regular forty francs a day?"

"Yes, the regular forty francs."

She stared at him a moment, and her lips grew tight. "How much are they paying you, Andreas?"

Benner drew in a deep breath. "Nothing," he said.

In the beginning she had shouted at him. Then, for a day and a night, she refused to speak at all. Then she shook her head grimly and muttered, "I am the wife of a lunatic." But when the time came for him to leave, there was his old rucksack neatly packed with his extra shirt and socks and Kletterschuhe and pipe tobacco, and, in his buttonhole, the blue cornflower that she had put there each time in nineteen years that he had started off for the mountains.

"Be careful," she said, as she came with him into the dooryard. "Be careful and say your prayers each morning and evening and do not climb on Sunday, and you will get to the top."

146

He looked at her in surprise. "But we are going only to the—"

"I know where you are going," she said.

"But—"

"Go on now. Your other crazy ones are waiting for you." She kissed him quickly on the cheek and gave him a push down the path. "Perhaps when you come back you will be worrying not so much about this verdammte mountain of yours and a little more about the vegetables and the goats."

Back in the storeroom at the inn he set to work sorting the equipment and loading the rucksacks and packboards, but every so often his eyes wandered to the little blue cornflower on the old belted jacket that he had hung on a nail in the wall, and he shook his head in slow puzzlement. If a man could not understand a woman after nineteen years, Andreas Benner wondered, when was he going to start?

On the first day of their preparations they worked through until after midnight, and the next morning they began with the sunrise. Herr Knubel shuttled briskly between storeroom and kitchen, laden with foodstuffs and suggestions. Ordway and Benner finished the loading of the first two packboards, tried them out on a ten-minute walk down the road and came back to reload them. Toward noon Nicholas Radcliffe appeared in a cart with his climbing gear, his flute and a stack of blankets, and Carla and Frau Knubel set about stitching the blankets together into makeshift bedding rolls. Delambre brought a variety of jars and tins down from his room to augment the food supply and, as an afterthought, added two bottles of Courvoisier.

"One for medicinal purposes," he explained. "And one for celebration when we reach the top."

"And if we don't reach it?" Ordway asked.

"Then for consolation."

It had been after dinner the previous night that Ordway had spoken to him about the climb, and the Frenchman, like Benner and Radcliffe before him, had seemed almost to know in advance what it was that he was going to ask him. He had been neither doubtful and hesitant, however, like the guide, nor calmly acquiescent, like the Englishman. Instead, he had sat motionless and tense while Ordway told him briefly of their plans, his knuckles white against his chair-arm and his eyes seeming to grow slowly

147

darker and brighter behind the heavy lenses of his glasses; and when Ordway had finished he had risen slowly to his feet, his whole body tight-strung with emotion.

"I shall never be able to express my gratitude for this," he said.

Ordway smiled slightly. "I don't know that it's anything to be grateful for. We're certain to have a rough time of it. And we'll probably fail."

"Nevertheless, Monsieur Ordway—"

"You'd like to come then?"

"Yes. Yes." Delambre's long, slender hand reached out and grasped Ordway's tightly; then he turned abruptly away. "I cannot tell you what this means to me," he said, his voice curiously thick and muffled.

Later, when Ordway told Carla about it, she had nodded quietly and without surprise.

"And the other?" she asked.

"Hein?"

"Yes. Have you asked him?"

He shook his head.

"Aren't you going to?"

"I don't know."

He had seen the German in the dining room at dinner and again at breakfast the next morning, but on both occasions had merely nodded to him as he came and went. Toward mid-morning, when he finally decided to speak to him, he had not been able to find him anywhere about the inn. Then Radcliffe had appeared with his blankets, there had been a minor crisis about boots that did not fit and another about punctured meat tins, and in the resulting activity he dismissed the matter from his mind.

After lunch he, Radcliffe and Benner sat with paper and pencil at a table on the verandah, working out the schedule for the next few days. Their food and equipment, after all possible eliminations and the most careful distribution, still required five packing boards, three large rucksacks and four small ones, and it was therefore obvious that they would have to make at least two trips up to the Heilweg Hut before everything could be assembled there.

"Can we do it in a day?" Ordway asked.

"It is possible," said Andreas. "But I think it is perhaps better we make it two. They are heavy, these things we must carry, and for Herr Delambre and yourself, who have not climbed so much recently—"

Ordway grinned wryly. *To the Heilweg—two days,* he wrote.

From the Heilweg Hut their route would run through the gorge to the saddle between the Himmelshorn and the Karlsberg; then down to the Blausee and across the miles of the wasteland to a second, long-abandoned hut near the snout of the Dornel Glacier.

"You remember it, Herr Martin?" Benner asked. "From the time when—"

Ordway nodded.

"We'll have to make a couple of trips there too," said Radcliffe. "That will take two days, surely."

"*Ja,* it is a long way," the guide agreed.

Valley to glacier, Ordway wrote. *Four days.*

Radcliffe unrolled a 1/50,000-scale Geographic Society map that he had brought with him and marked the approximate location of the Dornel hut with his pencil. Then he slowly traced their course up the white avenue of the glacier toward the base of the White Tower's southerly precipices.

"I imagine we're all agreed that the southeast ridge is our best bet?" he asked.

Ordway looked at Benner.

"*Ja,*" said the guide. "For a beginning, at any rate. Later—" he shrugged, "—who can tell?"

The Englishman nodded, and the point of his pencil crept onward across the ever-thickening lines of the altitude contours. "From here on, of course," he said, "maps won't be of much use. The details have been filled in mostly by aerial survey and triangulation, but there are one or two features that—"

The voice went on. The pencil moved on. Martin Ordway's head was bent intently over the map between Benner's and Radcliffe's. But as he looked now, the intricate pattern of lines, dots and shadings seemed slowly and subtly to be rearranging itself under his eyes. It was no longer glaciers and buttresses, ridges and precipices that rose toward him from the symbols on the paper, but buildings, factory sheds, docks, railway sidings. The black point of graphite moved slowly on over Lille, Aachen, Cologne, Essen. . . .

Clear now, boys? he was asking.

Yes, sir.

Any questions?

Do we come in from the west or northwest? (That was Harry)

The northwest, dope. (Bix)

Bearing three-fifteen. (Ted)

Okay, then . . .

The pencil had stopped moving at last. It had crept on beyond the innermost of the wavering concentric ellipses and was pointing to a minute blue-inked X. Then quickly it ringed the X with a black circle.

"Target," said Ordway.

A few moments passed before he realized that Radcliffe and Benner had raised their heads and were looking at him curiously.

The Delambres, husband and wife, were in their room on the second floor. Paul Delambre was moving back and forth between the closet and the chiffonier, selecting articles of clothing which he then laid in neat geometric rows on the bed. His wife, Astrid, lay on the chaise by the window, knitting. She was wearing a plum-colored house-coat that, like most of her clothes, was cut low at the throat and shoulders and clung closely to the full curves of her body. The late afternoon sunlight, sloping into the room between the net curtains, danced and glittered in the rich golden coils of her hair.

Delambre brought a pair of nailed boots from the closet, placed them on the floor and stood looking at the clothing on the bed. There were two thick woolen shirts and one flannel one, a pair of heavy corduroy trousers, a waterproof jacket, three sweaters, long woolen underwear, woolen socks, mittens. Presently he took off the gabardine slacks and soft sport shirt he was wearing and put on one of the wool shirts and the corduroy trousers. Crossing to the mirror, he stood looking at his reflection for a moment; then he stretched slowly and flexed his arms and shoulders. The feel of the rough fabric caused a warm, pleasant glow to spread through his body. It was almost as pleasant as the glow of a good cognac. Yes, he thought, there were times when a man needed such things. Rough wool and canvas; leather and steel.

"Have you seen that old pigskin belt of mine?" he asked.

"It may be in the trunk," his wife said, without looking up. "The sun is in my eyes. Will you pull the shade, please?"

He crossed to the window and pulled the shade halfway down. Then he turned and leaned back against the sill, watching the swift play of her needles. "Astrid—" he said.

Her deep violet eyes looked up at him incuriously.

"We may be gone almost two weeks, you know."

She nodded.

"You don't mind?"

"Why should I mind?" she asked.

"You seem a little—well—resentful."

"I am not resentful. I just don't understand it. It seems such a strange notion."

Delambre winced at the word. "It is not a notion, Astrid," he said patiently.

"Whatever you want to call it then."

Madame Delambre had continued knitting as they spoke. For a few moments now the only sound in the room was the thin, measured clicking of her needles.

"You do not understand, *ma petite*," Delambre said quietly. "To climb this mountain, this monstrous and beautiful *Tour Blanche*—it is a thing that I want to do most terribly. Ever since we came to this valley, from that first morning when we drove up along the road from the village and I saw it there white and shining in the sky, I have wanted to climb it. I have known that I must climb it."

"Before this you have always been saying the one thing you wanted was to write your book."

A shadow crossed the Frenchman's face. "Yes, there is the book too," he said.

"You are still planning to write it, then?"

"Of course I am going to write it."

"You have been saying that now for almost four years."

Delambre's long fingers closed slowly into fists, and his eyes, behind the lenses of his glasses, seemed to grow larger and darker. "Yes, and I shall go on saying it. And I shall do it," he said, his voice suddenly strained and a little shrill. "*Nom de dieu*, what is it that you expect of a man? That he create literature or philosophy while the world explodes around him? Or sitting here, year after year in a forgotten little pocket of the earth, like a stone, a stick of wood, a vegetable? Can you not see what I am talking about? What I am trying to do? I must feel again, fight again, come alive again. . . ."

"And you think you will come alive again, as you call it, by breaking your neck on a mountain?"

As he talked, Delambre had risen from the window sill and begun pacing slowly about the room. Now he stopped suddenly and stared across the room at his wife. "Yes, precisely," he said. "By breaking my neck. By standing on my hands on the edge of precipices. By spattering my brains over the rocks below."

"It is useless for us to talk if you will not talk sense," his wife said placidly.

"It is useless for us to talk—ever."

He sat down on the edge of the bed and gazed out the window at the strip of forest and pastureland that showed between the shade and the sill. It was silent again in the room, except for the tiny clicking of the needles.

"It is because of this American, isn't it?" Madame Delambre said presently.

"What is?"

"That you are going to the mountain."

"Partly."

"It was he who asked you, wasn't it?"

"Yes."

"And he suggested that you might pay for it, perhaps?"

"Pay for it?"

"There will be expenses, no? The guide, food, whatever else it is you take on mountains."

"Perhaps. I don't know." Delambre shrugged in annoyance. "You see how it is," he said, "we cannot talk together. We cannot think together. I try to speak to you of the things that are inside of me—of real things, important things—and all you are thinking of is the money."

"Many people think that money is important."

He was about to speak angrily again, but stopped himself. No, he thought, it was senseless to become upset about such things. It was senseless, after so many years, to go on expecting the impossible.

"I have been watching this young American," he said presently. "I think he is in love with the Austrian girl."

"I don't know anything about that. What I mean is that I have been studying the sort of man he is." Delambre paused a moment. "Do you remember what I was saying to you the other night? That he was strong, integrated, a doer. Well, I was right, you see. How long has he been here? Three days? Four? Yet in that time more things have happened in this valley than in months and years before. The rest of us, we sit and stare up through the blue miles at the Tour Blanche and dream that some day, perhaps, we shall climb it. Then this American comes, and we set out to climb it."

He paused again, looking thoughtfully out the window. "Do you know what I have been thinking? I have been thinking that after the war I should like to go to America."

"Go there?" His wife looked up at him, but the soft clicking of the needles continued.

"Yes—why not? Why do you say it in that tone?"

"America is a long way off. For the past two months now we could have gone back to France, and you have not even been willing to do that."

"France!" Delambre made an impatient gesture with his long hands. "What is there left for us in France? Or anywhere in Europe? . . . America may be big, raw, turbulent; but it is alive. France may be free again, but it is still dying. Europe is dying. Its young men put on their uniforms. Faceless, nameless, mindless, they crowd into their phalanxes and battalions and march off to kill and die. Those who remain have become either brutalized thugs or bloodless, impotent intellectuals. And what is left for us? Hunger, perhaps, and beyond it nothingness. A few piddling appetites and fears, and beyond them nothingness. Our cities are the shattered mausoleums of dead cultures. Our churches and libraries are the skeletons of dead faiths. Nothing is left—nothing."

Delambre rose and crossed again to the window. Raising the shade, he sat on the broad sill and looked out across the peaceful valley of Kandermatt. . . . It is all bloodless, rootless, seedless, he thought. Even the green sweetness of the fields has become the sweetness of the stench of death. Even the mountains, rising cold

153

and gleaming out of the dead heart of Europe, are like heaps of whitened bones.

It was very still now in the room. The knitting needles clicked. Paul Delambre looked down the long green valley into the distance; into the past . . .

In everyone's memory of his own life there is a node, a starting point—a sure and always rediscoverable landmark in the blurred wilderness of time. For some it may be a mother's caress, a new toy, a certain day in school; for others a train trip, a party, a boat on a lake, a laughing girl. For him it was, simply and unalterably, a room. His fourth-floor-rear room in his parents' home on the Rue Castellane in Paris.

Of his parents themselves and the rest of the house he remembered almost nothing. His father, senior partner of the industrial banking firm of Delambre Frères, existed in his memory only as pince-nez and a voice; his mother only as clothes; the house as an immense, vague labyrinth of chandeliers and Empire furniture, peopled by day with dusting servants and by night with gleaming shirtfronts and jewelled gowns. But his own room was real, vividly, unfadingly real—as much a part of him still as his clothing, his voice, his very body. In the beginning it had been his oldest brother Charles' room, and later, for a year his second brother Marius'. But Charles had gone away to war in 1914 and never come back, and Marius had gone off to school in 1915, and thereafter it had been his, his only, his completely.

The mere thought of it moved him almost to tears. The long secret hours he had spent there; the enchanted sun-flecked afternoons; the dark soundless nights when he turned on the carefully screened bed-lamp and read and read, until his heart was pounding wildly and his flesh almost crawled, partly because of the mystery and wonder of what he was reading and partly because it seemed to him that that tiny secret light beside him was not just the only light burning in all that great dark silent house, but the only one burning in all Paris, in all the world. He had not counted the months and years by the war or peace, or even by schools or vacation trips or his growing body or the clothes he wore, but only by the books he read. First Hugo, Scott, Dickens, Stendhal. Then Shakespeare, Goethe, Balzac, Voltaire. Then Baudelaire, Byron, Rimbaud, Wedekind. The list was as endless as his appetite was insatiable. And slowly, magically, year by year, the walls of that little room had seemed to expand around him, until all the wisdom and sorrow, all the beauty and terror of the world were contained for him, indissolubly, within its prosaic, familiar confines.

Yes, terror had been there too, along with the rest: in the pages of the books; in the sunlight and shadows; in the soft, crowding darkness beyond the circumference of the yellow night-light. But most of all it dwelt in the mirror that rose smooth and faintly gleaming from the top of the old walnut chiffonier. Hour after hour, during those years of boyhood and adolescence, he would stand motionless before it, staring and wondering, trying to find in its still silver depths the key to the mysteries of flesh and spirit that were tormenting him. It was himself at which he was looking, of course, and yet, in a profound and subtle way it was not himself —or it was more than himself. For always, as he watched, the image in the glass would begin to take on a strange and indefinable depth—a thickness, almost—and from behind the familiar face and features there would emerge slowly another image, another *thing*, that was not he at all. And he would stand rooted, scarcely breathing, while this inwardness moved silently forward toward him through the still, frozen world behind the glass—hostile, alien, unreal, and yet at the same time far more real than reality—until suddenly terror would mount through him in a slow, icy wave, and he would tear himself away at last and throw himself face downward on the bed, spent and trembling.

Later, when he was a man, he learned that it was an experience that came to many children, in one form or another, at the beginning of self-awareness. But in his own case it was an experience that was never to be outgrown. On the contrary, as he grew older it became ever more frequent and more intense, until the actual physical world itself slowly began to take on for him many of the elusive and ambiguous qualities of a mirror. A face, a landscape, a painting, the body of a woman—even the commonest objects of daily use—would often appear to him, as he contemplated them, to be somehow changing, dissolving, disintegrating before his eyes. The object itself would cease to exist, and in its place was the depth, the shadow, the inwardness, that it contained. He would stare, motionless and entranced, realizing with part of his mind that it was mere hallucination, but at the same time knowing that in some arcane and half-comprehended fashion he was penetrating to the reality behind the image, the substance within the form. And with it always, mounting, spreading, the still, cold wave of fear. . . .

At fifteen he left home for the first time, for three years at an aristocratic school for rich men's sons in the pleasant Loire countryside near Blois. He neither liked nor disliked it, neither profited nor suffered from the experience. He moved physically in a different world, spoke different words, saw different sights, but his real life went on almost unchanged from that which he had known in the quiet secret room of his boyhood, plunging ever deeper into the multiform and inexhaustible world of the mind and the imagination. There were times when he was lonely. There were times when he was miserable and afraid. But even stronger than loneliness and fear was pride, for he knew already that he could say with Descartes, *"Je pense, donc je suis,"* and with Verlaine, *"J'ai plus de souvenirs que si j'avais mille ans."*

Then came the university years: two at the Sorbonne, one each at Cambridge, Göttingen and Bologna. He did not follow prescribed courses of study or take degrees, but browsed eclectically through the treasure bins of history, taking from each such gold as it seemed to him it had to offer. There were periods when he worked with immense and feverish concentration, burning with the resolve to be another Aristotle, Leonardo or Goethe and encompass within himself the very sum-total of human wisdom and experience. There were others when his energies were scattered and diffused, when all the springs of thought and effort seemed to have dried up within him, and he seemed capable only of perception and sensation—nothing more. These were the years in which music, painting, sculpture and architecture became a part of his life; and the soft, ever-changing landscapes of Europe, in their antiquity, their loveliness, their poignant and piercing sadness.

These were the years, too, of his first knowledge of women. His earliest affair was with a barmaid in a Cambridge pub, his second with the daughter of a history professor at Göttingen, his third with a café dancer in Munich. To all of them, and the others that followed, he came with a curious anguished mixture of desire and fear, and all of them left him shaken and dissatisfied. It was not that he fell in love. He was too deeply involved with his own thoughts and emotions ever to lose himself so completely in another. But always he was conscious in the end of frustration; of something promised, hinted at, and then left unrealized. Always, as in his solitary vigils before his mirror, there seemed to be another image behind the visible image, an inwardness behind the reality, a hidden essence of mystery, unknowableness and nameless terror. One night in a hotel in Milan he was making love to a ballet dancer from the Scala, an exquisite and delicate girl with the features of a half-grown madonna, when, in the very act of coitus, a beam of light fell through the window onto her face and it seemed to him that it was contorted with lust into the semblance of a fleshless death's head. Trembling and sweating, he snatched up his clothes and ran out into the night; and for months thereafter he fought down his recurring desire and lived a life of continence and troubled dreams.

By the time he returned to Paris to live his father had died and his mother had remarried. He paid her a single, almost laughably formal visit at her new home, and another, equally meaningless, to his brother Marius in the gilt-and-mahogany offices of Delambre Frères. Then he shut himself away in two tiny sequestered rooms overlooking the Quai Voltaire and launched at last into the sustained creative writing which he had known since boyhood was to be his true life's work.

For three years then he lived what was almost the existence of a recluse among his books and manuscripts. His father had left him a sizable fortune, on the income of which he could have moved in the most fashionable and exclusive circles of the city; but he cared nothing about such things. His money he spent on his painstakingly chosen and ever growing collection of paintings, sculptures and records, and his time he spent on his work. By the end of the first year he had sold an essay on Rimbaud and another on Mallarmé to two of the more experimental literary magazines, and six months later he brought out a slim morocco-bound volume of his poems in a privately printed edition. The poems did not cause the stir that he had hoped; indeed they went quite unnoticed. But it did not matter to him, really. All that mattered was his long philosophical novel, *L'Ame Qui Rie*, which was his major task and into which he was pouring the distillation of all his years of living, thinking and feeling. He went on working at it, unruffled and serene.

Toward the end of the third year, however, he realized that he had arrived at a period of stagnation. Somewhere along the line he had begun to bog down in the subtleties and tortuosities of his own thought. "The world has receded too far from me," he told himself, "I have lost it and I must get it back." Gradually forsaking his ingrown hermetic life, he began to mingle in the artistic and intellectual life of the city, attending the openings at the theatres and galleries, devoting more time to his collections, and moving on the fringes of that glittering and frenetic coterie of cosmopolitans whose vortex was the ateliers of Cocteau and Maritain, Picasso and Gertrude Stein. He developed an interest in several young writers and artists of talent and found satisfaction in assisting them over their financial difficulties. He helped sponsor a string quartet and an intimate gallery in which only cubist and abstractionist painters would be hung. For eighteen months he was backer and co-editor of a highly regarded, but unfortunately never popular, literary and artistic revue called *Approches Nouvelles.*

Meanwhile he planned and replanned, wrote and rewrote his novel, but still its progress did not satisfy him, and still he could not seem to recapture the first fine concentration and consecration with which he had begun it. I have not yet found what I am searching for, he thought. This tight, self-absorbed little cosmos of artists and intellectuals is no more the real world than my solitary rooms above the Quai Voltaire. If I do not wish to atrophy altogether I must get away from it and stay away. . . . And he began to travel. Spending only two or three months of each year in Paris, he set out on one journey after another to all the places, near and remote, toward which imagination had beckoned him since early boyhood: to Scandinavia, Lapland and the empty northern tundras; to Algiers, Cairo and Damascus in the scented, swarming south; to the Nile and the Tigris, the Caucasus and the Himalayas, the hot, murmurous cities of old Asia and the soft, shining islands in the sea. Occasionally during his journeyings he would sit down to write. But for the most part he did not even try, for it was no longer writing, or even thinking, about the world that mattered to him, but simply the world itself. Moving from land to land and continent to continent, he steeped himself in its variousness, its distances, its vast and encompassing anonymity.

It was in Sweden, at an obscure summer resort on the silver Baltic beaches, that he had met Astrid Varnholm. She was one of the three waitresses at the tiny seaside inn at which he stayed, and he had not been there more than a day or two before he was aware of an attraction, almost a compulsion, toward her that he had never before experienced toward any woman. In the years since his university days his few sexual relationships had been casual and desultory. *Jeunes filles* bored him, prostitutes disgusted him, and the quick, brittle, thin-fibred women of the Parisian social and intellectual worlds filled him only with a sense of fecklessness and frustration. There had been a time when he felt a strong and peculiarly emotional attachment for a certain young painter whom he was subsidizing, and he had wondered if he were perhaps, after all, a homosexual. Then the phase passed, as suddenly and inexplicably as it had begun, and he entered into the period of his travels and, with it, a period of almost complete celibacy. . . . But in the presence of this placid, full-bodied, blond and violet-eyed Swedish girl all the old anguish of desire arose to torment him again, far stronger and more imperious than he had ever known it before. On his third night at the inn he invited her to a motion-picture show, and she accepted. Two nights later he made love to her for the first time, and she acquiesced. And on the last day of August, 1937, exactly three weeks to the day after he had met her, they were married in the registry office of the near-by town of Kristianstad.

Early in the fall he took her back to Paris with him, and through the following winter they lived quietly in his old rooms above the Quai Voltaire. He taught her how to speak French, how to dress and do her hair, how to act with servants, tradesmen, officials, acquaintances, friends. In the beginning he had been plagued by fears that she had married him only for his money, but never once, either by word or act, did she give any indication that this was so. She accepted his gifts and his instruction as she accepted him into her bed and body—quietly, matter-of-factly, showing neither avidity nor reluctance. She fitted herself, without so much as a visible tremor of adjustment, into the routine of life which he chose to live.

She was never aroused, never passionate; but passion was not what he wanted. She was simply the passive receptacle of his desire, and into her, physically and spiritually, he poured the accumulated pent-up tides of his torment and unrest. Alone of all the women he had ever known, she seemed to him complete and whole and utterly possessable. Here at last there was no second, secret image behind the image in the glass, no shadows and depths beneath the unclouded violet eyes and soft white palpable flesh. Whether or not he loved her he did not know nor even ask himself. If indeed it was love, it was love as an animal might experience it— a thing of desire and satisfaction, need and fulfillment, unblemished by thought. But this much he did know: that in the body and substance of this woman he had found an anodyne for which he had been searching blindly throughout his life; and that in those first few months of their life together he had almost succeeded in forgetting, for at least a little time, the loneliness and emptiness that he seemed doomed to carry with him forever in his mind and heart.

All that autumn and winter he did not work at all. There were his books, his paintings, his music, his brandy. There was the loveliness of Paris on blue-and-gold October afternoons and black-and-silver January nights. Above all, there was Astrid. But with the coming of spring he began to feel again the stirrings of ambition and unrest. He wrote an essay or two, a book review which he sold to *Figaro*, and a few poems. Then he got out the manuscript of his novel, reread what he had written, destroyed it and began again. "Now at last I am at peace with myself," he thought. "Now at last it will come."

But once again he found that it was impossible for him to concentrate. Paris was filled with noise and distraction, all Europe with the clangor of politicians and armies, and he realized that he must get away from it if he were to work steadily and productively—that he must stand a little outside the world; as it were, if he were to see that world clearly and whole. So, accompanied now by Astrid, he set out on his journeyings again. First to Tunisia, but it was too hot. Then to Minorca, but it was still too scarred and shaken by the violence of the Spanish War. Finally to Naxos, in the Grecian Cyclades. Here they spent the summer, in a pink stucco villa on a hillside above the Aegean, and here again, for a time, he found a measure of contentment and peace. Looking back through the years, he could remember the long golden hours drifting slowly past; the jacaranda and bougainvillea in the garden; the hammock between the mandarin trees; the brown cliffs and the white beaches; the long swims to the rock in the bay, and Astrid, her white body gleaming, rising like a reincarnated Aphrodite from the sun-flecked surf.

And then at last, suddenly and incredibly, the still, sun-flooded morning of September second and Christopher, their houseman, running wild-eyed and babbling up the dusty road from the village. Delambre had been sitting in the garden when the news came, listening to one of DeFalla's flamencos on the portable phonograph, and after Christopher had gone again he continued sitting there until the music was finished, feeling neither surprised nor shocked nor horrified, but only gently pensive and a little tired. *Eh bien*, he thought. *C'est arrivé.*

And a week later they were on their way again: by steam-launch to Piræus, by Lloyd Triestino to Genoa, by *wagon-lits* to Paris.

A few days after he arrived home his brother Marius telephoned and asked him to come to see him, and for the first time in ten years he found himself sitting in the executive offices of Delambre Frères, while a stranger, who happened also to be the son of his parents, presented a cogent list of reasons why he should enter the firm. "We are desperately shorthanded," Marius declared, "and even you must want to be of some service now." Paul listened courteously, if a trifle abstractedly, and when his brother had finished explained that he had other plans. And the following week he enlisted in the army as a private.

They put him in an office because of his eyes and wanted to make him an officer because of his name. But he struggled against both, and finally, in the spring of the following year, he was sent to a regiment stationed in the Maginot Line. Now at last, he thought, I am a *poilu*; now at last I am a part of France. But he was a part of nothing. He wore the same uniform as the men around him and lived through the same physical routine. But he could neither communicate his thoughts to them nor apprehend theirs. He did not understand their jokes, their amusements, their grousings or, half the time, the very words they spoke. He shrank from the loutish peasant coarseness of their bodies and minds.

Among thousands and millions of his fellow-men he was more alone than he had ever been in the years of his solitude.

And then, suddenly, monstrously, the cataclysm. Gunfire and bomb-burst; plane and tank; maneuver and withdrawal; order and counter-order; and then no orders at all. Now there was not even anything left to be a part of. No line, no regiment, no army, no France, nothing.

"Where are the officers?"

"The officers—*merde!*"

"Where are the guns—the planes—the tanks?"

"*Merde!*"

"What is happening to us?"

"*Merde!*"

He stumbled along the choked and flaming roads, not even bothering to take cover when the Stukas and Messerschmitts came down. He felt no fear, scarcely even dismay, but rather a dull acceptance and recognition. What did it matter if it all ended a day sooner or a day later? It was the end, in any case. After its appointed millions of years life was dissolving again into the chaos of mud and fire from which it had risen. From behind the bright deceptive images in the mirror the truth was relentlessly emerging, all its hideous sterility and corruption laid bare at last.

Yet it was not the end. His legs carried him on. His heart and lungs and body and brain still carried him on. The sun still rose each morning and shone in dancing summer splendor on the plane-wings and the gun-snouts, the carnage and the despair, the dying and the dead. And at last he reached Paris. He locked himself into his house, drew all the blinds and curtains, took off his uniform and burned it, and for forty-eight hours he remained there, shut away from the crumbling world, with his books, his paintings, his music, his brandy, and Astrid's gold and ivory body clasped hot and living and yielding to his own.

"We will stay here until they come and get us," he thought. But they did not stay there. On the morning of the third day he said, "Come, we must be going again."

Astrid packed quietly. "Where?" she asked.

He did not know where. Emerging again into the streets of the paralyzed city, it seemed to him at first that they would never get anywhere—not so much as a block. But presently he discovered that even in the midst of chaos and death one thing still retained its power. Money still lived. Money got him a van, gasoline, food, permits, more money. At first he had not cared if they got away or not, but gradually the fever of flight possessed him, and he stripped the house of possessions until the van was overloaded almost to bursting. As they drew away through the darkness of the following night a dull orange glow was slowly mounting the horizon to the north and east.

Then there were the roads again. For five days they crept on through a nightmare of dust, rain, mud, ditches, blown tires, snapped springs, arguments, threats, bribes, and the endless fleeing hordes. They came to Orleans and were turned back. They tried to cut across the country lanes to Bourges and bogged down. There were Nevers, Monthuçon, Lyons and at last the frontier. There were Geneva, Lausanne, Berne, Interlaken. . . .

And then, finally, Kandermatt. The peaks, the valley, the remote empty inn. . . . The months passed, and then the years, and the fury and clangor of a world at war became no more than a half-remembered nightmare hidden away behind the white mountain walls. And when at last the great counter-invasion came and France was free again, that too seemed less reality than a dream.

"We must go back," he had said. But they did not go back. He *could* not go back. . . .

Paul Delambre turned away from the window. While he had been looking out the sun had sloped away behind the high ridges to the west, and the room was now soft with evening light. His wife was still lying quietly on the chaise, her lovely, placid face half-turned toward him, the thin amber needles moving rhythmically in her hands.

Sudden white-hot fury seized him. "In the name of Christ," he almost shouted, "will you lie there knitting forever?"

Her cool violet eyes looked up at him. "I did not know it was upsetting you," she said.

He opened his mouth to speak, but no words came. For a few moments he sat motionless, the palms of his hands tight and flat against the sill beside him. Then the wave of anger ebbed as suddenly as it had risen. In its place was only a gray tiredness flowing slowly through his body and brain.

"Do you want me to stop knitting?" his wife asked.

"No," he said quietly. "There is no need to stop. . . . I am sorry."

"You are on edge today."

"Yes, perhaps I am, a little."

The needles clicked on.

Delambre watched her in silence. It was almost dusk in the room now, but the skin of her face and throat and the coiled masses of her hair seemed to him to be still shining with a rich inward glow of their own. Under the clinging silk of her gown her full, flawless woman-body stirred gently with her breathing. The blue and russet trees of his bookshelves rose into shadow behind the chaise. The Van Gogh and Toulouse-Lautrec glowed on the walls, and the Sung horses and Tanagra dancers loomed from their darkening corners in slender, frozen loveliness. Beyond the window were the green valley, the white peaks and the stainless, deepening ocean of the sky.

There was no sound. Nothing moved. Paul Delambre cupped his hands, covered his face with them and closed his eyes.

It was after dinner that evening that Siegfried Hein asked to join them. Or perhaps it was the other way around. Recalling the event later, Martin Ordway was never altogether sure.

He had been to the storehouse again, making a few last-minute additions to the packs with Benner and Carla, and was crossing the dark terrace toward the inn when he became aware of a figure sitting on the verandah steps.

"Nick?" he asked, approaching.

"No, it is I," the German's voice answered. "I think Herr Radcliffe is in the lounge."

Ordway murmured his thanks and began ascending the steps.

"You will start off in the morning?" Hein asked.

"Yes. After breakfast."

"You will have good weather for it."

Ordway paused and turned, looking out across the terrace to the mountains and sky above. Since the afternoon, four days before, when the mist had lifted not so much as a white shard of cloud had appeared above the valley, and tonight the stars hung bright as lanterns in windless blue-black space. "I only hope it holds," he said.

"It should be good for a little while yet. A day or two of fog perhaps. But in the Oberland the storms usually do not come until after the middle of October." Hein was speaking in English, with only a slight accent, but slowly and with a careful choice of words. "Well, I wish you good luck," he said.

"Thanks. We'll need it, I'm sure." Ordway turned to continue up the steps, then found that he had stopped and was looking down at the German. "I haven't seen you up on the slopes since that day on the Aarntal path," he said. "Haven't you been doing any climbing?"

"A little," said Hein. "Up to the moraine and glaciers. One cannot do much on the peaks by oneself."

"Your friend has gone, hasn't he?"

"Yes, he was called back to—" Hein paused. "He was called away suddenly."

"You could climb with a guide, couldn't you?"

"I am afraid we Germans do not have the money for such luxuries as guides. Besides, these Swiss peasants—they are really no good, you know."

"Andreas Benner's good. He's damned good."

Hein nodded. "Yes, this Benner is perhaps the exception. He has what none of the others have. *Eine Funke*—how do you call it?—a spark. But I had not known he was willing to go on the Weissturm."

"He's going."

"He thinks it can be climbed from this side, then?"

"He thinks it's possible. So do I."

"Could I ask, Herr Ordway, which route you intend to try?"

"Across the wasteland and up the Dornel Glacier. Then the southeast ridge."

Hein nodded again, slowly. "Yes," he said, "that is the best route."

"You've been on it yourself, then?"

"Once, many years ago. But only a little way up, to reconnoitre. I have never tried for the top."

"I'd have thought you had. Andreas has told me a little about your other climbs—the Matterhorn faces, the Eigerwand, the Grandes Jorasses. It would seem natural for you to have tried the Weissturm too."

It was a moment before the German spoke again. He was sitting bent forward, elbows on knees; but his eyes were raised to the distant, jagged white line where the mountain ridges met the night. "All my life I have wanted to climb the Weissturm," he said quietly. "More than any other mountain. More than anything I have ever done. When I was still a boy, twelve and fifteen years ago, and I used to come in the summers to Switzerland, I would stand and look up to it, high and white there in the sky above all the rest, and I would say to myself, 'Yes, there are many mountains in the Alps, but for me there is only one mountain. And to climb it, if need be, I shall give up my life.'"

"What's kept you from it then?" asked Ordway.

"To climb such a mountain as the Weissturm, after all, is very much more than a matter of wanting to. This much I knew even as a boy, and this much I still know: that he who will at last get to the top must be a mountaineer of the very first order. He must have skill, strength, endurance, but even they are not enough. He must also be ready to climb it, in his mind and spirit as well as in his body. He must be without fear or weakness of any sort." Hein paused, turning his head slightly, and Ordway felt, rather than saw, his gray eyes looking at him. "Herr Knubel tells me you too have known the Weissturm for many years, Herr Ordway," the German said. "Do you not agree with me?"

Ordway nodded. They were not the words he himself would have used. It was not the way an American, or for that matter an Englishman, thought. Yet it was true.

"Yes, I agree with you," he said.

"For many years, therefore, I climbed in the Alps," the German went on. "From the Dauphiné to the Dolomites. The snow peaks and the rock peaks. First the easy ones, then the harder, finally the hardest. Always it was the Weissturm of which I thought and dreamed, but I had resolved that I would never try it until I had earned the right to try it. Until I was ready. I went to the Alpen-verein with my plans, and they approved them. A small group was gotten together—six men—the best climbers in Germany, with myself as leader. All the arrangements were made, and in another week we were to leave for Kandermatt."

Hein paused and shrugged. "That was in the last week in August, 1939," he said.

"And you've never had a chance since, of course?"

"No."

"Were you and your friend planning to try it?"

"We thought and talked about it sometimes. When we first came here ten days ago we even climbed up to the glaciers to reconnoitre. But the Weissturm is no undertaking for only two men."

"It can't be very easy for you to sit by and watch others try it."

"No," said Hein. "It is not easy."

There was a sudden silence. He wants to come, Ordway thought. He is going to ask to come. . . . But the German did not speak again.

Ordway reached into his pocket and brought out his pack of Camels. "Cigarette?" he asked.

Hein hesitated momentarily, then took one. "Amerikanische," he said.

"Yes. Have you ever smoked them?"

"A few times, before the war. They must be hard to get these days in Switzerland, no?"

"You can find them occasionally, in the cities."

"It is in Zurich or Geneva that you are stationed, then?"

"Geneva," said Ordway.

"So? It is with the consulate, perhaps?"

"No, the International Red Cross."

They were silent again. As they spoke Ordway had struck a match and given Hein a light, and now he held the flame to his own cigarette. Suddenly, beyond the wavering yellow cone, he was again aware of the German's gray eyes, watching him. This time, however, they did not seem to be fixed on his face, but lower; on his throat, perhaps, or his chest. Martin Ordway glanced down to where his two army dog-tags were gleaming dully in the open V of his shirt collar.

Presently he looked up again, and for an instant the men's eyes met. Neither said anything. Ordway lighted his cigarette, drew in a deep breath of smoke and flicked the match away into the darkness.

"Well?" he asked.

The German remained silent.

"What do you propose to do about it, Herr Hein?"

167

Still another moment passed before Hein answered. Then he said: "It is a very fine organization, the Red Cross. It has done excellent work for both sides."

Ordway studied the glowing tip of his cigarette. "Meaning that you intend to do nothing?" he asked.

"That would depend largely on you yourself, Herr Ordway."

"You work for the Red Cross too. Is that it?"

Hein shrugged a little. "Each of us does his work," he said. "The Red Cross, perhaps—the consular service—whatever it is. It seems to me that, meeting here quite by accident in this mountain valley in Switzerland, we have one of two choices. Either we may ask each other questions or not. Either we may continue to be what we are elsewhere, or we are both simply—how shall I say it—Turisten."

"And you're suggesting the second?"

"I think you know perfectly well what I am suggesting, Herr Ordway."

"That we climb the Weissturm together."

"Yes."

Ordway snapped his cigarette away and watched its thin orange arc curve off into darkness. In his mind he was suddenly sitting again beside Carla Dehn on a rickety stile in the upper pasture. *"Until a few days ago my job was killing his kind, and his job was killing mine. In another couple of weeks it will be our job again. . . ."*

But here . . . now? . . .

"How much longer will you be here?" he asked.

"About two weeks," said Hein.

"You could be ready to start out tomorrow morning?"

"Yes."

"And you agree that, if you come, we will be simply two men climbing a mountain together? Only that and nothing more?"

"Yes, I agree."

A long moment passed before Ordway spoke again. . . . You want him, he thought. It's cockeyed; it's senseless; it's damnfoolishness. But you want him. . . .

"All right," he said quietly.

And they shook hands.

168

The rucksacks and packboards lay in a neat row on the storeroom floor. The dull gold of the ropes lay in coils in the corner and the sharp steel of the ice axes gleamed along the wall. Martin Ordway glanced at his watch. It was almost midnight. After a last look around he snapped off the light and walked back across the dark terrace toward the inn.

He walked slowly, hands thrust deep in his pockets, thinking.

Is it all foolishness? he thought. Is it all damnfoolishness and amateur playacting and what the people who have read the right books call Escape? They were going to climb a mountain. More accurately, they were going to try to climb a mountain. For a little while they would pretend that nothing else existed; that the world, the war, the past, the future, everything they knew and were, did not exist. They would, each in his own fashion, narrow down the focus of their minds, as a photographer narrows down the circular shutter of his camera to the minutest pinpoint, until only one thing would be visible to them: a blue-inked X on a curlycued map; a wind-ruffled crest of snow against an ocean of sky. They would put one foot before the other, one groping hand above the other, clawing with their fingers into the crevices of the rock and with their spiked toes into the blue, ancient ice, struggling upward toward that blue X, that white crest, with the blind, mindless desire of a moth for a candle or a lemming for the sea. Until they climbed it; or did not climb it; or were killed. . . .

Six characters in search of a blue X, he thought, sardonically. An architect who had destroyed a thousand homes. A guide to forgotten ranges. A bedevilled, self-exiled dilettante who dipped his pen in brandy. A geologist who was trying to shut out the world behind a wall of stones and fossils. A girl who was trying to shut it out behind a wall of years. An American, an Englishman, a Frenchman, a Swiss, an Austrian . . .

And now a German. An enemy.

Yes, it was foolishness. It was escape and unreality and illusion —a fantastic dumb-show, to be acted out by six lost, impotent human fragments, washed meaninglessly up into this uttermost outpost of the world by the immense tides of war. . . . "There is an emptiness," Andreas Benner had said. And all that they were doing was to exchange a flaming, exploding emptiness for an emptiness of cold, white stillness. . . . He came to the verandah steps and ascended them slowly. At the top he turned and stood with his hands on the railing, looking out across the terrace to the valley and mountains beyond. The valley was dark and still, the mountains white and still. High above the rest loomed the Weissturm, whitest and stillest of all against the oceanic blackness of the sky. Yes, he thought—it is all space and silence, all emptiness and nothingness.

And yet . . . .

What was it, then, that was suddenly holding his hands there, tight and tense against the verandah railing? What was the thing that he could feel now, slowly rising within him, swelling and brightening like an aching fire through his flesh and bones and blood?

Chapter 10

They came down the verandah steps and their nailed boots scuffed in the gravel of the driveway. They moved silently about in the gray twilight of the storeroom, lifting the packboards and rucksacks and adjusting their leather straps.

"Herr Martin and Herr Hein can each carry a packboard," Andreas Benner suggested, "and I will take a packboard and a small rucksack. Doktor Radcliffe and Herr Delambre will each have a large rucksack and Fräulein Dehn a small one." He counted carefully through the piles on the floor. "That will leave two boards, one heavy rucksack and two light ones for the second trip."

"And you to carry all of them," Radcliffe added wryly.

"How long do you figure for the first round-trip, Andreas?" Ordway asked.

The guide rubbed his chin reflectively. "That will depend of course, Herr Martin. It has been done in six hours. Also in ten or twelve. It is my suggestion each one should go at his own pace up to the hut. There is only the one path, so that no one can get lost, and in such a way everyone can find out how it goes best for him. If we are all back here again by, say, two or three o'clock and not feeling tired, we can perhaps then make the second trip. Otherwise we make the second tomorrow morning."

"It should not be necessary for Fräulein Dehn to make the two trips," Delambre suggested.

171

"No, it may be best if the *Fräulein* goes only once to the hut and stays there."

"I have a vague idea," said Ordway, "that the *Fräulein* is going to hold her own very nicely with at least one or two of the *Herren*."

Outside on the terrace the last wisps of dawn fog were dissolving, and though the sun had not yet risen, the valley walls to the north and south were slowly sucking color from the brightening sky. High above them the snowfields gleamed with a delicate pink flame in the light from beyond the horizon.

"*Ja*, the weather still holds," said Benner, squinting upward.

They hoisted their loads onto their backs, shifted the straps, and hefted their ice axes in their hands. Herr Knubel, in pajamas and bathrobe, had been standing on the verandah, watching them, and now he was joined by his wife and the waitress, Annamarie. They waved, and the six on the terrace below waved back at them. Then there was a brief, curious moment in which no one spoke or moved. It was almost as if they had suddenly remembered something—or were waiting for something. In the gray distance Ordway could hear the low, even rumbling of the Aarn.

"Well—" he said.

They crossed the terrace and started off down the winding road: first Andreas Benner, with his measured, bow-legged, trudge; then Radcliffe and Delambre, with Siegfried Hein a few paces behind; lastly, Carla and Ordway. But Ordway had gone no more than a few yards when there was a shout from the verandah, and a moment later Herr Knubel came hurrying after him, his bathrobe hobbling his knees and his slippers slapping violently against the gravel.

"It will be tonight or tomorrow that you are coming down again?" the innkeeper asked.

"I don't know," said Ordway. "It depends how things go."

"I will be down in the village the whole day tomorrow. So if you do not come back until then—" Herr Knubel extended his hand—"I wish you the most great success."

"Thanks."

"Beginning the day after tomorrow I shall be watching for you every day through the telescope."

Ordway smiled. "We'll be counting on that."

172

"And if before you return there should come instructions for you—"

"Instructions?"

"From Interlaken."

It was a moment before Ordway spoke. "Yes," he said. "Of course."

"Then I shall send Christian Mehrwalder at once up to the glacier. If you are already too high on the mountain, he has already made his arrangements with Andreas and will signal up to you."

"Andreas seemed to think it would be ten days or more before we could expect anything."

"Yes, that is the likelihood apparently. Still, in such things one can never tell, and it is better that one's plans are laid in advance."

Ordway nodded.

"They are satisfactory to you then?"

"Yes, quite satisfactory."

"Also—" The innkeeper extended his hand again. "Grüss Gott."

"Grüss Gott," said Martin Ordway. "And thanks."

"It has been nothing, my old friend."

"It's been everything."

He and Carla swung down the knoll onto the valley road, and the terrace and verandah and prim white gables of the inn faded gradually from view behind the intervening trees. The others were out of sight ahead, and there was no sound except the sharp chirping of finches and pipits and the murmuring of the still-unseen river. The meadows on either side of the road spread empty and utterly quiet in the gray twilight, transfixed by a hundred million silver drops of dew. Then, by almost imperceptible degrees, the grayness began to thin and brighten; a tide of light poured down the valley walls, like a golden liquid into a deep cup, and suddenly there was the sun, resting red and enormous on the ridges to the east.

Leaving the road, they turned into a forest path and followed its dark windings between tall walls of larch and maple. The sound of the Aarn grew louder in their ears, rose to sudden roaring thunder as they crossed it on the slender suspension bridge, and faded away again as they ascended on the far side toward the steep green slopes of the upper pastures. Here the path narrowed to a point where they could no longer walk abreast, and Ordway took the lead. They climbed the bright mountainside slowly and in silence, and above them the sun slowly climbed the blue miles of the sky.

When the instructions came, Martin Ordway thought. . . .

He repeated the innkeeper's words in his mind, but they were only words. Europe, the war, bombs and bombers—they were all words—a remote and half-remembered nightmare without substance or reality. Reality was the gentle upward thrust of the earth beneath his boots; the swaying of the packboard and the soft creak of its straps; the sun, warm and caressing on his face and neck and shoulders. It was the green, slanting pasture and the forest above the pasture and the rock above the forest and the snow-peaks above the rock. It was himself climbing slowly upward through that still, glittering world, and Carla Dehn climbing slowly behind him. . . .

He was suddenly aware that he had stopped and was standing quite still. Then he heard her voice.

"Is anything the matter, Martin?" she asked.

He turned and looked at the slender girl who stood a few yards behind him on the path. He looked at her boots and rough woolen trousers and gray flannel shirt, and at the warm brown of her arms and throat, and at her faintly flushed face and her deep gray-green eyes and her hair gleaming with sunlight.

He shook his head slowly. "I'm just making sure you're still there," he told her.

"You can't lose me that easily," she said, smiling.

And they climbed on.

In the forest above the pasture, Radcliffe, Delambre, Hein and Benner moved steadily upward along dark aisles of pine and fir. For perhaps the first hour they had kept close together, talking desultorily, but now they had spread out until they were separated by intervals of fifty to a hundred yards. They climbed singly and in silence, their eyes on the ground and their thoughts turned inward.

Andreas Benner trudged along in the lead, his back bent forward under his fifty-pound load, his stubby legs moving with the slow, inexorable beat of pendulums. How many times in forty years had he ascended and descended that path? A thousand, perhaps? Or fifteen hundred? Every foot of it, every pitch and bend and tree and rock and stream, was as familiar to him as the lineaments of his own face and body. The swaying of the packboard, the coiled rope on his shoulder, the smooth steel of the ice ax against his hand were as much a part of him as his arms or legs or the tide of mountain air pouring gently down from the glaciers and sucking sweet and cool into his lungs.

As he walked along now, his mind was occupied with the details of his trade. The thirty-meter ropes, would be best on the glaciers, he decided. Two thirty-meter ropes, three climbers on each, with himself leading the first and Herr Ordway the second. . . . Or would the German be better for the second? He weighed the matter carefully in his mind. . . . Yes, the German was probably the wiser choice. In the beginning, at least. For the actual mountain they could wait and see how things went.

Six climbers, he thought: yes, that was the right number for such a mountain as the Weissturm. But five *Herren* to one guide —or, rather, four *Herren* and one *Dame*—that was not so good. In ordinary times no first-class conscientious guide would take on a party of more than two, even on a familiar and easy mountain; and for a long or difficult ascent the usual ratio was one to one. . . . But these were not ordinary times, of course. Nor an ordinary party. The German, Hein, for instance—he was the sort who would never have climbed with a guide at all before the war. The sort who thought themselves better than any guide. The Frenchman, on the other hand, was probably the kind who was used to being hauled up a mountain by a whole regiment of professionals, like a sack of chicken-meal. The Englishman was a fine mountaineer, but old. The American had not climbed for years. And the girl . . .

Well, there was no use worrying about it; they would find out in God's own good time how things would go. It was enough for the moment that they were on their way; that mountain earth was rising and swelling beneath their feet; that each step they took brought them one step higher, one step nearer to their goal.

Andreas Benner looked down through the trees that screened the mountainside at the valley that was his home. Then he looked up past their tapering summits toward the world of rock and ice that was his home as well. And he trudged on. His pace remained even and unhurried, but apparently he was walking faster than the others, for by the time he came to the bold outcropping ledge of the Drachenfels he could neither see them nor hear their footsteps on the path below. Continuing on for another few hundred yards, he came to a small clearing in the forest and stopped.

Near the center of the clearing, beside the path, stood a shrine. It was a small and simple structure, little more than an oblong box on a low fieldstone base, and inside it were only a roughly hewn wooden cross and a chipped and faded image of the Virgin. Benner took off his hat, crossed himself and for a little while stood quite still, staring into the dark and musty-smelling interior. On the floor-board, scattered about the Virgin's feet, lay the stalks of a few long-withered wildflowers, and on the walls beside her, carved in the dark, weathered wood, were the names of generations of Kandermatt guides, half obliterated by the quiet hand of time. There were Mehrwalders, Kronigs, Burgners, Zurneisens, Rushlis, Lochmatters, Benners. There was *Franz Benner, 1871—1913.*

With his pack still on his shoulders Andreas Benner knelt and prayed. Rising again, he reached into the shrine and with a gentle hand removed the dead flowerstalks and scattered them on the ground. Then he took from his lapel the cornflower his wife had given him and laid it at the feet of the Virgin. For a moment he stood looking at it, lying fresh and blue and gleaming in the dim stillness of the shrine; then he crossed himself again and put on his hat.

And he climbed on.

Nicholas Radcliffe had noticed the gap gradually opening between him and the guide, but he did not quicken his pace. They had all agreed that each would proceed at his own speed, and besides, he thought now, musingly, they were, in any real sense, no more separated from each other when they were physically apart than when they were gathered in a group. They had committed themselves, the six of them, to a common enterprise. They had talked and planned together; now they were setting out together; soon they would be eating, sleeping, climbing, struggling together, their destinies intertwined, their very lives dependent on one another. Still, each of them was alone. And their aloneness had nothing to do with yards and minutes, miles and years.

Benner had disappeared now, but, glancing back, Radcliffe could see Delambre trudging along some fifty or sixty yards behind him and Hein following about an equal distance behind the Frenchman. Both men were climbing with slow, measured strides, their heads bent to the path and their shoulders hunched forward under their loads.

They are alone, Radcliffe thought. Each one of us is alone. . . .

He was a man who was accustomed to solitude. For almost twenty years, since he had resigned his associate professorship at Cambridge, he had lived and worked by himself—at the writing table, in the laboratory, among the forests and glaciers of the Alps. There were those, perhaps, who would have called it an escape from reality, but he had not thought of it as such. In his own mind he had simply, and quite consciously, renounced the sterile, evanescent realities of the social and political world for the fundamental and abiding realities of nature and science. In any case, it had been the life he had chosen, the life he desired. And he had been content with it. He had built his house, solid and foursquare, and cultivated his garden of rocks.

What was it that had been happening to him, then, in the past few years? And to this house of his mind? It had been with the coming of war that the first chinks had appeared in the walls—the papers coming up from Zurich and Berne, the news of Dunkerque and the death of France, his abortive decision to return to England. He had not returned; he had come back to Kandermatt and his work and the only life he knew; and he had striven with all the power of his mind and will to close those chinks. But he had been unable to close them. They had widened and gaped, until at last it had come to seem to him that there were no walls left at all, and he was like a man standing in the ruins of some antique and abandoned temple, peering out into an alien landscape of darkness and confusion.

A few nights before—the night after Martin Ordway first visited him—he had dreamed that he was walking along a white, empty beach beside an ocean. It had not been an ocean of water, however, but an ocean of time, and as he turned toward it, it had parted and dissolved, and he was walking not along an ocean bed but across the corpse-strewn mud-flats beyond Ypres and there ahead of him in the twilight was the desolate fire-etched skyline of

177

Vimy Ridge. Then that too had dissolved, and he was walking, still walking, always walking, across the brown, rippling miles of Tibet. Behind him somewhere, on the empty plateau, there was a lama chanting and a prayer wheel turning, but he could not find them and could not stop to search. Still walking and always walking, he kept on toward the thin white gleaming line that showed on the horizon to the west. . . .

Radcliffe raised his eyes and gazed up the familiar vistas of the forest path. He looked at the pines and firs and the needle-strewn earth and the scattered gray rocks and the soft slanting bars of morning sunlight. No, he thought, this was not a lonely place. There was nothing lonely about a rock or tree or the sun or the sky. There was nothing lonely about an empty plain or an ocean bottom or an unclimbed mountaintop. No place on earth was lonely until man came to it, bringing his loneliness with him.

Now presently the path twisted back on itself and emerged from the forest onto the high, open promontory of the Drachenfels. Radcliffe stopped, took out his pipe and waited for Delambre to catch up with him.

"How's for a spot of rest?" he suggested as the Frenchman appeared.

Swinging their packs from their shoulders, they sat down on the springy turf that fringed the rock and looked out over the valley. Delambre was obviously tired. His forehead glistened with tiny drops of sweat and he was sucking the thin air into his mouth in slow, deep breaths.

Radcliffe lit his pipe and stretched his long legs out before him. "You've been up here before?" he asked.

"Oh yes. Several times."

"I've always found it a pleasant place to break a climb."

"Yes, it is very lovely." Delambre sat quietly for a few moments, gazing down the mountainside. "The valley is so still and small and full of peace."

"And yet at the same time it has a certain—well—sadness about it, don't you think?"

The Frenchman nodded slowly. "Yes," he said. "The lovely, peaceful things are always sad."

There was the sound of boots on the path below, and presently Siegfried Hein came out of the forest and stopped beside them.

"Any difficulties, gentlemen?" he asked.

Radcliffe shook his head. "Just loafing a bit. Like to join us?"

"Thank you, but I am not tired. And besides, I have always found that to stop too often for resting only makes the muscles more stiff when one starts off again."

"Oh quite," the Englishman agreed.

Hein stood beside them without removing his packboard, and a trace of a smile touched his cool gray eyes. "You find the loads a trifle heavy, perhaps?" he asked.

"Not at all," said Radcliffe.

"Herr Delambre?"

"No, I can manage," said the Frenchman.

"I should be glad to relieve you of part of it."

"No, thank you very much. I can manage."

"In any case, there's no hurry today," Radcliffe said. "And it's always pleasant to coddle one's bones a bit and look back over the way one has come."

Hein's gaze followed the Englishman's down the valley walls. "Yes, it is a fine sight," he agreed. Then his eyes smiled again. "But do not forget the old mountaineers' song, gentlemen: *"Blick immer aufwärts, nie zurück."* Turning, he pointed upward with his ax. "Look. Already between the treetops you can see the boulders and the cliffs."

Radcliffe and Delambre turned, and the three men stared silently at the gray slopes and battlements that tiered into the sky above them.

"It is like another world, is it not?" said Hein.

"The real world, perhaps," Delambre murmured.

"How do you mean, Monsieur?"

"A wilderness. A battlefield."

Hein nodded. "Yes, I am afraid we shall find it a battlefield, all right, before we are through with it—and it with us. A battlefield of rock and ice—"

"Instead of iron and fire."

Hein looked at the Frenchman curiously for a moment; then the smile returned to his eyes, and he turned away. "I shall see you gentlemen at the hut," he said.

He disappeared among the trees, and after a few minutes Radcliffe and Delambre arose and prepared to follow. The latter was still drawing the air into his lungs in slow, deliberate breaths, but he swung his pack with a vigorous motion and set off up the path behind Radcliffe at the same steady pace as before.

The trees thinned out rapidly now as they ascended, and soon all that was left were scattered dwarf-pine, rising like gnarled brown fingers from the steep tilt of the mountainside. The gorse and juniper bushes hugged the ground more closely, and the grass gave way to pale, tiny-flowered moss, checkered with small but ever-multiplying patches of gravel and stone. Everywhere around them the gray bones of the earth were thrusting gently but inexorably upward out of their soft sheath of living green.

Yes, it is lonely now, Nicholas Radcliffe thought. . . .

And they climbed on.

Siegfried Hein trudged up through the long slopes of violets and primulas toward the gray rim of rock above. He had been climbing at a deliberate, unhurried pace, but already the voices of the others had faded away behind him, and, turning, he saw that they had not yet emerged from the forest. On all sides of him the bright mountainsides slanted away, empty and still.

Without stopping, he hitched his shoulders slightly and shifted the weight of his packboard. It was a heavy load—the heaviest he had carried for any distance in several years—but he had been carrying it now for almost two hours without resting, and he knew already that any doubts he may have had about his physical condition were unfounded. With satisfaction he felt the bite of the broad pack-straps against his body and the supple play of his muscles answering their pressure. He felt the strong, even thrust of his thighs and knees and the rhythmic tramp of his boots on the earth and gravel of the path. . . . Yes, he thought, it would be all right. After the years and the war it was still all right.

As he climbed, his eyes moved slowly upward from the soft slopes of moss and flowers to the monstrous sweep of rock and ice above. . . . Rock and ice. Iron and fire. . . . Delambre's words came back to him, and a thin, tight smile played for a moment on his lips. What did these writers and professors, these soft, bloodless, boneless half-men, know of iron and fire? It was he, Siegfried Hein, who could tell them about such things. . . . Memories thronged up before him out of the dark gulf of the years: not blurred and shadowy, as memories often were, but clear-etched, indelible, branded forever on his brain. Munich in those long-gone winters of the early twenties. The lightless, heatless, waterless room in the attic above the Grenadierstrasse. His father, his mother, his brother Konrad, Annichen . . .

He had been just ten years old in that bitter January of 1924 when his sister Annichen had died. All day, like the day before and the day before that, he had walked the ice-glazed streets, a ten-million-mark note clenched in his numb blue hand, trying to buy the milk that Annichen needed. He had begged, cried, fought, tried to steal. But it was no use. There was no milk. And coming home that night and seeing his mother's face as he opened the door, he had known that it would never be necessary for him to go looking for milk for Annichen again.

That was only one day, but there were many more days. There were days and months and years. There was his mother, already more like a grandmother, gray-faced and patient. And his father sitting endlessly in the corner, wrapped in his old green service-coat, coughing. Sometimes his father would go to the cupboard and take out his Iron Cross with the two palms and sit for hours holding it in his hand, staring at it. "What have they done to us, Konrad?" he would ask dully. Then he would begin to cough again, until he was bent double in a paroxysm and a black, viscous liquid seeped out between his lips and dribbled down his chin.

Before the first war, which was also before he, Siegfried, had been born, his father had been the bookkeeper for an insurance and law firm on the Marienplatz; but after 1918 he had not been able to work. Two or three times a year he went to the offices of the Veterans' Bureau, and each time they promised him, yes, they would soon send him away to a mountain sanitarium where his gas-seared lungs would have a chance to heal. And each time nothing happened.

"Be patient, Father," Konrad would tell him, his hand hard and tight on the sick man's shoulder. "Our day will come. Germany will not belong forever to the politicians and the Jews."

Konrad had been eighteen then. From six to six each day he worked as a greaser and cleaner in the Munich railway yards, and in the evenings he drilled with his Party unit or attended meetings at the *Braunhaus*. And then one night he went out to a torchlight parade, handsome, and stalwart in his new uniform and shining boots, and this time he did not come home again. Three days later his mother received word from the police that she could claim his body at the morgue.

But Konrad had been right: things did get better—at last. Nineteen thirty-three came, and the Party rose to power, and a man could be a man again, and a German could hold up his head again. By this time only he and his mother were left, but he was almost fully grown now and able to take care of her. True, he would never go to the university and take his engineering degree, as his father had planned for him. There were plenty of jobs, however, in the newly constructed metallurgical and munitions plants, and life, for the first time, opened out before him, full of promise and meaning and hope. His character had been hammered out, like iron, on the bitter forge of poverty and suffering, and at last he was being given a chance to show its temper. Month by month now, almost day by day, he felt growing within him the strength and pride of that other Siegfried, the great and ancient Siegfried for whom he had been named.

"But you are still so young, *Liebchen*," his mother protested. "You should not be working so hard."

He patted her hand, smiling a little. "I don't mind it, Mother," he told her. "It isn't only for myself I'm working, but for the New Germany as well."

In the evenings he too now drilled and attended meetings. (His storm-troop unit was called the *Konrad Hein Gruppe* in memory of his martyred brother.) And weekends and holidays he ranged the countryside with the *Sportsverein* and the *Wandervögel*, and for the first time in his life he saw the rivers and fields, forests and hills of his native Bavaria.

And the mountains . . .

Yes, best of all, the great mountains to the south—the mountains which his father had never reached. He remembered as if it were yesterday that magical summer morning when he first gazed upon them, when his heart stopped and his eyes went up as if in prayer to those sublime, sombre crags and glittering snows. He had known then and there, once and for all, that he must climb and conquer them, that over and above all other things in life he would be a mountaineer. Pride and ambition had risen within him like a shining sword. Here, indeed, was a challenge worthy of a soldier of the Third Reich, a prize, shining and stern, for the breed of the Walsungs. For a moment, his emotion had been so great that he was close to tears; then his lips drew firm and his eyes went cold and gray. . . . Yes, he knew then. He must make himself a man who could do such things—not a boy, but a man, strong and fearless, with body and heart and will of steel.

The Alps! . . . The bright images of those stirring days thronged back to him. . . . The Silvretta, the Engadine, the great white domes of the Oberland tiering up in the distance against the sunset. And Hans Mohler, Gunther Steinle and himself pedalling swiftly toward them along the foothill roads that led gently upward from the dark green waters of the *Boden See*.

Their possessions were few: their patched-together bicycles, the clothes and boots they wore, the laden rucksacks on their backs. And their money was less. They lived on cheese, sausage and brown bread and, when they were lucky, an occasional fowl or bottle of red wine; on stormy nights they slept in the cheapest *Gasthaus* they could find, on fair ones, more often than not, under a tree in a pasture. But they were not ashamed of their poverty. They were proud of it. And they despised the rich Englishmen and Frenchmen and Americans who flashed by them in their *wagons-lits* expresses or watched them indolently from the verandahs of their luxurious resort hotels.

The first summer they had concentrated on the Tyrolean peaks, the second on Mont Blanc and the Chamonix *aiguilles*, the third on the great peaks of the Pennines—the Matterhorn, Monte Rosa, the Weisshorn, the Täschhorn, the Dom. And they did not climb, as the tourists climbed, with hired guides and by easy and familiar routes; they were their own guides, and, after the first season in which they tried their wings, they spurned any ridge or face which did not offer the very highest degree of mountaineering difficulty.

"But it has never been done," the guides and resort-trippers around the hotels would exclaim when they heard of their plans for a proposed new ascent.

"No," they would agree, "it has never been done."

"And it is impossible. Such a venture is madness—not sport."

But he and Hans and Gunther had merely smiled and shaken their heads. No, it was not sport, nor madness either. . . .

It was war.

Soon their names and exploits were known throughout the length and breadth of the Alps. In 1936 they had received gold Olympic medals from the hands of the *Führer* himself for having performed the outstanding mountaineering feats of the year. The following summer they had made the so-called "impossible" ascents of the notorious Eigerwand and the west face of the Matterhorn. And in 1939 he, individually, had been selected by the *Alpenverein* from among scores of aspirants to head an attack on the noblest of all Alpine prizes—the south face of the Weissturm.

For years past he had dreamed of it and laid his plans for it—that most beautiful and terrible of mountains. He knew every detail of its ten-thousand-foot vertical sweep, as time and again he had studied it through his binoculars from the valleys and glaciers below: the gray, smooth-worn rock, the green-glaring ice, the tiny ledges and the monstrous fluted precipices leading up and up and up to the solemn white dome in the very heart and sanctuary of the sky. Carefully and patiently he worked out the details of the attack, together with Hans and Gunther and the three other climbers who had been chosen as their companions. They knew that many men before them had tried to force a way up through that appalling wilderness of rock and snow; that all had failed, that many had died. But, as the moment approached, the pounding of their hearts was not the pounding of fear. "We will not fail," they whispered to each other. "We will be the first."

Then, on the very eve of their departure for Switzerland, came the war.

At first, to be sure, he had been bitterly, almost heartbrokenly, disappointed. But he did not allow himself to brood for long. For a German, after all, did not climb as an Englishman or a Frenchman or an American climbed, for the mere gratification of personal and selfish ambition. He climbed—yes, the *Führer* himself had said it—in the name of Germany. And now Germany needed him elsewhere, and in the truest, deepest sense there would be no difference for him, for it was all a part of the same mighty struggle. Whereas the antagonist, before, had been a mountain, it would now be men. In place of a battlefield of rock and ice there would be a far vaster and sterner battlefield of iron and fire.

He was not recalled to the artillery, in which he had served his training period several years before, but was assigned, together with most of the other younger Bavarian climbers, to the mountain-warfare troops. For three months, during the triumphal march through Poland and the early days of the west-front stalemate, he was in training again, this time among the slopes and valleys of the Tyrol. Then, in recognition of his mountaineering reputation and his qualities of leadership, he was sent as one of a small handpicked group to an officer-candidate school near Leipzig.

At the time he was burning with the desire for active service in the field and chafed under the monotonous ironbound routine of lectures and examinations. But later he had come to realize that this period was perhaps the most important and fruitful of his whole life. For the things that he learned during those months were far more than were embraced in the prescribed basic courses in tactics and organization, communications, map-reading and military law. There, for the first time, he had the opportunity to see behind the façade of outward events into the inner core of historic and racial truth that molded them. He became familiar with the great kings and warriors of German history—Arminius and Charlemagne, Barbarossa and Wallenstein, Frederick the Great and Bismarck—not merely as names in a dry text book, but as living forces in the unfolding history of a nation. He learned of the great philosophers—Fichte and Herder; and of the great strategists—Clausewitz, von Moltke, Schlieffen. He came to understand the menace of bolshevism, the machinations of international Jewry, the treachery of England, the infamy of Versailles. He had entered his officer's training an ambitious but ignorant boy; he came out of it a soldier and officer of the Reich. He knew now what the *Führer* had meant when he said, "There are those to whom things are given and those who must fight for them." And what the commandant of the training school meant in his farewell address, as he handed them their commissions: "Remember that there are only two kinds of men, *meine Herrschaften*—the leaders and the led."

In March of 1940 he had rejoined the mountain troops as an *Unterleutnant*, and six weeks later his regiment took part in the invasion of Norway. There followed a few stirring days in which they tasted the heady wine of attack, achievement, victory; but scarcely had they begun to fight and feel their strength when it was all over. Then came long months of inactivity and routine garrison duty, while the tides of war shifted elsewhere and they waited restlessly for a transfer to an active front and a further chance to show their mettle.

It did not come, however, until almost a year later, and it proved another disappointment. Sent to the Balkans for service in the mountains of northern Greece, they did not arrive there until the campaign was all but over, and once again, after a brief day or two of combat, they found themselves relegated to an inactive role of garrison and patrol. Subsequently they were shifted to Roumania, and then to the Hungarian Carpathians, but still nothing happened. By the time he had been in the *Wehrmacht* for two and a half years he had experienced a total of rather less than two weeks of actual combat.

And then at last came the great opportunity. The armies of the Reich were rolling eastward into Russia in a vast, irresistible wave: through the fields and the forests, across the plains and the rivers, through Kiev, Kharkov, Rostov, to the very gates of the remote Caucasus. When, in the early fall of 1942, the Seventh Alpine Infantry was sent forward, the front had been pushed beyond Novorossisk into the rolling foothills beyond, and the great snow-peaks of Elbruz and Dyktau were already visible on the horizon to the southeast.

They moved into their positions and readied their weapons and gear. Proud and confident, they awaited the order to plunge forward and storm the heights. But a week passed, and then another week, and the order did not come. Vague and disquieting rumors began trickling down from the north, where a vast battle was said to be raging around the ruined city of Stalingrad. Enemy planes and patrols were becoming daily more active in their own sector. And then one morning in early November came the stunning announcement that they were not to attack but retreat.

Bewildered and bitterly disappointed, they withdrew from the Caucasian foothills onto the open plains of the Black Sea littoral. "There is no work for mountain troops here," they said to one another dejectedly. "They will send us back home again."

But they were not sent home. Week followed week and month followed month as they slogged slowly westward, with their useless mountain guns and climbing gear, across the endless desolate flatland. Winter closed in on them with its cold and snow—not the bright gleaming snow of the mountains they knew and loved, but a thick damp veil that fell dismally from the iron skies, shrouding the earth in a perpetual sunless gloom. A Russian armored force bore down on them from the north, and the Roumanian division on their flank buckled and disintegrated in shameful rout. The mountaineers turned and fought, retreated again, turned and fought again. Early spring found them in the featureless valley of the lower Dnieper, bogged down in an ocean of gray mud.

"When the ground dries we shall go forward once more," they said. But they did not go forward. May came, and then June, and still they huddled, impotent and miserable, in their improvised pillboxes and slit-trenches, while the enemy pressed in upon them in an ever-tightening ring of fire and steel. Although they had still to launch their first offensive action, their casualties rose to twenty, then to thirty percent, and of their remaining number at least half were suffering from dysentery, jaundice and various types of fever. A few short months before, the Seventh Alpine Infantry had been a trained team of athletes, filled with strength and self-confidence, straining toward battle and glory. Now it was a battered remnant of disillusioned veterans, gray-faced, nerve-wracked and exhausted to the breaking point.

The colonel of the regiment was killed by a shrapnel burst, and his second-in-command was evacuated by ambulance, blinded and with a leg blown off. The following morning the senior major called the surviving line officers together.

"During the night we have been cut off from the rest of the division," he told them. "The enemy has occupied our last line of retreat."

The officers stood in silence.

"There is reason to believe that he will attack within a few hours," the major went on in a tired, flat voice. "We will remain in our positions, fighting, until they are no longer tenable. Then we will surrender."

Still there was silence. Standing there helplessly in that inferno of mud and shellfire, Siegfried Hein felt the anger rising like a dull red flame through the blood and bones of his exhausted body.

"Surrender?" he repeated.

"We have no choice," said the major.

"Can't we try to break through?"

"It would be suicidal."

"But—"

"There are no buts, Lieutenant Hein."

He was a soldier. He saluted and was silent. But when the attack began, and the gray fire-spouting tanks came rolling toward them over the shell-pocked fields, rage and frustration rose again within him and engulfed him like a wave. To die was one thing. He was not afraid to die. But to lie there cowering and helpless in the mud—to be killed or captured like animals by a horde of barbarian peasants, without so much as a chance to fight or to prove themselves—that was too much to be endured. . . .

Suddenly he was on his feet, brandishing his revolver, shouting to the remnants of his platoon. "*Soldaten des Reiches—vorwärts!*"

The gaunt, febrile-eyed men around him lurched forward out of their holes. But there were two who did not move.

He turned and stared at them. "Are you coming?" he asked.

"No, *mein Leutnant*," one said. "It is hopeless. We will surrender."

"I order you to come."

"No, *mein Leutnant*."

He raised his revolver and fired twice.

Then they were plunging forward through the mud and craters of the shattered field. They ran, slipped, staggered, fell, got up, ran on again. They flung themselves under the very snouts of the onrolling tanks, hurling their grenades. A cross-fire from a machine gun caught them, mowing them down like grain. Then an 88-millimeter shell exploded in their midst in a fountain of red death. Still those who were left kept going. He emptied his revolver and flung it after the bullets. An enemy infantryman loomed suddenly before him, and he ran him through with the bayonet he had snatched from a fallen trooper. A bullet ripped through the sleeve of his tunic, searing the flesh, but he scarcely noticed it. A flying fragment of steel crashed against his helmet, knocking him down, but he pulled himself up again and ran on. He could scarcely see any longer for the blood and sweat that covered his eyes. He could hear nothing except the hoarse shouting of his own voice. The very earth seemed to be dissolving around him in a vast mad roaring of thunder and flame.

And then, suddenly, miraculously, they were out of it. The thunder was gone; the flame was gone. They had reached the cover of a thickly wooded copse, and the battle was behind them, rolling steadily and rapidly away to the south. They lay on the ground, panting and retching, their eyes glazed. Of the fifty-two of them who had started out there were eleven left.

They had survived the onslaught, but three more long and terrible days were to pass before they found their way to safety. All that day they remained in hiding in the copse, and when night came they began beating their way furtively across-country to the west. Early the next morning they were spotted by a Red patrol, and three of them were killed before the others made their escape. Two more were picked off that same evening by guerilla snipers. Moreover, there was no food of any kind to be found in the scorched and desolate countryside, and hour by hour they felt themselves growing weaker from hunger and exposure. Two of the men collapsed and had to be left behind, lying helplessly by a roadside. Another became delirious during the second night, and they were compelled to smother him, lest his cries reveal their whereabouts to the enemy. And in the end there were only three of them, three tattered bloodstained ghosts of men, who staggered across the last mile of open fire-raked battlefield and into the newly dug German positions.

The sentries called stretcher bearers for them, but he waved them off. "I must report to the brigade commander," he said.

"But, Herr Leutnant—" they protested.

"Take me to brigade headquarters," he ordered them.

As he approached the headquarters tent he felt his knees buckling beneath him and thought for a moment that he would fall in his tracks. But he did not fall. He continued walking to the tent, entered it and drew himself up to attention before the brigadier. Shoulders square, head high, he saluted him.

"Heil Hitler!" he said. Then the darkness closed in around him and he sank to the ground.

They had given him the medal of valor, mentioned his name in dispatches and sent him back to Germany. And in Stuttgart, at the reallocation center, the doctors questioned him and tapped him and stroked their chins over him and prescribed that he spend a month at a convalescent camp.

"But I am not wounded," he told them angrily. "There is nothing wrong with me."

"Of course not," they agreed.

"Then why—"

"You are suffering from what we call battle fatigue. The rest will do you good."

Battle fatigue—that was the fancy new name they had for it. For shellshock, funk, cowardice. In his bitterness he almost laughed in their faces.

"And when I come back?" he asked.

"You will be reassigned."

"To a desk, I suppose?"

"That will depend."

"I am a line-officer," he told them. "Do you understand? *Ich bin Soldat.*"

"You will be reassigned when you return," they said.

In the end they had stopped insisting on the convalescent camp and decreed for him, instead, an indefinite period of inactive status. He had not decided in advance what he would do; in his conscious mind he had not even thought about it. But the day after they let him go he had looked up Hans Mohler's family and learned from them that Hans also was temporarily out of service and had left ten days before for Switzerland. He drew his back pay, bought civilian clothes, made his arrangements. And that same night he was aboard a train, speeding southward. Speeding toward the mountains again; the mountains which he had never forgotten and of which he had dreamed every night in the terrible desolation of the Russian plains; the cold and glittering mountains; the bright white magic mountains; the mountains of his youth. . . .

Now Siegfried Hein trudged up out of the flowering slopes into the gray wilderness of rock above. . . . So it was to be a battlefield, this mountain, he thought. Rock and ice. Iron and fire. Well, there was one among them, at least, who knew the meaning of the words. There was a whole great nation. . . . His gaze moved slowly upward again over the vast and august grandeur of the range: glacier upon glacier, ridge upon ridge, precipice upon precipice, peak upon peak, and at last, unbelievably high and remote above them, the still white summit of the Weissturm suspended in the sky. And, gazing, he felt once more the old fierce pride of his boyhood rising cold and hard within him, like a sword of steel. . . .

Like Nothung, the sword of Siegfried.

Without his having willed it his lips were moving, forming words: "*Heil Hitler! Heil Deutschland! Vater und Mutter, Konrad und Annichen, Führer und Vaterland—heil!*"

<hr />

Chapter 11

"It is now almost twelve o'clock," Andreas Benner said,
squinting up at the sun. Ordway glanced at his wristwatch and it
showed eleven fifty-eight. "We should be going down again,
meine Herrschaften."

They had eaten their lunch of sausage, cheese and bread and
were sitting beside the little stream in front of the Heilweg Hut.
On his flat boulder on the slope above, the marmot sat watching
them, waiting patiently for them to go away.

"Do you think we can get back here before dark?" Ordway
asked.

Benner shrugged. "Offhand I would say no. We will wait,
though, and see how it goes on the way down. And how tired we
are."

"The editorial we," said Radcliffe.

"In any case, there is no need for Fräulein Dehn to go down
again."

"I am not tired," Carla said.

"Even so, *Fräulein*—there are only the five packs remaining. It
is much better that you stay here and rest."

"Whatever you think best," she agreed. "Some of the loads
need repacking, I've noticed. I can have them all ready by the
time you get back."

"It is not necessary, *Fräulein*. Tomorrow we can—"

"Someone must do it, and it will be something to keep me

busy." She looked from one to another of them, smiling. "All right, gentlemen, about your business now! You are dismissed."

The five men rose and prepared to leave.

"I don't like it," Ordway said to her.

"What don't you like?"

"Leaving you here alone."

"Silly! Nothing can happen."

"But we may not get back tonight."

"Then I shall spend the night alone." She pointed to the marmot on the rock and smiled again. "With my watchdog."

"Sure you don't mind?"

"Of course not."

She walked with them to the low ridge of boulders that ringed the hut and stood looking after them as they threaded their way across the moraine. For perhaps fifteen minutes Ordway, glancing back, could see her slender figure and her hair glinting in the sunlight against the gray wilderness of rock. Then she was gone, and there were only the boulders, and then the moss and wildflowers again, and the dwarf-pine and the forests again, and at last the valley and the Aarn. The file of men swung down the mountainside in silence.

Herr and Frau Knubel were on the verandah when they reached the inn, and tea and cakes were awaiting them in the dining room.

"Fräulein Dehn has remained at the hut?" the innkeeper asked.

Benner nodded. "There was no need for her to make the second trip."

"And you will go up again today?"

The guide peered out the broad plate-glass window at the sun, and Ordway looked at his watch. It was a quarter of four. The guide stroked his square chin reflectively.

"With the packs it is a climb of four hours," he said. "Perhaps more." He looked from one to another of them. "What do you say, gentlemen? In the morning we will all be fresher—no?"

Radcliffe and Delambre nodded. "We can leave at dawn again and be at the hut by ten-thirty," the Englishman said.

"Herr Hein?"

The German shrugged. "It is only a little walk, of course. But whatever the rest of you prefer—"

"And Herr Martin?"

Looking at Radcliffe and Delambre, Ordway could see plainly the tiredness in their faces and bodies.

"Whatever you think best, Andreas," he said.

But when the others had gone to their rooms he again sought out the guide, who had gone out onto the verandah and was now sitting on the steps sucking his pipe and talking with the Knubels.

"I think I'll go on up this evening," he told him.

Benner looked at him in surprise. "This evening, Herr Martin?"

"I don't like the idea of Fräulein Dehn spending the night at the hut alone."

"But I assure you she will be all right. She has been many times by herself in the mountains. And besides, the others, they are already—"

"There's no need for the others to come. I'll go by myself and the rest of you can come up as we planned in the morning."

"It is not at all necessary," Benner persisted. "Believe me, at the Heilweg Fräulein Dehn will be perfectly safe and comfortable. Is it not so, Herr Knubel?"

The innkeeper nodded vigorously. "Perfectly. She has spent the night there alone several times."

"Still I prefer going," Ordway said.

Benner stroked his chin and shrugged. "As you say, Herr Martin," he murmured. "I shall tell the others, and then you and I will start off."

"There's no need for you to come either."

"But of course I shall come with you."

"No, really, I'd rather you didn't."

"But—"

Benner started to rise, but paused and turned as Frau Knubel cleared her throat loudly.

"Let him go alone," she told him.

Benner shook his head. "I think I should go with him."

"Let him go," Frau Knubel repeated sharply. "Let him go—Dummkopf!"

The early mountain sunset had come before he reached timberline, but he kept climbing steadily and the sky was still gray with daylight as he topped the last crest of the Dürren moraine and looked down at the lonely squat shape of the Heilweg Hut. He stopped for an instant, cupped his hand around his mouth and shouted.

Carla came from the hut as he trudged down the boulder-slope and stood waiting for him by the door. He saw that she had changed from heavy climbing clothes to her short tweed skirt and green pullover sweater and that, in place of boots and woolen socks, she wore only light, rope-soled espadrilles on her stocking-less feet. Her face and arms seemed whiter, her hair darker and richer, than in the bright sunlight of the mountain day.

"I didn't just want to walk in and startle you," he explained.

"Thank you," she said, smiling.

They were silent a moment, looking at each other.

"You look—very nice," he said.

"Thank you again."

"You don't mind my coming, do you?"

"Mind?"

"I'm alone."

"Oh."

"You do then?"

She did not answer his question. "The others are not coming until tomorrow?" she asked.

"First thing in the morning."

"They were tired?"

"Old Nick and Delambre—a little."

"But you were not?"

"Yes, a little, too. But I didn't like the idea of your being here alone."

"You were afraid the marmot might eat me, perhaps?"

Ordway shook his head. "The rats," he said. "They've always had designs on you."

She laughed. For a moment she stood looking up at him, her eyes smiling and deep with memories. Then she turned her head away. "Still, it was foolish of you to come," she said.

"Do you really think so?"

She did not answer, and he took her head lightly between his hands and turned it toward him.

"Do you?" he asked.

"No," she said.

They went into the hut and he dropped his packboard on the

195

stone flagging of the floor. Then he stood looking about him in the dim light at the familiar cement-splotched walls, the fireplace and iron stove, the carved table and benches and the stack of straw mattresses in the corner. Everything was the same as on that afternoon when they had been there, three days before; and at the same time everything was different. The packboards and rucksacks which they had carried up on their first trip stood in a bulging, friendly file along the wall. The lower shelf of the once-bare cupboard was lined with pots and frying pans, tins and jars, and on a row of nails beyong hung ropes and axes and toilet kits and Carla's climbing clothes. There was a green-brown pile of furze and juniper twigs in the fireplace. There were knives and forks and tin cups and plates on the table and, in the center, a kerosene lamp and two white-enamelled tin dishes overflowing with violet-flowered campion moss.

Ordway started to speak, stopped, and stood looking at the girl beside him.

"It is better now, isn't it?" she asked.

He nodded slowly. "It's—itself."

"But getting too dark." Carla crossed to the table and lighted the kerosene lamp, and a warm orange glow seeped through the shadows. "Now—"

She went to one of the rucksacks, brought out a pair of espadrilles and handed them to him. "Take those boots off while I get supper started," she told him.

"Don't bother with much—really."

"In this Gasthof, Herr Kapitän, the guests eat what they are given."

He changed to the light rope-and-canvas climbing shoes and went out and washed in the stream. Then he came back into the hut and sat at the table watching Carla prepare their meal over the black, pot-bellied stove.

"You've kept busy," he said.

"While I was alone? Oh my, yes."

"Tell me everything you did."

"Well—first I unpacked the things we would need here at the hut, and then I changed the other things around in the packs the way Andreas wanted. Then—let me see—I brought some water up from the stream and set out the dishes, and after that I went look-

ing for branches and twigs for a fire. . . . Some for the stove and
some for the fireplace, if it gets cold later. . . . When I got back
the marmot was inside, even though I had closed the door, and I
spent ten minutes chasing him out and the next half hour cleaning
up after him. Then I cleaned myself up. Then I changed clothes
and had a cup of tea. Then—" Carla paused and smiled "—I sat
down to wait for company."

"And look what showed up."

"A first-class *Gasthof* must be prepared for anything."

She brought a pot of soup from the stove and poured it into two
of the tin cups, and they sat drinking it. Then he took the cups
down to the brook and rinsed them, and when he came back there
were two plates of fried ham and beans and bread and cheese on
the table. Carla filled the two cups with steaming sweet tea, and
when they were empty she filled them again.

"There are some tinned cherries," she said.

"God, no."

"*Speisekuchen?* Chocolate?"

"Look," he said, "the idea is to climb a mountain—not to eat
one."

He brought out two cigarettes and lighted them, and they sat
watching the blue smoke curl softly through the orange lamp-
glow.

"I am going to do the dishes," he announced.

"No."

"Yes."

He took the plates and cups and pans and went down again
through the gathering dusk to the brook and washed them, squatting low above the water. It was not like washing dishes anywhere
else. The dark water swooped into the plates, tugged at them
briefly and disappeared, and what was left in the plates disappeared
with it, instantly and completely. When he had finished he
brought the dishes back to the hut, and Carla dried them and
stacked them on the cupboard shelf.

"For breakfast," he said, "I believe I'll have orange juice, ba-
nanas with heavy cream, two eggs over with deerfoot sausages and
three cups of non-ersatz coffee."

"No waffles with syrup?"

"No, we'll save the waffles to have with our champagne cocktails on the summit."

Carla finished putting away the dishes, and they turned down the lamp and left the hut. It was almost dark now, and yet not wholly dark. The valley, far below, was filled with night, and night was slowly climbing the meadows and forest-slopes that ringed it; but it had not yet quite reached the level at which they stood. A last soft gleam of daylight still spread across the stillness of the mountain-world, touching the stream, the boulders, the distant glacier, the gray rock-walls that seemed, moment by moment, to be closing in nearer and taller around them. Ridge and precipice hung suspended in oceanic twilight. High above them the peaks leaned, white and transfixed, against the brightening stars.

"Do you remember?" he asked.

Carla nodded.

"The Blue Hour . . ."

They sat on the flowered moss beside the stream and stared down through the darkness and the tiny pinpricks of the lights in the valley.

"I know a lie," Martin Ordway said quietly. "The name of the lie is the map of the world, and it says that out there beyond that valley are places called Berlin and Stalingrad and Alamein and Tarawa and Lidice. It says there are two billion human beings out there hating and fearing and destroying one another. It says that peace and happiness are the fairy stories of children." He was silent a moment, and a thin smile touched his lips. "All right then —we're a fairy story."

She turned and looked at him, and her hand touched his lightly. Then she withdrew it and looked away.

"You are happy, aren't you?" he asked.

"Yes, Martin."

"Truly happy?"

She nodded, slowly, staring down again into the darkness. "Yes," she said very softly. "I am happy that you have come back. I am happy that we are here together."

"It's like—well—coming home, in a way."

"I know you feel that. And I am glad."

"Don't you feel it too?"

"A little, yes. Only—"

198

"Only what?"

"Only it is different for me, Martin, can't you see that?" She kept her head turned from him and her voice was suddenly tight and low. "I have been here for almost two years. It is the only home I know now."

"It's where you belong," he said.

"Belong?" She shook her head slowly. "No, that is the trouble, you see—I no longer belong anywhere. Vienna, the war, Stefan, my baby: I have run away from all of them; from everything that is real."

"This is real too, Carla. Here. Now."

"No, it is what you said before. A fairy story."

He started to speak, stopped himself, and they were silent for a while, sitting on the moss-bank in the blue darkness. He listened to the sound of the little stream, running fresh and cool beside them over its bed of stones. Then he turned his head a little and sat watching the girl beside him, and she too was fresh and cool and young, and the night was glinting faintly in her eyes and moving softly in her hair, and, looking at her, it was bitterly, achingly impossible for him to believe the things that had happened to her, and to them both.

He reached out his hand and laid it over hers. "Don't, Carla," he said.

She looked at him questioningly.

"Don't keep living in the past."

She shook her head slowly. "It is not the past," she said. "The past is gone. And this much I have always known and still know: if I had it all to do over again I would do the same thing again. I would leave Stefan. I would—" she paused almost imperceptibly —"not have his child."

"And you would come back to Kandermatt?"

She did not answer.

"You are sorry you came back, then?"

"I am not sorry tonight."

"But usually?"

"I don't know."

"Where else could you have gone?" he asked.

It was a moment before she answered. "Where else? Yes, that is it, isn't it? There is nowhere else. One runs away and there is nowhere to run to. One runs and runs and there is nothing beyond the running."

"Or one fights and fights and there is nothing beyond the fighting."

"No, in fighting it is different."

"Not so very."

"Yes, it is altogether different. When you fight you are doing something. And it is for something."

"That's what the speeches say."

"You are not fighting for nothing, Martin."

You fight to win—period, he thought. You fight to live—period. You fight to die—period. "I've stopped thinking about it," he said.

Carla shook her head. "You are tired now. You have been fighting too long—killing too long. But it will not always be like that. Some day the war will be over, and it will be different. Some day the war will be over, and you will go home." She paused, and he felt her eyes searching his face in the darkness. "What will you do when you are home again, Martin?"

"I've stopped thinking about that too."

"You will be an architect again?"

"I suppose so."

"And fall in love and get married and have children?"

He laughed a little. "You have it all figured out, haven't you?"

"No, I just want to know."

Ordway was silent, staring down into the deep, light-pricked well of the valley. "There are exactly three things I've learned out of three years of war," he said quietly. "The first is how to mooch cigarettes. The second is that most men know how to die a lot better than they know how to live. The third is to let the future take care of itself."

"And meanwhile?"

"Pick up the cards the way they lie. Play them the best you can. Do your job."

"And that is all?"

"Yes, that's all."

"And it is enough?"

Ordway shook his head. "No, it's not enough," he said. "Maybe that's the goddamned trouble with the goddamned human race. Nothing is ever enough."

While they sat there beside the stream the last faint blueness had faded from the sky, and it was now full night. The moon had not yet risen, but the stars shone sharp and bright as diamonds and the snow-peaks loomed white and rigid against the blackness of the sky. A cold soundless tide of air seemed to be pouring down into the little pocket in the mountainside from the glaciers above.

They arose presently and walked hand in hand up the dark mossy slope to the hut. It was even chillier inside. Ordway felt his way to the table, lighted the kerosene lamp and stood looking around him.

"Cold?" he asked.

"A little."

"Let's make a fire."

Stooping, he stacked the furze and juniper twigs, and soon bright darts of flame were fingering upward in the broad fireplace.

"What, no sofa?" he said.

He turned down the lamp again, and they sat on one of the long benches with their backs to the table, their eyes gazing, narrowed, into the flickering glow. The fresh wood burned slowly, popping and crackling, and soon the pungent dry fragrance of juniper filled the room.

After a while he got up and, going to the packs, took out two blankets. Then he selected two mattresses from the stack against the wall.

"The usual corner suite for Madame?" he asked.

"No, near the fire, I think, please."

The firelight was glinting in her eyes, but from where he stood he could not tell if they were smiling. He laid one mattress a little to the right of the fireplace and the other a little to the left, and spread a blanket on each.

"They're going to scratch," he said.

As the fire burned low they took off their espadrilles and lay down. For a few minutes there was no sound in the hut except the soft crackle of burning wood.

"Carla," he said.

"Yes, Martin?"

"No rats?"

"No. No rats."

"But there should be rats."

201

"How could there be, silly? There hasn't been anything for them to eat here for three years."

"But that's what I'm here for—to stand guard against rats."

"Shut up," she said.

They were quiet again, and the fire popped and crackled.

"Warm now?" he asked.

"Yes."

"Comfortable?"

"Yes."

"But what would Herr Doktor Naffziger say?"

"Herr Doktor Naffziger always knew that I was an abandoned woman."

"Unverschämt."

"Yes, unverschämt."

It was a long moment before he spoke again.

"Carla," he said.

"Yes?"

"Good night."

"Good night, Martin."

Now he was lying still, his body stretched long and straight on the lumpy straw mattress, with the blanket over his legs and a rolled sweater under his head and his hands clasped lightly under the sweater. He felt his tiredness flowing like a slow sweet liquid through his body. He felt the hot fragrant air from the fireplace and the cold thin air from the open window mingling and moving softly over his face and arms with a gentle warm coolness. He lay watching the weaving patterns of firelight on the dark shingles of the sloping ceiling.

. . . . And here we are again, Martin Ordway thought. Twelve years have passed, and we are here again in the quiet darkness of the Heilweg Hut—and nothing has changed—and everything has changed. We are here alone in the stillness of the mountain night, and the war and the world are far away, they are a million miles away, and still they are here. And Stefan is here. And Ted and Bix and Harry and Joan Nettleton and the Grimbacks' garage and the lots at Pawtucket and the Piper Cub and the bombsights and the bombs and the Jewish grandmothers and the Hungarian midwife —they are all here. Twelve years are here, lying still and enormous beside us in the darkness.

You could put out your hand and touch her, he thought; you could speak and she would answer you. She was there—a body and a voice. They were there together—two bodies and two voices in the deep enveloping stillness of the mountain night. . . . There is an emptiness, Andreas Benner had said. . . . In the emptiness there were bombs and burning cities and the dark roar of planes. There were sleeping and eating and drinking and doing your job and killing and not getting killed. There were bodies and voices and behind them the emptiness again, the ancient and ineffable loneliness. . . .

He watched the fading glow on the shingles above him. The fire was dying.

You lived your life, he thought, and you were a part of the world in which you lived it. You were a part of a time, a place, a society, a family, a profession, a crew, a squadron, a group, an army, a nation. You were biological man, political man, economic man, social man, psychological man, home-building man, bomb-dropping man, mountain-climbing man. You were all these things, you were the sum-total of them, and because you were you lived your life in a certain way and did the things you had to do. You were all of them—and at the same time you were none of them. You lay in the still darkness and were a part of nothing. You lay in the darkness and you were alone.

"Carla," he said softly.

"Yes?"

"All right?"

"Yes. Are you all right too."

"Yes," he said.

There was silence again, and he closed his eyes. When I open them again, he thought, I shall be lying on my bunk in the Quonset hut, and the whole hut will be trembling with the roaring from the airstrip, and Ted will be shaking my shoulder and swearing at me. He lay waiting for the sound, the touch, the familiar voice; but they did not come. Instead of growing closer and more real as he tried to focus his mind upon them, they seemed to be slipping away from him, fading and receding, behind the curtain of a dream.

He opened his eyes again, and it was all gone, lost, without substance or reality. There was only the faint firelight on the shingles, and the night and the mountains beyond the window, and the girl lying beside him. There was only emptiness and aloneness and within them and beyond them that other thing—that emptiest and most-alone of all things, growing and swelling now within him until it seemed to him that his whole body was filled with an aching hollowness of wanting.

He got up and stood for a few moments looking at the embers in the fireplace and for another few moments looking down at Carla. She was lying half turned on her side, with one arm stretched out away from her and her head resting on it. He could see the low rising and falling of her breath beneath the blanket that covered her and the faint crimson glow of the embers moving gently across her cheek and through the darkness of her hair. And then her head moved, so slightly that the motion was almost imperceptible, but enough so that the glow touched her eyes, and he could see that they were open and looking at him.

He did not speak, and the girl did not speak either. He stooped and pulled back the blanket and lay down beside her on the straw mattress. He drew her very gently, very tenderly to him, and now his arms were around her and his hands flat and tight against her back, and he felt the length of her body long and straight and slender against his own, and her head was pressed against his shoulder and her arms were tight around his neck. Still they did not speak, nor even move again, but only lay there close against each other, holding each other.

Then—"Martin," she said, very softly.

"Yes?"

But she only repeated his name.

"I love you, Carla," he said.

"You do not have to say that."

"I love you."

"You do not have to love me. You have only to want me."

"I love you," he said.

He moved his hands slowly upward along her back and shoulders and through her hair, and then he kissed her hair, and then his hands were holding her head and raising it from his shoulder and he was brushing his lips lightly along her throat and cheek and kissing her eyes and then her lips. He felt her bare feet pressed tight and cool against his own. He felt her knees against his and

204

her thighs against his and her belly against his belly and the soft rounded pointed firmness of her breasts against his chest through their two flannel shirts. His hands held her and moved over her, feeling the roughness of the blanket and the soft yielding roughness of her clothing; and then presently the roughness was all gone and where it had been there was only smoothness, only a soft warm coolness and a soft cool warmness; and now their flesh was together, long and close and tight-locked, and their mouths were together, and her mouth softly opened to him, and it seemed that the whole soft, supple smoothness of her body was opening to him too.

Then she turned her head from his and pressed it against his chest. "Oh, Martin," she murmured. "Martin . . ."

"My Carla," he said.

She began suddenly to tremble, her face still hidden and her body quivering long and smooth against his own, and for a moment he thought she was sobbing, as she had sobbed that afternoon three days before on the path through the meadows. But when he raised her head and kissed her again her eyes were dry, and when he held her close again her arms moved slowly down from around his neck across his shoulders and back, straining him to her.

"Come to me, Martin," she whispered. "Martin—my lover—please . . ."

He held her and felt her and she was there. And now everything was close and tender, with a gentle tenderness of hands and mouth and body; and then presently it was no longer gentle and tender but tight and tender, and then not tight and tender but tight and fierce; it was fierce and young and tender and hard and thrusting with life, and he thought fiercely, yes, this is real—this is everything there is—this is life and all there is to life and all the rest is death. The tiredness was gone now. The loneliness and hollowness were gone. The war and the bombs and the gray dead men and the gray dead earth—they were all gone. There were only two bodies; only one body; one body within another body, one life within another life. There was only wanting, seeking, thrusting, down and down ever deeper, up and up ever higher, through the flesh, through the soft darkness, through the bright hot shining living darkness, swelling, boundless, timeless. . . .

And then, presently, there was only softness and peace; darkness and peace; Carla and peace. There was only the quiet rhythm of their breathing and the embers in the fireplace and, very faint and deep and far away, like the sound of the earth's turning, the rumbling of the glaciers in the night.

He woke once toward morning, and the hut was cold and filled with moonlight. Propping himself on one elbow, he reached out and took the blanket from the other mattress and spread it over them. Carla did not wake. He lay beside her, feeling her breathing and the touch of her body, and presently he bent his head and kissed her lightly on the shoulder. But she did not move. He lay quietly, with his legs stretched out straight under the rough blankets and the air cold and sharp in his nostrils, and slipped gently away toward sleep.

When he woke again the sun was shining and Carla was gone. There were plates and cups on the table, and water was boiling on the lighted stove.

He lay for a few moments with his hands clasped behind his head; then he got up and dressed quickly and went to the door. Carla was at the stream, washing. She was again wearing her flannel shirt and rough woolen climbing trousers, but the trousers were rolled up to her knees, and she was standing with her bare brown legs in the stream. As she heard the door open she raised her head, and the sun flamed suddenly in her hair. On a boulder on the far side of the stream the fat marmot sat watching her with brown, patient eyes.

He went down to the stream, and she raised her head again and smiled at him, and he kissed her lightly on the nose, and then he stooped over and began to wash.

"Take off your shoes, as I have," she told him.

He shook his head. "It's too cold."

"Nonsense! Besides, your feet are the important thing when you're climbing—not that whiskery face of yours."

He took off his espadrilles, rolled up his trousers and stepped into the stream. There was the sharp, sudden spasm of the living water against the flesh, and the feel of rough gravel against his soles, and then a soft coolness creeping deliciously upward through his legs and body. Bending so that his face almost touched the sur-

206

face of the stream, he scooped great handfuls of water over his arms and face and hair.

"Think you will survive it?" Carla asked.

"I'll let you know later—when the feeling comes back."

They stood in the soft moss and dried themselves, using only a small corner of the towel because one towel was all that each of them would have for as long as they were on the mountain. Then she was standing straight and still, and he was standing behind her, his arms around her waist, holding her close against him.

"Good morning," he said.

"Good morning, Martin."

"Did you sleep well?"

"Yes, very well."

"It's a beautiful morning."

"Yes, very beautiful."

Below them the sun had not yet struck into the valley, and a milk-blue dawn mist was still curling softly up the mountainsides. But around them and above them it was full day. The moss bank rose clear and gleaming to the boulder-slopes, the boulder-slopes to the glaciers, the glaciers to the ridges, the ridges to the peaks.

"The Rotalp," he said, pointing.

"The Karlsberg."

"The Graf."

"The Gräfin."

"The Wunderhorn."

"The Dornelberg."

"The Himmelshorn."

Their eyes moved slowly upward until they were high above them all. They stood silently staring at the great white shape that rose, blinding and pure, into the heart of the newborn day.

"We're going there," said Ordway.

Carla nodded a little and turned and smiled at him. "But not until after breakfast," she said.

Chapter 12

A few minutes after ten they saw four specks moving across the talus-slopes below. The specks grew gradually larger, disappeared, reappeared, vanished again; presently a faint shout came up to them, reverberating in hollow waves against the rocks; and at exactly half-past ten the four men came trudging into the green pocket among the boulders and dropped their loads on the worn stone steps of the hut.

"You have hurt yourself," Carla said to Delambre.

"I am all right, mademoiselle."

"But you were limping, I noticed it."

"It is nothing, really. Only a bruise."

"Herr Delambre had a small slip crossing the moraine," Benner said.

Carla brought the first-aid kit from the hut and made the Frenchman remove the boot and sock from his right foot. Then she examined the purplish discoloration above his ankle, smeared it with a salve and bound it with gauze and adhesive tape.

"It will feel better now," she told him.

"Thank you, mademoiselle. It is nothing, though."

Carla looked around, smiling. "Any more ailments?" she inquired.

The others shook their heads.

"Except malnutrition," said Radcliffe.

"That we can cure too."

They sat at the rough-hewn table in the hut and ate a second breakfast of eggs and pork-strips, bread, jam and tea. When he had finished the Englishman lighted his pipe, stretched his long legs out before him and gazed meditatively at the ceiling. "Back in Flanders in the last war," he murmured, "there was a young subaltern chap in my regiment, good friend of mine, who used to keep saying to me: 'You know, old boy, this war business wouldn't be half bad if it weren't for all the killing.'" Radcliffe sighed a little. "Sometimes I think this mountaineering business wouldn't be half bad either, if it weren't for all the climbing."

The meal over, they cleaned up and sorted and repacked their loads.

"Think we'll get back here tonight?" Ordway asked. "Or not till tomorrow?"

He put the question to Benner, but it was Hein who answered. "I have been thinking about this second round-trip," the German said, "and it seems to me it should not be necessary to come back at all. The loads have been how much so far? Forty pounds the first trip, perhaps—thirty pounds the second. Figuring sixty pounds say, for everyone except the *Fräulein*, we can make it to the upper hut in one trip."

Ordway glanced questioningly at Benner, and the guide hesitated, rubbing his chin. "I do not think," he began—

"I will carry seventy pounds," Hein said. "You and Herr Ordway can take fifty each. Then the other gentlemen—"

"I intend to carry my share," Delambre interrupted.

"So do we all," said Radcliffe.

There was a moment's silence.

"It is not only a question of the packs," said Benner. "In any case it would not be a good thing to begin the real climbing tomorrow."

"What's the matter with tomorrow?" the German asked.

"It is Sunday, Herr Hein."

"So?"

"So, if the *Herrschaften* will agree, I think it is better that we go up with the first loads today, come back with no loads tomorrow, and go up for the second time on Monday."

"But—"

Hein broke off, tightening his lips, and Benner looked apologetically at the others. "You see, it is—"

"I don't think there's any need to explain, Andreas," said Radcliffe. "The Herrschaften agree."

Carla and Delambre nodded.

"Hell, yes," said Ordway.

He turned away; then paused and looked back at Hein.

"You are the leader," the German said, shrugging. "In any case, we should be going soon, no? It is already late?"

Radcliffe brought out his map, and Andreas Benner moved a brown, knotted finger slowly across its whorls and hatchings. "From here to the Himmelshorn pass it should take us an hour," he said. "From the pass to the Blausee—that is downhill—another hour. Then over to the north here and along the west slopes of the Graf to the saddle between—"

"Why not straight across?" asked Hein.

"Through the wasteland?"

"Yes. It is shorter."

"A little, perhaps. But the way along the slopes is easier and more pleasant. It is the way one has always gone to the Dornel Hut."

"The way the guides have gone—is that not what you mean?"

"Yes, naturally, the guides."

"And because the guides have gone one way for a hundred years that means it is the best way, of course?"

"It is the best—yes."

"Let's not get into an argument about it," Ordway put in. "There can't be more than a half hour's difference in any case." He turned to Radcliffe. "What do you think, Nick?"

"There's not much to choose," said the Englishman. "I'd say Andreas is best qualified to judge."

"Paul?"

"That would be my feeling," Delambre said.

"Carla?"

The girl nodded.

"Okay—Andreas' way it is." Ordway turned back to the German. "All right with you?" he asked.

"You are the leader," Hein said.

"You said that a few minutes ago."

"It is true, is it not?"

"No, it isn't true. I'm not the leader here and neither is anyone else. We're six people trying to climb a mountain together, and that's all we are. Everyone has a perfect right to make all the suggestions and objections he wants to."

"And if we disagree?"

"We'll continue doing what we did just now. Talk things over and see what the majority thinks."

"The democratic process, eh, *Herr Kapitän?*"

"You can call it that if you like."

Hein was silent a moment; then he shrugged again. "As you say," he murmured.

"You don't think much of the idea, I gather."

"It does not matter greatly. As you say, there are six of us, and I am only one." The shadow of a smile crossed the German's gray eyes. "I have never tried voting myself to the top of a peak before, but it may prove an enlightening experience. May I express the hope, though, Herr Ordway, that for all our sakes the Weissturm turns out to be a democratic mountain?"

"Amen," said Radcliffe.

There was another brief silence; then Ordway turned back to the row of sacks and packboards. "And now if congress has adjourned," he said, smiling, "may I respectfully submit a motion that we get the hell out of here?"

They emerged from the twisting gorge onto the saddle between the Karlsberg and the Himmelshorn and stood staring out across the long corridor of the wasteland and the converging ranges at the great white mass that rose into the sky beyond. They descended to the Blausee, dark and gleaming as an amethyst against the gray desolation of rock.

"Beyond here there is only snow and glacier-water," said Andreas Benner, as they stopped to drink and fill their canteens.

On the far side of the lake the path forked, one branch leading straight ahead through the tumbled debris of the plateau, the other bearing to the right and curving gradually upward toward the rock-choked slopes above. Following the latter, they soon found themselves moving obliquely across a gray, sea-like expanse of shallow troughs and low, serrated ridges. The lake disappeared behind. Then the worn granite walls of the Graf and Gräfin shouldered into the sky above them, and the Weissturm, too, was gone. The path climbed and dipped, climbed again, dipped again. But always when it climbed it was to a point a little higher than before.

They were walking in single file at intervals of about five yards, with Andreas Benner in the lead, Radcliffe, Delambre, Hein and Ordway following in that order, and Carla in the rear. It was the position she had always preferred when walking or climbing with a group, and she had kept it since they left the hut in spite of repeated male protests. When one was last in a party one was part of it and at the same time, in a sense, independent of it. She could stop briefly for any reason, or no reason, without causing any one else to stop behind her. She could adjust a bootlace or shift the straps of her rucksack without anyone's asking about it or wanting to help. To be last was to be together with others and yet apart from them, one of many and yet alone.

And on this day, on this gray twisting path through the high wasteland, Carla Dehn wanted to be alone.

She had tried to think, until there was no thought left in her. She had let her eyes and mind roam idly across the immense and solemn vistas of rock and sky. And now, as the minutes and then the hours crept by, her gaze moved slowly from one to another of the five men who trudged in line before her. They were all walking at the same pace. Their packs all swayed gently on their backs and their bootnails all scraped with the same monotonous rasp against the shale and gravel of the path. To a stranger, watching them, they would have appeared almost indistinguishable, one from another. Yet no two of them walked alike.

Andreas Benner walking was a man performing his habitual and natural life-function. His heavy, bowed peasant's legs moved as a pendulum or metronome moves, a phenomenon of beat and measure, devoid alike of either spring or strain. His boots, his pack, the ice ax swinging slowly in his hand seemed as much a part of him as his own body, and his legs and trunk and shoulders gave the impression, with each succeeding step, of subtly moulding themselves to the changing contours of the earth. It was almost impossible, Carla thought, to imagine his ever stopping, or ever tiring. He would simply plod on forever as he was plodding now

—a man with a load, a man walking—a traveler in some antique and patient caravan moving on its immemorial journey through the miles and years.

Nicholas Radcliffe, following a few yards behind was as lank and loose-jointed as the guide was stubby and compact. Wearing a light khaki shirt and a pair of old army shorts, he seemed from behind to consist exclusively of great lengths of bony brown arms and legs, held together somehow in the center by an ingenious arrangement of ribs and shoulder blades, wire and adhesive tape. He was tall and stooped. He was thin almost to emaciation. And yet the man's predominant physical quality, Carla recognized, was, strangely, not awkwardness, nor even angularity, but grace. It was in his high, gaunt shoulders, his free-swinging arms, his long, sure, casual stride. It was in the lean, weather-beaten hawk's face and the bright wintry blue of the eyes. It was the grace of the British, Carla thought—cool and elusive, shy and proud—and she was sure that Radcliffe's gait and bearing would not have been in the slightest degree different had he been walking across a brown Devonshire moor or up the glaciers of Everest or along the beaches of Gallipoli or Dunkerque. The long bones still moved in their easy rhythm. The wire and adhesive tape still somehow held together—scrawny, bloodless and indestructible.

The girl's eyes moved on to Paul Delambre. The Frenchman was walking with shorter, quicker steps than either Benner or Radcliffe, which created the impression that he was going faster than they, although he was not. His back was bent well forward under his rucksack, his eyes were on the ground, and the point of his ice ax bit sharply into the scree and gravel as he swung it vigorously in his hand. He is still limping a little, Carla thought. And then, almost at the same instant that she noticed it, a curious thing happened. Delambre seemed suddenly to have stopped limping. Almost as if he were conscious of being watched, he abruptly altered his stride so that he was no longer favoring his bruised right foot but appeared actually to be putting more pressure on it than on the left. His back and head were bent forward a little more now. She could see his right boot grinding deep into the gravel, as his legs drove him forward with sharp, almost vicious thrusts.

Behind the Frenchman walked Siegfried Hein, and although

213

she knew him less well than any of the others his appearance and manner of walking were still the most familiar of all to her. Like Radcliffe he was wearing shorts. They were not khaki, however, but Bavarian *Lederhosen*, and the bare legs below were not long and bony but smooth-skinned, heavily muscled and compact. His booted feet rose and fell with a strong, even rhythm. His shoulders were broad and straight under his pack, and he held his head high. He is marching, she thought. Up a mountain, through a meadow, along a city street, across a battlefield—it is all the same. He is a German and he is marching. He is a soldier, and the mountain is the enemy, and he is marching to war.

And now she was looking again at Martin Ordway, trudging along directly before her on the path.

He is a soldier too, she said to herself, musingly. He is *Hauptman* Ordway, Captain Martin Ordway, of the American Air Forces. It was the first time in the week that they had been together that she had thought of him in terms of his occupation or rank, and even now, as she repeated the words in her mind, they were without meaning or reality for her. He did not walk like a soldier, talk like a soldier, think like a soldier. Perhaps it was because he was a flyer, she mused—flyers were always supposed to be different from the others. No, she decided, it was not that, or at least only a little bit that; mostly it was because he was an American. She had not known a great many Americans in her life, but she knew that being one accounted for a great many things, whether you quite understood them or not.

The way he walks now, she thought. Not tirelessly, like Andreas; not gracefully, like Radcliffe; not tensely, like Delambre, not proudly, like Hein. His stride was long, careless and uneven, his hands were thrust deep into his trouser pockets, and he was whistling softly. As if he were on some sort of Sunday outing, or strolling down the street to call on a girl. He did not care if he led or followed. Ambling along now, he did not even seem to care if it was to one place or another that his long legs carried him. . . . And yet, she thought, it is because of him, and him only, that we are here. It is he, alone among us, who has had the power to will into being the thing that all of us have wanted.

Martin . . . Martin . . .

It was as if her voice had suddenly cried out within her, strong and importunate, filling her body and tearing at the very roots of her heart. Martin . . . Martin. . . . It was softer now, receding, fading away. She felt its echoes surging through her in a slow, pulsing tide. She stopped quite still on the path and closed her eyes.

The thing that we have wanted, she thought. . . . All that she had wanted through those long years had been forgetfulness and peace. All that she had wanted was to shut out the past and the future, as hermetically as the white ridges that ringed the valley of Kandermatt shut out the world beyond. Yet now, in a few brief days, in a few tiny moments in a sunlit meadow and a night-filled hut, the whole world that she had struggled so hard to build for herself had crumbled, disintegrated, vanished forever. A parachute had floated down between the valley walls, and the walls were gone. A man had stood suddenly before her and reached out his hand to her and led her up out of the valley. With her eyes closed now she could hear his easy, smiling American voice; she could see his eyes, tired and yet smiling, dark and bitter and yet smiling, looking down into her own and then up toward the mountaintop; she could feel his hands touching her, his arms around her, his body warm and hard and tender against her own.

With an almost physical effort she wrenched her mind away. It is wrong, she thought. It is wrong, fruitless and hopeless. . . . But the thoughts were only words; no sooner had she spoken them than they spun away into nothingness, and in their place was his name again, his voice, his face, his body again. She felt the palms of her hands pressed flat and tight against her sides. She felt the beating of her heart and the tears welling up, hot and sudden, behind her closed lids. No, she thought, it was no use pretending, no use trying to go back. After all the years the walls that she had built around herself were down at last; her peace was gone, the emptiness and nothingness were gone, and where they had been were a voice and an image, tenderness and fierceness, joy and pain.

She spoke his name again. Then she opened her eyes and saw the figures of the five men ahead of her, no more than moving brown blurs now against the gray wastes of rock beyond. She began walking again. It is hopeless and I am afraid, the words said in her mind. But the beat of her feet and the beat of her heart said: I am glad, I am glad, I am glad. . . .

They trudged on through the afternoon. The path climbed the side of a steep scree-slope, descended again into a boulder-choked gorge and climbed still another scree-slope on the far side. Here it petered out almost to invisibility, and for almost an hour they barely crept upwards, while their boots grated and scraped ankle-deep in rubble and slipped back half a step for almost every step forward.

Carla had been climbing with her eyes on the slope, but now presently, as they came out on the shale onto smoother ground, she raised them and saw that Ordway had dropped back and was walking almost beside her. He was breathing a little heavily and his face glistened with sweat, but his dark eyes were smiling.

"Tired?" he asked.

She smiled back at him and shook her head.

"Sure you don't want to rest?"

"No, I am fine. Really."

"I'm afraid Hein was right," he said.

"About the route?"

"Yes. The other would have been better."

Carla shook her head. "I am still glad we didn't take it," she said.

"Why?"

"Because it was his route."

"That's a foolish thing to say."

"No, I do not think it is so foolish."

He looked at her a moment, curiously. "Why do you feel this way about him?" he asked.

"Because he is a German."

"It's only that?"

"Because he is a certain kind of German. A kind I know."

"You distrust him?"

"I am afraid of him."

"What is it you expect him to do? Pull a revolver suddenly? Or shove us off a ledge?"

He was smiling again, but this time she did not smile back. "No," she said, "it is nothing like that. It is just that he does not belong with us. That he does not belong—here."

Ordway was silent.

"He is an enemy, Martin."

216

"Yes, I suppose so."

"But you are still glad you asked him along?"

"I didn't ask him. It just sort of—well—happened that way."

"But you want him along."

Ordway shrugged. "He's a first-rate mountaineer."

"And that's all that matters to you?"

"Yes."

"Is it really, Martin?" She was looking up at him now, her eyes steady and intent on his face.

"No," he said.

"You want him because he is an enemy, don't you?"

It was a little while before he answered her. "In a way, yes," he said slowly and thoughtfully. "I want him because he has been my enemy for three years. Because in another few weeks he will be my enemy again."

"But here and now he is not?"

"Here and now he's a man who wants to climb a mountain. He's one of six people who want to climb a mountain and who're climbing it together because they can't climb it alone."

"Together—" She repeated the word softly and was silent for a moment looking away from him at the figures on the path ahead. "But are we, Martin? Are we together? A little while ago, before we came up through the scree, I was watching the five of you moving along in front of me. The way each of you walked. The way you held your heads and carried your packs. And do you know how I felt? I felt, here we are, all in a line together, all doing the same thing, all with the same purpose. And still alone. Each one of us together with the others, and each one still alone."

He nodded slowly. "Yes, you're right," he said. "I've felt it too. But it will change soon. When we're on the mountain it will change."

"Perhaps."

"No, it will have to. We're all in this together: Andreas, Old Nick, Delambre, Hein, ourselves. And we're going to climb it together, or we're going to fail together."

"You feel sure of that, don't you, Martin?"

"Yes, I feel very sure of it."

They had come off the open slopes into a cleft between two shouldering ridges, and the sun was hidden by the mountain-masses above. Somewhere ahead they could hear the deep rumbling of a glacial stream.

Presently he took Carla's hand and held it in his own as they walked. "There's another thing I'm very sure of," he said.

She looked up at him quickly, looked away and did not speak.

"Have you been thinking about us?" he asked.

"A little."

"Why only a little?"

"I don't know. Because—" she hesitated "—because I'm afraid, perhaps."

"Sounds to me as if you're afraid of just about everything today."

"Perhaps that is what is the matter with me—that I am afraid of everything."

"Including me?"

She shook her head.

"Of what, then?"

"Of what has happened to us. Of what is going to happen."

"We're going to climb a mountain," he said.

"And then?"

"We're going to come down the mountain."

"And then?"

He did not answer.

"And then it is all over," she said.

"No."

"Yes. Then you will go away. There will be only the war again, and emptiness again."

"Now you're talking like a woman."

"How else should I talk?"

"Don't talk at all." He stopped and looked down at her. "Kiss me," he said.

"No, I am serious."

"And you think I'm not?"

"I don't know." She held her head turned away from him. "I don't seem able to think at all any more."

They were silent for a moment. The four men ahead disappeared around a bend in the path.

"Carla," he said quietly.

She did not answer him.

"Carla . . ."

She raised her face and kissed him lightly and turned away again. Releasing her hand, he placed both his hands along her cheeks and bent her head back and drew her close to him and kissed her on the mouth. His hands moved very slowly, very gently across the smoothness of her cheeks, over her ears and hair, then down along the brown smoothness of her neck and throat. He felt the length of her body close against him and her hands pressed flat against his sides, and then he felt them on his back and on his shoulders, under the rucksack, and then suddenly her arms were around his neck, holding him tightly and tenderly and fiercely.

"I love you, Carla," he said.

"You do not need—"

"Yes," he said, "I do need to say it. I need to say it more than anything I've ever said in my life."

She was silent again, standing quietly against him with her face pressed to his shoulder.

"And you love me," he said.

"Yes, Martin."

"And you're glad of it."

"Yes."

"And we'll think about the rest of it later."

"Yes."

He released her, and for a moment they stood there close together on the path looking at each other. And then she smiled and kissed him again, lightly, and said, "We had better go on now —the others will be wondering about us."

Then they were trudging on again, at first side by side holding hands, and then, when the path narrowed once more, with Carla in front and Ordway behind; and as they walked again he watched the lightness of her step and the soft firmness of her shoulders under the straps of her pack and the soft richness of her copper hair against the grayness of the mountain rock. She is lovely, he thought. She is loveliness and love, and she is yours. Watching her now, he waited for the bright warm fire to stir within him—the fire that coursed like an electric current through his blood whenever he had touched her or looked at her or so much as thought of her during these last golden dreamlike days. He waited, but where the bright fire should have been there was only an aching hollow emptiness.

Yes, we'll think about all the rest later, he thought. A little later; much later; any time but now. That was one of the three great things that war taught you, along with mooching cigarettes and how men die. Jiggle your joystick. Drop your bombs. Climb your mountain. Kiss your girl. But don't think about them. Don't think about that convent you hit instead of the railway siding. Don't think about the Focke-Wulff pilot you fried alive the other day or the Focke-Wulff pilot who will probably fry you alive next week. Don't think about Biscuit or Mrs. Wasniewicz or Madame Duval or Frau Schultz. Don't think about Temples of Science or the Grimbacks' garage or the bungalows at Pawtucket. Don't think about Stefan Raudiger or Mrs. Carla Raudiger or Mrs. Martin Ordway or New York or Vienna or where you've come from or where you're going. Never think about them. For Christalmighty's sake, don't think about them!

You had learned that. You knew that.

And still you thought about them.

You thought about them in the deep sleepless dark of the Quonset hut, with the roaring from the airstrip and the Canadian Club whisky and the reverberation of a thousand bomb-bursts all weaving and vibrating together through your blood and brain. You thought about them in the shattered cockpit of The Spirit of Perth Amboy, with Ted Riggs hunched and still in the seat beside you and Harry and Bix two sprawled shapes on the trembling floor-plates. You thought about them as you looked into Carla's eyes, as you held her body, as you watched her now, light and bright and lovely, walking before you through the gray wilderness of mountain rock. Let the dead past •bury its dead, you said. And then you thought about the past. Let the future take care of itself, you said. And then you thought about the future. You knew your thinking was not going to get you anywhere; you knew you were better off not thinking at all. And still you went on thinking. Still you went on and on, because, however much you tried to pretend otherwise, you were not simply an airplane pilot or a bomb-dropper or an architect or a mountain-climber or a girl-kisser; you were not a character in an Ernest Hemingway novel or someone being interviewed for the Times or Producing-Consuming-Unit-Number-One-Billion-and-Something in Professor So-and-So's

Brave New Chart for a Brave New World—but you were a man, God help you, and that was the way you were made.

You love this girl, Martin Ordway said to himself quietly. You don't know quite how it happened, or why it happened, but that's the way it is. You've found her and you love her and the thing you want most of anything in the world is to have her with you, beside you, a part of you, for the rest of your life. But you're not going to have her. You're going to lose her. You're going to lose her the same as you've always lost everything you've ever truly wanted.

That's what living is, he thought—a losing. Haven't you found that out yet, after thirty-one years? That isn't what it says in the book, of course. That isn't what the Reverend Doctor Michelson used to tell you on those long-ago Sunday mornings in his neat little First Congregational Church on neat little Maple Street in neat little Larchmont. The Reverend Doctor Michelson's favorite sermon topic was that life was a growing and a becoming; but his sermons, it so happened, were not written or delivered in the cockpit of a bombing plane or the black crater of a shellhole. . . . No, that might be all good and well for the pastor of the First Congregational Church on Maple Street, but in the world in which he, Martin Ordway, had lived a man's life was measured not by what he had gained or achieved, but by what he had lost. You lost the Reverend Doctor Michelson, for one thing. You lost that home run with the bases full. You lost Lindbergh. You lost the Temple of Science and the Grimbacks' garage and the bungalows at Pawtucket and the sweet clean thrill of flight. You lost Stefan and Carla and Joan Nettleton and Ted and Harry and Bix. You lost the ideas you believed in and the people you loved, the things you were fighting for and the things you were living for, until all that was left to you were a few technical skills and a few physical appetites and a carefully tended garden of platitudes on letting the future take care of itself.

And now you were going to lose Carla again. . . .

He looked at the girl walking along before him. He looked at the lightness of her step and the curve of her back and shoulders and the soft brightness of her hair against the gray rock and the sky beyond, and the emptiness within him swelled until it seemed that he could bear it no longer; and then slowly it contracted and closed in upon itself until presently all that was left of it was a thin, bitter smile. Those are two of the nice things about a war, he thought: you meet such interesting people and it keeps you out in the open air.

Carla turned her head a little and pointed. "They have stopped," she said.

He looked past her, along the path, and saw that they were coming out from between the shouldering walls of the defile and that before them again were sunlight and the spreading sky. Perhaps a hundred yards ahead the four men stood in a motionless group at a bend in the path, looking upward at what lay beyond.

"Wait," Ordway said.

Carla stopped and turned, and he came up to her and stood looking down at her for a moment silently and then he kissed her again, lightly, on the lips.

Her eyes searched his face questioningly.

"That's all," he said.

She smiled a little and they began walking again. Presently they came up to the others and stood beside them, looking upward.

Chapter 13

The days followed one another, full of stillness and space, as identical as the beads of a blue, shining necklace. On the first they reached the upper hut on the low saddle between the Dornelberg and the Wunderhorn, near the snout of the Dornel Glacier. On the second they returned to the Heilweg Hut for the remaining packs, and on the third, they went up again. Each day they climbed for about eight hours and covered some twelve miles. But by this time the very concept of "hour" or "mile" had become meaningless to them, mere arbitrary and artificial patterns of numbers on the dials of their watches and the margins of Radcliffe's map. There were no hours or miles in the world through which they were now moving; there were only light and darkness and the slow rhythm of their steps. They measured their marches as the travelers of five thousand years ago had measured theirs: by landmarks on the earth about them and the wheeling of the sun.

"Einstein has spent his life trying to prove the oneness of time and space," said Radcliffe, "and the rest of the mathematicians have spent theirs trying to understand him. They've been wasting their time; they should have climbed mountains." The Englishman smiled as he spoke, but his blue eyes were quiet with contemplation as they moved slowly across the ranges.

They climbed. They reached the upper hut, ate, slept, descended again, climbed again. Nothing seemed to happen.

And yet, Ordway realized almost with surprise, one thing or another was constantly happening.

223

On the second day they encountered a brief and curious thunderstorm. All morning they had trudged along under a brassy, glittering sky; then in the early afternoon, quite without warning, the sky to the south turned a dark purplish hue, the sun flickered and went out like a guttering candle, and a tide of air poured down upon them from the high passes above. For ten minutes they groped half blindly along the path, while dust and grit swooped around them in vicious gray whorls. A monstrous clap of thunder shattered the atmosphere, then another and another, until the seething, opaque air vibrated with their roar. But no rain fell. And as suddenly as it had come the storm passed on. They stood for a little while rubbing the film of dust from their eyes and lips and watching the dark compact mass race like a projectile up the long ridges to the north. Then they moved on again under the stainless glazed bowl of the sky.

Early the next morning, ascending for the second time from the Heilweg Hut, they came to one of the brawling streams that foamed down from the Dornel Glacier into the Blausee. On the previous days' climbs Delambre had borne one of the lighter rucksacks, but now, at his own insistence, he was carrying a packboard, and as he stepped out onto the first of the boulders that forded the stream the unwieldy load began to sway dangerously on his back.

"Need a hand?" asked Radcliffe, who was behind him.

The Frenchman shook his head.

"Why not let me take the pack until you get by that tricky spot?"

"I can manage quite well," Delambre said.

He hesitated briefly, then took a long step forward to the next boulder. His foot slipped slightly as it struck the smooth wet stone, and he struggled to regain his balance; but the weight of the packboard pulled him over to the left, and an instant later he was floundering in the water up to his waist. Radcliffe leaned forward to give him a hand, and Ordway, a little way behind hurried up to help. In a matter of moments Delambre, pack and all were safely on the far side of the stream.

"No damage," said Ordway, smiling.

But the Frenchman did not smile back. He stood silently with his dark eyes on the ground, and his face was white and taut beneath the stubble of his three-day beard.

"You didn't hurt yourself?" Carla asked.

"No, it is nothing," said Delambre.

"The sun will dry you off in a few minutes," Ordway said.

"Of course. It is nothing." He picked up the packboard, which they had set on the ground, and began to sling it on again.

"Take one of the lighter ones for a while," Radcliffe suggested.

"No, this one is mine."

Benner and Hein, who had crossed the stream before the mishap occurred, had retraced their steps from up the path and were standing by, watching. "It would perhaps be wiser, monsieur," the guide began—

"I am all right," Delambre said. Suddenly he raised his eyes and looked at them, and Ordway saw that his lips were compressed into a thin white line and that his hands, fumbling with the pack-straps, were trembling. "Will you not leave me alone, please?" he cried, his voice almost breaking. "Nom de dieu, leave me alone!"

A few hours later the same day a second incident occurred. They had stopped for one of their periodic rests and were sitting among the stones beside the path, when a mountain hare appeared suddenly from behind a near-by boulder and crouched motionlessly, staring at them. Hein was the only one of the six who moved. Reaching quickly into his pack, which lay beside him, he brought out a heavy, black-metalled revolver, took aim and fired. The hare made a single leap; then it struck the ground again, crept for a few feet along the broken shale beside the path and lay still.

Hein went over to the dying animal, finished it off with a blow of the revolver butt and brought it back to the others, "Rabbit stew for supper," he said.

"Hasenpfeffer," nodded Benner.

"If we had the Pfeffer," said Radcliffe.

Hein fastened the hare to his pack with a length of twine, and presently they started off again. Ordway fell into line behind the German and for several minutes trudged silently behind him while the path looped upward across a long slope of tumbled rock. Then the path levelled off and widened, and he quickened his pace slightly until he was abreast of him.

"The Swiss customs officers must have been a little near-sighted," he said.

Hein's metal-gray eyes looked at him questioningly. "The customs officers?" he repeated.

"Not to have noticed your Luger."

"Oh, that."

"Yes, that."

The German shrugged. "It is almost five years that I have had it with me. From Leipzig to Athens. From the Lofotens to the Caucasus."

"When you were an officer of the *Wehrmacht*."

"I am still an—"

"No," said Ordway. "That's just the point. Not here."

It was a moment before Hein spoke again. "In other words, you object to my revolver," he said.

"Yes."

"You are afraid I might decide to do something melodramatic with it—is that it?" A thin smile played for a moment on the German's lips, but his eyes remained cool and level.

"No," said Ordway, "that isn't it. It's simply that a gun has no place here."

"I see. And how about your own, may I ask?"

"I have none."

"How do I know that?"

"You know it because I'm telling it to you."

Hein was silent again for a moment. "And what is it you want me to do with mine?" he asked.

"I don't care what you do with it. Except that you leave it behind when we reach the mountain."

"You are ordering me to?"

"I've already told you no one is giving orders here. I'm asking you to."

"And if I refuse?"

"I don't think you'll refuse."

They trudged on a little way without speaking. Then Hein stopped, unslung his pack and took out his revolver again. He held it for a moment in his hand, looking at it, and then with a sudden gesture threw it from him. It arched, spinning, through the air, struck a rock, rebounded and disappeared. When he turned back to Ordway the thin smile was on his lips again. "Satisfied?" he asked.

226

"I can't quite see the need of making a big gesture out of it."

"It does not matter, *Herr Kapitän*. There are plenty more where it came from."

Ordway did not speak again. Hein closed the flap of his pack, slung it onto his shoulders, and they continued along the path.

There were other incidents, other conversations. A pack-strap broke and spilled half a load of food and equipment out onto the ground. Radcliffe burned his hand on the Primus stove. Three tins of pressed beef were discovered to have been punctured and their contents spoiled. On the morning of the second ascent from the Heilweg there was a protracted argument as to whether Benner's or Hein's route to the upper hut was the more practicable.

But no sooner had anything happened, it seemed to Ordway, than it almost vanished from the memory. The discussions and frictions, the invariable daily mishaps and occasional flashes of ill temper—in retrospect they were all mere scraps and fragments in the empty blue chain of the hours. There appeared to be no meaning or substance to them, no reality that held the mind.

Only their progress was real: the day's climb, the next, the next. . . . "A collection of bloody walking-machines," Radcliffe chuckled. And it was true. . . . On the march they were usually in single file, widely spaced, and even when they walked together the roughness of the trail and the weight of the packs left them with little energy or desire for talk. At night, in the huts, there were the packs to be unloaded, and supper to be prepared, and tiredness, and sleep.

But the silence in which they habitually moved had far deeper roots even than these. It was a silence, indeed, not so much of their own making as of the world around them, of the illimitable naked loneliness of rock and sky. They had come to this place, each in his own fashion, from many parts of the earth. They had crossed oceans and continents, groped their way through battlefields and gutted cities, crept slowly, painfully upward out of the fever and clangor of a world at war. And now at last they had left it behind. The sound and fury of man-made strife were far away, infinitely remote and inconsequential beyond the encircling immensities of rock and ice. Here in the high, still places man was no longer the center and focus, the prime-mover and destroyer of the world;

he was barely suffered to exist, to crawl minutely and laboriously against the ground across a gigantic unhuman planet of earth and air. Something of this vastness, of this ancient monolithic loneliness, had communicated itself to their spirits. It brooded above them, spun itself into them, sealed each of them into his own secret self as if by gray impenetrable walls.

They trudged on, silently and steadily, through the hours. The only sound beween earth and sky was the creaking of their pack-straps and the dry rasp of rock beneath their boots.

Ordway picked his way mechanically over the broken ground. It was late afternoon of their third day in the wasteland, and they were approaching the upper hut on the saddle for the second time. A few minutes before he had stopped to remove a pebble from one of his boots, and now, as he continued along the path, the others were already out of sight ahead. Presently, however, he rounded a sharp bend and found Andreas Benner waiting for him.

"There is something I have been wanting to speak with you about, Herr Martin," the guide said.

Ordway looked at him inquiringly. Benner held a gnarled brown hand out in front of him and studied it silently while he selected his words.

"It is about Monsieur Delambre," he said.

"What about Monsieur Delambre?"

"I am worried about him, Herr Martin."

"You mean the bruises on his ankle?"

The guide shook his head.

"He didn't hurt himself in that fall in the stream?"

"No, it is not that either. It is nothing physical." Benner paused again, choosing his words. "He is—too—how do you say it?—gespannt."

"Tight?"

"Ja—tight. Stiff. Like some rope that has been pulled out with a great heaviness and is ready to break. . . . You have noticed it, Herr Martin?"

"Yes, of course I've noticed it."

"It is not good."

"No."

"And on a mountain it is especially not good," said Benner in

228

his quiet, grave voice. "For twenty-five years now I have been a mountaineer and guide, and always it has been this one sort of man with whom it is the trouble. The fat ones, they are sometimes all right. The old ones, the weak ones, even the ones with feet and stomachs and dizziness. But this one kind, no. The man with the tight hands and the white, hungry face—no, never."

"He hasn't been drinking anything, has he?"

"No, he has not been drinking. The two bottles of cognac that he brought—I should not have, perhaps, but I looked for them in his rucksack this morning, and they were both still full. Still there is something about him, Herr Martin. In the way he walks; in his eyes . . ."

"In other words, you don't think he's going to be able to make it?" said Ordway.

"Make it?" Benner shrugged. "We do not know if any of us can make it, Herr Martin. But on a great mountain it is more than getting to the top. You know that from when you were a boy. Herr Radcliffe and Herr Hein know it. Fräulein Dehn knows it. But with Monsieur Delambre it is different. He is not made for the mountains. He does not—how shall I say it?—belong here."

"And you think we should leave him behind?"

Benner stared at his hands.

"Is that it, Andreas?"

"I am only the guide and you are the Herr. Such a thing is for you to decide."

"It would mean an uneven number for the ropes."

"Yes."

"And heavier packs for the rest of us."

"Yes."

"And he wants so terribly to do this thing."

"So do we all, Herr Martin."

Ordway was silent again, musing. "Let's think it over a bit," he said at last. "We've still got a day on the glacier and probably another of reconnoitring, before we get into the real climbing. Suppose we wait and see how things go."

"As you say," Benner agreed.

"And we'll decide later."

The guide nodded, and they began walking again. They walked side by side, and then the path steepened and narrowed and they

229

walked singly, with Benner ahead and Ordway a few yards behind; and there was stillness again, trudging again, the gray boulders again. . . .

And then, presently, it was no longer the boulders or Andreas Benner at which Martin Ordway was looking, but the image of Paul Delambre. He saw the Frenchman clambering jerkily up onto the bank of the stream, his cheeks taut and white under the stubble and his trousers plastered tightly against his thin legs. He saw him limping up the broken slope beyond the Blausee, and then changing his pace suddenly, as if conscious of being watched, and grinding his bruised right foot deep into the gravel of the path. He saw his long fingers slowly turning the pages of *L'Immoraliste*, his dark eyes gazing at the brandy in the crested glass; his face turned, lean and thirsting, toward the tranquil golden loveliness of the woman who was his wife. He heard his voice, curiously thick and muffled, saying, "I cannot tell you what this means to me."

We'll decide later, he had said.

Yes, of course, he thought. Later. You would decide about Delambre later. You would think about yourself and Carla—later. You would fight the war again—later. Everything was later. Nothing was now. Now was blue sky and gray rock. It was your right boot swinging slowly past your left and then your left swinging slowly past your right. It was the crunch of pebbles, the bite of pack-straps on your shoulders, the brown dot of the upper hut moving slowly into view on the crest of the saddle above.

They had come around a bend in the path, and then another and another and a fifth and a tenth, and now they were coming around the last bend, and the high boulders were falling away, and there before them was the last long bare slope and the white snout of the Dornel Glacier and the end of the day's journey. A few yards ahead of him Benner's heavy shoulders and pack swung rhythmically against gray distance. Far beyond and above he could see the minute insect-like figures of the others moving slowly upward across the scree.

In a few minutes they will be at the hut, he thought. . . .

They would reach the hut and drop their packs and lean back against them, watching the blue and gold of the late afternoon sky fade imperceptibly into gray and feeling the tiredness flow in slow, languid currents through their blood. They would prepare supper, eat supper, clean up after supper and sit again, their backs against the stone of the hut walls, watching the gray of the evening sky turn imperceptibly to blue again, and then to purple, and then to black. They would talk desultorily about routes and blisters and the increasing coldness and whether they should have pork and beans or tinned bacon for breakfast. They would sleep, get up again, eat again, sling on their packs again, climb again. They would climb through the next day and the next day and the next —six minute moving dots against the scree-slopes and boulder-slopes, against the glaciers and snowfields, against the ridges and precipices, against the ice-walls and rock-walls.

"There is an emptiness," Andreas Benner had said. There was an emptiness and six dots and a blue X. There was a mountain and the six of them moving slowly upward toward that mountain. . . .

Why? Martin Ordway asked himself.

In a war you lost the habit of asking why. You asked when and where and which and how and how much and how long (yes, more than any of the others that was what you asked: how long) —but after a certain length of time and a certain length of experience you gave up asking why. You left that to the politicians and the editorial writers. You left it to that other remote, half-forgotten world of living rooms and striped neckties and weekly magazines and concentrated on your own world of cockpit and bomb-bay, throttle and tachometer. Partly you did this because you were too busy to care, too tired to care, too close to death to care. But there was another, deeper reason as well. You did not ask why, because you knew why. You flew because you were a flyer. You fought because the world was fighting. You did what you did because that was the way things were.

But here, now, it was different. You were not doing what you were doing now because it was your job; or because you had been ordered to do it; or because everyone was doing it. It was not a means to an end. It was not a step on the road toward victory or peace or home or the Four Freedoms or the More Abundant Life or the Brave New World or anything else, capitalized or otherwise. . . . What was it, then? And why were you doing it? . . .

231

You were doing it because you wanted to. You were doing it for its own sake.

How many things were there in a lifetime, he mused, that you did purely and wholly for their own sakes? Damned few. The more so-called civilized and educated you were, the fewer there were—the more everything was tangled up with money and ambition and duty and service and what-was-expected-of-you and God knew what else. You got drunk sometimes—that was one thing you did for its own sake. You ate certain things that disagreed with your stomach. You read a few books, played a few games, nursed a few ideas, cherished a few friends.

What else?

You fell in love.

What else?

You climbed a mountain. . . .

Martin Ordway's eyes moved slowly across the desolation of the wasteland. They travelled over the boulders and the slag, the long slopes and twisting ridges, the gray rock-faces of the precipices and the coldly gleaming rivers of the glaciers. They climbed past the crests of the Rotalp, the Karlsberg, the Dornelberg, the Himmelshorn, the Wunderhorn and came to rest at last on the great shape that rose before him, white and gigantic, out of the tortured earth. More than a week had passed now since that afternoon when he had sat alone beside the rumbling Aarn and seen the White Tower for the first time, emerging like an immense and shining spectre from the mist. And in the days that followed he had stared upward at it from many places and at many hours. He had seen it at night from the deep valley, as cold and remote from earth as the stars that rimmed its ridges. He had seen it in the thin dawnlight, rising in delicate façade, without depth or substance, into the brightening sky. He had seen it transfixed and frozen and streaming with cloud and spindrift, withdrawn and sombre in twilight and blazing in the incandescent splendor of noon. A thing of rock and ice, it was also a thing of light and color. Untouched by the centuries, it altered its aspect from hour to hour. It was never the same and still always the same; ever-changing, yet changeless.

And now, towering close and immense above him, the mountain was as he had always known it, and at the same time utterly different. The shape was there, and the familiar distinguishing features: the tumbled moraines and the great avenues of the glaciers; the soaring buttresses and tilted snowfields; the monstrous precipices of its fluted trunk and the jagged ice-spine of the east ridge; finally the shoulder and the upper snow-slopes, and the dark battlements of the Citadel and the ultimate white pyramid that stabbed the sky. But whereas from the valley and the lower slopes it had always seemed remote and insubstantial, a half-real, half-imagined image of snow and sunlight, it was now no longer an image at all. It was a mass: solid, imminent, appalling; a vast vertical wilderness of stone and snow. For all its thousands of feet of soaring height, it seemed now suddenly to Ordway less to tower than to crouch—a white-hooded giant, secret and remote, but living. Living and on guard.

His eyes moved downward to the hut on the saddle ahead. He was looking again at the scree-slope and the four moving dots and the gently swaying pack on Andreas Benner's shoulder. He felt the pull of his own pack-straps and the pebbles beneath his feet and the cool steel of the ax blade in his hand.

All right, he thought—you climbed a mountain. You climbed it for its own sake. Because you wanted to. Because you had to.

George Mallory had said it: *Because it is there.* . . .

They cooked their supper over the humming Primus in the bare cubicle of the Dornel Hut. Then they sat among the rocks outside, watching the light drain slowly from the evening sky. There was no wind—there had been none since they left the valley, except for the curious rainless thunderstorm that had swirled briefly past them the afternoon before—but a great slow-moving tide of air seemed to be flowing down upon them from the glacier above, penetrating the chinks of their clothing and pressing gently against the sunburnt skin of their faces and hands.

"Perhaps we could find something for a little fire," Carla had said as they finished their meal.

But there was nothing. The interior of the hut was an empty rectangle of stone walls and stale-smelling air, and outside there were only rock and scattered patches of old snow and the gathering darkness.

233

"They used to keep a few things here," Radcliffe said. "A bit of firewood, mattresses, a couple of pots."

Benner nodded. "In the old days, yes. But now even the patrols do not come here any more."

"How long is it since you've been up?" Ordway asked.

The guide shrugged a little. "Four years," he said. "Perhaps five."

"That's a long time."

"Ja, it is a long time."

They pulled off their boots and then their woolen socks and sat with their tired feet pressed against the soothing coldness of the rocks. Benner brought out his stub of a pipe and lighted it. Carla changed the dressing on Radcliffe's burned hand and the adhesive tape on Delambre's ankle. They talked desultorily about the broken pack-strap and the next day's route and whether they should have the bacon or the pork and beans for breakfast. Then they fell silent again, watching the dusk.

The low saddle on which the upper hut was placed marked the northern end of the great corridor of the wasteland. On either side of it long ridges climbed in broken arcs to the precipices of the Dornelberg and the Wunderhorn; and beyond them, framed by the outlines of the lesser peaks and filling the sky with its frozen symmetry, rose the White Tower. The central mass of the mountain, however, did not spring up directly behind the saddle, as it appeared to do from the wasteland, but was still some four or five miles away, to the north. Across this intervening distance, descending in great curving ramps from the south face to the plateau, stretched two roughly parallel granite spurs, and deep between the spurs, as if between the forepaws of an immense crouching beast, lay the undulating, twisting ice-sea of the Dornel Glacier. Glacier, spurs and the mountain behind them were transfixed in stillness and space. Only the dusk lived and moved. As Martin Ordway stared upward now from among the forlorn rocks of the saddle he could see it slowly deepening, thickening, moving upward: over the blue glint of ice, the gray gleam of rock, climbing like a great dark sea from the glacier to the spurs to the solemn walls and battlements above. For a few moments it almost seemed to him that the mountain itself was moving, withdrawing itself majestically and relentlessly into the veils of twilight. Then, presently, it was still again—frozen again. Beyond its white-looming skyline ridges the stars brightened swiftly into night.

Benner's seamed face glowed faintly above the orange disc of his pipe-bowl. Ordway could hear the sound of his watch ticking against his wrist.

"Om mane padme hum," Radcliffe murmured.

The others turned their eyes to him, but he did not go on.

"Om mane—?" It was Carla's voice.

"It's the beginning of an old Tibetan chant." The Englishman stared musingly before him, as if puzzled by his own thoughts. "The lamas in the Himalayan monasteries used to repeat it over and over every day at sunset while they turned their prayer wheels."

"What does it mean?"

"The actual words mean, 'the jewel is in the lotus.' But as the priests of the Rongbuk used it, it meant 'the goddess is in her sanctuary.'"

"The goddess?"

"Chomolungma—Goddess Mother of the World."

"That is the Tibetan name for Everest," said Delambre. Radcliffe nodded.

"It is a better name."

"And they worshipped it?" Carla asked.

"In their own fashion, yes—not in the way a European or a Christian thinks of worship. The peasants and herdsmen filled it with all kinds of spirits and demons. The lamas—well—contemplated it." Radcliffe was silent a moment, gazing up at the mountain and the night. "There was a famous hermit monk who lived in a rock cell in the cliffs, a few miles above the Rongbuk monastery. Every day for more than twenty years he'd sat from sunrise to sunset at the mouth of his cell, staring up across the glaciers at the summit of Everest. At the time we passed through the valley, in 1924, he'd already long since been blinded by the glare of snow and ice, but he still sat there, cross-legged and slowly turning his prayer wheel, with his empty eyes raised to the mountain. If he's still living, I know he's sitting there in the same position today."

"Still searching for Nirvana," Delambre murmured.

The Englishman shrugged. "Nirvana—understanding—liberation from the Wheel of Life. It can be called by many names."

"But what a terrible way to seek it," said Carla softly.

"It's not our way, of course. What to the Eastern mind is a holy man or a saint is to us simply a fanatical disease-ridden old creature with a broken body and a brain full of devils. And yet—" Radcliffe paused again and smiled a little "—yet I hardly think anyone could deny that in the last five years we have learned a few things ourselves about the mortification of the flesh."

"With scientific improvements," added Ordway.

"Oh yes, of course. With the most ingenious scientific and technological improvements.

"And then too," Radcliffe went on, "I'm wondering, when you come right down to it, how much real difference there is between what that blind old lama was seeking, sitting there beside his prayer wheel in his Himalayan valley, and what we ourselves, the six of us, are looking for here and now. We don't call it Nirvana —no. We don't turn prayer wheels, or starve our bodies or blind our eyes if we can help it; but aren't we too, each in his own way, struggling for liberation from our own Wheel of Life?"

"For 'liberation' read 'escape,' " said Delambre. "And for 'the Wheel of Life' read 'reality.' "

The Englishman regarded him curiously for a moment. "You're quite sure then, old boy," he asked, "of what comprises reality?"

"If you are speaking of ultimates, monsieur—no, I am not. If you are speaking of the world in which we are unfortunate enough to live, I am afraid I am."

"The war, you mean?"

"The war—" Delambre shrugged. "Yes, that is one word for it, I suppose. The war around us, and the war within. For myself, however, there are two other words that I would select. The one is 'anarchy,' and the other is 'guilt.' "

Andreas Benner nodded and spoke for the first time. "Die Schuld—ja. The blood-guilt. The curse of Cain."

"The guilt of what we have done with this life that has been given us," said Delambre.

They lapsed into silence again. While they talked the last shreds of daylight had seeped from the western sky, and it was full night now: black, sharp and unchanging. Glaciers and peaks gleamed whitely around them, as if lighted by a ghostly inner incandescence of their own.

"That, of course, is the bitterest thing of all," Radcliffe said presently in a quiet voice. "That the more we accomplish the less we have; that the more we know, the less we understand."

"That hardly sounds like a scientist," said Carla.

"No, it doesn't, does it? And I can remember a time not so very long ago when I'd have thought it hellfire-and-damnation heresy. When I believed that the reasonableness and objectivity and equanimity of science were the one and only hope of the world."

"You do not believe it any longer, then?"

"I believe in its methodology. I believe in the factual knowledge which is its end. But as for its benefits, its meaningfulness in human life—" Radcliffe paused and shrugged his bony shoulders "—about that I'm no longer so very sure."

"Because it has been perverted to war?"

"It's partly that, I suppose. But also a great deal more than that." The Englishman paused again, gazing out beyond the boulders of the saddle at the mountains and the night. "Sometimes it seems to me that man—all of us together and each one of us in himself—can be compared to a candle in a dark room. The flame of the candle is his spirit, his awareness, his comprehension —whatever you choose to call it—and the room is the world or universe he inhabits. The flame is not a particularly bright one, to be sure, but neither, in the beginning, is the room a very large one, and the candle serves to light it fairly well. Gradually, however, as the years and the centuries pass, the room begins to grow larger, its walls begin to recede and its ceiling to rise, at first very slowly, very haltingly, and then faster and faster, until presently it is no longer a room at all, but a limitless expanse, a plain, a waste. But the candle is still only a candle. Man is still only man. And the little flame that once threw its beams, however faintly, to the four walls and corners of a room is now nothing but a tiny lost flickering in unbounded, untracked darkness."

"And your solution, Doctor Radcliffe?" The voice was Siegfried Hein's. "Is it, perhaps, that we should all go back once more into our snug little room of the past?"

"There are times when I think it might be rather pleasant." Radcliffe smiled slightly. "As pleasant as it is impossible."

"And granting that it is impossible—what then?"

"We must rediscover a purpose, a direction, in our living. We must allow our—forgive the word—souls to catch up with the things our hands and brains have accomplished. To know a little less and to understand a little more: that, it seems to me, is our greatest need. It may be faith that I'm talking about. I'm not quite sure."

"And has it not occurred to you that there are perhaps many in the world who have already found it?"

"In the new political philosophies, I suppose you mean? In leaders, nations, causes?" Radcliffe shook his head and smiled again. "*Sie gefielen mir vielleicht, wenn ich andere Ohren hätte.*"

"You speak German well, *Herr Doktor.*"

"I'm not really speaking it. Merely quoting it. . . . You recognize the quotation, perhaps?"

Hein shook his head.

"It is from one of your greatest German poets, with a name, coincidentally, very similar to your own. You have heard of him, I imagine—Heinrich Heine."

It was a moment before the German answered. "Yes, I have heard of him," he said.

"But you are not acquainted with his works?"

"No, I am not acquainted with them."

Radcliffe nodded but did not speak. In the stillness Ordway could again hear the soft pulse of his watch against his wrist.

"And this—well—faith that you believe so many have found," the Englishman said presently, "—that is enough to live your life by?"

"Enough for a whole people."

"I'm not speaking of whole peoples. I'm speaking of individual men."

"Individual men?" Hein shrugged. "What do individual men matter? Men come and go, but a great nation remains."

"I should say rather that nations, leaders, causes come and go —but men remain."

The voices continued speaking; but now Martin Ordway was conscious only of their sound and not their words. . . . *But men remain,* he repeated musingly in his mind. . . . Not all men, to be sure, he amended; not all of them, by a damn sight. Not Ted Riggs, for one; not Harry nor Bix nor several dozen others he could name, nor several million others he couldn't. But in the sense that Radcliffe had meant it, it was true. Men remained—and they remained the same; with all the changes that they had wrought in the world, with all that they had learned and suffered and achieved, their innate moral and mental capacities had not increased by one iota from the First Dynasty to the Third Reich, from Sinai to Stalingrad. The Twentieth Century had produced no greater minds than Aristotle or Copernicus, no greater spirits than Jesus or Socrates. Nor would the Fortieth, probably. Nor the Eightieth. And for the vast masses of humankind life would continue to be what it had always been: a mindless farrago of appetites and emotions; a brief, feverish scuttling about under the ageless, immutable goads of hunger and fear.

You fought a war. You fought the good fight. . . .

You fought it with a club, a sword, a spear, a longbow, a flint-lock, a gatling-gun, a Sherman tank, a B-29. You fought it at Thermopylæ, Cannæ, Roncesvalles, Blenheim, Austerlitz, Shiloh, Verdun, Anzio. You fought with such courage as God and your glands and your basal metabolism had endowed you with, and that courage was neither more nor less than that of a Bœotian hoplite of 800 B.C. or an interplanetary atom-bomber of the Twelfth World War. You fought in the sure conviction that what you were fighting for was good and what your enemy was fighting for was bad, but in the end there was neither good nor bad, but only history.

Om mane padme hum—were those the words? The jewel is in the lotus. . . . Or, as the lamas of Larchmont High used to put it: if we had some ham we could have ham and eggs—if we had some eggs.

He was pleased with the thought and smiled a little to himself, and then he came back to the others. He felt the cool hardness of the rocks against his bare feet and the cool softness of Carla's hand upon his own. The talking had stopped, and Radcliffe had gone into the hut and brought out his flute. Sitting on the stone steps, he played Debussy's *Fantôches* and Schubert's *Lorelei*, and the others sat listening quietly while the music spun out like a thin silver thread into the darkness. When he was finished the silence of the mountain night flowed back again—in a trickle, a stream, an immense black tide. Beyond the tumbled boulders of the saddle the long ridges climbed skyward, iron-brown and still under the stars.

Chapter 14

They descended the eroded slope beyond the saddle, crossed a milk-white, foaming stream and climbed up through the boulders and slag that formed the terminal moraine of the Dornel Glacier. In another ten minutes they emerged on the ancient green ice of the glacier's snout.

"Also," said Andreas Benner, unslinging his pack, "we shall rope up now."

For almost an hour in the first light of another cloudless morning they had stood on the flat promontory of a ridge above the hut, studying the details of the savage mountain-world that soared into the sky before them. Throughout the morning, and perhaps for part of the afternoon, their path would be along the twisting white ribbon of the glacier. Then, as the glacier narrowed to its apex, they would come to the final transverse crevasse of the Bergschrund and, beyond it, to the frozen cascade of the icefall, where the glacier's surface buckled upward and merged with the snow-slopes of the mountain proper.

Benner moved a stumpy brown finger upward and to the right. "There should not be much snow now on the icefall," he said. "With the crampons, and some step-cutting perhaps, we should be able to reach the southeast ridge in another two or three hours."

It was this southeast ridge, they had agreed after long discussion, that offered the most promising route of approach to the upper reaches of the mountain. Rising out of a jumbled wilderness of crags and gorges to the east of the glacier, it climbed in a steep, twisting spine of rock and ice to a point, about two-thirds of the way to the summit, where the main east ridge of the mountain swept in from the right and merged with it. Between the confluent ridges, narrowing to an apex at their point of juncture, were the beetling precipices of the east face; and to the left of the southeast ridge, and directly before them, was the south face.

It was this southern façade of the White Tower that was the most familiar to them all. It was the side that faced the valley of Kandermatt, the Heilweg Hut, the Blausee, the wasteland; it was the side that faced the upper hut and the Dornel Glacier, and during the long days through which they crept upward toward its base the outline and dimensions of its gigantic form had become an image indelibly limned into their consciousness. Now, however, for the first time, it was no longer simply an apparition—an entity—but an overwhelming complexity of detail; no longer merely a spectacle, but a mass. From the valley, and even from the high plateau, the south face had appeared as a single unbroken sweep of ice-sheathed granite, rising vertically from glacier to peak. Now they could see that it was divided into three separate and divided tiers of precipices, one above the other and each of them comprising roughly one-third the height of the mountain. Between the tiers, marking them off one from another, were two roughly horizontal white bands, indicating broad terraces or snow-slopes, and veining the rock-walls themselves were narrower perpendicular streaks that traced the course of great clefts and couloirs. The two lower belts of cliffs extended across the full breadth of the mountain's trunk, from the southeast ridge, on the right, to the distant skyline of the west ridge, on the left. The third belt, however, narrowed, as the mountain itself tapered toward its summit, and ended in a shining cornice of ice and snow. Above the cornice the eastern ridges that framed the face steepened abruptly and levelled off into a broad, almost flat shoulder that jutted like an immense sea-washed promontory into the sky. Then at last there was the summit pyramid: a whitely gleaming slope of snow; the final belt of rock that the guidebooks called the Citadel; another snow-slope, narrowing and tapering; an ultimate, remote pinprick of whiteness transfixed in the blue miles of the morning. . . .

It was their hope to set up their first camp that night at the point where the southeast ridge crossed the snow-slopes of the lower "terrace," their second at the end of the next day near the junction of the east and southeast ridges. Passing their three pairs of binoculars from hand to hand, they swept the lenses slowly upward over the desolation of rock and snow.

"You think it will be possible to stay on the ridge the whole way then?" Delambre asked Benner.

"The whole way?" The guide shrugged. "One cannot tell."

"And if not?"

"Then we must try the faces."

Siegfried Hein lowered his glasses and nodded. "After we pass the first band of snow I think we will find the south face is the only way."

"The ridge becomes unclimbable?" Radcliffe asked.

"Yes, it is too steep."

"And the face?"

"It is steep too, of course. But not quite so steep, perhaps, as it seems from here, seeing it straight on. Look—" the German pointed. "You see that long dark streak that looks like a shadow on the rock? The one between the first and second snow-bands just to the left of the ridge?"

The others nodded.

"That is called *die Röhre*. The Funnel. It is a deep couloir, or chimney, cutting up through the cliff-face for almost two thousand feet to the upper band. Once, many years ago when I was planning to climb the Weissturm, I went up almost to its base to reconnoitre, and I believe it can be climbed. It was the way I was going to try when the war came and everything was called off."

Benner nodded again.

"You know it too then?" Hein asked.

"It was the route my father always wished to try."

"But he never did?"

"No. He was never able to find a guide or *Herr* who would try it with him, and it was too much, of course, for a man alone."

"And you? What is your opinion about it?"

The guide hesitated, squinting upward. Then he lowered his

242

eyes and stared reflectively at the backs of his hands. "I think we can judge better when we get there," he said.

The discussion continued: about routes and camps, times and distances, probabilities and possibilities. The binoculars swung slowly upward, horizontally, downward again, upward again. Then the sun's rays, streaming from behind the long ridges of the Himmelshorn, struck the mountain as if with a thousand shattering spears, and all detail, all shading of depth and outline, vanished instantly in a consuming blaze of reflected light.

It was the last time that they would see it whole, Martin Ordway thought. From this point on they would be too close to it, too much a part of it, too deeply in its shadow. The White Tower would no longer be an entity, but only the sum of its parts: first a glacier, then an icefall, then a ridge, a precipice, a chimney, a cornice, a crag, a slab, rock, snow, ice. Its oneness would exist only in their memories, their goal only in their minds. . . .

When he turned back to the others it had been a few moments before he could see them clearly with his glare-blinded eyes. Carla was standing close beside him, watching him, her gray-green eyes smiling a little, her hair a soft copper gleaming against the desolation of mountain rock.

"Now for the second try," she said.

He smiled back at her. "Good luck, *gnädiges Fräulein*."

"Good luck—Binks."

Hein and Radcliffe had begun to sling on their packs. "Also—" said Benner, looking from one to another.

And now they were on the glacier at last; at the beginning of their real journey at last. Dropping their packs again, they removed two of the ropes, uncoiled them carefully and then looped them around their waists.

"You remember how, Herr Martin?" Benner asked.

"Of course I remember how," said Ordway.

But it turned out that he did not remember. First he tied a slide knot that almost cut him in two when he pulled against it. Then he tied a granny that promptly slid down to his feet. Finally he stood by, docile and deflated, while Carla laughingly made the proper knot with a few quick twists and pulls.

In accordance with Benner's suggestions made the night before, they teamed off so that each rope would be of approximately equal strength. On one of them Benner was in the lead, with Carla second and Ordway third; on the other were Hein, Delambre and Radcliffe, in that order. "With so little snow on the glacier," the guide said, "it is perhaps not necessary that we rope up at all. Still it is better always to be on the safe side, and it will get us used to working together."

They tested the knots, slung on the packs again and picked up their ice axes.

"Here goes," said Ordway.

And they started off.

The Dornel Glacier, in its lower reaches, was perhaps a third of a mile in width—an undulating, gently rising river of ice between the eroded rock-walls of its containing spurs. During the first hour of their ascent the crevasses were few and clearly visible, and they were able to proceed in a fairly straight course. Their progress, however, was far slower than on the boulder and shale-slopes of the previous days. This was due partly to the insecure footing of ice and granulated snow, partly to the increased weight of their packs. For today, for the first time, there would be no doubling back on a return trip for supplies, and, having left a second cache at the upper hut, they were now carrying with them the whole of their equipment and food for as long as they would be on the mountain.

They rested for five minutes at the end of the first hour, and again at the end of the second. Both the wasteland behind them and the base of the mountain ahead were now hidden from them by the twisting, shouldering spurs, and the glacier had become a narrow corridor, insulated from the rest of the world by ice, rock and sky.

"We are about halfway to the icefall now," said Benner.

Beyond their second resting place the going was even slower than before. The angle of ascent steepened perceptibly, the glacier's surface became warped and corrugated, and soon they were threading their way cautiously through an intricate network of crevasses. At one point they came to a great transverse fissure that necessitated their doubling back and forth across almost the whole breadth of the ice sheet before they could find a way around it. And further on there were crevasses covered with snow. Zigzagging, halting, retracing their steps, they were reduced to a progress of two or three strides at a time. Benner and Hein, at the head of the two ropes, walked with their eyes fixed on the white surface ahead, searching for the slight shadings and discolorations that would indicate a void below, sounding carefully with their axes before each forward step.

Coming out at last on a broad area of solid ice, they rested again and ate a few mouthfuls of bread and cheese. The surface of the glacier around them shone with a hard, cold gleam in the morning sunlight, but the long slanting rays were warm on their heads and shoulders, and Ordway, raising a hand to his face, realized for the first time that his cheeks and forehead were glazed with sweat. He lay back for a few moments with his hands cupped under his head, feeling the sunlight on his closed eyelids and the gentle, rather pleasant throbbing of fatigue in his legs and back. . . . This is going to be a lot of mountain, he thought, half-smiling. You know that, don't you, Ordway my boy?—and something tells me you're going to need every bit of that certified-Grade A-20/20-U.S.Army-Air-Corps-manpower before you're through with it and it with you. In fact, you're going to need most of it right this minute just to open your eyes and sit up.

He opened them and sat up, and there was Carla beside him, watching him and smiling.

"Elizabeth Arden would be proud of you," he said.

The smile changed to a puzzled questioning.

"You're not sweating?"

She shook her head.

"Or tired?"

"A little, maybe. Not very."

"Elizabeth Arden and I are *both* proud of you."

Sitting beside Carla on the other side, Benner was rummaging for something in his rucksack. Beyond him were Hein and Radcliffe, still eating, and farther off, half a rope's length away, Delambre was sitting with his elbows on his drawn-up knees, staring off up the glacier. Ordway's eyes rested on him for a few moments; then he stood up, untied himself from the rope and walked over and sat down beside him.

"It's a long way to Tipperary," he said, smiling.

"Pardon?"

"There's still a long way to go."

"But of course. We have only just started."

Delambre had not turned his head and seemed to be only half-hearing his own words. In the silence that followed Ordway looked at him curiously. The Frenchman's face, thin to begin with, had grown even thinner, it seemed to him, in the four days since they had left the valley, until now, in the harsh, flat light of sun and snow, the bones of his cheeks and jawline appeared actually to be pressing outward through the tight-drawn flesh. There were men —Benner for one, Hein for another—whose faces gained strength and dignity from a stubble of beard and wind-roughened skin. But Delambre's had become merely flyblown and unkempt. His complexion was sallow and mottled, his lips chapped and cracked, and his thin nose, protruding incongruously between the dark lenses of his goggles, was almost comically reddened and pinched. . . . The Exquisite in Exile, Ordway thought sardonically. The Boulevardier joins the Boy Scouts. . . . And in the next instant he was annoyed with himself for thinking it.

"It's going all right?" he asked.

Now at last the Frenchman turned and looked at him. "Oh yes, very well," he said.

"The pack's not bothering you?"

"No."

"Or your foot?"

"It does not bother me at all."

"Good." Ordway was silent, wondering what he could say next. Then he became aware that the other's eyes were still fixed on his face.

"You are worried, aren't you, Monsieur?" Delambre said.

"Worried?"

"That I shall hold you back." Ordway was about to speak, but the Frenchman continued in a quiet voice. "That I bruised my foot. That I slipped crossing a stream. That I am not—how shall I say it?—strong enough."

"It isn't a question of strength. Or of worrying either."

"Of what then?"

It was a moment before Ordway answered. "It's simply a matter of keeping one's sense of values," he said slowly. "Of recognizing one's capabilities and limitations and being—well—sensible."

"Ah yes, to be sure. Sensible." Ordway could not see Delambre's eyes behind the curved green glass of his goggles, but the low, even voice was edged with mockery. "As an American, I imagine you are a great believer in sensibleness, *mon Capitaine?*"

"In some things—yes."

"In the sensibleness of war, for example. In the sensibleness of hating, fearing, killing. In the sensibleness of what we have made of this world we live in."

"I'm not talking about—"

"No, of course: you are not talking about the world we live in. You are talking, unless I am very much mistaken, about getting rid of me." The Frenchman's voice, though still low, had become suddenly cracked and harsh. Now with equal abruptness it changed again. "I am sorry," he said, "I should not have said that. If the rest of you feel that I shall delay you or make things more difficult, then of course there is no choice left to me."

Ordway did not answer. Turning his head a little, he sat silently staring up the glacier.

"You want very much to climb this mountain, don't you?" he said at last.

"Yes," said Delambre. "I want very much to climb it."

"And you believe that you can?"

Delambre shrugged. "Do any of us know if we can?" he asked. "But this much I can promise you, Monsieur Ordway: Where the rest of you go, I can go too."

"You realize what lies ahead of us, of course."

"Yes."

"The danger, the uncertainties . . ."

"Yes."

"And that we'll probably fail—"

"Yes."

"And that even if at last we do get to the top there'll be nothing there but rock and snow and sky—"

"And ourselves," said Delambre.

In the silence that followed Ordway heard the others getting to their feet and the scraping of packs and bootnails against the ice. . . . And then, presently, they were climbing again, moving slowly and steadily up the white river through the still blue air of late morning. The glacier narrowed and steepened more rapidly now, and its spine began to undulate in great humps and hollows

247

beneath its thin sheath of snow. They leaped a long diagonal crevasse, circumvented another. Then they threaded their way tortuously through a belt of seracs—a frozen forest of weirdly contorted ice-towers, thrust up through the glacier's surface by the immense buckling pressure from below.

"Here it is best that we go quickly," Benner called back from the head of the first rope.

But they did not go quickly enough. While they were still in the midst of the jumbled white spires, they suddenly heard a low rumbling beneath them and felt the surface of the glacier trembling under their feet. An instant later there was rending sound, swelling to a roar, and a thirty-foot serac, halfway between the first and second ropes, toppled slowly over and shattered into a thousand shining blocks and shards of ice. The roaring faded, echoed, faded once more. Then there was Benner's voice again.

"Everyone all right?"

For a moment there was no answer.

"All right," Radcliffe called from the rear.

And they climbed on through the white silence. . . .

A short distance beyond the seracs both spurs that hemmed the glacier fell abruptly away, and two smaller tributary glaciers curved into the Dornel from east and west. Turning a little as he climbed, Ordway let his eyes move slowly up the eastern one to the point where it disappeared into the deep notch between the Wunderhorn and the main east ridge of the Weissturm. Then suddenly he realized that Benner and Carla, ahead of him, had stopped and were gazing at it too.

"Do you remember?" the guide asked.

Ordway nodded. "Shouldn't we be able to see the lean-to from here?"

"It is five years that the lean-to is gone."

"Gone?"

"It collapsed in a storm during the winter, and no one ever rebuilt it."

They stood silently, staring up across the glittering emptiness of ice and snow. . . . The lean-to was gone. It was gone, but it was still there. The boulders beyond—the snow-slope, the ridge, the ledge, the winking flashlight in the darkness—they were all still there. Two boys and a girl were there, and Andreas Benner shaking his brown, weather-beaten head. . . .

"*Verdammtes Kinderspiel*," Ordway said, barely audibly.

As they continued up the main glacier the containing rock-walls rose again. They twisted, straightened, twisted again, rising ever higher and closer above the narrowing glacier, until they shut out the sun, and the sky was merely a jagged blue slit between the dark scarps of their summit ridges. The base of the mountain was no more than a mile away now, and the vast expanse of the south face seemed to rise not so much in front of them as directly above their heads. But its very closeness foreshortened and distorted it out of all true proportion. The summit and upper slopes were hidden from their view. Ridges, precipices, ice-walls and couloirs tiered endlessly skyward, no longer in the familiar pattern which they had come to know so well, but in a monstrous jumbled confusion. Ordway's eyes searched for the southeast ridge. . . . Rock and snow. . . . For the first "terrace." . . . Rock and snow. . . .

They rested again.

And then they were trudging on again. They climbed, zigzagged, threaded their way between seracs, probed patiently and cautiously with their axes. They felt the still-converging walls above them drawing them relentlessly in and upward like two great dark arms. They were standing at last on a smooth bulge of powder-covered ice, looking at the broad gash in the glacier before them and the steep, tumbled cascade of the icefall beyond.

"*Also*," said Andreas Benner. "*Der Bergschrund.*"

Unslinging their packs, they walked back and forth along the rim of the great crevasse. Here at its apex the glacier was no more than a hundred yards in width, and, as they had expected, the Bergschrund extended the whole distance across it, ending only at the vertical, unclimbable rock-walls of the enclosing spurs. There was obviously no way around it. Returning to the middle of the glacier, they stopped at the point where a narrow bridge of bluish-gray snow formed the only span over the chasm. Seen from the side, it appeared to be about three feet in depth. "Enough to hold us," said Hein, "if it is frozen underneath."

Benner edged to the very rim of the solid ice, leaned carefully forward with his ax raised and drove it strongly downward. The haft plunged through the snow, unchecked. He moved a little to the right and tried again, a little to the left and tried again. The results were the same. Balancing on his left foot with the help of the ax, he moved his right foot forward and pressed it against the grayish surface. The snow tightened slightly around his boot, but did not hold. He allowed his foot to sink in another inch—then another. Then with a quick movement he jerked it away. The snow around the bootprint trembled, began to crumble, disintegrated suddenly before their eyes. With a soft hissing sound the whole mass of the bridge collapsed, and they stood on the rim of the *Bergschrund* staring downward into blue, ice-walled depths.

"*Verfluchtes Zeug!*" Benner growled.

They sat on a hummock of ice, their eyes measuring the width of the crevasse; then Benner, followed by Ordway and Carla, began walking slowly along its lip. It was virtually the same width all the way across: three meters, perhaps—a little less than ten feet. "It would be easy enough to jump," said Ordway, "if it weren't for our boots and—"

He broke off, hearing the sound of voices behind him, and the three of them turned and saw that Hein had untied himself from the other rope and was walking away from the *Bergschrund*, down the glacier. Suddenly, when he had gone about a dozen paces, he wheeled about and began running back up the slope.

"He's going to—"

It was Carla's voice. And in the same instant that she spoke, Hein jumped. His crouched body hurtled out from the lower lip of the crevasse, seemed to hang motionless for a moment above the blue depths and landed lightly in the snow on the other side, a good two feet beyond the farther rim. By the time they had retraced their steps to the point from which he had jumped, he had regained his feet, turned, and was gesturing at them.

"Throw over the ropes now," he called.

They tossed the ends of the two ropes across the chasm, tied their rucksacks and packboards to the other ends, and Hein pulled them over one by one. When all the gear was on the other side he straightened and gestured again.

"All right," he said. "Come on."

There was a moment's silence.

"I think we had better use the rope," Benner said.

"But there is nothing to it!"

The guide hesitated. "Still I think it is better to—"

He was interrupted by the quick thudding of boots against the snow. While he and Hein had been talking Delambre had moved a few paces back from the edge of the *Bergschrund*, and now, suddenly, he was running toward it, as the German had done a few minutes before. Ordway took a step forward to intercept him, but it was too late. His body taut and driving, his ice ax extended before him in his right hand, Delambre reached the edge and jumped. For an instant it seemed that he was going to make it easily. Then his momentum through the air appeared to lessen; his feet struck on the exact edge of the farther rim—and slipped. There was a sharp scraping sound and a flurry of white flakes as boots and ax dug into the smooth surface of the ice-wall. The point of the ax caught, slipped, caught again. Hein knelt, extended a hand, and a moment later Delambre was standing on the level snow of the farther lip.

There was another silence.

"*Bitte, das Seil,*" said Benner quietly.

Hein knotted the end of one of the ropes around his waist and threw the other end back across the crevasse. Then he braced himself behind a hummock of ice while Benner, Ordway and Carla in turn tied themselves on and jumped. All of them made it with inches to spare.

"You see?" said Hein. "There is nothing to it."

Benner nodded without speaking and threw the rope back across to Radcliffe. While the others watched, the Englishman fastened it on, walked back from the edge and turned. Then he paused, looking across at them, as if in indecision.

"Let her go!" Ordway called.

For another moment Radcliffe remained motionless; then suddenly he was running toward them. Ordway watched the angular long-boned stride, the forward-thrust head, the grizzled cheeks, hawk's nose and bright blue eyes, against the white background of the snow. . . . Like an old stork with rheumatism, he thought, smiling. . . . But in the next instant he was no longer smiling. Radcliffe had stopped.

"Did you slip?" Benner was calling.

Radcliffe did not answer.

"Anything wrong?"

251

The Englishman shook his head. "No. I'm quite all right. It was only"—his voice barely came to them across the ten feet of the crevasse—"I'm a little out of breath, I think."

He remained where he was for a little while, leaning on his ax and staring down at the snow at his feet. Then, walking slowly, he retraced his steps to the point where he had started his run.

Carla touched Ordway's arm. "Do you think one of you should—"

But before she could finish Radcliffe was running again. Once more the tall, angular figure loped forward to the edge of the Bergschrund; once more it seemed to hesitate, to be about to stop. But this time it did not stop. It thrust itself forward again, reached the brink, jumped. Benner and Ordway took hold of the rope in front of Hein, braced their feet in the snow and pulled in. Radcliffe's boots hit the near rim, and the rope jerked him forward. He tripped, fell to his knees momentarily and then got slowly to his feet.

"For a new Olympic record," said Ordway, grinning.

The Englishman smiled back at him, but did not speak, and Ordway suddenly saw that there was sweat beading his forehead and that the knuckles of his bare right hand were showing white against the haft of his ax.

"We'll rest here for a few minutes," he said.

Radcliffe shook his head. "No, we should be getting on."

"That is true," said Siegfried Hein, looking at his watch. "It is half-past eleven now; that means we are already half an hour behind schedule."

"So we will be thirty-five minutes behind," Carla said. "Even if the rest of you don't want to rest, I am quite sure that I do."

She sat down on a hummock of ice, and after a moment the others followed suit. Radcliffe sat for a while without moving, his arms folded across his knees and his eyes on the ground. Then he raised his head and looked around at the others.

"Sorry," he said.

"What's there to be sorry for?" Ordway asked.

"This—damnfoolishness."

"Nonsense. Anyone can slip."

"It's a wonder all of us didn't," said Carla. "Racing along like that over the ice."

Radcliffe did not say anything, and they sat for a few more minutes in silence. Then the Englishman got to his feet.

"All right," he said.

"Sure?"

"Oh yes. Quite sure."

They roped up again, slung on their packs and started off.

Through the bright, still hours of midday they wound their way upward between the towers and clefts of the icefall. They were no longer walking now, but actually climbing, and their progress was correspondingly slow; but the angle of their ascent was now so steep that when, after an hour, they turned to look back, they saw that they were already higher than the crests of the two spurs that flanked the glacier. The glacier itself appeared flattened and remote—a mere streak of undulating white at the foot of towering rock-walls. The *Bergschrund*, at its apex, showed only as a thin bluish line, almost directly below.

Then, as they climbed still farther, the world beneath them disappeared altogether behind the shouldering masses of ice. What lay ahead and on either side was concealed as well. They moved tortuously through a frozen wilderness of towers, spires and gargoyles that rose monstrous and glittering above them into the sky.

They bore to the right, then straight up, then to the right again, stopping every few minutes while Benner, in the lead, reconnoitred a way through a labyrinth of clefts and gullies. Presently they came to a pitch of such steepness that they could climb only one at a time. Then the ice became so slippery that it was necessary for them to halt and lash their steel-spiked crampons onto their boots. But they did not pause to rest.

"It is best we get out on the open slopes as quickly as we can," said Benner, looking about him warily. "In the afternoon with the sun shining is no time to be in the middle of an icefall."

No seracs fell, however. Occasionally they would hear a distant, hollow rumbling off to the right or left, but the frozen towers around them loomed massive and motionless, as if made of stone. They climbed on, steadily and in silence.

And finally, some two hours after leaving the *Bergschrund*, they came out on the upper margin of the icefall. The bristling white forest of seracs fell away behind; before them now, instead of cliffs and towers, was a long smooth slope of snow; and at the crest of the slope, high above them and to the right, was the southeast ridge slanting jagged and immense into the sky. Ordway drove the shaft of his ax into the snow, and there was a muffled clinking sound as the steel tip met a solid surface below. Scraping away the loose powder, he stood looking down at the gray gleam of wet rock.

They were on the mountain itself at last.

They rested, ate again and drank a few metallic-tasting mouthfuls of water from their canteens. "Now begins the dull work," said Benner.

Ordway squinted up the slope. "You think we can go straight up?"

The guide shrugged. "It depends if there is snow the whole way, or later ice."

"In any case, it shouldn't take more than an hour to the ridge."

"An hour. Two. Maybe still longer. On a mountain, Herr Martin, one soon discovers that the eyes can climb much faster than the feet."

"And the feet faster than the backside," said Hein.

He stood up and began readjusting his pack and rope, and after a moment the others did likewise.

Ordway looked at Radcliffe. "All right?" he asked.

The Englishman nodded. Ordway's eyes moved to Delambre, but he had already adjusted his pack and climbed a few yards up the slope after Hein.

"You would perhaps like to lead for a while?" Benner asked the German.

"If you wish."

"It is better, I think, to change positions sometimes."

Hein nodded and moved on up the slope a little. "Die Herrschaften will please tell me if I should go too fast for them," he said turning.

And then they were climbing again. Their axes swung in slow rhythm, and their heads were bent to the incline of the mountainside. Their boots scuffed through the snow, at first laboriously and strainingly, as their briefly relaxed muscles tightened again to the effort, and then presently with a slow, unvarying, mechanical beat, until, as time passed, it almost seemed to Ordway that they were no longer actually climbing at all, but merely holding their own positions on an immense slanting treadmill. The ridge above appeared to grow no nearer. The white slope flowed down to them smoothly out the sky, lapped in soft powdery ripples about their feet and flowed away again behind and below. Down its center, dark and tiny, streamed the long undulating line that was the pattern of their boot-prints.

For perhaps half an hour they plodded straight up the slope. Then the angle of ascent steepened, and they began to zigzag. Gradually the consistency of the snow changed, first from powder to dry granules and then from granules to a hard-crusted glaze, and it became necessary for them to stop and lash on their crampons again. After another few minutes, however, the footing became so steep and slippery that even the steel prongs could no longer hold them securely to the slope. Their progress became a matter of a step, a pause, a step, a pause, while Hein, working skillfully and methodically with his ax, cut a ladder of footholds in the ice.

Time crept past. Mountainside and footholds crept past. . . .

And Martin Ordway, at the end of the second rope, thrust himself slowly, monotonously up from hold to hold. Above him, thirty feet ahead, Carla stepped and waited, stepped and waited, and beyond her were the four other figures moving jerkily up the ice-wall like a file of articulated marionettes behind the glinting rise and fall of the axhead. His eyes sought out Radcliffe and Delambre again. They must be tiring, he thought; the German is setting too relentless a pace. But even as he looked, he saw Hein move up again from one foothold to the next and the two figures behind move after him. Then they were motionless again. The ax was swinging again.

"Good boy, Delambre. Good boy, old Nick . . ."

He must have spoken aloud, for Carla had turned on her stance above and was looking down at him. He smiled and waved a hand at her, and she waved back.

"We're getting there," she called.

"Sure we are."

"Andreas says we're three-quarters of the way to the ridge."

Up ahead he saw the guide take another step. Carla turned and took another step. Ordway watched the slack of the rope slither up the ice-slope behind her; then he too took another step. Thrusting the prong of his ax into the ice, he bent forward and rested his forehead on the cool blade, waiting.

So we're getting there, he thought suddenly with a thin inward smile. So the Rover boys in Switzerland are three-quarters of the way to the ridge. Another hundred steps and they would be seven-eighths of the way. Then eight-ninths—then nine-tenths—then there. There on the southeast ridge, on the rock and snow, squinting up at the ten-tenths of the way of their next lap. . . . "There is an emptiness," Andreas had said. There was a hill of ice rising through the emptiness and six figures creeping like minute, grotesque insects up the hill. For a moment, as he crouched there on the white slope of the mountainside, Martin Ordway felt a cold, slow-flowing numbness spreading through his body and brain. It seemed to him that he was no longer climbing a mountain but standing off at a great distance watching a mountain, and that suddenly, as he watched, the glittering snow and ice that covered it peeled away in vast cascading avalanches, exposing the dark bare bones of ancient rock beneath. And yes, he thought, it was the truth he was seeing now. The White Tower was not white, but gray and black. It was not a tower, but a ruin; and they themselves, creeping insect-like up its desolate flanks, were no longer the conscious, waking men they conceived themselves to be, but merely sleepwalkers acting out some fantastic Freudian charade of their own illusions, driven on from emptiness to emptiness by the monstrous and feckless egotism that burned within them.

He felt the rope tighten about his waist. He looked up again, stepped up again. . . .

All right, he thought, it was the truth.

It was the truth, but it did not matter. He was tired; the thin air was bitter in his mouth and throat; the crampons dragged like leaden weights at his feet and the straps of his swaying packboard bit savagely into his shoulders. And that did not matter either. For now suddenly, as he stepped up once more, he felt the numbness and tiredness draining away from him, and in its place was a quiet happiness, a deep and pervading sense of well-being, such as he had not known for years. The figure of a girl outlined against the ice above—that was what mattered. The creeping, halting shapes beyond her, the brown arc of the rope, the bright rise and fall of the axhead—they were what mattered. His cracked lips were

spreading slowly into a smile, and the happiness within him swelled
into a fierce exultation.

Good boy, Delambre; good boy, old Nick . . .

The rope jerked and he stepped up.

The rope jerked. He stepped up.

And now at last there was the ridge. There were the dark twisting spine of the rocks, and the snow-slopes below the rocks, and
beyond the snow the peaks and valleys of the Oberland spread out
to meet the curving sky. They rested for fifteen minutes, unlashed
and stowed their crampons and fastened the axes to the webbing
of their packs. Then they began climbing again. And through the
long blue hours of the afternoon they wound their way upward
along rugged scarps of granite and gneiss.

The going, though often steep and tortuous, was not difficult,
and they made far faster progress than during the morning. Presently they were looking down at the uppermost fringes of the
snow-slope and, beyond it, at the bowl-like cirque of the névé that
was the source of the Dornel Glacier. Then all snow dropped away
behind. On either side of them the bare south and east walls of
the mountains rose sheer and monstrous from the white skirts of
their bases, and they were ascending between converging precipices
of smooth, gray-gleaming rock.

The section of the ridge on which they found themselves did
not rise at a steady gradient, but built itself upward in short pitches
of varying steepness, with the result that for most of the time their
view was limited to the stretch immediately ahead. The vast familiar features of the mountain that they had known from the
valley were all gone. Summit and citadel, shoulder and skyline
remained hidden behind the towering masonry of the cliffs. Occasionally, above the spurs and knobs of the ridge, they were able to
catch fleeting glimpses of gray battlements and slabbed rock-walls,
dark couloirs and snow-flecked buttresses, rising one above another
into blue distance. But that was all. Then the crests and bulges
loomed above them again. They climbed the next pitch. And the
next.

The dial of Ordway's watch showed three o'clock. Then four.
Then five. The westering sun touched a rim of rock high above,
shattered into a thousand fragments of orange fire, and disap-

peared. The violet-gray shadow that had been climbing the slopes below engulfed them and raced on up the mountainside ahead. It grew suddenly much colder, and they stopped to put on more clothing.

Ordway was carrying the pack in which the extra sweaters and windbreakers were kept. Opening it, he handed them one by one to the others, but when he came to the last he realized suddenly that someone was missing. Looking around, he saw that Radcliffe was sitting on a boulder a little distance away, with his arms folded across his knees and his head resting on his arms.

"Nick," he called.

Radcliffe did not move.

"Nick!"

The Englishman raised his head. His beaked face looked more than ever like the face of an ancient vulture, and the skin was the color of the rocks behind him. "Oh—thanks," he said.

Ordway brought the sweater to him. "You'd better put it on," he suggested.

"Yes. Thanks, old boy."

He unslung his pack slowly and pulled on the sweater.

"And now take a little cold tea," said Carla, who had come up beside him.

Radcliffe shook his head. "I don't think I care for any just now."

"Of course you do. Who ever heard of an Englishman who didn't want tea?"

She stooped and detached his canteen from the webbing of his pack. It was empty. Replacing it, she unfastened her own and handed it to him. Radcliffe protested, but she was insistent, and finally he drank. When he had finished he sat quietly for a few moments with his eyes on the ground; then he got slowly to his feet.

"Wait," said Ordway. "We'll rest a bit."

The Englishman shook his head again. "It's getting late."

"Still—"

"And I'm quite ready," he added. He picked up his pack and swung it to his shoulders, his long arms and legs moving awkwardly, like the wired wooden limbs of an outsized puppet. Then he walked over to where the others were waiting.

"It should not be much farther now," said Andreas Benner, squinting upward.

The ridge narrowed as they climbed again, and presently they were inching along a jagged saw-edge of rock between gray gulfs of twilight. The angle of ascent grew steeper, dipped abruptly to a deep notch, and steepened once more into the longest and most difficult pitch they had yet encountered. Beyond it the ridge grew slightly wider. They toiled up another pitch. And another. And then at last they came out on a bare knob of rock beyond the final tower and saw their goal before them. To the left of them the precipice walls were flaring gradually outward into the immense flat-topped cornice that marked their summit. Above, in the dusk, there was a bluish-white glint against the rocks.

In another ten minutes they had reached the snow. The ridge broadened and flattened out abruptly, as if its spine of rock had been shattered by some ancient and monstrous cataclysm, and continued before them for a few hundred yards, not as a ridge at all, but as a gentle white slope. To the right the snow ended abruptly against the unbroken cliff-faces, but on their left it curved on around the trunk of the mountain as far as they could see, forming the first band, or terrace, of the south face that they had studied earlier in the day from the glacier below. Above the terrace the rock walls sprang up in a second tier of precipices, and the ridge emerged again and twisted darkly upward. But in the fading light they could discern few details of form or structure.

"See—the Funnel," said Hein, pointing.

Peering upward, they could barely make out a long shadowed gash in the cliffs high above. Beginning at the summit of the snow-slope, it seemed to cut diagonally across the cliffs to the left of the ridge, veer suddenly upward at a point some thousand feet above their heads and continue straight up in a line roughly parallel to the ridge and perhaps a quarter of a mile distant from it. Its upper reaches were lost in distance. And whether even the lower section were climbable they could not tell.

"Time enough for the Funnel tomorrow," murmured Benner, lowering his gaze.

They pitched their camp on a level stretch of snow about a third of the way up the slope, well removed from the exposed bulge of the ridge and at the same time far enough from the cliffs to be clear of the danger of rockfall from above. Within half an hour two of their three tents had been set up, the groundcloths laid, their blanket-rolls stowed inside. Then they squatted on their half-emptied packs in the space between the tents and heated a supper of tinned stew and tea. By the time they had finished eating it was full night. The flame of the Primus threw a blue glare on the snow for a few yards around them, and beyond it they could see the long white band of the terrace tapering vaguely into the distance. Above and below was darkness.

"Also—" said Benner, getting slowly to his feet.

They crawled on hands and knees through the low sleeve-like entrances of the tents. They took off their boots and outer socks and crept into their blankets. They lay motionless in the black silence. They slept.

Chapter 15

Ordway awoke in the night.

He knew at once that it was a sound that had awakened him, but he had no intimation of what sort of sound it was. His eyes moved through the brown gloom of the tent and saw nothing. Then he lay still and listened.

A few feet away he could hear the low rise and fall of Benner's breathing, and then, presently, the faint rustling of blankets on the other side of him, as Carla shifted in her sleep. That was all. Yet in the next instant he was sitting upright, because he knew that it was not all. Another sound was there—or, if not a sound, a stirring, a presence—and as he listened now, motionless and straining, it swelled until it seemed to fill his ears and throb softly in the channels of his brain. It was not a loud sound, but low, persistent, pervading, and he had the impression that it was coming to him from very far away. It rose, undulated, fell, swept up again out of the stillness and subsided into it. Then it was gone.

You've been dreaming, he thought. You've been dreaming and the dream's still with you. Lie down. Go back to sleep. . . . But he did not lie down. For a few minutes he remained as he was, without moving. Then he quietly pushed back the blankets, pulled on his boots without lacing them and crept through the entrance of the tent.

Instantly the black, blazing night enveloped him. The stars were curved in a great dome over the mountainside, so huge and close

261

that it seemed to him that he could touch them if he but reached out his hand, and a three-quarter moon, hanging above the eastern ranges, threw its slanting light across the peaks and valleys as if over a frozen silver sea. On either side of the camp the white band of the terrace tapered away into distance; above, the rock-walls glinted grayly as they reared upward from the snow-slope and then lost themselves in night. Ordway stood motionless, watching and listening. There was no sound or movement either from the tent he had just left or from the other, in which Delambre, Radcliffe and Hein were sleeping. He began to circle the tents, walking carefully and noiselessly on the frozen snow.

And then he saw Radcliffe.

The Englishman had taken one of the rucksacks from the pile between the tents and was sitting on it, a few yards away, staring off down the slope. He raised his head as Ordway approached, but did not speak.

"Can't sleep?" Ordway asked.

Radcliffe shook his head. "Not much, I'm afraid. . . . Nor you either?"

Ordway hesitated a moment. "No, I keep waking up," he said. "It's hard to understand," he added, "after a day like we've had."

"Sometimes tiredness keeps one awake, of course."

"That's true."

"And sometimes—" Radcliffe did not finish the sentence, and the two men were silent, looking down the white slope into the darkness. Ordway fumbled with stiff fingers in the pocket of his windbreaker and brought out his pack of Camels.

"Cigarette?" he asked.

"No thanks, old boy."

Ordway lighted one and felt the smoke go down, harsh and burning, through his dry throat. When he blew it out it hung motionless before him, like a thin grayish cloud in the black air. For a few minutes he stood quite still, listening. Then he glanced at Radcliffe again and realized suddenly that he was listening too.

"The same thing used to happen occasionally on Everest," the Englishman said in a quiet voice. "We'd climb all day, carry loads and set up camps, work ourselves almost to the point of exhaustion. And then night would come at last, and we'd crawl into our tents to sleep—and couldn't sleep."

"You were too tired?"

"It was partly that, I suppose. But not only that." Radcliffe paused a moment. "We used to imagine we heard sounds."

"What sort of sounds?" Ordway asked.

"We were never quite sure—that was the trouble. Usually it was the wind, of course: the wind can do strange things moving over rock and ice. But sometimes we would hear them when there was no wind. When it was as still as—well—as it is tonight."

"Then you don't think—" Ordway broke off.

"That what you've been hearing is the wind?" The Englishman shrugged his bony shoulders. "If you're asking me as a scientist—yes, of course I do."

"And not as a scientist?"

"I don't know. There's always the imagination, of course."

Ordway flicked his cigarette away. A point of orange fire glowed for an instant against the snow and went out. The two men sat side by side in the stillness.

"Back on Everest," said Radcliffe, "we used to argue about it now and then. Some of the men claimed never to have heard anything. Others of us heard it many times—or thought we did. More and more frequently, the higher we climbed."

"But you couldn't describe its sound?"

"None of us was ever able to—no. I suppose it was actually less sound than feeling. The sense of a presence, almost. Of something being there with us—following us."

"Following you?"

Radcliffe smiled a little. "Mallory used to say it was ourselves. The selves that we were trying to leave behind. That we were running away from. It's as good an answer as any, don't you think?"

Ordway nodded but did not speak. High on the cliffs above their heads a patch of snow or mica-encrusted rock caught a beam of moonlight, glinted suddenly in the darkness and disappeared.

"Altitude can play queer tricks on a man," Radcliffe said musingly. "I remember when Norton and Somervell made their last try for the top, just before Mallory was lost. There were only the two of them on the whole mountain above Camp Five, and they knew it, but each of them said afterward that throughout the day he had had the recurring sensation that there was a third climber just behind them."

263

"The same sort of thing sometimes happens in high-altitude flying," said Ordway.

"Yes, so I've heard. And yet after one has flown a great deal—a chap like yourself, for instance—one must become pretty well acclimatized to lack of air."

Ordway shook his head. "Peculiarly enough, it works in exactly the opposite way."

"The opposite? How?"

"In the Air Force, at least. We always begin using the oxygen tanks when we get to eleven or twelve thousand feet. Take the mask off the average man suddenly at twenty thousand and he'll black out within ten seconds." Ordway paused a moment. "As soon as we came up off the glacier this morning something started to go wrong with my breathing, and my mouth and throat dried up. At first I couldn't understand what it was—I'm in good enough shape, as far as I know, and I've never had any trouble with altitude before. And then suddenly I realized the reason. . . . Strange in a way, isn't it?"

"Yes. But still logical, of course. That's a part of it I hadn't considered." Radcliffe stared off down the slope, and it seemed suddenly to Ordway that a thin smile was playing on his lips. "One of several things, I'm afraid, that I haven't considered."

Ordway looked at him curiously. "What do you mean?" he asked.

"Well, take the rest of us, for instance." The Englishman was still gazing down the mountainside. "If anyone had asked me a few days ago which one of us would be the most likely to hold us back, I am quite sure that I would have said Delambre."

"Well?"

"And not myself."

It was a moment before Ordway spoke. "Nonsense," he said. "You're doing fine."

"No, I'm holding you back, old boy, and you know it."

"I know nothing of the sort."

"I didn't realize myself that anything was wrong until we came to the Bergschrund. Then suddenly, as I stood there waiting to jump, I knew—"

"You made it, didn't you?"

"Oh yes—I made it. With a little help."

264

"And you made the icefall. And the ridge. And the terrace. I suppose you think the rest of us didn't get tired? It seems to me you did damn well, considering—"

"Considering that I'm an old man," said Radcliffe quietly.

Ordway started to speak, stopped himself and sat silently looking at the snow. He sat without moving, feeling the stillness of the night, and then presently again he felt the stillness swelling and thickening, and the remote, elusive, pervading sound behind the stillness. It rose, wavered, fell, rose again, seeming to draw ever closer and closer around them on the frozen strip of moonlit whiteness between the darkness above and the darkness below. His eyes went to Radcliffe. He was motionless and listening too.

. . . *to the selves that we are running away from*, Martin Ordway thought musingly.

Yes, it was as good an answer as any.

Suddenly he was aware of another sound, close at hand, and, turning, he saw a figure emerge from one of the tents and come toward them across the snow.

"There is nothing wrong, no?" said Andreas Benner's voice.

"No, we're just watching the moon."

The guide came up beside them and looked curiously from one to the other. "The moon will be shining also when we come down the mountain. It is better tonight that we get some rest."

"Much better. But neither Dr. Radcliffe nor I could sleep."

To Ordway's surprise, Benner nodded. "*Ja*," he said. "I know."

"What do you mean, you know?"

"It is so with many people the first night on a mountain. Especially when—" Benner broke off and stood peering up into the darkness, listening. The other two men watched him in silence.
. . . "Yes, it is stronger now," the guide said.

"What is stronger?"

"The wind."

"Oh. Then it *is* the wind?"

"Of course. It has been blowing now for almost three hours."

Ordway looked around at the black and silver whiteness. "But there isn't any—"

"Not here, no. But up above. And it is coming from the other side of the mountain."

"The northwest," said Radcliffe.

"*Ja.*"

They were silent again, listening.

"The northwest is bad, isn't it?" Ordway said.

Benner shrugged. "In the summer, no—it is seldom bad. But in October it is hard to tell." He narrowed his eyes and squinted off to the left. "So long it does not shift off more to the west . . ."

Ordway's eyes moved slowly across the winking constellations. Not a cloud, not a shred or wisp of vapor, marred the flawless shining blackness of the night. "I think it's even clearer tonight than on the others," he said.

"That is the thing I like least, Herr Martin. It has been clear —what is it?—almost ten days now. Since the evening after you came."

"I didn't think that was unusual in the Oberland at this season."

"No, ten days is not unusual. Or even two weeks. But always in October, sooner or later . . ." Benner broke off, and the tone of his voice changed abruptly. "Anyhow, there is nothing we can tell about it tonight. A mountain like the Weissturm, it makes its own sounds and its own weather. Come now—we should get some rest."

They walked toward their tents. Then they stood for a moment between the tents, and there was stillness again, and the distant wind through the stillness.

And then, suddenly, a low cry—a man's voice. Ordway wheeled around, startled.

"It's Delambre," Radcliffe said.

"Delambre?"

"He's been talking most of the night in his sleep."

There was silence again. Then, after a few moments, the voice from the tent again. This time it was louder, clearer, sharp with terror.

"*Voyez donc—la glace. La glace . . .*"

Ordway and Radcliffe looked at each other. "*La glace,*" the Englishman repeated softly. " 'The ice.' "

"Or 'the mirror.' "

They waited, but there was no further sound from the tent.

"Come," said Andreas Benner. "Now we too should sleep."

It was cold in the tent—colder, it seemed to Ordway, than it

266

had been outside—and he lay with the blankets pulled up to his chin, waiting for sleep. For a while he listened to the sound of the night; then Benner began to snore softly, and the other sound was gone. Carla shifted again in her sleep. He felt her shoulder touch his own, and he turned and moved toward her a little until he could feel the length of her body against his own through the thick layers of clothing and blankets. She moved over more but did not waken, and they lay quietly in the darkness. Above him, the roof of the tent seemed to be stirring slightly, as if a faint current of air were flowing gently along the slope of the canvas. Or it might have been only the moonlight.

. . . . And then presently there was a hand on his shoulder and a figure crouching over him in the gloom.

"Yes, Stefan?" he murmured.

But when he sat up the dream dissolved. "It is almost five," Andreas Benner's voice was saying. "We should be starting, Herr Martin."

Outside it was still night. There was no wind, no sound or movement of any kind, and moon and stars seemed frozen into the arching blackness of the sky. Moving about stiffly and in silence, they set the Primus to burning, rolled their blankets and struck and packed one of the tents. They would need only two tents for their second and final camp that night, and, having three altogether, they had decided to leave one standing at their present site as a cache for supplies for the return trip.

"Or in case—" Benner did not finish.

"In case," said Radcliffe.

They ate their breakfast huddled about the blue flame of the cooker, shuffling their boots in the snow and holding the warm tin cups tightly in their mittened hands. By the time they finished the night had begun to thin. Moon and stars paled and seemed to recede slowly into purple distance, and from behind the eastern ranges a vast tide of twilight seeped up across the sky. The faces of the five men emerged from the darkness that had hidden them: wooden, stubbled, heavy with cold and sleep. Ordway's eyes went to Radcliffe, then to Delambre, but he could discern nothing beneath the grayish masks of their features. The Englishman had taken a knife from his pocket and was punching a new hole in one of the straps of his rucksack. The Frenchman was sitting bent

267

forward a little, elbows on knees, staring expressionlessly across the brightening snow of the terrace.

Hein scooped up a handful of snow and rubbed his face with it, and Benner and Carla did likewise. Then Carla took a second handful and turned her attention to Ordway's.

"Ouch!" he protested.

But she kept on scouring until she was satisfied with her work. "Now you look lovely," she said, smiling up at him.

"I can imagine."

"No, really." The smile rippled into a little laugh. "And if I think you look lovely now—"

"Well?"

"Then there is obviously something the matter with me."

Suddenly he was laughing too. They stood close together, looking at each other, and their laughter mingled and became one. He heard the sound of it, bright, warm and living, in the still gray air. Then as abruptly as it had begun, it was gone, and the stillness flowed back again.

"*Also*—" said Benner, getting slowly to his feet.

They extinguished the Primus, stacked about a quarter of their remaining rations in the still-standing tent and stowed the rest in the rucksacks and packboards. They checked over their axes, ropes, crampons, helmets, goggles. Then they started obliquely upward across the long slope of the terrace. It was almost full daylight now, although the sun had not yet risen, and the cliffs and buttresses of the south face tiered away above them into clear, crystalline space. Ordway's gaze moved slowly upward along that immense façade. There was no mist, no cloud. He stopped and listened. There was no sound. And then suddenly, his eyes narrowing and straining, he saw, immeasurably far above, what appeared to be a cluster of tiny white ribbons streaming out from the hidden mountainside against the cold, slate-blue sky.

He turned to Benner, pointing, and the guide nodded. "*Ja*," he said. "It is the spume blowing off the upper snow-slopes."

They climbed on for a few moments in silence.

"The wind is still from the north then," Ordway said.

"*Ja*, it is still from the north."

Coming presently to the crest of a low rise, they stopped and surveyed the wilderness of rock that rose vertically before them.

To their right, soaring up out of the terrace, was the upper continuation of the southeast ridge, and even without binoculars they could see at once that Hein had been right the previous morning when he had said it was unclimbable. Indeed, from where they stood now, it appeared scarcely a ridge at all, but rather an immense serrated buttress, part vertical, part overhanging, sealing together the converging precipices of the south and east faces. To its left, directly above them, were sheer cliff-walls—also unclimbable. And beyond them The Funnel.

Passing the binoculars from hand to hand, they stared up at the great gash in the mountainside. Seeing it now for the first time from close at hand and in daylight, Ordway perceived that it did, in fact, have the shape of a gigantic inverted funnel, or cone, gouged out of the living rock. Flaring out at its base in a broad, boulder-choked gully, it tapered and steepened as it climbed, at first slowly, then more and more rapidly, until it was merely a deep and narrow cleft continuing up along the granite walls as far as the eye could see. At the extreme limit of visibility, where the upper scarps of the precipice jutted out to meet the sky, it seemed to bend sharply to the right and flare out again, but all detail was lost in a blue-gray blur of distance. It might come out on the ridge two thousand feet above; or on the upper terrace of the face; or simply peter out into smooth cliffs below the terrace. There was no way of telling until they got there.

Provided they could get there. . . .

Ordway passed the binoculars back to Benner. After a few minutes Benner passed them to Hein. Through the stillness, presently, Ordway could hear a faint moaning sound high above.

"There's no other way," Radcliffe said.

"No," said Benner, "there is no other way."

"And do you think—"

The guide shrugged. "It may go. It may not."

Siegfried Hein lowered the binoculars and looked around at them. His eyes were very gray and steady and his jawline was tight under the yellow stubble of his beard.

"It will go," he said. "We will make it go."

There was a silence again.

"Alors," said Delambre.

But Benner was standing motionless, his eyes on the snow, and, when after a moment he looked up, his face was thoughtful and grave.

"You are all very sure you want to try it?" he asked.

Ordway looked from Carla to Delambre to Radcliffe. For a moment no one spoke.

Then Hein said: "But you have just admitted yourself that there is no other way."

"No, there is no other way. But we do not yet know that the Funnel will be a way either. It may be impossible. In any case, it will be—difficult."

"It will go," said Hein.

Benner looked at Delambre. The Frenchman's reddened face was tense and strained, and his eyes seemed almost to be burning with a dark inward fire.

"We will make it," he said.

"Herr Doktor? You are sure?"

Radcliffe hesitated for an almost imperceptible moment. Then he nodded slowly. The guide's glance moved to Ordway, and Ordway looked at Carla. As their eyes met she smiled.

"I am sure," she said.

"I'm sure," said Ordway.

There was another pause.

"And you, Andreas?" asked the girl. "Don't you want to?"

"Ja," said Benner. "I want to too."

. . . . And now they were climbing again. They were climbing slowly, one behind the other, up the long rippling snow-slope of the terrace, and the snow was dropping away behind, and there was rock ahead and rock under their feet and rock above, growing always closer and steeper and taller, as the mountainside seemed to swing slowly and gently outward over their heads. The sky grew brighter. Then there was a glint of light high above; a great golden band raced toward them down the gray walls, and in the next instant the sun's rays were streaming horizontally across the distant white ridges of the Wunderhorn. The mouth of the gully flared out to receive them.

"Now we must watch out for the rockfalls," said Benner, peering upward.

For perhaps half an hour they threaded their way through a tumbled detritus of slag and boulders. Then the gully narrowed to its apex, and above them the Funnel itself rose in an immense sloping groove through the solid rock. They halted, lashed their axes to their packs, roped up and began to climb.

The lower pitches were easier than they had dared hope. Ledge led to ledge, hold to hold, crevice to crevice, and although the angle of ascent was now all but vertical they were always able to find a stance for their feet or a grip for their hands. At intervals they came to patches of old snow or slick greenish verglas and worked their way carefully around them. Occasionally, too, there would be a sudden rumbling above, and a shower of small stones and gravel would plunge past them, ricocheting wildly from wall to wall of the chimney. But no large rocks fell; and the warning sounds of the small slides gave them ample time to find protection in the many recesses of the walls or under the bulge of overhangs.

Insofar as they could, they kept well into the Funnel, following the twisting notched spine of rock that formed the trough between its two converging walls. More and more frequently as they advanced, however, its knobs and hollows petered out into smooth slabs, and they were compelled to veer away from it toward one or the other of the outer edges. Here the climbing was more exposed: glancing back over their shoulders or down between their legs, they could see the gray walls of the cliff-face dropping vertically away into space beneath. But the holds still proved adequate, and there was less danger of rockfall than in the center of the trough. Moving with careful deliberation from stance to stance, they made slow but steady progress. And when, presently, they stopped to rest on a narrow shelf and gazed down at the distant strip of the terrace, they estimated that they had already come almost a third of the way up the Funnel.

What lay ahead, however, they still had no way of telling. On either side of them the precipices of the south face rose unbroken to the morning sky. Straight above, in the shadowed couloir, they could see only more knobs and bulges, more patches of snow and ice, more rock. They drank sparingly from their canteens and shifted the pack-straps on their shoulders. Then there was Benner's voice murmuring, "Also—"

The Funnel walls narrowed, flared out, narrowed again. Then the ribbed granite of their surface gave way to a smooth, almost holdless limestone, and they were forced back once again into the trough. The cleft was deeper now—no longer a mere fissure in the cliff-face, but a great shaft cutting through the inner fabric of the mountain—and the sky was only a thin, remote ribbon at their backs. Foot by foot, yard by yard, they groped upward through a soundless rock-ribbed dusk.

Presently Benner, who was in the lead, stopped.

"Listen," he said.

Somewhere above them, in the gloom, they could hear a soft dripping sound, and a few minutes later, as they moved upward again, the walls that rose about them were no longer gray, but black with seeping water. Here, for the first time, the climbing was so difficult that they were able to move only one at a time. Their boots scraped and slipped on ooze-covered ledges, their hands and clothing became coated with slime, and the two ropes jerked and slithered almost uncontrollably as they belayed one another cautiously upward from one vantage point to the next. Half the time they were not climbing with hands and feet at all, but squirming slowly upward on elbows, knees and stomachs. Thin trickles of water dripped from above into their eyes and down their necks, and the air around them was heavy with the stench of rotting stone.

Ordway slipped, fell sidewise against a wet bulge of rock and swore softly.

"What did you say?" Carla asked from above.

"I'm composing a poem."

"About me, I hope."

"No, about the mountain. It's called *The Beautiful White Weissturm*."

"It sounds lovely. But I'm afraid we need a new name for it."

"What do you suggest?"

"How about *The Beautiful Black Schmutzturm*?"

They laughed, and the sound of their laughter echoed hollowly along the black rock-walls. Then there was silence again. There was the dripping of water and the scraping of bootnails. . . .

And then at last the wetness and ooze were dropping away behind them; the blue slit of the sky was widening and brightening, and presently they were emerging once more from the darkness of the Funnel's trough onto the firm dry granite of wide-flaring walls. Finding a sunlit ledge, they rested again and scraped what they could of the mud and slime from their faces and clothing. Ordway discovered that he had gashed his cheek slightly when he fell; Radcliffe had bruised a knee, and the others had accumulated a variety of cuts and abrasions on the exposed parts of their bodies. Carla took the first-aid kit from her rucksack and dabbed at them with iodine and cotton. Then they sat silently on the ledge, looking upward.

It was Benner who spoke first.

"It is best we change now to the Kletterschuhe," he said. "And that we go all together on one rope."

Hein looked at him in surprise. "On one rope?"

"Ja."

"But it will go much slower."

"A little slower perhaps. But safer too."

There was a brief silence, and Ordway watched the two curiously. Andreas doesn't trust him, he thought. He's afraid he'll take too many chances leading a rope on his own.

Hein seemed about to speak, changed his mind, and waited a moment. "As you say," he murmured, shrugging.

Removing their nailed boots, they put on their light rope-and-canvas espadrilles and tied themselves at evenly spaced intervals onto the two-hundred-foot rope that they had thus far carried with them without using. Benner took the first position, with Hein second and Delambre third. Then came Radcliffe, Carla and Ordway, in that order.

"So that there'll be all five of you to hoist me up," said Ordway, grinning.

But the guide did not smile back at him. "We will climb now only one person at a time," he said, looking soberly from one to another. "And no one should move until the one above him is in a good position and belaying the rope."

The others nodded. They stood for another minute or two jerking restlessly at their rope-knots and pack-straps. Then Benner raised a groping hand to the gray wall above.

The section of the couloir up which they now began to work their way was dry, and the rock sound; but the angle of ascent was now even steeper than before, and their position far more exposed. Indeed, the Funnel was soon no longer a couloir at all —nor even a deep cleft—but the merest shallow gully grooving the immense blank bastion of the south face. Above them wave upon wave of gray, snow-freckled stone rose endlessly into distance. Behind and below was space.

Their progress was creepingly slow and followed an unvarying pattern. First Benner would stand peering up at the next pitch above him, his keen mountaineer's eyes patiently searching out a feasible stance and the hand- and foot-holds that would get him there; then, very methodically and cautiously, he would begin inching his way upward through the confusion of slabs, cracks and crags. Sometimes he gained his next stance on less than the forty-odd feet of rope that joined him to Hein. More often his voice came down—"*mehr Seil*"—and Hein untied himself and played out an additional ten or twenty feet. Then at last the voice would come again—"*gut—komm*"—and Hein would begin climbing. And after him, one by one, the others. Only rarely did they come to a ledge or hollow broad enough to accommodate them all together. Usually by the time Ordway, at the end of the rope, reached the top of a pitch, Benner, Hein and Delambre had already disappeared up the next pitch. They crept upward as a caterpillar creeps, in articulated, separately moving sections, joined together only by an occasional glimpse or shout and by the vibrating, almost sentient spinal cord of the rope.

Pitch by pitch, too, the climbing was growing increasingly difficult. Cracks petered out into crevices, knobs into smooth bulges, ribs and ledges into the merest wrinkles, while the cliffs above them leaned ever farther and farther out against the sky and the rock to which they clung seemed to be pushing them away from it with gentle but relentless pressure. They surmounted a holdless overhang by jamming elbows and knees into a three-inch cleft that split its center. Then they came to a belt of slabs with crevices so narrow that they could grip them only with their fingernails; and beyond this to more slabs, with no crevices at all, to which they adhered merely by the friction of their spread hands and feet and of their clothing. Presently Ordway heard a new sound above: the dry clink of metal on stone. They are hammering in a piton, he thought. He climbed on again as the rope tightened, stopped again, climbed on again; and then he came up around a sharp corner of jutting rock and saw Carla crouched on a shelf above, pointing.

"It's above you to the right," she called. "You can't see it though until you're almost there."

He wormed up a marble-smooth bulge, found a crack for his fingers, lost it, began to slip, and in the same instant saw the steel eye of the piton protruding from a fissure, just within arm's reach. Seizing it, he pulled himself up, and in a moment the bulge was beneath him.

"All right," he called. "Go ahead."

Once more he waited until the rope went taut, indicating that Carla had reached another stance. Then he advanced again. Soon he came to a second holdless bulge with a piton projecting from it; then a third and a fourth. Almost every time he stopped now he could hear from far above him the faint, measured clinking of steel on rock.

Their progress was slower than ever now: out of every fifteen minutes he was actually climbing perhaps five, waiting ten. The watch on his wrist showed ten o'clock, then ten-thirty, then eleven. More than five hours had passed since they had begun the ascent of the Funnel, almost half that since they had left their last resting place above the wet rocks. He waited again, listening to the patient ticking of his watch, digging fingers and toes into the shallow crevices against the insidious outward push of the rock. It can't go on forever, he told himself. . . . Or maybe it can, he amended with a grim smile. But you can't.

He was growing tired, and he knew it. His arms and legs throbbed with a dull pervading ache; his breath rasped loudly in the dry knot of his throat, and, worst of all, he had developed a muscular twitch in his right thigh that made it increasingly difficult for him to keep his balance on the precarious sloping footholds. Also, the seemingly interminable waits between the brief bursts of climbing and struggling had had the effect of making him more and more conscious of the exposure of their position. As a flyer, he was used to height. But the height that one experienced in a plane was a thing of aloofness and separation, with no bond to the earth below; and the higher one climbed the greater was one's sense of detachment and freedom. Here, on the other hand, he belonged neither to earth nor sky. He was an intruder, an interloper—the merest midge of creeping, clinging flesh, lost in an ambiguous and hostile half-world of rock and space. He looked down over his arm and saw his feet projecting from their two minute niches in the stone. He saw the shallow trough of the Funnel dropping away beneath them, and the deeper gash farther down, and the endless gray continuity of descending rock-walls curving solemnly into emptiness below. And as he watched, motionless and staring, it seemed to him presently that the emptiness had begun almost imperceptibly to move, that the whole mountainside was flowing very slowly, very smoothly, downward, drawing his eyes after it, leading them on and on into emptiness, and more emptiness, plucking gently at his pack, his clothing, his legs, his arms . . .

He turned away, bending his forehead to the hard coldness of the rock, and his fingers dug, hooked and stiff, into the crevices that held them. He heard the rasp of his breathing and the faint clink of metal above. Then the rope stirred slightly around his chest, and he was climbing again. He clambered, crawled, slipped, struggled, stopped again.

And now presently, as he clung waiting to his next stance, some thirty or forty feet above the last, he became aware for the first time of a new sensation that was neither bodily tiredness nor vertigo. Or perhaps sensation was the wrong description for it. It was an intimation, rather—a subtle and undirected sense of uneasiness that was somehow communicating itself to him across that frozen, slanting stillness of rock and air. His eyes moved slowly upward, but the others were all hidden from view. There was only the bleak tide of the crags surging above him and the thin brown strand of the rope sloping up the slabs and disappearing behind a cornice overhead. Behind him were only the sky and the sun. . . . Or had the sun disappeared? . . . Suddenly he recognized the feeling that had come over him. It was the same that he had experienced occasionally while flying over hostile territory, when another plane interposed itself distantly between his own plane and the sun. There was no visible movement, no flash or glint or sharp differentiation of light or shade, but only a slight, scarcely perceptible graying of the atmosphere, the shadow of a shadow, the consciousness of a presence other than one's own that lived and moved within the void of space.

Turning, he looked over his shoulder. . . . Yes, the sun was still there. The sun and blue depths of sky, and that was all. . . .

And yet the feeling, the knowledge, remained that it was not all. For the light of its rays was now without warmth or lustre. The rock-walls around him were more desolate than before. The air was stiller, colder. Somewhere between himself and the sun, it seemed to him, a vast and formless mass was invisibly taking shape —a monstrous plane, perhaps, or a great hovering bird—approaching ever nearer and nearer to the mountainside, closing slowly in upon it, shutting it out from sky and sunlight and the earth below with the spread of immense gray wings. He stood waiting—not moving. Then he turned slowly and his eyes moved upward again. They moved across the frozen slabs, up the motionless rope. . . .

"Carla!" he called suddenly. "Carla!"

He heard his voice cutting like a blade through the stillness. And in the same instant he was climbing again. Taking in the slack of the rope as he went, he crawled across the slabs, struggled up a notched granite rib that rose beyond them and pulled himself on hands and knees to the top of the cornice above. Carla was standing on a narrow shelf another ten feet higher, facing in toward the mountain and peering upward.

"Are you all right?" he asked.

The girl turned with an expression of surprise. Then she smiled. "All right? Yes, of course." She looked down at him and her smile brightened a little; and then it faded. "But you should not have come up until—"

"Yes, I know. But I suddenly had the feeling that—" He broke off sharply and hesitated a moment. "I was wondering what was holding us up."

"I am afraid Nick is having some trouble."

"Who isn't?"

It was Ordway's turn to smile; but Carla did not smile back. "I think he is getting tired," she said.

"Really tired, you mean?"

"Yes, really tired."

They were silent a moment.

"How about Delambre?" he asked.

"I haven't been able to see him often. He seems to be doing all right."

"And you're doing all right?"

277

The flicker of a smile touched the girl's lips again. "We are both doing all right," she said.

They lapsed into silence once more. Presently the rope above Carla twitched, and she began climbing; and then, after a few minutes, there was a gentle pull on Ordway's rope, and he began climbing too. There were more slabs and a wait; more ribs, gullies, walls, cliffs, cornices—and after each a wait. There was the faint clink of steel on stone, and the cold eyes of the pitons in the crevices, and the thin brown line of the rope twisting endlessly onward up the gray desolation of the rock. And then, suddenly, there were voices directly above him, and he came up, crawling and grasping, onto yet another curving ledge between mountainside and space, and there were the other five, all together, crowded into a shadowed recess in the cliffs.

Or, rather, four of them were actually on the floor of the recess, with Andreas Benner clinging motionless to its right-hand wall some fifteen or twenty feet above their heads. The rope fell in a straight line from his waist to the foot of the wall, where Hein had belayed it, first around a jutting knob of granite and then in a double coil about his own body. As Ordway came up into the recess the German was pointing to the area of the wall above Benner's head and calling out suggestions, but the guide neither answered nor moved. Carla and Delambre stood close beside Hein, their heads craned upward. Radcliffe was squatting on the rocks a little distance away, staring out into space, his face gray and expressionless.

"To the right," Hein called, gesturing. "More out on the face and then to the right."

Following his pointing arm, Ordway's eyes moved over the vast surge of masonry that rose into the sky above them. The recess in which they stood, he saw, was a roughly rectangular niche, about ten feet across and five feet deep at its base, cut into the sheer rock-face of the Funnel. On its outer side, in front, was space—and themselves. On the other three sides its containing walls leapt upward on great arcs which curved gradually inward until they met in a dark, dome-like apex perhaps fifty feet above and in almost a direct line over their heads. Holdless and overhanging, nine-tenths of the area of the walls were obviously unclimbable. The only possible route of further ascent lay at the

278

far corner, where the right-hand wall joined the outer face of the precipice, and a series of minute nubs and bulges ran up the vertical line of juncture and disappeared from view beyond the sweeping in-curve of the arch. If a man could get high enough up on this corner, he might—just might—be able to reach up and around beyond the arch and, finding a hold, to pull himself back from the cliff-face onto the roof of the dome and safety. It was there only, Ordway recognized, that any chance of success was offered. And it was there, halfway up to the point where the dome curved inward, that Benner was now clinging precariously to the tiny roughnesses of the arching wall.

"To the right," Hein was repeating. "To the right now, and above."

For a long moment Benner still did not move. Then very slowly his right arm groped upward, exploring the surface of the wall above like the antenna of an insect; and very slowly—so slowly as to be scarcely perceptible as motion at all—his body and legs moved after it. There was a pause. Then he moved again. He was almost at the corner now, with one foot hooked over the edge onto the wall of the precipice beyond. Above him, still two arms' lengths away, was the cornice of the dome. Below was the outer lip of the recess floor and four thousand feet of nothingness.

"Twice more now," Hein called. "Twice more and you have it."

But this time Benner did not move up again. Thirty seconds may have passed, or a minute, or two minutes, while he clung, spread-eagled and transfixed, to that savage edge of rock. His hand groped out and returned to its hold; groped out once more, returned once more. "*Es geht nicht*," he said. His voice came down to them as a hollow, echoing whisper between the dark walls of the recess.

Hein's mouth was a thin, frozen line. "*Es muss gehen*," he called up. "*Es muss!*"

There was another silence. Nobody moved. Then Benner tried again. A hand moved upward; then a foot. His body arched backward into space as he struggled to hoist himself over the bulge of the corner. And suddenly he slipped.

For a terrible timeless instant those below heard the scraping of his shoes and clothing and saw his fingers clawing at the wall. Then, miraculously, his downward progress stopped. Something

—hand or foot or knee—had caught a minute projection in the rock, and held. He clung motionless to the corner again, as if pinioned there.

"Come down," Ordway shouted. "Andreas! Come down!"

Another several minutes passed before the guide moved. Then, almost as slowly as he had climbed, he began to descend. Exploring the rock below with toes and knees, he lowered himself inch by inch from the corner to the wall below, and then down the nubs and bulges of the wall to the floor of the recess. When at last he turned, facing the others, his brown face was streaked with sweat and a thin film of blood showed along the line of his lips.

"*Es geht nicht*," he repeated, shaking his head.

"There were no holds above?" Hein asked.

"Far above. But I could not reach them."

"You could not drive a piton?"

Benner shook his head again. "There was no crack."

He took a red rag of handkerchief from his pocket and slowly wiped his lips. The others stood watching him silently. Then Hein unslung his pack, adjusted the rope about his waist and approached the wall.

"You're not going to—" The voice was Carla's, but she did not finish.

"I am going to climb it," Hein said.

"But if it's impossible—" said Ordway.

"I do not believe it is impossible." Reaching the foot of the wall, the German turned and looked at him. "What is it that you suggest we do?" he asked. "Give up and go back?"

Ordway hesitated briefly. "No," he said.

"Or that we stay here and die, perhaps?"

Ordway did not answer. Hein's eyes rested on him for another moment, gray, cool, and faintly mocking; then he turned back to the wall, stared up at it with his hands resting on the rock above him, and began to climb. Benner seemed about to speak, but did not. Taking the length of the rope that dangled down from Hein's waist, he crept to the rear of the recess and belayed it around the knob of granite and his own body. The others stood motionless, looking upward.

And now Hein was creeping slowly up the wall above them toward the broken line of the corner and the precipice beyond.

His actual movements were as cautious and deliberate as Benner's had been, but he did not pause so long between them, and his arms, legs and body seemed to swing, one with the other, one after the other, in a coordinated, almost gentle rhythm. In perhaps three minutes he had reached the point where Benner had been clinging when Ordway first came up onto the shelf of the recess. In five more he was out on the corner, his knees gripping the angle between wall and outer precipice, his body outlined against the sky. He worked his way up a foot or two and paused. Another foot and paused. He was straddling the corner now at the highest point which Benner had reached, and the curved eaves of the overhanging dome were a scant two arms' lengths above him.

He hoisted himself up another foot.

Now, for the first time, there was a long wait. The watchers below saw a hand moving very slowly along a wrinkled bulge of the wall. Then a foot moved. Then a hand again. For a single timeless, endless instant Hein's body clung transfixed to the rock. . . . And then he lunged. . . . Like Benner before him, he arched backward, reached his arms high, seemed to give a mighty jerk. But, unlike Benner, he did not slip. His hands caught onto something above, pulled him up, swung him outward. For a moment the whole length of his twisting body hung suspended in space; then his arms pulled him up again. His head and shoulders disappeared over the rim of the dome. His trunk disappeared. His legs and feet disappeared. Where a few seconds before Hein's body had been there was now only the thin strand of the rope moving smoothly and steadily upward.

There was a long interval. Through the stillness they could hear the scratting of loose rock on the upper surface of the dome and the scrape of the rope against the rim. Then the rope hung still, and a faint cry came down to them.

"All right?" Ordway called.

There was no answer.

Ordway cupped his mouth with his hands. "Are you all right?" he shouted.

Hein's voice came down again, barely audible. "Yes—all right."

"Should we come up?"

"Yes, come up."

Benner uncoiled the rope from around the rock-belay and his

own body and tied it on again around his chest. There was an exchange of shouts in German between him and Hein, half swallowed by distance and echo. Then he began to climb again. This time, aided both by his previous experience and the taut pull of the rope from above, he ascended more steadily and rapidly than before, and in a few minutes he had reached the corner and was pulling himself up the sharp edge of rock beneath the coping of the dome. There was a pause again, the groping and maneuvering again. Then he reached up and out—and found his hold. His body swung out against the sky, supported not by the rope but by the grip of his own hands, and in another few moments he had hoisted himself up and disappeared onto the roof above.

Ordway looked at Carla and smiled. "*Es geht*," he said.

The girl smiled back at him.

There was another wait, punctuated by the gritting of gravel, and the remote sound of voices. Then the loose end of the rope appeared over the rim of the dome and snaked downward along the wall to the recess floor.

"*Komm!*" Benner called.

Delambre stepped forward and picked up the rope. Ordway watched him as his fingers fumbled stiffly with the knot. "Suppose I try it first," he suggested.

The Frenchman shook his head. "Thank you, no, Monsieur. It is my turn."

He gave the rope-knot a final tug, approached the base of the wall and began the ascent. Climbing faster than either Hein or Benner, he worked his way upward in a series of quick jerks and thrusts, seeming to propel himself less by actual physical pressure of hands and feet than by a compelling inner urgency of the will. Halfway to the corner he slipped; but the rope caught him immediately, and in an instant he had regained his holds and was climbing again. On the corner below the dome he slipped a second time. And as he made his final straining lunge for the rim above, Ordway could see the rope tightening about his chest and dragging him inward and upward.

Then he too was out of sight. They waited again. The rope came down again.

"Now the packs," Benner's voice echoed faintly.

They tied as much gear as they could to the rope, gave a signalling jerk and watched the clustered rucksacks and packboards scrape slowly up the wall and over the rim. When the rope came down they tied on a second load. And after it a third. Everything was up now, and only Ordway, Carla and Radcliffe were left in the shadowed stillness of the recess. Throughout the long struggle with the wall, the Englishman had remained sitting on the rocks near the inner angle of the recess, exactly as he had been when Ordway came up over the slabs below. Now, however, he got slowly to his feet. As the rope descended once more, he picked up its end and tied it about his chest. Then he approached the wall.

"Nick—"

Radcliffe turned and looked at Ordway. "Yes?" he asked.

"Don't try to—" Ordway hesitated and stopped. For a long moment he stood looking at the man before him: at the long, stooped figure; at the pale blue eyes and sunken gray-stubbled cheeks; at the veined bony hand, like a bird's claw, resting on the rock above. You shouldn't let him, he said to himself, almost savagely. You know damn well you shouldn't let him.

"Don't try to do what?" Radcliffe asked.

"To take it too fast."

"No," said Radcliffe quietly. "I won't take it too fast."

. . . . And now he too was slowly groping and grappling his way up the nubs and crevices of the arching wall. Climbing even more slowly than Benner on his first attempt, he crept from hold to hold like an immense ungainly spider, now tightly contracted, now spread-eagled on the gray rock face, seeming to move, not with his whole body or even limb by limb, but almost joint by separate joint. The seconds ticked away on Ordway's watch. The minutes ticked away. Radcliffe inched up from the wall to the corner, from the corner to the rim of the dome. His foot slipped, caught and held him. A body's length farther on, it slipped again. And held fast again. And now at last he was at the top of the corner, his head not more than two feet below the curve of the dome, his hands groping along the hidden rock above. For a final moment he clung motionless, gathering his strength. Then he swung up and out. His hands gripped something above, held him, pulled him slowly upward—very slowly upward—more and more slowly upward. He was not moving at all now. He was motionless again, hanging. . . .

"I'm done," he said.

It was not a cry. His voice came down to Ordway and Carla merely as an echoing whisper in the long sounding-box of the recess. And in the same instant he fell. There was the quick sickening flash of a plummeting body, a grotesque contortion of arms and legs, the rope spinning off into space over the rim of the dome. Men have lived and died in the eternity that that rope spun. And then the shock came. In a fraction of a second, so instantaneous that it was no part of time at all, Radcliffe was no longer falling. The rope braked, held him motionless, seemed almost to be flinging him back upward again in one monstrous convulsive jerk. There was a spatter of falling gravel and the slow creaking of hempen strands. Radcliffe hung suspended from the end of the rope, revolving slowly in the air under the gray eaves of the dome.

An enormous stillness filled the recess.

"Nick!" Ordway called.

There was no answer.

"Nick! Can you hear me?"

Still Radcliffe did not answer. And Ordway suddenly realized that the jerk of the rope as it caught his fall and its present constriction about his chest could scarcely have left him with the power to breathe, much less to speak. But in the next instant, staring helplessly upward, he saw the dangling figure move. An arm groped out toward the rock-wall, struggled to reach it, and fell back. A moment later it tried again. And failed again. And then at last there was the sound of movement and voices on the roof of the dome, and the rope began to pull Radcliffe slowly upward toward the cornice above.

The rope gained two feet, and stopped, another two feet and stopped. Radcliffe's head was now no more than an arm's length from the jut of rock, and another single pull would bring him up to it. But the seconds ticked past, and the pull did not come. And suddenly Ordway saw that the rope was wedged into a deep crevice at the very lip of the cornice. It trembled and strained, as the men above hauled in on it with all their strength. But it did not budge.

Once again Radcliffe's arm moved slowly upward. But he could not reach the lip.

"He's stuck!" Ordway shouted up through cupped hands. "The rope's stuck!"

There was the hollow echo, a remote answering shout, echo again, silence. Ordway took a sudden step toward the wall.

"Martin!" Carla's voice was quick and sharp. "What are you going to do?"

"I'm going up."

"But you can't possibly reach him."

"I can try."

"No—it's impossible."

He hesitated, staring upward again. And now at last he could hear once more the faint scraping of feet on stone, and after another few minutes Siegfried Hein's head moved slowly out against the sky beyond the rim of the dome.

"The rope's jammed," Ordway called. "Can you see it? Below and to your right."

Hein's head seemed to be nodding, but he did not answer. Ordway could hear the scratting of gravel again as he maneuvered for position, and then his head moved out still farther, followed by his shoulders and arms. He was on the very brink of the cornice now, with his hands reaching down onto the receding wall, and for a minute or more he struggled silently with the rope in the crevice below.

"He can't free it," Carla said.

Hein pulled himself back behind the rim, reappeared in a slightly different position and tried again. Then he withdrew for the second time.

"My God," Ordway murmured. "They must be able to figure out something!"

They waited. Radcliffe revolved slowly on his rope. And then at last Hein moved into view again. This time he wormed forward until not only his head and shoulders but the whole upper half of his body projected out beyond the rim and arched slowly downward. His thighs and legs were apparently prone on the slope of the dome above, but whether it was a second rope or merely a hidden toehold that kept him from plunging on into space Ordway could not tell. He worked out another inch. And then one more. Now his body was motionless, but his arms were moving slowly downward along the brown strand of the rope, and Radcliffe's were moving slowly up to meet them. Suddenly their hands locked. Hein was pulling. Inch by inch, foot by foot, he struggled upward and backward; and inch by inch, foot by foot, the dangling figure below him moved up out of the gray cavern of the recess. Presently Radcliffe's hands were no longer gripping Hein's, but the edge of the cornice. He had passed the crevice into which the rope had wedged, and the rope was free and pulling strongly. There was the sound of scraping and scratching, as first his arms, then his chest, then his waist and legs and finally his feet dragged up over the rim onto the slope above. And an instant later he and Hein had disappeared from view.

There was a distant shout; the shuffle of footsteps; silence. Ordway and Carla waited in the stillness of stone and air.

Then the rope came down. . . .

And there was Carla climbing . . . Carla moving very slowly, yet easily and gracefully, up the long gray slant of the wall . . . groping toward the corner, reaching it, straddling it . . . moving up again, clinging, stretching . . . There was the lunge and the swing and the taut, trembling rope . . . and then Ordway's eyes were closed, his heart pounding and swelling suffocatingly in his throat . . . and when he looked upward at last Carla was gone . . . and there was the stillness again, the waiting again. . . .

The rope descending again. . . .

There were the gray slabs of the recess floor receding slowly beneath him, and the stone of the wall pressing smooth and hard against his face and chest, and his fingers and toes clawing, stiff and straining, at the tiny nubs and cracks. . . . There were the nubs and the cracks, and more nubs and more cracks, and his fingers and toes aching, and the muscle in his right thigh twitching, and the breath rasping in his throat . . . and then at last the notched line of the corner moving slowly toward him out of the sky beyond . . . his legs scraping, slipping, thrusting him up onto the corner . . . and suddenly, sickeningly, the recess gone altogether, and in its place nothingness, and beyond nothingness the precipice, the sun, the white glaciers. . . . There was the next thrust, the next grasp . . . the second . . . the third . . . and the rim of rock above his head, and his hand groping upward, and

286

the sweat in his eyes and the thick bile in his throat . . . and the savage, voiceless *"Now!"*

There was the last thrust, the swing, the slip . . . and gray space revolving behind him . . . and the rope crushing his chest and thudding against his face. . . . There was the rim of rock under his fingers, under his palms, under his elbows, his ribs, his knees . . . a gentle slope of slabs before him . . . the slanting line of the rope . . . the five figures at the end of the rope, a scant ten feet away . . . there was Siegfried Hein's hand reaching out to him and Hein's cool, gray eyes on his face.

"Sieg heil, Herr Kapitän," he said, smiling.

Chapter 16

"Nick—"

Radcliffe did not answer.

"Are you all right, Nick?"

The Englishman's gaze came back from the depths of space and fastened, blue and steady, on Ordway's. He nodded slowly but did not speak.

"How about a little tea?"

"There isn't enough, is there?"

"Of course there is."

"Well—thanks then."

Radcliffe took the canteen and raised it to his lips. The others waited, watching him.

For perhaps fifteen minutes they had rested on the broad, gently sloping slabs that formed the upper surface of the dome. They had not talked; they had scarcely even raised their eyes to the gray walls of the Funnel that still rose massively above them into the sky. They had simply sat or lain motionless, propped against their packs and rucksacks, waiting for strength and will to flow back again into muscles and lungs and hearts. And now at last they had risen again, slung on the packs again.

All except Radcliffe . . .

The Englishman drank, lowered the canteen and sat motionless once more, staring out beyond the rim of the dome.

"We ought to get going, Nick," Ordway said.

The older man nodded, remained as he was for another moment or two and got slowly to his feet. "Yes," he said, his voice very quiet and even. "You must get going."

There was a silence.

"And I'll get going down," said Nicholas Radcliffe.

He turned away suddenly.

"But, Nick—"

There was silence again. Then Radcliffe turned back to them. "I've funked it, old boy, and I know it. . . . And you know it."

"Funked it? Ridiculous! I don't know what you're talking about."

"Yes you do. And so do I. I knew it yesterday morning at the *Bergschrund*; I knew it last night down there on the terrace when we sat listening to the wind; I've known it all morning, coming up the Funnel. But I was too damned pigheaded to admit it. So I kept on going. I kept on fumbling, funking, holding you up. . . ."

"You haven't held us up, I tell you. You've done wonderfully considering—"

"Considering that I'm an old man," said Radcliffe. He paused, smiling thinly. "I found out long ago that there's one thing a mountain can teach a man better than anything else in the world, except perhaps war; and that's the measure of his own strength . . . or weakness."

"But—"

Ordway broke off. He looked at Benner, then at the others, then back at Radcliffe. He started to speak again and stopped.

"Oh no, Nick!" Carla cried suddenly. "You mustn't do this! You can't!"

The Englishman did not answer.

"We'll take it slower than we have," said Ordway. "Andreas thinks the Funnel will be easier from here on, and we'll camp for the night on the upper terrace."

"And tomorrow you will feel stronger again," the girl added.

Radcliffe's eyes moved from one to the other of them, and a long moment passed before he spoke.

"You want to get to the top, don't you?" he asked, very quietly.

"Of course," said Ordway.

"And don't you realize by now that you'll never get there with me?" Radcliffe's glance went to Benner. "Isn't that true, Andreas? Tell them."

The guide hesitated.

"Yes, it is true," Siegfried Hein said suddenly.

The others looked at him. "Thank you, Hein," said Radcliffe.

"It is foolishness to go on with this pretending," the German continued, "because you are right, Herr Radcliffe—you will not make the top. And it is far better you understand it now than later."

Carla broke in angrily. "You haven't any right—"

"On the contrary, my dear," Radcliffe said gently, "Mr. Hein has a perfect right. A few minutes ago he risked his life to pull me up onto this rock. It would only be a question of time before he would have to risk it again—or the rest of you would have to risk yours—to get me out of some new difficulty." He paused and stroked his hand slowly over the ragged gray stubble of his jaw. "No, it is better this way. . . . And now get along with you. You're wasting time."

There was another silence.

"But you can't stay here," Ordway said.

"No, not here. But I can go back to the tent on the terrace and wait for you there."

"Down the Funnel?" Ordway's glance moved to the cornice of the dome and the blue emptiness beyond.

"You can let me down into the recess on one of the ropes. Below that it isn't too bad, and there are the pitons to help. If I take it slowly I shan't have any trouble."

"But even when you get there," Carla protested, "it will be three more days, perhaps four—"

"Don't worry about that," Radcliffe interrupted. "I'm used to being alone in the mountains, after all." He counted off on his fingers, smiling a little. "I shall have my rock specimens to collect; I shall have my flute; and I shall have a five-course victory dinner to prepare for your return."

The girl looked at him without speaking, and there were tears in her eyes. The Englishman reached out and took her hand, in an almost awkward gesture. "And besides," he went on, still smiling a crooked smile, "I'm an old hand at retreat, you know. I had plenty of practice in the last war. And on Everest. And not so long ago in Geneva. So don't look so sad about it—please. The Old Guard may not be very strong on advancing, but it always retreats in good order."

He let go her hand and turned to Benner. "All right, Andreas," he said, his voice suddenly very clipped and British. "If you'll be good enough to let me down now—"

The guide had been standing by silently, his eyes bent to the rock. Now he began slowly to uncoil a spare rope from his shoulders.

"I am coming with you, *Herr Doktor*," he said.

"No."

"*Ja, Herr Doktor.*"

"We will all come," said Carla.

"That's ridiculous!" Radcliffe exclaimed.

"And it is not necessary," the guide said, continuing to uncoil the rope. "Herr Radcliffe and I, we will go down together. With the pitons and some roping down we will be over the steep parts in an hour, and from there Herr Radcliffe can go on to the tent alone. It is now what time?—a little after twelve. The four of you will wait and rest, and I will be back by three; perhaps even sooner."

"I won't hear of it," said Radcliffe.

"I am sorry, *Herr Doktor*, but in this I must insist. I am a guide of Kandermatt, and a guide of Kandermatt does not leave one of his *Herren* to go down a great mountain alone. Such a thing I will not have."

The Englishman continued to protest, but Benner was adamant. While the others watched, he tied one rope around Radcliffe and himself and looped a second behind a projecting boss of rock for the rappel down into the recess.

"All right," he said finally. "We are ready now."

Radcliffe's eyes moved from the guide to Ordway and from Ordway to the others. He seemed about to speak again, but stopped himself and stood motionless. His thin hawk's face, framed in its gray stubble, was as seamed and gray as mountain rock.

Then with a sudden angular movement he turned to Hein and extended his hand. "Good luck," he said. "And thank you. I've been privileged to know many great climbers in my time, but none any greater than you."

"Thank you," said Hein.

Radcliffe turned to Delambre.

"Good luck," he said.

"Thank you. I am sorry—"

The Englishman shook hands with Ordway and then with Carla. "Oh, Nick, Nick," the girl murmured. "You shouldn't do this. You know you could make it, if you would only—"

Radcliffe shook his head. "That's something we're never going to find out," he said. "But I know that you and Martin can—and that's much more important, my dear."

She raised herself suddenly on her toes, kissed him on the cheek and turned away.

"All ready, Andreas?" Radcliffe asked.

"All ready, *Herr Doktor*."

Benner took his stance in a niche in the rocks, ready to belay the guide-rope. Radcliffe picked up the doubled strand of the other rope, wrapped it about him in rappel position and backed slowly toward the rim of the dome. At the very edge he stopped, knelt, and began lowering himself into space below. His long legs disappeared; then his thighs and waist and chest. Only his head and shoulders were now above the level of the rim, and his eyes, as they fastened suddenly on Ordway, were as blue and bright as the sky behind him.

"Good luck, Mallory, old—"

He broke off.

"Good luck, old boy," he said quietly.

And he was gone.

For a while, leaning out over the cornice, they could see the two tiny figures moving down the wall of the Funnel far below. One of them seemed to turn and wave. Then they disappeared. Beneath the cornice the south face of the mountain fell away, empty and still, into the ocean of space.

Carla opened one of the rucksacks and brought out cheese, crackers and a tin of smoked tongue. They ate slowly and in silence, and when they had finished they took a sip of tea apiece from the canteen.

"We should have gone down with him," Carla said.

Ordway shook his head. "What good would it have done? And besides, he'd rather be alone."

"He is a courageous man," said Delambre.

"Yes."

"But without the strength," Hein said. "And without the will." They fell silent again, staring out into the emptiness of sky. Then Hein got to his feet.

"Shall we be starting now?" he asked.

Ordway looked at him in surprise. "Starting?"

"Up. There is still a quarter or more of the Funnel to go."

"But we're going to wait here for Andreas."

"Here?" It was the German's turn to show surprise. "But that is senseless. We will lose the best hours of the day."

"He's only going part way down. He said he'd be back by three."

"Three?" Hein shrugged. "Or perhaps four. He is like all the old guides, this Benner: a steady climber, but slow. But anyhow —to waste three hours here, that is foolishness. We can leave a note for him and mark our route as we go. Also, we will leave one of the packs with a tent and enough food, so he will be able to make his own camp if he does not catch up with us tonight."

He looked from Ordway to Carla, then back to Ordway again. The latter shook his head.

"If we wait here for three or four hours we will never reach the upper ridge before dark."

"Then we'll reach it after dark. Or tomorrow."

"Tomorrow? . . . But we are a day behind our schedule already. This weather will not last forever. Nor our food either." Hein paused again, and his thin lips tightened slightly against his teeth. "Do not take offense if I tell you something, Captain Ordway. This is no tea-party, or even an ordinary mountain ascent, that we are on. An adversary like the Weissturm one does not conquer except by fighting."

"And you suggest we do this fighting by leaving our guide behind?"

"Not by leaving him, no. Simply by pushing on as far as we can each day. The Englishman was weak and holding us up, but now that he has gone we must take advantage of our opportunities. Benner will catch up with us, do not worry. One man can

293

climb much faster than four, and besides we will mark out the route for him."

Hein stopped and waited, but Ordway did not answer.

"You will not go?"

"No."

"Have you any objections then if I go alone?"

"Alone?"

"Why not?" The faint smile came again into the German's gray eyes. "If our aging friend Benner can come up the Funnel by himself, do you think perhaps that I am not competent to go on alone?"

"I don't question your competence. But I'm familiar enough with mountains to know that a climbing party should stay together, insofar as possible."

"Is it not perhaps better to say 'insofar as sensible'? Surely you do not believe that on a mountain, any more than in war, the weaker should be permitted to pull down the stronger?"

Ordway looked at Hein curiously. "Are we talking about the war now," he asked, "or about climbing a mountain?"

"About both. And I do not think you will find so great a difference between the two by the time we are through with the Weissturm, and it with us."

Ordway was silent for a few moments, his eyes on the veined gray pattern of the rocks. "Do as you like," he said. "As I told you once before, I'm not running this show any more than anyone else."

"In that case—"

Hein picked up one of the packboards and slung it on his shoulders. At the same time Delambre, who had been sitting by, listening quietly, got to his feet and approached him.

"I shall go too," he said.

The German eyed him in surprise. "With me? . . . You are sure you want to?"

"If you do not object. Nor the others." Delambre's glance went to Ordway, but the latter did not speak. "It is better, if we are to split for a while, that we do it two by two. And besides—" He hesitated, and his whole body seemed to go suddenly tense. "—Besides, I agree with you. To climb such a mountain as this, one must push on—one must struggle."

294

Hein looked at him curiously; the gray smile flickered again across his eyes and disappeared. "With only two of us we may be climbing faster than before," he said.

"Yes, I know."

"And there will be less protection from the rope."

Delambre nodded, and there was another pause.

"As you say then," said Hein.

Ordway watched silently while the Frenchman made his preparations. Climbing first on a different rope and then at the extreme end after they joined ropes, he had had little chance to observe Delambre during the long, arduous hours of the morning, and was aware now, for the first time, of the remarkable change that had come over him. The signs of fatigue and distress that he had shown so plainly on the wasteland and the glacier were altogether gone. While Radcliffe, hour by hour, step by step, had grown tireder and weaker, he, apparently, had gained in strength and endurance with every new difficulty that confronted him. Not comparable in his technique as a climber to either Benner or Hein, nor even to Carla or Radcliffe, he had nevertheless fared as well as any of them on that savage vertical waste of rock and ice: inching steadily, doggedly upward, bearing his share of the burdens and hardships without complaint, compensating for his lack of skill and experience by the sheer drive and determination of his will.

Even his face, it seemed to Ordway, had changed. True, the skin was still sallow and bloodless, the lips cracked, the stubbled flesh drawn parchment-tight over the jawline. But whereas the previous day these had added up to an appearance of almost comic dishevelment, their effect now was to give his thin, fine-boned features a strength and rough-edged distinction that they had not possessed before. Slinging on his pack and taking ax and rope-end in his hand, he stood motionless for a few moments staring up at the mountainside above them. . . . Like a pointer freezing, Ordway thought. Or like a fine coiled spring at the heart of an intricate and delicate machine. . . . *Gespannt*, Andreas Benner had called it. Tight. And he had been right and at the same time wrong. For the weighted rope had not broken; the coiled spring had not snapped. The gray time-weathered iron of which Nicholas Radcliffe was made had slowly rusted and dissolved in that sterile, pitiless emptiness of rock and space, but the thin steel and platinum strands of Paul Delambre's spirit had seemed to grow ever tighter, tauter, stronger.

Now the Frenchman turned his head a little, so that Ordway could see his eyes. They were gazing upward, dark and unmoving. And once again, as he watched him, Ordway remembered those same eyes, dark and large behind their lenses, staring at the brandy in a crested glass, at the gold-and-white loveliness of the woman who was his wife, at the remote and shining snows of the Weissturm above the green slopes and meadows of the valley of Kandermatt. He saw them again, dark with hunger—dark with doubt and desire and dreams. And then suddenly he heard again the voice from the tent on the terrace, clear and terror-laden in the mountain night: "Voyez donc—la glace. La glace . . ."

Hein's voice broke abruptly in upon his thoughts. "You are ready now?" he asked Delambre.

"Yes, I am ready."

"Let us start then." Hein turned to Ordway. "We will continue straight up the Funnel, I think. From its appearance it will be easier from here on, but if there should be any difficulties we will leave pitons and markers for you."

Ordway nodded, without speaking.

"At the top we will try to cross over the upper terrace to the ridge. If we cannot reach it before dark we will make camp somewhere on the terrace and flash a light down so that you can find us."

"And if you do reach the ridge, but we can't?"

"Then we will make separate camps for the night, and in the morning I will come down early and lead you up."

"I see. Thanks," said Ordway. He looked at Hein quizzically. "Is there anything else?"

The German hesitated. "Only that I suggest you do not wait after three o'clock for your giude. The Funnel is no place to be caught by the darkness."

"He'll be back by three."

"Perhaps yes. Perhaps no."

It was a moment before Ordway spoke again. "You don't think much of Benner as a mountaineer, do you?" he asked.

Hein shrugged. "As I said before, he is like all the Swiss guides:

296

steady but plodding, and tied down with all manners of peasant traditions and superstitions. And also—"

"Yes?"

"Also he is afraid of the mountain."

Ordway did not answer, and Hein turned away. "We will see you later then," he said.

"Yes."

"Either tonight or in the morning."

"Yes."

Hein scrambled up the slabs to the rear of the ledge and stood briefly squinting upward. Then he began to climb, and Delambre climbed after him. In a few minutes they were fifty feet up on the rock-face; in another few, almost a hundred. . . .

And then they too were gone. Above and below the ledge there was now only the stillness of rock and blue air.

"I suppose I was wrong," Ordway said presently.

Carla looked at him questioningly.

"I could have kept them from going."

"If you had wanted to."

"Then why didn't I want to?"

"I think it was for the reason that you gave before: that you do not wish to tell others what to do."

"No, I don't want to tell others what to do." Ordway was silent a moment, gazing out across the gray rim of the ledge. "This Hein bird—" he asked musingly; "what do you make of him?"

"I have told you before: he is a German."

"And that explains everything?"

"It explains a lot."

"He's an army officer—did you know that?"

"Yes."

"How?"

"I have known a great many German officers, Martin."

"And he wants awfully damn badly to climb this mountain. You know that too?"

Carla nodded. "Yes, he wants very much to climb it; and because he is a German he shows it in a different way from other people."

"Different from Nick's way, for instance."

"Yes, different from Nick's," she said. "Poor Nick . . ."

They were silent again, sitting side by side on the broad shelf of the rock, and he was thinking about Radcliffe and then about Siegfried Hein and then about Radcliffe again and Andreas Benner and the Frenchman Delambre. Or, more accurately, he was trying to think of them, but with very little success; for the more he thought now the vaguer their faces and shapes and voices became in his mind; the more he struggled to bring them into focus the farther they seemed to recede into blurred, misty distance. He looked up and down, and there was rock and space. He looked around him. There was an island in the sky. The others were gone, everything else was gone and remote and insubstantial beyond the white ranges and the blue sea of air—in that half-remembered other world where war was, and *The Spirit of Perth Amboy*, and Ted and Harry and Bix. . . . .

There was a girl beside him, watching him.

"What is the matter, Martin?" she asked.

"Nothing," he said.

"What is it that you want?"

He looked at the girl's face, at her hair, at her faded flannel shirt and the brown V of her throat. "I want to look at you," he said.

"You may look at me."

"And I want to touch you."

"You may touch me too."

He reached out his hand and ran a finger downward around the line of her ear. Then he let it run lightly along her throat and up to her cheek and along the cheek to the mouth and across the mouth. And then he was holding her very closely and tightly to him and kissing the cool soft warmness of her mouth.

When he let her go and looked at her his eyes were smiling. "It's nice to see you again," he said.

"You have seen me all the time the last few days."

"But not the right parts of you. All I see when we're climbing are your backside and the nails of your boots."

"Oh. And those parts do not please you?"

"They please me very much—especially those lovely tricouni nails. But I get a little tired of them after a while."

"You will get tired of my face after a while too."

"No. Your face is beautiful."

"It is chapped and dirty."

"It's chapped and dirty and beautiful, all at the same time." He bent and kissed her again on the mouth. Then, very lightly and gently, he kissed her eyelids and the tip of her nose and her ear and the soft hollow beneath the ear and the soft brown V of her throat. And as he kissed her he felt her body trembling and her hands holding his head, and he put his arms around her and held her again, tight and close.

"Shall I tell you some other things I want?" he said.

"Yes."

"I want to dance with you."

"We are dancing now."

"I want to dance with you on a late June night on the terrace of a little roadhouse on Long Island Sound. I want to drive back to New York in the moonlight along the Hutchinson River Parkway and keep trying to put my arm around you while you keep reminding me of the traffic. I want to stop off for a nightcap at Tony's and a bowl of cornflakes at Childs'. And then I want to go to bed and wake up in the morning, and there's the sun shining over the Third Avenue El, and there's the orange juice and coffee and the Sunday Times, and maybe even the comic section of the Journal, and you."

He paused a moment.

"I want to marry you, Carla," he said.

She did not speak, but sat very quietly beside him with her head bent over so that it rested against his shoulder. And then suddenly her body began to tremble again, very gently, and he realized that she was crying.

"Carla," he said. "Carla, sweet—"

"Oh, Martin, Martin," she murmured. "What is this thing that has happened to us?"

"A very simple thing. We've fallen in love."

"But we can't."

"We have."

He raised her head and kissed her again and sat looking at her without speaking, smiling a little. But she did not smile back at him.

"And now?" she said.

"Now we both know it."

"But I am—" She broke off and looked away from him, and when she spoke again her voice was almost inaudible. "I am a married woman, Martin."

"You were a married woman. Soon you'll be a married woman again."

"Soon?"

"We'll work things out somehow."

"How? When?"

"We'll work it out, I tell you."

"When the war is over, you mean. When you have gone away again and will never come back." A sudden convulsive sob shook the girl's body, and she covered her face with her hands. "Yes, I know it. That is the way it will be."

"Carla—" he said.

"That is the only way it can be. And it is better—better—better. . . . Oh, can't you see, Martin? This thing is no good for us. It is no good for you. . . . You are an American. You will fight this terrible war to the end, and win it, and go home and begin your life again. I am an Austrian, and for the rest of the world that is no different from a German. I am a German without a country —a refugee—a fugitive. Remember what I am, Martin, and what I have done. Remember Stefan—and that I have killed my child. . . ."

"Stop it!" Ordway put his hands on her shoulders and drew her toward him again. "Carla—stop."

"What I am saying is true."

"What you're saying is about what's past. It has nothing to do with the future. Nothing to do with you and me."

She began to speak, but he bent quickly and kissed her, and then pulled her head down so that it rested against his chest. "Don't talk about it any more," he told her.

Her shoulders were still trembling a little as he held her, but she did not speak.

"Don't think about it any more," he said.

. . . . And now the girl was quiet in his arms, and he sat looking out over her head at the gray rim of the ledge and the emptiness beyond. And as the minutes passed it seemed to him that once again the emptiness was closing slowly in about him, as it had done so often before in the plane, in the valley, in the wasteland, on the glaciers and walls and ridges of the mountain—except that this time, within it and behind the emptiness, there were the sound of Carla's voice and the fear in Carla's eyes. He looked down, and there was her body against his own; there were her arms and the line of her cheek and the glowing coppery softness of her hair. But beyond them there was still emptiness. And as he stared upward and outward again it seemed to him almost as if, far in the depths of space, an immense violin string had suddenly been drawn taut and snapped, and that where its music had been was now only a low, fading reverberation, and that where the bright sun and blue sky had been were once again the gray shadow of immense spreading wings.

Don't think about it, he had said. . . .

Not about the past, not about the future. Not about the world, the war, the bomb-run, the plane, the dead. Not of the dark recess below or the savage heights above, but only of here and now —the girl in your arms—your bright, tight sunlit little hour on your island in the sky.

He squinted upward, not moving. . . . Was it only his imagination again, or was there actually a shadow, a thin, gently moving veil interposing itself between them and the sun? Its face seemed less golden now than yellow, the sky no longer ocean-blue but a remote and lustreless gray. He listened—and there was only stillness. He continued listening—and presently, very faint and elusive within the stillness, there was the same distant sound that he had heard the previous night on the terrace far below. It rose, wavered, subsided, rose again, fell. Then there was only stillness again. There was only rock and sky and the yellow sunlight, and high on the mountainside above them, a long whitish scarf of vapor trailing out to the east.

Carla stirred slightly in his arms.

"Martin—" she said.

"Yes, sweet?"

"I am sorry."

"Stop it," he said.

"No, truly, I am sorry. We are so happy—so very happy—and each time I spoil it because I am afraid of our happiness."

"Stop it, stop it, stop it," he said.

"Because I am a coward and a—"

He bent and covered her mouth with his. He drew her to him,

gently at first, then more strongly and more tightly, and still more strongly and still more tightly, until he was holding her with an aching tenderness and fierceness of desire. And then he raised his head a little and looked down at her and smiled and said, "Hello, Carla, my wife."

"Hello, Martin, my husband."

Her eyes smiled back at him and then closed, and she lay still again, and he sat holding her in the stillness on the gray rock of the mountainside.

Look at her, he said to himself. Look at her now. . . .

He looked at her hair and her eyelids and the brown softness of her cheek and throat and the slow rise and fall of her breathing under her flannel shirt. You're dreaming it, he thought. You're back on your bunk in the Quonset hut beside the strip, and you're dreaming. In the long lonely nights of those past two years he had held many women in his arms. Sometimes it had been Joan Nettleton and sometimes May (or Kay), the Powers (or Conover) girl; sometimes it had been Rita Hayworth or Ingrid Bergman and once even Catherine the Great; and sometimes a woman without a name—any woman—everywoman; but always in the end it was no woman; always in the end there was only the dark bunk and yourself and your loneliness and womanlessness crying out at you in the night. . . . Yes, he thought, it was the dream again. It was the same again. . . . Only not quite the same—the ending not the same—because this dream was real; the woman was real.

Because the woman was Carla.

She is real, he thought, looking down at her. She is real and she is yours and she is everything there is. No—keep the record straight —not everything. But a part of everything; a hell of a big part of everything. Part of all you have ever been, and are, and ever will be. Part of the Temple of Science and the Grimbacks' garage and that first solo flight long ago in the Piper Cub. Part of New York in an October dusk and Long Island Sound in the summer sunlight and the Hudson Valley in the spring. Part of the war, even. Not the bloody, dirty, roaring day-to-day war of killing and dying —but the other war, the war you had once believed in and thought worth the fighting, the war that had to do not with death but with life. Part of living itself, of wanting itself. Part of the White Tower, rising shining and serene into the emptiness of space. . . .

He looked upward again; listened again. The whitish scarf of vapor high above was longer and denser, and he could hear the sound of the distant wind. . . . It's growing stronger, he thought. It's growing stronger and it's blowing from the west.

Yes, she was part of everything, he thought. And she was not a dream, but real. Only she wasn't going to stay real very much longer if he didn't start doing some pretty fast deciding about what they were going to do. . . . You've got to do more thinking, he told himself. You've got to think clearly and honestly and truly, without always getting yourself fouled up in your goddamned emotions. . . . Sure, that was fine. You could think about Carla without emotion just as easily as you could eat your food without chewing or climb a mountain without using your feet. . . . Still he had to try. Perhaps he could do it in a roundabout way. Perhaps he could start by thinking about something else—about one of those any-number-of-things that Carla was a part of—and work back to her gradually.

All right. What was there? . . . There was the war. . . . There was always the war. But what were you supposed to think about it? There had been a time, two years, three years ago, when he had thought about it a great deal; when he had thought about it in terms of strategy and campaigns and nations and history and ultimate purpose. Later he had thought of it in terms of missions, targets, interphones, R.P.M.'s, fuel-gauge readings, and still later in terms of burst, flame, concussion, dying, death. Now he scarcely thought about it at all. He could fight it, experience it, live or die in it, but he could not think about it. Certainly he could not think about it in reference to Carla. The hell with the war.

What else was there? . . . Politics. . . . Politics were damned important. The smaller and more entangled and more bloody the world got, the more important they were. Politics were himself and Carla multiplied a billion times; two billion people, instead of two, struggling to find a way of living together and not being very successful about it. What were his politics then? Not much of anything, when you came down to it. Most of all he believed in a free society; but he also knew that it had become the sort of a world in which you had to have a planned, controlled society, and how you could have both of them at the same time he did not know. Probably it was democracy he believed in: the big vague editorial-page sort of democracy. Certainly not in Democrats. Nor in Republicans. Nor in socialism or communism or—God help him—fascism. It is strange, he thought. You were willing to fight politically. You were willing, if you had to, to die politically. But you were not willing, you would never be willing, to live or think politically. That was for other people; you had something else to do. You had a girl to marry, a living to earn, garages to build, bungalows in Pawtucket to build. You would be a moderately good citizen, you hoped. You would vote when the time came, and for the right man. You would read, discuss, argue, even fight again. But you would never, truly and wholly, belong anywhere politically—and you knew it—because the world that you yourself inhabited was composed primarily, not of parties, causes, systems, nations, but of individual human beings, and you could never believe that any governmental system, however sound and enlightened, held the ultimate key to their salvation.

Politics. And after that, what? . . . Religion. . . . It was the same thing, really, in a different dimension. The need of the many to identify themselves with something greater than themselves. The ability of the few to use that need to gain power over the many. In the war-books he occasionally read pilots were supposed to do a lot of praying. He had never prayed, though. And he was willing to bet that, outside of the Catholics, practically no one he had known in the squadron ever prayed. Not that a lot of them wouldn't have liked to. Not that he hadn't often wanted to himself. The trouble was, there was plenty to pray for but nothing to pray with. The religion people like himself had been brought up in had to do with christenings, weddings, funerals. It had to do with Bible stories, organ recitals, the election of vestrymen, charity pageants, servicemens' canteens. There was nothing wrong about any of it. It was all fine, admirable, okay. But what good did it do a man holding his intestines in his lap or frying to death in the jammed turret of a bomber? What did it have to do with pain or evil or fear or faith?

Faith—that was it. Christalmighty how you needed it in the bloody, cockeyed, fouled-up world in which you lived. . . . Faith in yourself; in what you were doing; in your fellow-men in something above and beyond yourself and all men. . . . But where were you going to find it? There were many men, there were whole nations, who no longer found it in religion at all, but in their politics. There were many, too, who still found it in the rituals and patterns of their ancient creeds. Andreas, for example. Where, anywhere, could you find a man with a deeper strength and serenity than Andreas Benner drew from the depths of his simple peasant piety? The only difficulty, of course, was that what worked for others wouldn't work for you. Andreas' faith wouldn't be strength for you. It would be hypocrisy and weakness.

You're doing fine, aren't you, Ordway old boy? he told himself savagely. Do you know what the trouble with you is? There are two troubles with you. The first is that you don't believe in anything. And the second is that you can't think straight about anything. Every time you try to stand off and look at yourself—or at other people or the war or the world or any damn thing—the same thing happens. It's like holding a book up to a mirror and trying to read it. Everything is there: letters, words, punctuation marks, all of it, familiar and unchanged. And still you can't read it. It's no longer a pattern, but a hieroglyphic; no longer a symbolic representation of intelligible ideas, but an indecipherable mess of strokes, dots and curlycues.

Yes, he thought, that's what has happened. All design has disappeared. All meaning has disappeared.

And yet . . .

Somewhere still, somewhere always, there was design and meaning and a vast, deep, secret harmony. That much he knew, and that much he had always known. It was not a thing that you could understand or embrace or possess, but that came to you out of the unknowable in the merest fragments and intimations. In your dreams, sometimes. In a face, a voice, a scene, a shared experience. You had heard it in the bars of certain symphonies and the lines of certain poems and the hooting of a great foghorn on a ship at night. You had seen it in the prim lines of a blueprint on a drafting board and in the clean bright sweep of plane-wings across a sunlit sky. You saw it in Carla's eyes, heard it in her voice, felt it in her body. You saw and heard and felt it as you stared up at the White Tower, rising immense and gleaming above the valleys and the ranges. . . .

He looked up again. The sun was yellower and the sky was grayer. The streak of vapor had multiplied into many streaks, and they were streaming out like great white pennons from the mountainside. When he looked down Carla had opened her eyes.

"You can hear the wind," she said.

He nodded.

"It is from the west."

"Yes."

"What are we going to do if the weather turns?" she asked.

"Wait here for Andreas."

"And when he comes?"

He was silent a moment. "What do you want to do?" he asked.

"Go on."

"You're sure?"

"I am sure. Aren't you?"

"Yes, I'm sure too."

There was another pause.

"Martin—" she said.

"Yes?"

"Kiss me."

He bent and kissed her and held her close to him again, and then he let her gently down and sat looking at her, and she lay quietly in his arms looking up at the mountainside.

"Do you remember the last time we were together on a mountain ledge?" she asked.

"Of course."

"That is what I have been thinking about while my eyes were closed. How we shivered there all night in the darkness. And how frightened we were, although none of us would admit it. And then in the morning, how we waited for Andreas—"

"As we're waiting now."

"Except that this time Andreas is not coming to take us down."

"No."

"And this time we are not frightened."

"No."

Carla's eyes were on him now, very deep and gray and still. "This time we are going to climb the White Tower, aren't we, Martin?"

"Yes, this time we're going to climb it."

She closed her eyes again, and when she reopened them they were smiling a little.

"Martin," she said.

"Yes?"

"Martin—"

Chapter 17

Three o'clock came; a quarter past three; half past. The mountainside fell away, empty and still, below them. The only sounds were the faint hum of wind above and the quiet ticking on Ordway's wrist.

Creeping to the rim of the ledge, he peered downward again, but there was only rock and space. . . . And then, suddenly, in the stillness, the tiniest flicker of movement. . . . He waited, eyes straining, and there was another movement.

"He's coming!" he called to Carla.

She came forward and lay prone beside him on the rim, and they watched the blurred movement become a definable speck and the speck become a human figure and the figure become Andreas Benner. They shouted and waved, and Benner waved back. In ten minutes he was working slowly up the slabs below the recess; in another ten he was out of sight on the recess floor. Ordway let down one of the ropes and belayed it from the niche at the back of the ledge, but there was no pull on it as the guide came up the wall and corner beneath them. Presently his square brown face appeared above the edge of the cornice; then his shoulders and chest and a crooked, thrusting knee. In another moment he was sitting beside them on the smooth slabs of the ledge.

Ordway laid a tight hand on his shoulder.

"I am sorry, Herr Martin—" Benner began.

"You can talk in a minute," Carla interrupted. "First there are more important things."

She handed him an opened canteen of tea, and he sipped it slowly. Ordway noticed that he held the canteen in both hands and that his massive chest was rising and falling in deep, slow breaths.

"I am sorry—" he began again.

"The hell with that," Ordway said. "How did it go?"

"It went all right. But slow."

"And how's Nick?"

"The *Herr Doktor* is at the tent now. There is nothing to worry about. . . . But he was tired, Herr Martin. He was very tired."

"How far down did you go with him?" Carla asked.

"In the beginning I had thought I would go only past the wet section—you remember it? Well, we get past it, and I let Doktor Radcliffe off the rope to see how he will do alone; but almost the first step he takes he slips and begins to fall. So I go on with him to the big boulders below."

"You went the whole way down the Funnel then?"

"To the boulders, ja. From there it was only walking, and no difficulties. As I was climbing up again I kept looking back and saw him coming to the tent. There are plenty of food and supplies there. He will rest and be all right."

"How were his spirits?" asked Ordway.

"*Bitte?*"

"His spirits. How did he feel?"

Benner shrugged. "He was tired. He was very tired. All the way down we did not speak at all. Only at the end, when we were saying good-bye."

"What did he say then?"

"He said, 'Andreas, you are going to climb the Weissturm. You and Herr Ordway and Fräulein Dehn—you are going to climb it.' "

"That's all?"

"*Ja*, Herr Martin, that is all."

While they talked Carla had taken chocolate and dried fruit from one of the packs. Now she offered them to Benner, but he shook his head.

"You should," she told him.

308

"Later, danke. I am not hungry now. Besides—" He stopped, looking around him. "The others—where are they?"

"They've gone on," Ordway said.

"On? Up?"

Ordway nodded. "Hein practically insisted on going. And Delambre wanted to string along. They're to wait for us either on the upper terrace or the ridge."

"So?" Benner was silent a moment, his square face clouded and his eyes on the rocks. "Herr Hein is a fine climber, to be sure. He is one of the finest climbers I have seen in almost thirty years as a guide. Still I do not like such things. A party it should stay together on a mountain like the Weissturm."

Ordway nodded.

"And Monsieur Delambre?" the guide asked. "What did he say?"

"He didn't say much of anything. But he wanted to keep on, and as long as Hein was going anyhow I didn't see any harm in it. If he's going to get into any trouble Hein can be of more help to him than I could."

"He has done well so far, Monsieur Delambre."

"Yes."

"And he did not seem tired?"

"Not especially."

Benner stroked his chin slowly. "It is remarkable," he said. "Very remarkable. Perhaps I was wrong when I spoke to you about him the other day on the wasteland."

"He's been damn good so far. No doubt about it."

There was another silence.

"You should eat something, Andreas," Carla said.

"Later, danke."

"Some more tea then."

"There is enough?"

"Of course."

Benner took the canteen and drank again. Then he got to his feet. "Also—" he said.

"You should rest some more."

"I have rested enough. And besides, it is already late. We must be out of the Funnel before dark."

For a little while he stood peering up at the rock-walls above them. Then his gaze moved slowly outward to the long vapor-trails that streaked the sky and the pale westering disc of the sun.

"Not good," said Ordway.

"No, it is not good."

"The wind's from the west now."

"*Ja.*"

They were quiet, listening.

"And stronger."

"*Ja.*"

"What do you think, Andreas?"

The guide shrugged. "In the winter a wind from the west is always bad. In the summer, no. In the spring and fall one cannot tell—especially from this side of the mountain. Sometimes I have seen it like this, and it is all clear again by evening. Sometimes it is a little squall or a snow flurry—"

"And sometimes it's a storm."

It was not a question, but a statement, and Benner did not answer. "In any case," Ordway continued, "there's nothing to do but go on."

"No. With the others above, that is all we can do."

"And keep our fingers crossed."

"*Bitte?*"

"And hope for the best."

"*Ja*—and hope for the best."

They slung on the packs again, tied themselves to the rope again. Then they were climbing again. Benner went first, Carla next, Ordway last. The ledge receded slowly beneath them. The rock-walls flowed slowly past.

For the first few minutes Ordway could scarcely drag himself upward. After the long rest on the ledge his whole body was tight and stiff; his bones seemed almost to be locked in their sockets, and the muscular twitch in his right thigh that had bothered him earlier in the day returned suddenly with increased, almost ludicrous violence. Calling up to the others to stop, he flexed and rubbed the leg vigorously, and presently the twitching subsided. When he moved on again it did not return, and some of the stiffness and numbness seemed to have drained from him. His body was still tired, and he was still conscious of a dull throbbing ache

310

deep within his bones. But at least they were doing the job they had to do.

He glanced up at Carla, clambering over the rocks some thirty feet above. She was tired too, he knew. He had felt the tiredness in her body as she lay quietly and with closed eyes in his arms on the sunlit ledge below. Yet now that they were climbing again, she did not show it in any way. Her body moved as lightly and gracefully as if she had just come out of the inn for an afternoon's walk along the paths beside the Aarn. . . . What the hell is she made of, he wondered. Steel? . . . No—he smiled to himself a little—not steel. Most definitely and definitively Carla's body was not made of steel. Of what, then? Silk and radium maybe. Whatever it was, it was wonderful.

As Hein had prophesied, the climbing in the section of the Funnel in which they now found themselves was not particularly difficult. The walls rising above them were still steep, almost to verticality, and on either side of the shallow couloir the precipices of the south face swept sheer and unbroken from space above into space below. But the rock was sound under their hands and feet. Always, where they needed it, there was a ledge, a crack, a knob, a bulge, a platform, and nowhere did they encounter a problem comparable to the climb up out of the recess, or even to the ascent of the almost holdless slabs below it. Benner still worked his way upward with patient care and deliberation, and their actual movements were no faster than before. Climbing three on a rope, however, was a much simpler matter than with six; there was less belaying and shorter waits between pitches; and their progress was correspondingly quickened. They climbed for twenty-five minutes, rested for five, climbed on again. . . .

And now, presently, the Funnel began to grow narrower and deeper again. Its trough bit further and further into the mountainside, and its walls slowly converged, until it was no longer a mere groove but once again a deep shaft in the rock, as it had been in its lower reaches above the snow-slope of the terrace. Above and below them now were only long vistas of shouldering stone, behind them the thin slit of the sky. The slit, however, was no longer the shining blue it had been before, but as gray as the rock that framed it.

Ordway looked at his watch. It was almost five. Leaning out

from his holds, he twisted his neck and peered upward, but he could not find the sun. It was impossible to tell how much of the grayness was caused by clouds or mist and how much by the approach of dusk. He clung motionless to the rock, listening. He could hear the faint scraping of bootnails above, and, through it, the sound of the wind. The sound no longer seemed to come from far overhead, but from all around him—above and below and on every side. Its hollow moaning filled the dark shaft of the Funnel; it was almost as if he could feel it vibrating within the solid, looming walls of mountain rock.

With an involuntary gesture he moved his hand slowly over the rough granite before his face. It was hard and still and very cold. Suddenly he became aware that the air had grown much colder too. There was no wind in the Funnel—only the sound of the wind —but a gray tide of coldness seemed to be pouring down along the walls from its upper reaches, pressing gently against his face and hands and fumbling at the crevices of his clothing. Holding on with one hand at a time, he held the other for a few moments in his armpit. Then the rope jerked softly at his waist.

For a little while now the going grew harder. It became necessary in places to climb not only with hands and feet, but also with elbows, knees and the friction of chest and thighs, and there were occasional long pauses during which he could hear Benner scratting about above in search of holds and stances. In the middle of a particularly ugly, almost holdless pitch he became aware of Carla calling down to him and pointing, and in the gloom ahead he saw the steel head of a piton protruding from the rock. He reached for it, grasped it, pulled himself up. And as he did so he realized suddenly that there had been no sound of hammering. The piton was not Benner's, but someone else's . . . Hein's. . . . Thirty feet higher up there was another, and beyond that a third. Then the angle of ascent began to ease off again. There were more holds, broader ledges. The rock-walls sloped sharply to the left, and he came out on a broad, almost level platform and stood beside Benner and Carla, peering upward.

The top of the Funnel was in sight. Directly over their heads its containing walls flared out again, but this time far more widely than before, and in the broad angle that they formed, perhaps a hundred feet above, was a curving rim of snow, and beyond it the slate-gray sky.

"The upper terrace," said Ordway.

Benner nodded. His eyes moved slowly up the sloping walls, first to the left and then to the right. Suddenly they stopped, and, following his gaze, Ordway saw a small cairn of five or six loose stones piled on a level shelf about a third of the way up the right-hand wall.

It was no longer a question of climbing, but simply of scrambling up over gently sloping slabs, and they went one directly behind another, holding the slack of the rope in coils over their arms. But now for the first time they felt, as well as heard, the wind. A sudden bitter gust swooped down from the terrace above, caught Ordway's pack sidewise and almost threw him from his feet. He caught and steadied himself just in time for a second and a third. The sound above them was no longer a humming but a roar, and then no longer a roar but a thin vibrating scream. Like a Focke-Wulff diving, Ordway thought. Like a whole damned skyful of Focke-Wulffs. . . .

They passed the guiding cairn, threaded a short stretch of tumbled boulders and worked their way up a deep gully that cut transversely upward toward the crest of the slope. The walls of the Funnel were beneath them now. The Funnel itself was beneath them, and on either side the precipices of the east face fell away, sheer and unbroken, into space. Ordway looked down. There was snow under his feet. He looked up, and there was snow ahead. He moved forward, crouching, into a wall of wind.

Suddenly his bent head bumped into something. Carla. She had stopped, and Benner, ahead of her, had stopped too, and was peering around him. After a few moments he pointed off to the right and began moving again. They cut off diagonally across the slope for perhaps twenty paces, rounded an outcropping of white-powdered boulders and descended behind them into a small hollow in the snow. Benner unslung his pack and sat down on it. "It is at least a little shelter," he said.

"See any signs of them?" Ordway asked.

"Not yet."

"The snow is too hard for footprints," said Carla.

They sat close together, staring out into the scudding dusk. To the right and left of them, rimming the mountainside, the snow band of the upper terrace curved white and faintly gleaming into the distance. Far narrower and steeper than the terrace below, it was, indeed, scarcely a terrace at all, but merely a sharply tilted ramp, perhaps fifty feet in breadth, cutting horizontally across the east face between its middle and upper tiers of precipices. Below them, on both sides of the opening of the Funnel, were white eaves and space; above them sheer rock, rising out of sight into the dusk above. It was not on these, however, that their eyes were fixed, but on the long ribbon of the ramp itself; on the point, far off to the right, where the gleam of snow suddenly stopped and an immense, soaring arc of rock clove through it and climbed upward against the sky. The ridge, Ordway thought, his heart suddenly pounding. It was the southeast ridge, at last. . . .

"The terrace goes all the way," Carla was saying.

Benner nodded.

"We can make it then."

"Ja, we should be able to make it. Provided—"

The guide broke off and squinted upward, studying the sky. The sun was gone. No trace remained of it, or even of its afterglow, and in its place was only the vast and unrelieved grayness of distance and dusk. Ordway's eyes searched the horizon for clouds; but there were none—or at least no individual and recognizable cloud-shapes. Rather did the sky itself seem to be a cloud, opaque and brooding, arching from horizon to horizon. There was no movement anywhere, except the wind; no sound except the wind. Snow-slope and rock-wall, peak, valley and glacier sprawled away into the gray miles, wrapped in a frozen arctic twilight.

Now Benner was gazing at the ridge again. "What is the time, Herr Martin?" he asked.

Ordway looked at his watch. "Ten of six."

The guide nodded. "At this height there will still be a little light until after seven. If the wind does not get any stronger we may be all right."

"It can't get much stronger than this, can it?"

"Very much stronger. But whether it will or not—" Benner shrugged. "In any case, we should be going now."

They drank a mouthful of tea apiece, put on their woolen helmets and extra sweaters and loosened the ice axes from the webbing of their packs. Then they got stiffly to their feet.

"How about the others?" Carla asked.

"Ja," said Benner. "First we should look for signs of the others."

The wind lashed at them as they came up out of the hollow. Separating, they moved slowly up and down at rope's length from one another, searching for tracks or markers; but whatever loose snow had once lain on the terrace had long since blown away, and the old crust that remained was frozen almost to the consistency of ice. When he turned, every few paces, to look behind him, Ordway could not see the prints of his own boots. To look for those of men who had passed by two or three hours before was obviously hopeless.

A moment later, however, Carla's voice was calling out to him, and as he and Benner rejoined her he saw that there was a trail and that she had found it. Running in an almost straight line along the center of the snow-ramp was a clearly visible chain, not of footprints, but of minute, evenly-spaced holes.

"Gut," said Benner, nodding. "Their axes."

Taking out a pair of binoculars, they swept them slowly along the terrace, but there was no other sign of Hein and Delambre. Before them was the empty white ribbon of snow. To the left, rock-walls. To the right, nothingness. They put away the binoculars, readjusted their packs and rope and started off.

For the first time now since they had left the lower reaches of the glacier they were not climbing but walking virtually on the level, and the effect, after the long hours of watching the mountainside rise up before them, was almost that of moving downhill. There was nothing easy about the going, however. The sharp outward tilt of the ramp and the hard-packed surface made it necessary for them to proceed with great caution, making sure of each foothold before trusting their weight to it and steadying themselves constantly with their axes. Also, and much worse, there was the wind. Fortunately it was coming mostly from behind them—they would scarcely have been able to advance at all if they had been meeting it head on—but the very momentum that it gave them added to the difficulties of balance and the danger of a slip. For minutes on end it would beat in a steady roaring tide at their backs. Then, suddenly and unpredictably, it would drop, only to be followed a moment later by wild gusts beating at them from in front and both sides. Another lull would follow, and then again the steady torrent from behind. Sometimes its initial blast, catching them unprepared, all but knocked them forward onto their knees.

Ordway walked with his head bent, his eyes on the jerking strands of the rope and the tiny dark holes in the snow that flowed slowly past his feet. There was a whole mosaic of ax-marks now—not only Hein's and Delambre's but also Benner's and Carla's, and then finally his own. He began counting them, lost track, began counting them again. Then he noticed that the natural swing of his arms brought the point of his ax down at the exactly same spacing as another set of holes. He found himself wondering whose they were. Carla's, he hoped. There's a fine start for a marriage already, he told himself, smiling a little: you swing your ice axes so that they come down in the same holes.

Except that they weren't Carla's. Looking ahead at her he could see that at once. Carla's stride wasn't that long, and neither were her arms. Oh, well, there had probably been plenty of marriages that survived even worse disillusionments. . . . Marriages, he thought. Sure. It's simple, isn't it? . . . He stopped thinking about Carla and thought about the holes again. He was becoming extremely fond of those ax-holes, he decided. They were very comforting, warming little things in the immense emptiness and loneliness of that mountainside.

A new sound came to him suddenly through the wind, and, raising his head again, he saw that Benner and Carla had stopped.

"It is getting more icy," the guide called to him. "We had best put on crampons."

Clinging to the steep tilt of the ramp, they got out their spiked climbing-irons and strapped them to their boots. The wind tore at their packs and clothing and numbed their bare hands. Before replacing his mittens Ordway looked at his watch. It showed exactly seven, and the phosphorescent hands and figures were glowing faintly. The sky, he realized, was much darker now—a sombre iron gray poised between dusk and night—and the ridge ahead rose up against it like a black headland into the sea.

"We can't make it before night," he said to Benner.

The guide shook his head.

"What should we do?"

"There is nothing to do but go on. We cannot camp here."

"It should not be more than another hour," Carla said.

Ordway turned and looked down at her. He saw her eyes smile up at him. He saw her face, soft and glowing against the white wool of her helmet and the snow and the rock beyond. Bending, he touched his cold nose to hers. "Hello baby," he said.

"Hello, Binks."

"Having fun, baby?"

"Great fun, Binks."

"Also," said Andreas Benner, picking up his ax and knocking the frozen snow from the rope.

They trudged on again. The wind howled. It grew still darker. Then it was night.

Ordway was thinking about the previous night: about the clearness and the stars and the silence and the faint humming beyond the silence. And then suddenly he was struggling to remember where that had been. . . . Had it been the lower terrace? Yes, of course it had. Their camp on the terrace seemed immeasurably remote to him now, and yet it had been that very same morning that they had left it. It had been that same day—merely a few hours ago—that they had begun the ascent of the Funnel, that they had fought their way up out of the recess, that Radcliffe had gone down, that he and Carla had sat side by side in the bland afternoon sunshine on the ledge. And only yesterday that they had been on the glacier and the icefall. And only—what was it?—five days since they had left the inn and the valley. Those were the facts; they were facts you could count on the fingers of one hand. And yet he could scarcely believe them. The lower terrace, the huts, Kandermatt; the chute, the plane, the war; New York, Paris, Larchmont. They all seemed equally far away. They were all so very far away. . . .

He looked up, squinting through the darkness. The damned ridge was still so far away. . . .

The white ribbon of the ramp moved toward them out of the obscurity ahead, glinted for a moment in white crystals underfoot and slipped away into obscurity behind. Its surface, as Benner had said, was now even harder than before—no longer snow at all, in fact, but a slanting, windswept catwalk of burnished ice. Looking

317

down again, Ordway realized that the pattern of ax-holes was gone and that in their place was only a white flowing smoothness marked by the faintest of nicks and indentations. Andreas must be having trouble following the trail, he thought. And yet their pace did not seem to have slackened. He trudged on, watching the slow, measured swing of his boots and ax-haft. Through the wind he could hear the faint metallic clank of his crampons against the ice.

The crampons were heavy. The pack on his back was heavy, and the ax felt like a bar of iron in his hand. He squared his shoulders a little and drew in a long, deliberate breath, but the air seemed to catch in a tight, cold knot in his throat. Coughing suddenly, he felt the knot moving slowly downward into his lungs and stomach. There seemed to be no air at all to breathe; only coldness and wind.

You're getting tired, he thought. You're getting very, very, very damned tired. . . .

Fatigue was enveloping him now in an almost tangible wave. He felt it clinging to his steel-shod boots, tugging gently and persistently at the pack-straps, muffling his thoughts, sensations and movements as the thick layers of wool and flannel muffled the surface of his body. It was not fatigue in the sharp, urgent sense of physical discomfort that he had experienced during the strenuous climbing earlier in the day. The knot in his throat did not actually pain him; there was no twitching of muscles or ache of bones. It was a far deeper tiredness than that—far subtler and more pervading. Soon I shall simply stop walking and sit down, he thought. It was as simple as that. He would stop. He would sit down.

Or was he sitting down already? . . . Apparently he had had his eyes closed, because now, suddenly, he was aware of opening them and looking down. . . . No, he was still walking. There were his boots still moving, his ax still swinging. There were the blue-white glinting crystals of the ice still flowing past beneath them.

He shook his head and drew in another deep breath, opening his mouth wide until he felt the dry lips cracking. The air caught in his throat, and he coughed again. For a moment the ice went black before his eyes and a dark wheel seemed to be spinning in his brain; then his throat opened a little, and he was drawing the air down in quick, shallow gasps. It's the wind, he thought—the wind and the lack of oxygen. Yes, even more than the wind, the lack of

318

anything in it to breathe. It was ridiculous,
he, a flyer, who had spent uncounted hours at
thirty thousand feet, should find himself bala
hairline of blacking-out at a mere thirteen or fou
with the solid earth under his feet. And yet there it
the way it worked. And far from being able to do any
it, he did not even feel anger or determination within
could think them; he could put them into words. But he c
feel them. All he could feel was numbness. All he could he
the wind and the clank of his crampons and the rasping of b
in his throat.

They trudged on. Through the wind. Through the darkness.
Somewhere, he was thinking presently, he had felt like this be
fore. As numb as this. As tired as this. Somewhere, sometime, long
ago. . . . His mind went back, groping, but he could not remember . . . And then, in the next instant, he did remember. It had
not been long ago at all, but merely a few short days before. It had
been in the plane, in *The Spirit of Perth Amboy*, crippled and lost
in the night over Europe, with the drone of the engines in his ear
and the mist in his face and the dead men around him. He h
been numb and tired then too—tireder than he had ever belie
a man could be and still live—spent with a tiredness that w
deeper than body, deeper than mind; a suspension of all facu
a lethargy, a trance. . . . His eyes were closed now. A cool, s
ing darkness was rising around him and through it the deep
of the engines. Ted—Harry—Bix, he thought. He was trying
speak their names aloud, but the wind snatched them from h
lips. He was trying to hold their faces before him, but they slipped
away into darkness.

And now he too was slipping away after them. Very softly. Very
gently and peacefully. He felt the darkness rising up to receive
him, and the wind—or was it the engine?—behind the darkness.
And then, suddenly, there was something hard and flat striking up
at his knee from below, and a firm hand in his armpit. "It is getting steep now," Andreas Benner's voice was saying. "We must
take it slower and have care."

Opening his eyes, he saw the glint of ice rising before him. The
surface of the ramp was no longer level, but sharply tilted. A few
hundred feet ahead it ended abruptly in what appeared to be a

...mbled boulders, and at the summit of the
...k line cut diagonally upward against the softer
...ky beyond.

...ge," Ordway said.

...Martin, we are almost there."

...n of them?"

...et."

...ou think they have gone all the way to the crest?" Carla

...ot all the way, no," said Benner. "The wind would be too
...ng there. They are probably among the rocks just below."

...Ie took a flashlight from his pocket and beamed it upwards. A
...ong spear of light glittered over the ice-slope and moved slowly
across the desolation of rock beyond. But there was no answering
beam from the ridge. Benner snapped the light off, waited for a
few moments and tried again. And again there was only darkness.

"Also," he said. "We shall go up."

Carla looked anxiously at Ordway. "You did not hurt your
knee?" she asked.

"No. It was only a stumble."

"You would like to rest a little perhaps?"

"No, I'm all right. Really."

...et us go then," said Benner. "On the rocks at least we will
...some protection from the wind."

...he last hundred yards of the ramp not only steepened but nar-
...ed abruptly, until finally it was no more than a slanting ten-
...ot shelf between the mountain walls and space. Hugging its inner
margin, however, they ascended it without mishap or difficulty
and came up at last off the ice onto a dark, spreading slope of
boulders and shale. Here they stopped briefly to remove their
crampons, and Benner brought out his torch and flashed it upward
again. They waited, but there was no answer. Then they climbed
on up the slope.

The boulders closed in around them, black and looming, having
less the appearance of actual rock than of mere insubstantial
shadow-masses in the blowing night. It was much darker now than
on the white strip of the terrace. Their boots gritted and slipped
on unseen obstacles, and their hands groped for holds and supports
that as often as not existed only in their imaginations. Benner

320

flashed his light upward once more, then held it to the slope immediately before them, searching out the next turn and the next step. But even the rocks themselves seemed black. The tiny circle of the beam flickered over them, illuminating a crevice here, a knob or corner there, but around it, on all sides, remained impenetrable darkness. They stumbled on, climbing and twisting, through a shrouded labyrinth of stone.

At least, Ordway thought, Benner had been right about the wind. The rock-masses rising around them protected them from its full blast, so that it no longer beat down on them in a steady, relentless tide, but merely in intermittent gusts. Its sound, however, was even louder and wilder than before. Along the smooth curve of the ramp it had dinned in their ears with an even, almost monotonous howling; but here on the cragged eaves of the ridge it alternately roared and shrieked, piped and moaned, as it swept in a thousand vagrant currents over the immense slanting keyboard of slabs and gullies, clefts, cornices and pinnacles. Two or three times they stopped and listened, thinking they had heard a voice calling from above. But each time it was only the wind. Once, beaming the light upward again, they cupped their hands and shouted themselves. The wind shouted back at them.

The boulders grew larger as they ascended—taller, more contorted, pressed closer and closer together. Then, presently, they were no longer boulders at all, but great scarps and towers of living rock, rising black and gnarled out of the buckling mountainside. The crest of the ridge, almost directly above them now, reared up against the sky like the silhouette of a tremendous ruined castle. The dark slope tiering up to it seemed no longer a mere maze of clustered stone, but a host of guardian shadows huddled waiting in wind and night.

They paused, leaning on their axes, peering upward. "*Der Riesensteg,*" said Benner. "Do you remember?"

Ordway nodded. . . . The Giant's Causeway. . . . Through the telescope from the valley it had showed merely as a tiny smudge of rough darkness against the soaring arc of the southeast ridge. Now it had become almost a mountain in itself. Another mountain. An ancient and evil mountain wrapped in desolation and decay. It was almost impossible to believe that a few thousand feet below there could have been sunlight and glinting snowfields and the clean bright sweep of cliff and precipice; or that a few thousand feet above them there was an immense white dome rising serene and changeless into the winds and nights of the centuries. Most of all, it was impossible to believe that Hein and Delambre were somewhere there in the darkness above them; that, indeed, any living things before themselves had ever penetrated into that lost, night-shrouded world of wind and shadow and crumbling stone.

And then suddenly, incredibly, there was a flash of light above. A slender beam slanted down at them across the rocks, swung to the right, then back to the left again, and vanished. Benner snapped on his own torch, flashed it upward, and after a moment the light above reappeared. Then they were climbing again, scrambling straight up over the dark masses of the slope toward the yellow eye that gleamed steadily above them. They heard a faint shout, saw an arm waving. Threading a narrow cleft between two black shouldering ramparts, they came down into a sheltered hollow beside Siegfried Hein and Paul Delambre.

"*Wilkommen in unserern Schloss,*" said the German. "We were becoming afraid that you had lost the way."

They swung their packs to the ground and sat down on them. The wind was howling on all sides and over their heads, but in the little hollow between the rock-walls the air was almost still. For a few moments no one spoke.

"You are all three all right?" asked Hein.

"*Ja,*" Benner said. "And you?"

"All right too. A little cold and stiff perhaps. We have been waiting here almost three hours."

The guide nodded without speaking. Then he looked slowly around. "Where is the tent?" he asked.

"The tent?"

"*Ja.* Where have you set it up?"

"We have not." Hein's voice sounded surprised. "I had not thought we would camp here."

"It is a good enough place, no?"

"Good enough? If it is for the wind you mean—yes. But we must go higher."

"Tonight?"

"Yes, of course. Tonight." Hein paused, looking from one to

322

another of them. "Before it was dark I climbed up to the ridge and looked around. It is still another thousand feet—maybe more—to where it meets the main east ridge."

"Well?"

"That is where we long ago decided we must make our second camp. If we do not get at least that far tonight, there will be no chance in the world of making the top tomorrow."

"Then we will make it the next day," said Benner.

"The next day? Of course." Hein's voice was growing edged. "The weather will hold good just as long as we want it to, I suppose?"

"It is still too soon to tell what the weather will do. In any case, it is no good now for climbing in the dark."

"So it is dark. And it is blowing a little. Are you telling me that in thirty years as a guide you have never climbed on a windy night?" Hein paused again, but Benner did not answer. "Look," he went on, "It is what time now? A quarter of nine. In two hours, by eleven at the most, we can be where the ridges meet."

"Or lying six thousand feet down on the glacier," said Benner.

"Nonsense! I have looked at the ridge, I tell you. There is no difficulty or danger."

"There is always danger on a mountain when a party is tired."

"Tired? Oh, so that is it then? When one is tired on a mountain one sits down. When one is tired in a war one surrenders. . . ."

The voices went on, now sharp and clear, now almost lost in the moaning and piping of the wind. Ordway sat hunched forward, his arms folded on the blade of his ax, half-listening. His body felt hollow and weak and his legs like two slabs of stone, but he was breathing almost normally again, and his head was clear. It had been the oxygen all right, he thought. Or the lack of it, rather. When he was climbing automatically, without thinking, his body was all right, and when he was sitting quietly, as he was now, his thinking was all right. It was when it became necessary to do the two together—climb and think, do and be aware of doing—that the trouble started. There simply wasn't enough fuel. Or enough engine.

He looked at Carla, sitting quietly beside him, and reached out a mittened hand and put it over hers.

"Still there?" he asked.

"Oh yes—still here."

She smiled at him, and he pressed her hand a little, and then his eyes went back to the others. Hein and Benner were crouched in the center of the hollow, talking now in German, and beyond them, against the far wall, was Delambre. The Frenchman sat motionless, his face a faint whitish blob in the shadows, his shapeless body scarcely distinguishable from the rocks that rose around him. It suddenly occurred to Ordway that he had neither spoken nor moved since the five of them had come together. He must be tired too, he thought. He must be awfully goddamned tired. . . .

"Paul—" he said.

"Yes?"

"Okay?"

"Yes—of course."

"How did it go?"

"All right, thanks. And with you?"

"All right too."

The wind rose to a sudden shriek over their heads, and a gust of icy air struck down, circling, into the hollow. Hein and Benner had half risen, and the German was pointing off up the slope toward the ridge. Crouching side by side in the darkness, muffled and featureless, they looked less like human figures than like two padded, wind-battered scarecrows.

Yet even now, Ordway thought, watching them, there was no mistaking one for the other. One thing they had in common: they were mountaineers. They were the two greatest mountaineers he had ever known, or probably ever would know in his lifetime. But in every other respect they were as unalike as two men could be. One was massive, the other slender; one slow, the other quick; one patient, the other— He broke off. There was no use putting it into words. It had nothing to do with words. It was in every contour of their bodies, every step they took, every gesture they made. Hein was neither moving nor speaking now, but his arm was still pointed upward. *Let us storm it,* said the arm. Benner did not move either. His face, raised a little to the darkness and wind, was as immobile as mountain rock. *Let us wear it down,* it said.

. . . . And then, presently, both men were moving. They were approaching him and squatting down beside him.

"And you, Ordway?" Hein asked. "You are tired too?"

324

"Yes, I'm tired," he said.

"And you are unwilling to go on?"

Ordway hesitated, looking from one to the other. "Unwilling? No. I'm willing to do what the two of you think best."

"Unfortunately we cannot agree."

"You're convinced that we should keep going?"

"Yes."

Ordway's eyes went to Benner. "And you think we should stay?"

"Ja, Herr Martin."

"Because of the wind?"

"Because of the wind and the darkness and the chance that it will really storm. But most of all because we are very tired."

"There's no possibility of making the top from here?"

"In one day? To the top and back? No, it could not be done."

"Whereas if we went on further tonight—to where Hein wants to go—"

"Then we could—yes," the German put in. "In one day, with even fair weather. Up and back."

"You sound very sure of it."

"Sure? Of course I am sure." Hein's voice became suddenly sharp and strained. "Gottverdammt, man, I have studied this mountain for years. Planned for it. Dreamed of it. To climb the Weissturm from Kandermatt—that is what I have wanted most in the world ever since I have been a boy of ten. . . . And now you ask me, am I sure?"

There was a short silence. Ordway peered up into the night and the wind.

"How do the rest of you feel about it?" he asked.

No one answered.

"Paul?"

"I am willing to go on," said Delambre.

"Carla?"

The girl hesitated. Then she nodded.

"You aren't too tired?"

"I am tired—yes—of course. But if it makes the difference between—"

"And you, Ordway?" Hein asked. "You are for it too, then?"

Ordway drew in a long, deep breath. "Well, Andreas—" he said.

It was a moment before Benner spoke. Then he shook his head very slowly. "I am sorry, Herr Martin."

"You mean you won't go?"

"No, I will not go."

"But—"

"I am a guide, Herr Martin," Benner said quietly. "For almost thirty years I have been a guide in the Oberland, and for a hundred years my father and grandfather before me. My father was killed on the Weissturm. Like Herr Hein here, I have said to myself since I was a boy: 'You will climb this mountain. With the help of merciful God you will some day climb this beautiful terrible mountain that has killed your father.' . . . But not foolishly —no. Not recklessly and with pride and vainglory. Not to risk the lives of my *Herren* so that I may stand at last on a point of snow in the sky and shout, 'Look, *du lieber Gott*: look, I have done it!' "

There was silence again. Hein began to speak, but stopped himself. Another gust of wind swooped down into the hollow, plucking at their packs and clothing.

"And you believe it would be foolish and reckless to go on tonight?" Ordway asked.

"*Ja*."

"And as a professional guide you refuse to do it?"

"*Ja*, Herr Martin. I refuse."

"All right," said Ordway, looking around at the others. "That's that."

He could hear Hein drawing in his breath sharply and see his gray eyes fixed on him through the darkness. "You mean we will stay here?" the German burst out suddenly. "When all of us want to go, and only this one old man—"

"Andreas is our guide. He knows these mountains, and he knows his responsibilities."

"Responsibilities? For what? For his own skin, perhaps. But not for me, Herr Kapitän Ordway—I assure you, not for me. For eight years before the war I climbed in these mountains. I am a leader-first-class of the *Deutsch-Österreichischer Alpenverein*, and do you know what that means? It means that I have climbed guideless on the Eigerwand, the Matterhorn faces, the Grandes Jorasses, all of them—ascents that these old Swiss tourist-nurses would have apoplexy even thinking about." Hein's voice had risen as he spoke,

326

but now he checked it sharply, and when he resumed speaking it was in a low, even tone. "I have told you once before and I tell you once again: one does not conquer a mountain like the Weissturm except by fighting for it."

"We have been fighting for it, and we're going to go on fighting for it. Tomorrow."

"That is your last word?"

"Yes."

"And the rest of you? It needs only two of us to go on, and the rest can stay here. Who of you will go with me?"

No one answered. Hein had risen to his feet and stood facing them, looking from one to another. In the darkness Ordway could see his mittened hands slowly opening and closing at his sides.

He stood up and laid a hand on the German's shoulder. "Let's make it everyone's last word," he said. "I'm tired. You're tired. We're all tired. Let's get something to eat and some sleep, and in the morning we'll see how things are and make our decisions."

Hein remained motionless for a few moments, staring at the ground. Then he raised his head a little, and once again it seemed to Ordway that there was a faint mocking glint in the gray eyes. "The democratic system again," he said. "Eh, Herr Kapitän?"

They opened the packs and pitched their two tents, wedging the poles into deep crevices in the rock and weighting the wall-flaps with heavy stones. Then they crouched around the blue flame of the Primus and prepared themselves a warm meal from their tins and jars. They ate in silence, listening to the intermittent battering of the wind on the sloping roof and the deeper, steadier sound of its floodtide overhead.

"It is getting stronger," Carla said a little later, after Hein and Delambre had gone to the other tent and she, Ordway and Benner were kneeling to unroll their blankets.

Ordway nodded. "Yes, it's stronger now."

In the blackness he lay quietly beside her, his cheek against her blanketed shoulder, listening again. He heard the wind howling out of the void beyond them, shrieking in the guy ropes and jerking at their fragile canvas shell, sweeping on again in wild, piping music up the black desolation of the ridge.

I should go out and take a look at the stones, he thought.

Then he closed his eyes.

Chapter 18

It seemed to Paul Delambre that he was standing on the cliff at Naxos looking out to sea. Directly beneath him was a strip of golden beach, and beyond it the bay with its yellow-sailed fishing boats, and beyond that the channel and the island of Dionysus and the blue miles of the Mediterranean. Everything was utterly still. For a long time he remained motionless, watching; then he turned to Astrid, standing beside him, and watched the cool, violet-blue of her eyes and the sun dancing lightly in the bright aureole of her hair. She smiled at him a little, but did not speak, and presently he took her hand and they walked back toward the little house through the garden. There were the bougainvillea and jacaranda around them, the hammock between the mandarin trees, his table in the shade with the jade cigarette box, the bottle of Courvoisier and the neat white stack of foolscap. There was sunlight and stillness—and then suddenly, through the stillness, the houseman, Christopher running toward them up the dusty hill.

There was Christopher talking, his dark eyes wide, his lips jerking excitedly over his white teeth. But no words came from him. He talked voicelessly and soundlessly, like an image in a mirror. The sea beyond him was like a mirror too. Astrid's violet eyes, watching him, were as cool and deep as a mirror. Christopher went on talking, the lips and teeth went on jerking, but around them the stillness moved ever closer and closer out of sunlit distance. . . .

Delambre opened his eyes and lay listening. The sunlight was gone, but the stillness remained. The wind has stopped, he thought.

Raising himself on one elbow, he peered around him in the darkness. Hein's form was huddled motionless under the blankets. The roof and walls of the tent were motionless. It must be almost morning, he thought. Groping for his flashlight, he snapped it on and looked at his watch. It was a few minutes after four. He pulled up the blankets, closed his eyes and lay quietly, struggling back toward the sunlight. But the sunlight was gone. Sleep was gone. The stillness swelled slowly around him, filling the tent, pressing gently against the canvas walls.

Presently he got up, pulled on his boots and crept noiselessly toward the sleeve of the entrance. A moment later the brown darkness of the tent was gone too, and in its place was a gray, weaving darkness of night and mist. Yes, the wind has stopped, he thought. There was no breath or intimation of wind; and yet the air could not have been wholly still, because great streaks and billows of whitish vapor were moving slowly upward across the mountainside. He listened again, but there was no sound. Crossing the hollow, he sat down on the far slope, in the same spot he had sat earlier in the night before they had put up the tents. It is colder, he thought. I should have put on a helmet and outer jacket.

He did not feel cold, however. He did not even feel particularly tired, and the deep, dull bone-ache that had filled him throughout most of the day's climbing had disappeared. His body felt light and insubstantial—as insubstantial as the drifting mist.

He sat without moving, watching the mist. It seemed to be coming from below, rising in long twining scarves from the black void beyond the south face and drifting very slowly upward across the hollow toward the ridge above. The ridge itself showed as a faint, dark mass behind it. The towers and parapets of the slope raised their twisted black shapes out of its billows as if from the depths of a gray and desolate sea.

"*Mais où sont les neiges d'antan?*" Paul Delambre said quietly. He listened to the sound of his voice as it seemed to drift away into the darkness. Then he bent his head and covered his face with his hands.

It was the same, he thought. On a Parisian boulevard, a Baltic beach, an island in the Cyclades, a mountain in the Alps—wherever he went and whatever he did—it was always and forever the same. There was the sunlight on the sea. There was a field of wildflowers, a glowing painting on a wall, a woman's eyes smiling, a mountain rising white and shining into the blue miles of the sky. He saw them, felt them, knew them. His mind encompassed them. He reached out his arms to possess them. . . . And in the same instant lost them. . . . It was no longer the sea at which he was gazing, but a mirror; no longer a flower, a picture, a woman, a mountaintop, but images in a glass. Snow and sunlight faded, all color and texture and brightness faded, and in their place was mist.

He raised his eyes again. In the darkness behind the mist it seemed to him that a face was slowly taking shape. It was the face of a girl, the girl from the Scala ballet in Milan: young, fragile, exquisite. Her name had been Antonia, but he had called her Ariel —*Ariella ballanta*—and she was still, now, no less than on those long-gone enchanted nights of his youth, the brightest and loveliest thing he had ever looked upon. Through the years and the mist he saw her dancing and whirling across that great darkened stage, her silver toes scarcely seeming to touch the boards, her body a flashing arrow of light; and then, presently, no longer dancing, but smiling at him with the dark eyes of a madonna, and then no longer smiling, but lying slender and cool beside him, her body sealed to his own, her face a pale, faintly glowing petal in the darkness. He was bending over her, caressing her. "*Ariella*," he whispered, "*amore mia, vita mia . . .*" And then the beam in the dark —the rift in the mist—and where the face of a child had been, the face of ancient lust. Where Ariel had been, the mate of Caliban. . . .

Delambre sat motionless, staring upward at the shrouded ridge. A face, he thought. A face, a flower, a painting, a meadow, a sea: it was all the same. And now a mountain. And that was the same. The snows of yesteryear were gone, the sun and stars were gone, the White Tower was gone. Where they had been was darkness; the black bones of earth; mist.

"You want very much to climb this mountain?" the American had asked on the glacier.

"Yes," he had said. "I want very much to climb it."

"And you believe you can?"

330

He had shrugged. "Where the rest of you can go, monsieur, I can go too."

And he could. He had. Through the forests and meadows, across the passes and wastes, up the glacier and snow-slopes and ridges and precipices, he had gone along with the others; tiring occasionally, perhaps, stumbling and faltering occasionally; but always keeping the pace, always doing his share. It had pleased him a little, but not surprised him, because he had known he could do it. If climbing was putting one foot before the other, one hand above the other, he could climb. If writing was setting down one word after another, he could write. If fighting was striking one blow after another, he could fight, and if loving was embracing the body of one woman after another, he could love. And yet he was neither mountaineer, author, soldier, lover. He had never climbed to the summit of any great peak. He had never written a book, defeated an enemy, found or engendered happiness in any woman. Always between desire and fulfillment there was the shadow. Always between the image and the substance there was the stillness and emptiness of the mirror, the gray mist rising out of the depths of the mirror, deeper and more terrible than emptiness.

He saw Siegfried Hein standing beside him on the ledge in the Funnel. "With only two of us we may be climbing faster," the German had said.

"Yes, I know."

"And there will be less protection from the rope."

He had nodded.

And he had gone with him. Step by step, pitch by pitch, he had followed Hein up the long slanting walls of the upper Funnel toward the graying sky and the sound of the wind. He had not slipped nor fumbled. He had not asked to rest. And in the end it was side by side, both of them together, that they came out of the great cleft onto the narrow, tilted snow-band of the second terrace.

Here they had rested briefly, hunched over against the wind. Hein studied the white arc of the ramp beyond, then presently turned and looked at Delambre. His eyes, in his bronzed, square-lined face, were very gray, very cool, faintly mocking.

"We should be able to reach the ridge before dark," he said.

Delambre nodded.

"You would perhaps rather wait here for the others?"

"No, I will go with you."

And they had gone on, again without resting: along the curving ribbon of the ramp, up the steep ice-slope at its eastern end, among the twisted, blackened rock-masses rising to the desolation of the ridge. He had put one foot in front of the other; raised his ax, swung it, set it down, raised it again; bent head and shoulders and thrusting knees into the battering, bitter tide of the wind. And when at last they reached the hollow beneath the ridge and sat down to wait for the others, Hein's eyes were no longer mocking, but fixed on him with a new, almost admiring curiosity.

"It has been a long climb," the German said.

"Yes, it has been long."

"And you have done well."

"Thank you."

He was conscious of a fleeting sense of pleasure and pride. . . . Yes, you have done well, he thought. You have done all that he did. You have shown him. . . . Then he stopped thinking and for a long time sat staring quietly up at the darkening ridge.

All right, he had shown him. Why? And to what end? To know that he could put one foot in front of the other as often as another man? To win a grudging glance of approval from a mindless clod of a Boche superman? To sit, spent and freezing, on the outermost rim of earth and stare up at a black ridge rising, ancient and forlorn, against the winds of night?

They had waited. The sky grew darker and the wind howled among the rocks. He must have closed his eyes and dozed, because presently it seemed to him that the mountain was no longer black, but white and glittering, and he was moving toward it across a broad, gentle slope of flowered meadows. When he came closer, however, he saw that it was not a mountain at all, but a great sea shining in the sunlight. He reached the shore of the sea, entered it, moved over it and through it, and its surface lay spread around him like a sparkling silver-blue mirror. But gradually now, as he advanced, the sea became higher and deeper. He was no longer on its surface at all, but within it, beneath it, and its sunlit glitter was a mere distant and receding gleam above his head; and then there was no longer any gleam at all, but only darkness; and he was moving through the darkness beneath the mirror of the sea, in the soundless black stillness of the ocean depths. . . .

When he had opened his eyes again it was full night. There was the black ridge and the rocks and the wind, and then presently the thin finger of light in the darkness and the hunched shadows in the hollow, talking.

"I am willing to go on," he had said.

He was willing to go; he was willing to stay. It did not matter. There was the brown gloom of the tent and the wind beyond the tent, and the sunlight beyond the wind, and the garden and the bay spreading many-hued and lovely in the sunlight. There was no need to climb higher, to put one foot in front of the other, to struggle on. He had only to lie back with closed eyes and everything was there before him: the house on the Rue Castellane; the villa at Naxos; the Bois in April; the colors of Gaugin and the music of Debussy; the face of his mother, of Ariel, of Astrid; the shining mountain and the shining sea. They were all there, deep in memory and desire—one behind the other, one within the other —brightening, fading, returning, fading again. . . .

He sat with his back against the slope of the hollow, staring upward. They had all faded now. They were gone. Even the wind was gone. There were only the two tents and the black rocks and the mist.

Yes, it is colder, he thought. Even without the wind it is colder.

After a few minutes he arose, crossed the hollow and crept through the entrance of his tent. Hein lay motionless under his blankets, in the same position as before. Feeling his way along the canvas wall, he came to his rucksack, groped in it and presently found what he was looking for. The glass of the bottle was cold as ice, but it almost seemed to him, as he lifted it gently from the pack, that he could already feel an inner warmth spreading from his hand through all his spent and hollow body. Creeping from the tent again, he returned to where he had been sitting before, took his knife from his pocket and pried out the cork. Then he held the bottle up before him. At first it appeared only as a black, opaque shape in his hand, but as he turned it slowly, watching, there was a sudden, tiny flickering within the blackness—the merest glint of amber light against the darkness of rock and mist.

He smiled a little as he tilted the brandy to his lips. "To our white, beautiful mountain, Monsieur Ordway," he said.

Once again Ordway awoke to the touch of a hand on his shoulder.

"Andreas?" he murmured.

Carla's voice answered him. "No, it is I."

He raised himself on his elbow and saw the face of the girl close beside him. The interior of the tent was filled with a brownish, filtered twilight.

"It's morning," he said.

"Yes."

"We've overslept."

"No. Andreas said to let you sleep. There has been much fog, and there was nothing we could do until it was light."

He was quiet a moment, listening. "The wind's gone," he said.

"Yes, there is none at all now."

"Where's Andreas?"

"Andreas and Hein have gone up to the ridge to see how things are. I have just waked Paul, and now I am getting breakfast."

She turned to go, but Ordway reached out and held her hand. "You haven't told me good morning," he said.

"Good morning, Martin."

"You can do better than that, old lady."

He pulled her down to him and kissed her, and she lay quietly in his arms, smiling. "Good morning, my lover," she said.

"I've got an idea," he told her.

"What?"

"We'll ring for room service and have breakfast in bed."

"All right." She raised her lips, and he kissed her again. "There's one trouble, though."

"What's that?"

"I'm room service." She gave a little laugh, kissed him lightly on the nose and crawled toward the entrance of the tent. "And I'm the chef besides, and the water is going to boil over any minute."

"This is a hell of a way to spend a honeymoon."

"Next time we'll go to a better hotel."

She disappeared through the sleeve, and he sat up and began

334

pulling on his boots and outer clothing. As he did so he became aware for the first time of various bodily sensations. His arms and legs ached, his brain felt heavy and clogged, and the knot in his throat was tighter and drier than ever. Suddenly he began to cough. He struggled to control it, but couldn't, and sat hunched over upon the blankets in a hacking, retching paroxysm. When at last it subsided he remained sitting quietly for a few minutes, shaking his head to clear it and drawing slow, deep breaths down into his lungs. The air smelt stale, and there was a bitter, almost rancid taste in his mouth. Lacing his boots and pulling on mittens and helmet, he crept across the dishevelled blankets and out through the sleeve of the tent.

For an instant it seemed to him that he had come from the out-of-doors into a dim, smoke-filled room. There was fog everywhere—a great opaque pall of it, filling the hollow and rising in gray, frozen billows up the mountainside beyond. The tents, the surrounding rocks, the figure of Carla bent over the Primus between the tents were the merest blurred shadows, seeming less material, tangible objects than accidental thickenings and shadings of the mist. The ridge above and the black towers of the Riesensteg were hidden entirely; in all the shrouded sweep of desolation around them there was no movement, no faintest stirring of air and light. Ordway looked at his watch. It was a quarter of seven. Somewhere above and about them, unimaginably far away, the dawn was brightening slowly over the valleys and ranges. But there was no brightening here. The night was gone, and still it was not day. It was as if they were no longer on a mountainside at all, but on the bottom of an immense stagnant sea, shut out from sky and sun by gray depths of watery twilight.

"Tea's ready!"

Carla's voice came to him muffled and unfamiliar through the veils of vapor. "Here, honeymooner," she said, smiling up at him as he approached.

He took the cup that she handed him and stood sipping from it slowly and pressing his mittened hand against the warm enamel. Carla bent to the stove again and stirred the stew that was warming over the blue flame.

"They're not back yet?" he asked.

"No, not yet."

"It's godawful, isn't it?"

"Andreas thought it might be a little better up above."

"It can't be much worse, anyhow."

She ladled the stew onto two plates, and they sat eating and drinking in silence. On the third or fourth mouthful he gagged and began to cough again, but this time he was able to control it a little more quickly.

"Your throat is bad," Carla said.

"Not bad. Just annoying."

"Try gargling with the tea a little."

He tried, gagged again, then tried a second time. The hot liquid burned like a searing iron, but once it was down the tightness seemed to have relaxed a little.

"Better?" she asked.

"Yes, it's better now."

"I'll paint it later with the argyrol."

He shook his head. "There's another treatment I like better."

She looked at him questioningly and saw that he was grinning; and then, still grinning, he leaned over and kissed her.

"I'm beginning to think you are a very difficult person," she said.

He was about to speak again, but stopped himself suddenly and raised a hand, listening. A faint voice came down to them from the shrouded slope above.

"Hal-loo—" he shouted.

The voice came down again, a little louder now, and he kept on shouting. And presently there was a flicker of movement in the mist above, and the muffled figures of Benner and Hein appeared on the rim of the hollow. Letting themselves down the wall, they untied themselves from their rope and approached the stove.

"It is like trying to find a beetle in a woodlot," said Benner.

The two men stood close to the Primus, warming themselves, while Carla readied the tea and stew.

"How is it on the ridge?" Ordway asked.

The guide shrugged. "Mist. Fog. More fog."

"But not so thick as here," said Hein.

"No, not quite so thick any more. It is lifting a little."

"Any wind?"

"Ja, there is a little wind too. It is following along the line of the ridge though, so one cannot tell from what direction it is really coming."

"Do you think it will blow up stronger again?"

"Sooner or later, *ja*, it will blow stronger. On a mountain like the Weissturm it cannot stay so quiet for very long. But whether it will blow clear or with a storm—" Benner broke off, shrugging again. "As I have said, Herr Martin, October it is a bad season. One can never be sure."

Carla handed the two men their plates and cups, and they stood eating and drinking in silence. Ordway sat staring up into the gray depths of the mist. He was not certain whether it was his imagination or if he could actually see the black towers of the Riesensteg looming dimly above them. . . . Yes it was thinning, he thought. Not much, but a little. Not clearing, but still thinning. . . .

"If we had gone on last night," said Hein suddenly, "we could be now not just a few hours ahead, but a whole day."

"And if it had stormed last night," Benner began—

"Anyhow, we didn't go last night," Ordway broke in, a little sharply. "So there's no point arguing about it again. Let's start from where we are."

"Start from where we are, yes," said the German. "But stay where we are—no." He paused, looking from one to another of them. "There is something that I am going to tell you right now, my friends. If we are going to climb to the top of the Weissturm we must go up and make our last camp today."

"You think we can then?" Carla asked.

"Can? . . . On a mountain one does not speak of 'can,' *Fräulein*. One speaks of 'will.'"

"To Wagnerian music," said Ordway.

"*Bitte?*" Hein's gray eyes turned toward him curiously. "You disagree perhaps, Herr Ordway?"

"Not at all. Nothing I like better than *Götterdämmerung* for breakfast."

"Apparently I have said something that amuses you. For myself, however, I find nothing amusing about defeat. Or about starving to death either, for that matter."

"Starving?"

"I think the *Fräulein* here knows what I am speaking about." Hein looked at Carla. "How many days' food have we?" he asked.

337

"Four."

"Today and three more, no?" He turned back to Ordway. "We go up to where the ridges meet today—that is one. Tomorrow to the top—two. And two more down to the lower tent where we have supplies. Figure it out."

"It is four days' food if we eat as we have been," Carla said. "If we do with less it can stretch for five or perhaps six."

"All right, six. And if a storm comes up? Or some other emergency—" Hein's eyes went to Benner. "You are a mountain man," he said. "Tell them."

The guide was silent a moment, slowly stroking the gingery stubble of his beard. "*Ja*," he said quietly, "it is true. There is not much time to be spared."

"In other words, you're for starting right now?" Ordway asked.

"It may go. It may not. One cannot tell."

"But you think it's worth the chance?"

"It is our only chance, Herr Martin."

Ordway looked from Benner to Hein and from Hein to Carla. Then he got to his feet. "Let's get going," he said.

He started for the nearest tent, stopped and looked around him again. He was suddenly aware that Delambre had not joined them. "Paul isn't—"

He was interrupted by an exclamation from Carla. "How stupid of me!" she said. "He must have fallen asleep again."

"Paul!" Ordway called. "Paul!" There was no answer. "I'll get him," he said.

Approaching the tent, he stooped and crept through the entrance. In place of the limitless gray twilight of mist there was now a brown, stale twilight between sloping canvas. Delambre, fully clothed, was lying on the blankets along the far wall. Ordway crawled across to him and reached out an arm to touch his shoulder. "Paul," he said—

Then he saw that the Frenchman's eyes were open.

"We thought you were asleep."

"No," Delambre said, "I am not asleep."

"We're getting ready to leave."

"Yes, of course." There was a pause, but Delambre made no move to get up. His thin, bearded face, turned to Ordway, was expressionless, but in the gloom the pupils of his eyes seemed

338

darker and larger than ever. "Of course," he repeated quietly. "It is time."

Ordway waited, watching him. "Is there anything wrong?" he asked.

"Wrong? But no. What is there that could be wrong, mon vieux?" Delambre turned away a little and closed his eyes. "The sun is shining, is it not? The white mountain rises out of the green valleys. God is in his heaven and man in his hell."

Ordway reached out a hand again. "Paul," he said—

There was a sound behind him, and Carla was creeping through the entrance carrying a plate and cup. "We are packing the cooking things now," she announced. "Here is your breakfast." She stopped suddenly, looking from one to the other of the two men. Then she crawled to Delambre's side and bent over him. "Paul—breakfast," she said.

The Frenchman did not answer.

"Paul, do you hear me?"

He opened his eyes and smiled at her. "Hallo, ma jolie," he said. "You are going to eat now."

"Thank you, I am not hungry."

"You must. Come, sit up now." Setting down the plate and cup, she took his hands and half coaxed, half pulled him into a sitting position; then she picked up the cup again and handed it to him. "The tea is good and hot. You will feel better when you have drunk it."

Delambre held the cup in both hands, staring down at it with a peculiar, almost frozen fixity. "You are kind to me, mademoiselle," he said, without looking up at her. "You have all been very kind to me."

"Drink it now," Carla told him.

He raised the cup slowly to his lips and drank. Ordway watched him for a few moments, then gestured to Carla and crept from the tent. Benner and Hein were crouched in the mist where the stove had been, lashing foodstuffs and utensils onto the packboards, but glanced up as he approached them.

"Something's the matter with Delambre," he said.

"The matter?" Benner repeated, rising. "He is sick?"

"I'm not sure. But something's wrong with him." He recounted briefly what had happened in the tent. The guide listened quietly,

339

his leathery face clouded with worry, and Hein's lips narrowed until they were a tight, colorless line.

"It is mountain-sickness perhaps," Benner said when he had finished.

"Perhaps. But it seems more—well—mental than actually being sick."

"With the mountain-sickness it is sometimes the head more than the stomach. Do you know if he has been—how do you say it?" Benner touched his mouth with his hand.

"Vomiting? No, I don't think so." Ordway looked at Hein. "Did you hear him at all during the night?"

The German shook his head. "No, I heard nothing." He stood silently looking out into the mist beyond the hollow, his hands slowly opening and closing at his sides. "Gottverdammt!" he burst out suddenly. "Es ist immer etwas los mit diesen Idioten und Schwächlingen . . ."

Ordway felt the blood rushing to his cheeks. "Shut up!" he snapped. "I've had just about enough of your—"

"Do not upset yourselves, messieurs," a quiet voice said behind them. Turning, they realized that Delambre had come from the tent and was standing a few yards away, watching them and smiling a little. "Believe me, there is no need to. I am not going to hold you back from your mountaintop."

The three men stared at him.

"You're feeling better now?" Ordway asked.

"Quite well," said Delambre. "Quite well, indeed, thank you."

"You should have rested a while longer."

"No, I have rested enough for the time. Perhaps later I shall rest some more." The Frenchman came a few steps nearer, walking with a curiously deliberate, almost mechanical motion. The trace of a smile still lingered on his lips, but his eyes, as he looked from one to another of them, were sombre and very steady. "You see how I get about, messieurs? Like a chamois on a cliff. You must not worry about me, please."

He stopped and stood motionless, his gaze going out past them into the gray emptiness of fog. "Yes," he said, "the sun is shining. And the sea is blue and gold." He sat down abruptly on the flat shelf of a boulder and buried his face in his hands.

"Paul—" said Ordway.

340

Delambre did not answer.

"Ja—it is a touch of the mountain-sickness," Benner murmured.

"Or exhaustion," said Hein.

Ordway put his hand on the Frenchman's shoulder, and at the same moment Carla appeared in the tent entrance and came quickly toward them. "Martin," she began—

Delambre raised his head and looked at her. "It is not necessary for you to tell them, ma petite. I shall be the patient and the diagnostician too." He paused, the faint smile returning to his lips, and when he spoke again it was in the quiet, precise tone of a teacher addressing a classroom of children. "I am not suffering from mountain-sickness," he said. "I am not exhausted, as Monsieur Hein here thinks. I am merely drunk. Merely very, very drunk."

The three men stared down at him without speaking. Then Ordway's eyes went to Carla, and she nodded slightly. "I looked in the rucksack for the bottles."

"And they weren't there?"

"No."

There was another silence. Ordway looked at Delambre again. "You poor damn fool," he said quietly.

Time and again, time without number in the days to come, he was to find himself struggling to remember the details of that hour that followed. When had this decision been made? When had that one been abandoned? Just what had Andreas said? And Hein? And Carla? And he himself? Above all, what exact word or thought or act had it been that crystallized their final resolve. The more he thought about it later, the further he was to be from an answer. In retrospect it came to seem to him almost as if he had been drunk himself; as if everything that had been said and done were shrouded in the same gray, ambiguous pall of unreality that had veiled the mountainside around them.

They squatted on the stones in the mist, arguing. They decided to wait, to go down, to go on. They decided that Carla would stay while the others went on, and then that Carla and Benner would stay, and then that everyone would stay. They finished loading the packboards and sat on them, staring silently up toward the hidden ridge. They took down one of the tents, started packing it, argued again. Hein rose suddenly, picked up his rucksack and ax and began climbing the upper slope of the hollow. Benner followed and all but pulled him down. There was indecision again. Silence again. There was Delambre hunched on the boulder with his hands over his face; walking with careful, deliberate steps toward the still-standing tent; lying on his back in the brown twilight staring up at the canvas of the roof.

"*Ma petite—*" he said presently.

"Yes?" said Carla.

"You will go now."

"No."

"Yes, you will go."

The girl did not answer. Ordway and Benner crouched silently near the entrance, behind her.

"You must go, do you hear me?" Delambre raised himself slowly to a sitting position. "You see—I am able to sit up, to walk, to talk. I am all right, believe me. I cannot go with you, but I am all right. I am drunk and good for nothing, but I am all right."

"We will wait until you are able to go with us."

"But I will not be able."

"Then we will not go either."

A long moment passed before Delambre spoke again. Then he reached out toward her and said, "Give me your hand. I know you do not want to, but give it to me anyhow. For just a minute." Carla extended a hand silently, and he took it in his own. "There. That is better. Thank you, *ma petite.*" He paused again, his eyes dark and steady on her face. "Now listen to me," he said. "It is one of my misfortunes that I am a wiser man when I am drunk than when I am sober, so listen to what I have to say. . . . Whether or not I climb this mountain means nothing. Do you understand? Nothing. But that you and your Martin climb it— that is everything. I do not mean simply for yourselves, but for me—for everyone. I do not mean simply because it is a mountain, but because you are what you are and this is a thing that you must do. You know the kind of man I am now. I should not have come with you. I should have known that I would bring you only trouble and unhappiness. You may think of me what you like; you owe me nothing but anger and contempt. But there is one thing only that

342

you cannot do, and that is to let me keep you from climbing this mountain. That you cannot do to me—or to yourselves."

Delambre paused, but his eyes did not waver from Carla's face. She felt his long fingers tighten around her mittened hand. "You will go now?" he asked very quietly.

She did not answer.

"You will go—please?"

Carla turned and looked at Ordway and Benner. There was a long silence before her eyes went back to the Frenchman.

"All right, Paul," she said. "We will go."

Outside in the gray hollow they finished loading the packboards and rucksacks. Presently Delambre came from the tent again and sat on a flat stone near the entrance, watching them. When they had finished Benner walked slowly over and squatted down beside him. "Herr Delambre," he said—

"Yes?"

"You can understand what I am saying?"

A smile touched the Frenchman's lips again. "Yes," he said, "I can understand."

"Today we will go only a short way up the ridge for our last camp. Tomorrow, if the weather is good, we will try for the top. If it is bad, we will wait and either try the next day or come down. The latest we will be back here will be the day after tomorrow in the evening."

Delambre nodded.

"All that you will need we are putting in the tent. There is food for five days, a fireless cooker, all your clothes, blankets, equipment. The tent is in a sheltered place, but if it blows again you should keep the ropes tight and weight the bottom of the walls with stones. Above all, do not leave here—for any reason. Neither to go up nor down." Benner paused, his blue eyes searching the Frenchman's face. "You will promise me that, Herr Delambre?"

Delambre nodded again.

"You will not leave here?"

"No."

Benner hesitated, and for an instant it seemed that he was about to speak again. Then he got to his feet. The others were standing beside him, ropes and packs on their shoulders and their axes in their hands.

343

"Get some sleep, Paul," said Ordway.

"Yes," Delambre answered, "perhaps I shall sleep a little now."

"We will be back before you know it," Carla said.

"From the top."

"All right. From the top."

"Yes, that is the way it must be. That is the—" Delambre faltered and stopped, but his dark eyes remained fixed on the girl's face. "You are a very lovely thing," he said softly.

They stood watching him in silence for another moment.

"*Also,*" said Andreas Benner.

. . . . And they were climbing again. Their boots were gritting on the rim of the hollow, and then on the boulders beyond the rim; and when Ordway turned to look back Delambre was gone, and when he turned the second time the tent and the hollow were gone; and where they had been was only mist. They threaded their way tortuously up the steep, tumbled labyrinth of the slope. The twisted towers of the Riesensteg floated down toward them out of the obscurity above, closed in about them in black, looming shapelessness, and floated away again into obscurity below. The prongs of their axes clicked in slow, broken rhythm against the flinty rocks.

After perhaps five minutes it seemed to Ordway that he would be unable to go on. His feet were like blocks of stone, his pack like a giant boulder strapped to his shoulders, and the thick, choking dampness of the fog seemed to be seeping through his clothing to his skin and then through his skin into his very bones and blood. Presently he stopped and leaned forward on his ax, coughing. A few paces farther on he slipped, came down heavily on one knee and had to rest again.

If it gets any worse, he thought . . .

But it did not get worse. Just as he reached the point where he was wondering dully if he could take so much as another step, the strength began to flow back into his body. His feet felt lighter. The drag of the pack lessened. His body, stiffened and enervated by the long hours of inactivity, responded once more to the demands of his will and was functioning again, thrusting forward again. It was better now. Not good, but at least better. Better than when they had first started; better than sitting and waiting; better than sitting and looking at Paul Delambre as he sat hunched on a stone with his hands over his face.

344

The fool, Ordway thought. The poor damn fool. . . .

His boots swung slowly in and out of view beneath him. His ax clicked dully against the rocks. And then presently he stopped again, not because he had to this time, but because the others had stopped ahead of him, and he could see Benner's muffled figure pointing, and suddenly he realized that they had reached the ridge.

The towers of the Riesensteg still rose on either side of them, black and gnarled, but the ground under their feet was level, and a few yards farther on it tilted away abruptly into gray depths of space. There was no wind—at least Ordway could feel none—and yet he was conscious at once of a difference in the mist. It was no longer a shroud, but a veil; no longer motionless, but slowly weaving and churning, as if propelled, now one way, now another, by some immense but undirected force in the void beyond.

They stood silently, listening.

"You can hear it?" Benner asked.

The others nodded.

"When we come up out of the towers we will feel it. It is stronger than before."

Veering sharply to the left, they began the ascent of the ridge. The actual angle of its incline was not precipitous, for the Riesensteg, as they had observed from below, marked a continuation across the ridge of the upper terrace of the south face. But its crest was so deeply crenellated with towers and clefts, spires and notches that there was scarcely a moment in which they were not clambering steeply up or steeply down. They groped their way slowly from pitch to pitch, from platform to platform, as if along the parapet of an ancient, crumbling castle.

The sound of the wind grew louder as they advanced—a deep, hollow moaning that seemed to fill the air around them as densely as the mist itself—and the mist above them was no longer simply weaving and churning, but spun revolving through space in immense streaming whorls. A sudden gust struck down at them from a cleft between two of the towers. It was followed after a few moments by a second and then a third. The towers were growing lower now, the notches between them wider; then towers and notches alike dropped away behind them. The ridge became a gently undulating rib of black rock slanting up into the grayness. The gusts became a tide.

345

They climbed with backs bent, their eyes on the slope before them. In the strict climbing sense the going was easier than before, but the battering of the wind made balance precarious, and the rock, which on the Riesensteg had been of an almost flinty hardness, was now soft and rotted and kept breaking away in thick lumps and slabs under their feet. It was as if the mist that enveloped them were a distillation not so much of air and cloud as of the mountain itself. It seemed not merely to be clinging to its surface, but to be oozing out from the very stones; to be spreading downward, damp and mouldering, into its deep inner core of granite and iron.

After perhaps an hour they rested for a few minutes in a shallow half-sheltered recess between two tilted boulders. Then they climbed on. The ridge buckled sharply upward, twisted to the right, straightened again, levelled off again. And then suddenly it began to narrow. The gray emptiness on either side edged in closer and closer, until only the narrowest catwalk remained under their feet. Above and ahead they could see it as a thin black line, less a ridge-crest than the top of a stone wall, slanting tenuously off into the mist.

Benner, in the lead, slackened his pace, testing the rocks in front of him before each forward step. Then he stopped and waited for the others to come up to him. "It is better we crawl here," he said. "Keep the rope tight between you, and watch out for when the wind changes."

Dropping to his hands and knees, he crept on along the ribbon of stone, and the others followed at intervals of a few yards. The wind lashed at them, first from one direction, then from the other, swinging their packs back and forth on their shoulders and making it necessary for them to lean sharply into its blast to keep from being thrown bodily off the ridge on the far side. A knob of rock came loose under Ordway's hand, teetered for an instant on the rim of space, and fell. He stopped, listening, but there was no sound from below, and he crept on again. The ridge, he noticed, was narrowing still farther, and he could see that Carla, ahead of him, was no longer crawling on hands and knees, but had straddled the thin wedge of rock and was hunching herself along it with her hands. Carefully shifting his position, he let his own legs down the sides and gripped the slender saw-edge with his knees. He raised 'and pushed; raised again, pushed again. Foot by foot, rock by rock, the black line of the ridge moved down toward him out of the wind and the fog.

And then at last it began to broaden once more. Presently they were no longer straddling it, but creeping, and then no longer creeping but on their feet again, thrusting forward, foot by foot, step by step, their heads bent low into the gray tide of the wind. The black, jagged line of the knife-edge faded away behind them. The rock beneath their boots was sound and firm again, and the ridge steepened abruptly. Above their heads they could see it tiering away into distance, like a gigantic granite stairway.

Finding a sheltered niche beneath an overhang, they rested again and munched at the raisins and shreds of chocolate that they carried in their pockets. Ordway pushed back the wristlet of his mitten and looked at his watch. It was exactly noon. His first reaction was surprise, for it was not what he had expected; but what he had expected, he realized suddenly, he did not know. Morning, noon, evening: they were all the same. There was nothing to distinguish them one from another. Time was simply the monotonous ticking of a tiny mechanism on his wrist. It was the next rock, the next step, the next breath. And that was all it was. Minutes and hours, sunshine and shadow, light and darkness were part of another lost, dimly remembered world that they had left behind them, immeasurably far below. In the world through which they now were moving there was only rock and mist and wind. There was only twilight, impenetrable and changeless.

And yet, as they began climbing again and he raised his eyes searchingly to the emptiness above, he began very slowly to become aware that something was changing. At first he thought it was merely that the rocks around them were of a lighter color than before. Then it seemed to him that the mist itself was brightening a little—or, if not brightening, thinning. The wind still drove it in scudding waves across the crest of the ridge, but there were jagged rents now between the waves, and through them, for an instant here, another instant there, he could see the dark, looming rock-faces of the mountainside above. Then, suddenly, he realized that still another thing was happening—or had already happened. One moment the air, the mist, the whole shrouded world around them had been a sombre, uniform gray; the next it was a dully gleaming yellowish brown. His clothing, his boots and the stones beneath his boots seemed to have changed subtly in texture and color. The ridge ahead and the three figures moving up it appeared clearer and more sharply defined, and yet, at the same time, curiously insubstantial and unreal, as if all dimension of depth had been taken from them. As he stared upward there was a quick silvery glint from the blade of an ice ax and, an instant later, a second, darker glow, as Carla turned her head and the copper of her hair shone vividly against the rocks beyond. There was no sun, no sky or brightness anywhere. And still, moment by moment, the mist grew thinner and more luminous, the vista before him clearer and more unreal. He was seized by a strange and indefinable sensation that the mountain was no longer a mountain at all, the ridge no longer a ridge, the rocks no longer rocks, but all of them mere painted images on an immense slanting stage, bathed in desolate amber twilight.

They trudged on up the great stairway, into the wind. . . . And then, suddenly, no longer into the wind. . . . For it had dropped. Instead of the steady tide beating down upon them there were now only light, fitful gusts plucking at their packs and clothing. Instead of the pervading roar in their ears there was stillness. Coming up over the crest of a steep pitch, Benner paused and stood motionless, peering up into the mist. The others, below, stopped and waited. The mountain itself seemed to be waiting. . . .

A deep, hollow moaning filled the very core of emptiness above them. The mist trembled and began to churn again, and the light behind it changed from amber to a livid green. It was as if all that shrouded world—air, mist, twilight, the mountain itself—were poised in swollen suspension above them, waiting only for the snap of a fuse to dissolve in one monstrous shattering explosion of thunder and lightning. But the explosion did not come. The moaning rose to a howl, the howl to a shrill, insane piping, and air and rock alike seemed suddenly to be vibrating with a deep inner tremor, as the torrent of sound poured down on them from the invisible heights above. For an instant the mist overhead thinned and parted, revealing depth beyond depth of tumultuous green twilight. Then it closed in again, thickened, surged down. Behind the mist came the ocean of the wind, and behind the wind, the snow.

It might have been thirty seconds, a minute, two minutes that Ordway crouched motionless in the blast. The ridge had disappeared; the figures of the others had disappeared; everything beyond a radius of a yard was blotted out by a wall of seething greenish whiteness. He leaned forward, balancing himself against the wind, and took a few steps forward. Then suddenly he stopped, realizing that a slip would endanger the others, if it caught them unprepared. He crouched waiting again, watching the rope that trailed over the rocks above him, his eyes slitted against the stinging snow. And at last the rope moved. Bent almost double and steadying himself with his ax, he followed it slowly upward into the howling emptiness ahead.

He half expected to find the others waiting for him at the top of the pitch where he had last seen Benner. But they were not there. The ridge levelled off briefly, then began to rise in a second pitch, but the yellow strand still slid slowly on up the gray, snow-lashed rocks. He counted his steps . . . fifty . . . a hundred. . . . He lost count, started over, stumbled, fell, picked himself up and crept on again. The wind was so violent now that he could breathe only by pushing the neck-piece of his helmet up over his nose and mouth. His eyelashes were so beaded with snow that he was barely able to see the rope at his feet.

And then suddenly he realized that the rope was motionless again. What he had taken for the outline of jutting rocks a few feet ahead were the figures of the three others crouched close together in a shallow depression between two tilted boulders.

Benner reached out an arm and drew him down beside them.

"You're going to wait here?" Ordway asked. Wind and snow tore the words from his lips, and he repeated them, shouting.

The guide shook his head. "There is not enough protection."

"What then?"

"There is no shelter anywhere on the ridge. We must get off it as soon as we can."

"Down, you mean?"

But in the same instant that he spoke he realized that Benner did not—and could not—mean down. There was no more possibility of their getting back over the knife-edge in the teeth of the storm than of simply standing up and walking down the precipices on either side of them.

"We must be getting near to where the ridges meet," Carla said. The guide nodded. "*Ja*, it cannot be so far now."

"Then the only thing—"

The rest of her words were lost in the howling of the wind, but there was no need to talk further. Struggling to their feet again, they faced upward into the blast.

"I will lead if you like," said Hein.

Benner shook his head without answering and took a few steps up the ridge. "Hold the rope short," he called back, turning, "and keep the one ahead always in sight."

Ordway watched his muffled figure fade into the grayness above; then Hein's; then Carla's. Then he too was climbing again, feet thrusting, head bent to the rocks and the rope.

He counted a hundred steps.

He counted a second hundred. . . .

The juncture of the east and southeast ridges, as Benner had said, may not have been far above them; but their progress was creepingly slow. For a distance of a few hundred feet the ridge flared up in a steep pitch of crests and notches that offered a slight protection against the wind. It was necessary here, however, to use the hands as well as the feet; the rock, though firm, was smooth and filmed with snow, and the sudden, unpredictable gusts that swooped in on them from both sides were so violent as almost to wrench them bodily from their holds. Then they came up onto a gentler gradient where the climbing itself was easier, but they were once again exposed to the full tide of the wind. It was not blowing down upon them now, but horizontally, out of the void to the west. The snow lashed stinging into their eyes and noses and mouths and beat against their clothing with the rataplan of machine-gun fire.

Ordway counted another hundred.

The ridge seemed to be curving slowly to the right and flattening out. The rough, spinelike protuberances of its crest had almost disappeared, and in their place was a patchwork of smooth, almost rectangular slabs, not unlike the shingles of a steeply sloping roof. As with shingles, too, the slabs were all joined in such a way that the thicker, protruding edges were on the downward side, offering no hold to either boot-edge or hand. For a few precarious minutes they groped and slipped helplessly, while the wind nudged them nearer and nearer to the gray emptiness on their right. Then they went down on all fours and crept onward, clinging to the slabs by the friction of palms and knees.

Now Ordway was counting the forward thrusts of his hands. The left hand was the odd numbers, the right hand the even, and when he reached a hundred once more he realized that he must have been counting aloud, because his mouth was filled with snow. Or perhaps he had been holding it open to breathe. There was a tight, throbbing knot in his throat again, and the trickle of air sucking down into his lungs burned with an icy fire. . . . One, he started over again. Two, three, four, five . . . sixseveneightnineten. . . . When he got to fifty, he decided, they would be there. Fifty—or was it five hundred? That was the trouble, of course: he not only didn't know what he was counting for, but not even what he was counting to. There were 365 days to a year, 5280 feet to a mile, nine innings to a ball game, two halves to a whole. But how many steps made a mountainside? How many arm's lengths got you 'there'? . . . "Using Peck's Flight Manual and the table of logarithms, Captin Ordway, will you be good enough to tell the class how many R.P.M.'s make a war?"

It did not matter, of course. It did not matter at all. The numbers blurred, streaming past him like the snow, and blew away. They had climbed beyond numbers, as they had climbed beyond time and the sun.

He stopped for a moment, letting the slack of the rope run out over the slabs ahead, turned his head from the wind and drew in two or three deep, burning breaths. Steady now, he told himself quietly. Very slow and steady and sure. . . .

He knew that he could not go on much farther.

And yet it was not tiredness of which he was most conscious as he crept on again, groping and thrusting, up the rocks. It was not the aching of arms and legs nor the leaden weight of the pack nor the pain in his throat and lungs nor the snow lashing into the numbed thickness of his face, but, curiously and inexplicably, the same pervading sense of well-being that he had experienced once or twice before on the mountain when his body had been on the verge of exhaustion. A wave of exhilaration, almost of exultation, seemed to be slowly rising within him, filling his bones and blood, carrying him strongly, irresistibly on. Each slab moving slowly

351

downward beneath his bent head was another enemy vanquished, each groove and crevice and tiny flickering snowpatch a milestone on an immense and portentous journey. He was not recoiling from the wind now, but breasting it, subduing it. Its wild strength was no longer fighting against his body, but with it; entering into him, becoming a part of him.

One, two, he counted . . .

He was watching the rope again—a yellow, snow-rimed thread of twisted hemp inching tortuously up over the rocks ahead. . . . A-hundred-and-one. A-hundred-and-two. . . . It led up into roaring emptiness; to Carla, creeping on hands and knees through the emptiness above him; to Hein, above Carla; to Benner, above Hein. . . . A thousand and one. A thousand and two. . . . It was a bridge, a messenger, an artery; an umbilical cord joining them together in the emptiness, waist to waist, body to body, life to life. . . . Ten-thousand-and-one. Ten-thousand-and-two. . . . A slight tremor came down the cord to him, and, raising his eyes, he saw that Carla was no longer on her hands and knees, but walking again. He struggled to his feet, leaned into the wind and lurched forward. The smooth slabs were gone now, and the ridge ahead appeared to be buckling up in a jagged crest. To the right and above, the enormous, dark shape of the main east ridge was moving very slowly toward them out of the gray ocean of space.

Then they were together again, crouched with their backs to the wind on a great promontory of stormswept rock. Below them the two diverging ridges slanted away into the opaque depths of distance. Above, the single ridge into which they now fused climbed on into the wind and snow.

Ordway peered around him through the scudding twilight.

"There is no shelter," Benner said. "I have looked."

"Can't we get off the ridge?"

"We must get off it," said Hein.

The guide nodded. "Ja, we must. To stay on it any longer is to—" He broke off, looking from one to another. "You are all right?" he asked.

Hein nodded. Ordway nodded. Then Ordway looked at Carla. Her face was merely a snow-streaked mask in the white circle of her helmet, but as she raised it to him he could see that her lips were smiling a little, and her half-opened eyes seemed to be glowing with dark green fire.

"All right?" he said.

"Yes, Binks—all right."

The words were barely audible, but whether it was because of the faintness of her voice or the tumult of the storm he could not tell.

"Let me take your pack," he said.

She shook her head.

"I think there is a snow-slope and a big cornice up to the left," said Hein.

Facing into the storm again, they crossed the narrow platform of the promontory, clambered up over the serrated crest of the ridge and bore left and upward for a distance of perhaps fifty feet. Here, as Hein had said, there was snow—a broad, steeply rising band of whiteness slanting away almost at right-angles to the ridge —and at its top, dimly visible in the gloom, an immense ice-cornice curling out against the sky. Benner balanced himself carefully and tested the footing. The surface was little more than a mass of churning spume, but beneath it was old, firm snow into which their boots bit securely, and, half climbing and half floundering, they were able to zigzag slowly upward. In perhaps fifteen minutes they reached the top of the slope and began hacking their way up an ice-cleft in the cornice. In another fifteen they stumbled out on its summit into a small snow-filled depression between the upper rim and a dark outcropping of rock that rose like a low, curving wall beyond.

Benner stopped, peering around him; then he stooped close to the snow and turned his face to the wind. "*Ja*, there is a little protection," he said. "If we dig down it may be enough." He rose and walked toward the lip of the cornice, trampling heavily and probing with his ax. When he turned back to the others he was nodding slowly.

"It's solid?" Ordway asked.

"*Ja*, it is solid."

With hands, feet and axes they cleared away a few square feet of new-fallen snow. Then, huddling in the hollow they had formed, they unstrapped the largest of the packs and brought out their sole remaining tent. Lying prostrate on the wildly whipping canvas, they adjusted the guy ropes with stiff, fumbling fingers, and drove the steel pegs, one by one, into the old, frozen snow that formed the base beneath the drifts. When the last one was in, the tent itself was almost buried beneath a thick coating of white. Pushing their packs before them, they burrowed beneath it, and groped for the two poles.

"Also," said Benner, his voice a hoarse whisper in the darkness. "Very slow and careful now."

He and Carla took one pole, Ordway and Hein the other. Bracing with their feet and clinging to them with hands and knees and bodies, they began to raise them. The slender wood swayed and trembled, and the tent billowed suddenly out above them with a savage lunge. But their grip held. Wood and canvas held. They strained at the poles until they were vertical, swivelled their pointed ends deep into the snow and weighted the bottoms of the walls with the packs and axes.

"Better to keep holding on for a while," Benner said.

They crouched motionless in their pocket of darkness, two of them gripping each pole with both hands. The snow battered against the canvas. The wind howled.

Chapter 19

The wind howls. The sun recedes into gray mist, and
spatters of rain drive down the valleys of the Danube, the Rhine,
the Rhone, the Po. As the hours pass the wind grows stronger
and colder, the rain swells from a drizzle to a slanting torrent.
The bombers and fighters stand motionless on a hundred shrouded
airstrips. Along a thousand bomb-pocked roads the yellow dust
thickens slowly into slime and rises toward the hubs and axles of
the creeping trucks. In his slit trench beside an olive tree in an
orchard above Viareggio, Private Floyd Murdock of Delphi, Indiana, scowls at the sky, throws away a sudden pulp of his last
ration cigarette and announces: "Here come another goddamn
Eyetie winter."

Above Viareggio the storm blows from one direction, at Strasbourg from another, in the Hurtgen Forest from still another. It
sprawls across a million square miles of western Europe in a seemingly unrelated confusion of squalls and gales. But fundamentally
there are only two winds. From the south a tide of warm, moist
air is moving up out of the Mediterranean over the Pyrenees and
Balkans, the Apennines and the Alps. And from the north and
east the first great cold front of approaching winter is pushing
massively down across the brown plains of Russia and Poland.
Where the two meet, above the heart of the continent, the cold
air, rising, grows colder itself and condenses into cloud. This con-
densation, however, warms the colder air below, and it in turn

355

begins to rise and condense. Warmth and cold, dryness and moisture intermingle and struggle. The conflicting winds merge in an immense vortex and begin to whirl counterclockwise, faster and faster.

On the frontier between north and south stand the Alps. The cold front beats down upon their northern slopes; the warm front, or *Föhn*, streams up on the other side from Italy and the sea, and at their apex the two meet and do battle. Here, indeed, fifteen thousand feet above the lowland plains, is the very node and fulcrum of the storm. It is no longer rain that falls, but snow and sleet. The clouds are not merely above the earth, but around it and on all sides, and with each hundred and thousand and ten thousand feet that they ascend, the winds blow with a wilder and intenser fury. There is still an overall pattern to the storm—still the interlocking grapple of *Föhn* and northwind and the gigantic vortex spinning slowly to the east. But on any individual mountain the pattern is lost in chaos. Ridge, pinnacle and buttress tear the wind into innumerable currents and cross-currents. Cornice and couloir pour down their burden of snow, no less than the sky. On the flatland the storm is almost wholly a thing of the elements and the earth a mere passive recipient of its violence, but the great peaks take the elements to them and remake them in their own vaster, more terrible image. The whole range seems almost to rear back and strike. The mountains themselves storm.

The White Tower storms. . . .

High above the surrounding crests of the Oberland its ancient walls catch the wildest blasts of wind and snow, wrench them and tear them and fling them back, reeling. It is no longer an insensate mass, but a thing alive. A vast, hollow moaning seems to emanate from its innermost core, thinning and heightening as it rises, until it becomes a wild, piping skirl along its curving precipices and skyline ridges. Deep tremors wrench its snow-slopes and ice-walls; white cataracts stream down gully and chimney, and avalanches plunge, thundering, onto the glaciers. But every patch and shred that its sloughs off is replaced tenfold from the wind and sky. Pouring its life down into the valleys, it yet does not diminish, but rather increases, itself. Spending its strength, it becomes, not weaker, but ever stronger.

The hours pass. The storm rages on, unslackening. And then

abruptly, inexplicably slackens. The wind drops, and the snow falls in immense, gentle flakes through the motionless air. Even the clouds are lighter now—scarcely clouds at all any more, but a thin mist again, diamond-bright with the pinpricks of a hundred million ice crystals. Where a few minutes before all was violence and tumult, there is now only a shrouded white stillness. . . . But the storm has not passed. It has merely withdrawn itself temporarily into the depths of the sky, drawing its scattered forces together, remarshalling its powers. Nor has the mountain spent its strength. It is merely waiting. . . . And then, as suddenly as they stopped, they strike again. The clouds turn from silver to sullen gray and from gray to a green-tinged black. The wind swoops down again —first with a whine, then with a wail, finally in a rending, shattering roar—and the snow lashes in savage horizontal waves against precipice and ice-wall. The false peace of the lull is over. Mountain and sky strike out at each other again, locked in the blind fury of war.

The hours pass. It is day and then night and then day again. But there are neither hours nor day nor night in this lost, primordial world that rises above the world.

There are only the mountain and the storm.

The wind piped among the white gables of the Gasthof zum blauen Himmel. It soughed through the slanting forests, raged across boulder-slope and wasteland, glacier and icefall, and battered at the tent on the lower terrace, in which Nicholas Radcliffe sat brewing himself a cup of tea. Four thousand feet higher up the mountain it moaned in the guy ropes of the second tent that crouched in the snow-choked hollow beneath the towers of the Riesensteg.

Paul Delambre lay motionless with his eyes closed, listening. Anything was better than the stillness, he thought. Anything was better than the stillness. . . .

He had slept, wakened, sat up listening to the storm, and lain down again, half-sleeping, and half-waking. The sound of the wind receded slowly, and in its place was the distant booming of surf, the hum of cicadas in the jacaranda trees, the rumble of traffic as it poured out of the Champs Elysées into the Place de la Concorde. Then these too were gone, and there was a woman's voice calling to him from very far away. Was it Ariel's or Astrid's? Presently he realized that it was neither, but the Austrian girl's: Carla Dehn's. Yes, he thought, smiling to himself a little—she is lovely too. . . .

When he sat up again there was no sound at all. Not even the wind. Snapping on his flashlight, he saw that it was eleven o'clock. Whether it was morning or night, however, he did not know, for the snow was drifted so thickly over the tent that no faintest gleam of light could have penetrated down through the canvas. He began winding the watch, and the stem turned for a long time before it was tight. A whole day had passed, he decided, and it was morning again. Feeling his way to the entrance, he crept through the sleeve and pushed his way upward through the white powder of the drifts. The hollow was a hollow no longer, but a smooth-surfaced pond of feathery whiteness. Above it the not-yet-fallen snow seemed to be hanging almost motionless in the air, like the dots in an enormous white veil. And behind the veil was blackness.

Delambre turned, crawled back into the tent and sat motionless again in the dark. All right, he thought—it was night. It did not matter.

In any case, he should eat. Snapping on the flashlight again, he fumbled in the rucksack and brought out a tin of stew, a packet of tea and the fireless cooker, but once they lay on the blankets before him he merely sat staring at them. The more you eat, he told himself, the less there will be for the others.

He snapped off the light. And then suddenly he laughed. Yes, of course, he thought—you are a very noble fellow, mon brave. . . . He could not have forced so much as a mouthful down his burning throat.

He sat cross-legged on the rumpled blankets in the darkness, and both his brain and stomach seemed to be revolving slowly within him with a slow, elliptical motion. It was the cognac, of course—the after-effects of the full bottle of undiluted Courvoisier. Yet he had drunk as much, and more, many times, and it had never before affected him in quite this way. . . . What was it, then? . . . It is the altitude, imbécile, he told himself. The altitude, and that you are tired.

He was very tired. It was dark and absolutely still. As he sat listening it seemed to him that the darkness and the stillness were

358

slowly thickening around him, pressing gently downward, entering into him in a soft black tide. If only it would blow again, he thought. . . .

He lay down and closed his eyes.

And when he awoke again it was blowing. An immense, deep moaning filled the air around him, and the walls and roof of the tent were trembling and creaking in the wind. Opening his eyes, he saw that the tent was no longer black, but filled with a faint brown twilight. The drifts on the roof have blown away, he thought. In a moment the tent itself would blow away too.

He lay quietly, waiting. The wind rose to a shuddering roar in his ears, and with each succeeding gust and blast it seemed certain that the thin shell of canvas would break loose from the earth and spin wildly away into space. But the minutes passed, and the ropes still held. Poles and canvas held. And presently he sat up and looked around him in the gloom. There were the blankets and the rucksack and his ax and boots and a coil of rope. There were the packet of tea and the tin of stew and the fireless cooker. Against the wall, in a far corner, stood the empty bottle of Courvoisier.

For a little while Delambre stared at it dully. And then, suddenly, his heart began to pound. The second bottle . . . he had forgotten it. There was still the second bottle, if the others had not found and taken it. And they could not have found it because he had hidden it, against exactly that possibility. On the rim of the hollow; in a crevice between the rocks. . . . In the next instant he was on his knees, crawling toward the entrance of the tent, shouldering through the sleeve. The storm struck at him when he rose to his feet outside, but he scarcely noticed it as he floundered straight ahead through the drifts toward the far side of the hollow. Then, abruptly, he stopped, peering around him. Hollow, slope, rocks, every familiar feature of the campsite were gone, and in their place was a bare, trackless bowl of wind-riffled snow. He took a few steps forward, glanced back at the tent, took another few steps to the left. Then, crouching, he began to dig. He dug for two or three minutes, patiently and methodically at first, and then more and more hurriedly, until his arms were flailing through the soft powder and his breath was coming in short, harsh gasps. But there was only snow. He moved five paces farther on and dug again; then five to the right, and another five. He was digging without plan now, in loops, circles and crisscrosses, with an intense, almost demonic ferocity.

And at last he struck rock. His hand was groping over the roughness of a boulder, a second boulder, a third; then plunging deep and searching into the pockets between them. In the first there was only snow. In the second and third, snow. He crawled on, digging and groping, from one rock to the next, one pocket to the next, and in the seventh or eighth his fingers came in touch with a smooth, rounded surface. For a moment he lay motionless in the drift. Then, very slowly and carefully, he brought up the bottle.

He got to his feet, holding it close against him in his mittened hand. The pounding of his heart had stopped, and he felt the feverish tenseness that had filled him draining like a thin liquid from his limbs. His head felt suddenly clear, his body relaxed and strangely hollow. Calmly, almost defiantly, he raised his head to the storm.

The wind lashed at him and drove the snow in long stinging spears into his face; but, squinting his eyes, he could see the brown triangle of the tent-roof rising from the drifts, and beyond it the steepening billows of the slope and the lower towers of the Riesensteg. The towers were no longer black, but white and ghostly behind the scudding grayness. From their hooded crests long scarves and pennons of spindrift streamed out into the void beyond.

A blast of air, stronger than any before, caught him and sent him reeling. When he picked himself up, however, he still did not start for the tent, but stood braced against the storm, his face raised again, his eyes closed. He felt the storm against his lids, tasted it on his lips, listened to its roaring in his ears. He listened to it howling among the towers above, climbing through them to the ridge, wailing across the ridge, descending on the far side, pouring down the precipices, down the ice-walls, down the snow-slopes and boulder-slopes and glaciers, pouring across the wastelands and the valleys, across the ranges and the forests and the rivers and the cities, through the dark, sunless skies of Europe. He heard it beating in cold rain on the cobbles of Montmartre, on the rubble of London, Rotterdam, Hamburg, Warsaw; on the concrete of pillboxes; the steel of tank-plates, the aluminum of plane-wings; on gun-barrels and helmets and hunched shoulders and the quiet gray faces turned to the gray sky. He heard it everywhere—*all* of it—not merely the wind or the rain or the snow, but the storm itself; the essence; the noumenon. Sweeping over the old, scarred shell of the earth; through the misery and corruption of mankind. . . .

He opened his eyes and looked down, feeling a tingling numbness in his feet. He had forgotten to put on his boots. Holding the bottle in one hand and pushing through the drifts with the other, he struggled back to the tent, crept through the sleeve and squatted down in the brown, creaking twilight. The bottle was like a cylinder of ice in his hands, and he wrapped it carefully in the blankets beside him.

For a little while he sat listening to the storm. Moment by moment it was increasing in intensity, growing louder and wilder, and then still louder, still wilder, until it seemed to him that earth and sky alike must be filled, choked, enveloped in an annihilation of wind and snow. Only the tent, and he himself within the tent, were not a part of it. The storm swooped down on them, battered them, tore at them, but left them untouched and undestroyed—a still, twilit hollowness in the very core of chaos.

Now the hollowness, too, seemed to be growing—swelling. . . . He crept across to where his rucksack stood, brought out his notebook and a pencil and squatted down again with the notebook open on his crossed legs.

Nous sommes les hommes vides, he wrote.

Nous sommes les hommes rembourrés . . .

The pencil stopped moving, and he sat staring intently at the two lines of small, precise script. "Yes, it is good," he said aloud. "Almost as good as when Eliot wrote it in English."

He thought he was going to laugh, but he did not laugh. Ripping the page from the notebook, he threw it into a corner and sat with eyes closed, listening to the wind.

. . . And voices are
In the wind's singing
More distant and more solemn
Than a fading star.

That was Eliot too. It was always Eliot. Or Gide. Or Verlaine or Baudelaire or Keats or Heine or Bach or Debussy or Matisse or Van Gogh or Joyce or the Book of Job. It was always someone else. Never himself. Never a word, an idea, a song, an image from the emptiness and hollowness of himself.

Save only the one image . . .

He unwrapped the bottle from the blanket. It was still cold, but not so cold as before, and holding it between his knees he pried out the cork, and then lifted it to his lips. The brandy was like liquid ice in his mouth, but as it spread downward it glowed in the emptiness and hollowness with a deep, secret fire.

He began to write again. He wrote swiftly, steadily, surely, in his fine, beautifully formed hand, pausing only to turn the pages and to drink. When he had done five pages he tore them from the book and laid them on the blanket beside him. He did the same after the next five, and the next, and the next, until presently the blanket was littered with small oblongs of paper. He knew neither how many there were nor how long he had been writing, but kept on without stopping for another five, and then another, and one more—and one more. At the bottom of the last page he wrote, very carefully: *Paul Delambre, Tour Blanche, Octobre, 1944.*

"Alors, mon brave," he said. "It is yours. All yours."

He sat quietly again; listened to the wind again. Then, smiling a little, he began to collect the scattered sheets. When at last he had them all, he crossed to the tent entrance, crept halfway through the sleeve, and, crouching, passed them, one by one, from his left hand to his right and from his right out into the storm. He did not throw them away. He merely opened his hand, the wind snatched at them, and they were gone. When his hands were empty and he crept back into the tent and picked up the bottle again, its glass was warm to the touch.

It was day, and then night, and then day again. The storm still howled among the towers of the Riesensteg. It swept over the rotting rocks and gleaming drifts, across the open ridge and the twisting line of the knife-edge and the naked shingles of the upper ridge beyond. It roared with an unremitting fury of wind and snow about the tent in the hollow above the lip of the great ice-cornice.

Andreas Benner peered, frowning, at the sagging canvas of the roof. "The snow is too heavy now," he said. "Another few inches and it will crack."

He pushed at the roof with his hands and shoulders, but the drift above did not budge. Pulling on his helmet, he crept from the tent, and a moment later the others could see the movement of his arm along the canvas, as he swept the snow away. When he came back through the entrance he was wiping his eyes, and his beard and eyebrows were flecked with white.

"No change?" said Ordway.

The guide shook his head.

"I think it is better we hold the poles again," he said presently.

It was lighter in the tent with the roof cleared, but there was also less protection from the wind, and the canvas whipped and snapped about them again with ominous jerks. The sound of the storm was louder, too, making it impossible for them to talk to to one another except by cupping their hands and shouting. But this did not matter, for they had long since passed the point where they either wanted or needed to talk. They sat silently, listening to the storm. They waited.

And waited. . . .

Late in the afternoon of the first day the wind had seemed to drop a little, and Benner got suddenly to his feet. "I am going down," he announced.

"Down?"

"To Herr Delambre."

"It is impossible," said Hein.

"Think of the knife-edge," Ordway said. "And the slabs."

"Still I must try."

Deaf to their protests, he made ready and, with the others following him, left the tent. But no sooner had he stepped out of the drifts of the hollow than a blast of wind struck him like an ax-blow, and he had to fall flat, with hands and feet dug into the snow, to keep from being blown out over the cornice.

"Come back, you fool!" Hein shouted.

Ordway started after him, but before he had taken more than a step or two the guide turned and struggled back to them through the drifts. He did not speak, but merely shook his snow-crusted head and crawled into the tent. For several minutes he sat silently in a corner, his blue eyes staring unseeingly at a crack in the groundcloth between his feet.

"He is one of my *Herren*," he murmured. "I am responsible for him."

"But there is nothing you can do, Andreas," said Carla. She put her hand lightly over his. "He will be all right. Stop worrying about him."

Benner shook his head again. "He is one of my *Herren*," he repeated.

The tent was designed to accommodate two people, or at the most three, and with the four of them crowded into it, it was impossible even to shift position without bumping into either the walls, the poles or one another. As time passed, too, the thin air grew stale and more difficult to breathe. Ordway's throat was contracting into a tight knot again, and presently he began to cough. Propping an ax in the entrance-sleeve, they tried to let in just enough air for ventilation, but the blast from outside was too strong for them to control, and in a few minutes everything in the tent was covered with a fine film of snow. When they closed up the vent, the air quickly grew stale again, and Ordway resumed his coughing.

They ate supper with each of them hunched into a corner and the Primus, food and utensils crowded into the little circle formed by their spread legs. Then they sat waiting again; listening again. When it became dark they lighted the kerosense lamp, but after fifteen or twenty minutes Benner reached out and turned down the wick. "It is perhaps better we save it," he said.

They slept in two-hour shifts, two of them rolling up in the blankets against the walls while the others sat guard over tent-poles, guy-ropes and canvas. Ordway and Carla slept first, and each time the former was awakened by Benner the guide whispered, "I will watch with you, Herr Martin. We will let her sleep." But no sooner had the men agreed than Carla woke by herself and insisted, over their protests, on taking her turn.

"It is not necessary, *Fräulein*."

"Nevertheless—"

"It is better for you to rest."

"And for you, too."

. . . . And for the next two hours, while Hein and Benner slept, she sat quietly beside Ordway, her head on his shoulder, her hand in his, in the roaring, creaking blackness.

Toward midnight the wind slackened. For perhaps half an hour it blew fitfully against the canvas in steadily diminishing gusts; then even the gusts dropped away, and in their place was an immense sounding silence.

"Let's have a look," Ordway whispered.

Moving carefully, so as not to disturb the others, he and Carla crept from the tent out into the waist-deep drifts. Not a wisp or shred of air was stirring. The night lay spread around them as black and still as an ocean depth, and through it the curtain of snow floated earthward so slowly and gently that it seemed scarcely to be moving at all.

They did not move either, but stood quietly, hand in hand watching. "The wedding guests are throwing rice," Carla said.

"And the bell is ringing. Hear it?"

"Yes, I hear it, Martin."

"Come on—we'll miss the train."

"To Niagara Falls?"

"Hell, no."

"I thought that was where Americans always went on their honeymoon."

"It's not where we're going."

"Where are we going, my husband?"

"Some place warm."

"And bright."

"And flat."

He laughed and bent to kiss her, and there was her face cold and sweet as the snow against his own, and the leather and flannel and wool of her muffled body in his arms. ". . . And where brides don't wear any damned clothes at all," he added.

When, a little while later, they lay down to sleep, there was still no wind. There was only darkness and stillness, and behind the stillness a single bell ringing, very faint and far away. But when they woke again, after two hours, the wind had returned; and in the morning the storm was raging about them as wildly as ever. For breakfast they had a cup of tea and two biscuits with marmalade apiece. Then they sat listening again; waiting again. . . .

After a while Ordway became aware that he had to urinate and struggled out through the entrance into the drifts. When he returned, Hein and Benner went out, and, after them, Carla. She was gone much longer than the others, and when at last she reappeared her clothing was plastered with snow and her lips purplish with cold. "Never believe that it isn't a man's world, meine Herrschaften," she said, wrapping herself in her blankets.

Almost an hour later Benner, who had been sitting motionless in his corner, reached suddenly for his ax. "I am going to reconnoitre," he announced.

This time, creeping the whole way on hands and knees, he succeeded in circling the ice-bulge above the rim of the cornice. But when he reached the top of the cleft that led down to the slope below, a blast of wind and spume roared up about him like a geyser; and after a half-dozen futile attempts to deploy his way around it he crawled slowly back to the tent. Once again they sat hunched in the stale, wind-battered gloom, their eyes closed or fixed, unseeing, on the canvas walls, moving only to relieve the cramped stiffness of their legs and bodies. Ordway's watch showed ten o'clock; eleven; eleven-thirty. . . .

At noon they ate again: another cup of tea and three tablespoonfuls of stew for each.

"Shall we finish the cheese now?" Carla asked.

"It is perhaps better we save it," said Benner.

They did not talk further about the food. They did not talk about Delambre. Or their plans.

Sitting wrapped in his blanket with his eyes closed, Ordway felt a gentle, almost luxurious torpor spreading slowly through his body and brain. Half asleep, half awake, he listened to the wind—to the sound of the snow in the wind—to the deep wild music beyond the snow and the storm. . . . Or was it music? he wondered. . . . It was deeper, more vibrant and pervading, than any music he had ever heard. It was a humming, rather—an immense yet elusive humming, such as he and Radcliffe had heard a few nights before in the dark stillness of the lower terrace. A humming that swelled slowly to a drone, and a drone that swelled slowly to a roar. . . . Suddenly the tent seemed to lurch and begin to fall. It was no longer a tent at all, but a cockpit, and the plane was falling, steep and twisting, through the roaring, wing-darkened sky.

Ted! a voice shouted. Harry! . . . Bix! . . .

The sound jerked him back to consciousness, and he opened his eyes. For a moment he was certain that he had called aloud, but the others, huddled in their corners, neither spoke nor moved. The wind was only wind again; the tent only a tent. As he looked around, it seemed to him that the sloping brown walls were closing in very slowly about them.

Throwing off the blanket, he crossed to the entrance and crept out into the storm. He remained there, crouched in the drifts, until the blast of wind and snow stung his mind to clarity, and then returned to the tent. The others had still not moved. He sat

366

down again and pulled the blanket over him. He sat listening and waiting.

Presently he became aware that he wanted a cigarette. He had smoked very little—in fact he had felt practically no desire to—during the past few days on the mountain, but now, suddenly, he needed a cigarette as he had never needed one before in his life. Fumbling in his pockets, he brought out his flattened pack and fingered it open. There were five left; two Camels and three German Abdullahs from a box that Herr Knubel had given him before they left the inn. He hesitated, took one of the Abdullahs, hesitated again, and crept to the tent entrance. Squatting beside it, he lit the cigarette and blew the smoke out into the flapping sleeve.

The first inhalation went down through his throat like a jet of flame. And on the second he began to cough. He waited for the spasm to pass; inhaled again; coughed again.

"That is foolish, Martin," Carla said.

"What's foolish?"

"To smoke. When your throat is bad."

"All right—so it's foolish."

The words came out strained and harsh, and ended in more coughing. Then he took another puff. Carla did not speak again, but he was conscious of her eyes watching him in the gloom.

With an abrupt, almost savage, gesture he crushed out the cigarette and crawled over beside her. "I'm sorry," he murmured.

"There is nothing to be sorry for," she said.

"I'm sorry, Carla."

She smiled a little, without speaking, and he moved his hand and laid it over hers.

"Carla—" he said.

"Yes?"

"Hello, Carla."

"Hello, Binks."

He shifted around and rested his head lightly against her shoulder. Then he closed his eyes.

When he awoke it was almost dark and very still. Carla was still sitting beside him, but Benner and Hein were gone.

"The wind's dropped again," he said.

Carla nodded.

"Like last night."

367

"No—the snow has stopped too."

He was wide awake now and sitting bolt upright. "Then the storm's over?" he said.

"Andreas thinks so."

Creeping from the tent, they found Benner and Hein standing side by side in the drift, staring upward. Only the faintest remnant of wind was blowing, and above them the mist was drifting slowly in great shreds and tatters across the mountainside. A sombre twilight still filled the air, but now it was the twilight of evening—not of storm. As they watched, it grew darker; but the snow-slopes around them, instead of fading into the darkness, seemed moment by moment to be growing whiter and brighter. Beyond the slopes the hooded pinnacles of the ridge were emerging one by one from their dissolving sheaths of vapor. And beyond the ridge a deep purple tide was seeping into the gunmetal grayness of the sky.

"At last," said Ordway.

Benner nodded.

"You don't think it might start up again?"

"No, it is finished now. It will be clear tomorrow."

"Then tomorrow we—" Ordway broke off, and the guide did not speak again.

"We should have some supper now," Carla said after a moment.

Back in the tent they lit the Primus and heated another meal of stew and tea. As they ate, slowly and in silence, the unaccustomed stillness of the night outside seemed to be pressing in against the canvas walls like a tangible weight.

"Ja, it will be clear," said Benner suddenly. "As soon as it is light I will start off."

"Start off?" Ordway repeated.

"Down to Herr Delambre."

No one spoke for a moment.

"No," said Hein. He paused, looking slowly from one to another, and when he spoke again his voice was low and even. "If we go down now we will never get back again. It will be the end."

"I did not say we, Herr Hein," said Benner. "I said that I would go down."

"Alone?"

"Ja—alone." The guide sat silently studying the backs of his hands, and when he raised his eyes again he was looking at Ord-

368

way. "I have been thinking about this thing all day, Herr Martin," he said, "and here is what I think we should do. Herr Hein is right when he says that if we all go down we will probably not be able to come up again. We will be tired. There are the tents and food and many other reasons. Also, the new snow will not yet be frozen tomorrow, and it will not be good for four people to be climbing together over the narrow places on the ridge. What is a better thing is this. I will go down to Herr Delambre in the morning. Alone a man can go more quickly, and it will take me only three hours—maybe four. If Herr Delambre is all right I will come back in the afternoon, either with him, if he wants to come, or alone again, if he does not, and the next day we will make the try for the summit. If he is not all right—if he is sick or there has been trouble with the tent or some other thing—I will stay there, and the next morning the three of you will come down."

"Without even trying for the top?" said Hein.

"If Herr Delambre is not all right, the most important thing is that we get him down off the mountain as quickly as possible. Also, there is food for—how did we figure it?—just for three more days now, if we go on eating only the little that we have been. Tomorrow, with the new snow, even to think of the top is useless. You agree with that, no?"

Hein nodded. "No," he agreed. "Tomorrow there is no chance."

"And after the next day there would be no food for the descent."

"Leaving the day-after-tomorrow," said Ordway.

"Ja—leaving the day-after-tomorrow. That is—"

"Sunday," Hein said.

There was a silence. The other three sat looking at Benner, and Benner sat looking at the backs of his hands.

"Ja, Sonntag," he said presently. "If the snow has frozen and Herr Delambre is all right."

The snow had already begun to freeze an hour later, when they came out of the tent for a few minutes before making ready for sleep. It was much colder than during the storm, and the last shreds of wind and mist had disappeared. The snow-slopes tiered above them, white and gleaming, to the jagged ridge. Beyond the ridge was blackness, and beyond the blackness were the stars.

Chapter 20

The sun rises over Europe, warm and golden in the blue October sky. Its long rays slant across the valleys of the Danube, the Rhine, the Rhone, the Po. They move gently over the swollen rivers, the drenched and gutted cities, the sodden fields, the brown and gray columns that crawl like huge serpents through the mud. They shine on the wet barrels of guns and the thick ochrish pools in the bomb craters and foxholes. They glint from the windshields of trucks and from the snouts of tanks and from the wings of planes and from the sightless blue eyes of Private Floyd Murdock of Delphi, Indiana, who lies staring at the sky beside a flooded slit-trench in an orchard beyond Viareggio. High above the plains and cities and armies, they stream in gleaming splendor upon the white shroud of the Alps.

In the valley of Kandermatt the Aarn pours in milky torrents over its ancient stones. The fields beside it spread green and shining under a billion round drops of moisture, and on the mountainsides above a hundred-thousand interlacing rivulets trickle downward through the spruce and rhododendron and juniper. Still higher, beyond the tree line, the minute flowers among the moss and furze suck color from the brightening sky; the gray wilderness of the boulder-slopes glitters with mica and long swathes of melting snow, and a thin gauze of snow whitens the desolation of the wasteland. Then, as the range buckles upward, the snow thickens and billows. It lies in deep, trackless rivers on the glaciers, filling

370

the crevasses and obliterating the seracs. It chokes the gorges and couloirs, trails in white scarves across the rock-walls and ice-walls and rises in a vast powdery sea to the ridges and the peaks.

For a few moments, as the sun comes up and its long rays stream horizontal across the ranges to the east, the entire mass of the Weissturm shines with a cold and glittering fire. Then all color fades. All life and movement fade. Wrapped in a white caul of stillness, the mountain stands against the brightening sky.

On the terrace of the Gasthof zum blauen Himmel broken branches, twigs and leaves lay in tangled confusion on the gravel and the grass. Emerging onto the verandah, Herr Knubel stood for a few minutes tugging at his nose and watching Annamarie, the waitress, as she raked the debris into small piles beside the driveway. Then he descended the steps.

"That will do now," he said.

The girl stared at him with blank blue eyes.

"The breakfast dishes and the beds are waiting."

"But Frau Knubel said—"

"Never mind what Frau Knubel said. Get along with you. This is a man's work." Taking the rake from her, Herr Knubel began scraping it across the soggy turf. Annamarie stared at him for another moment, giggled suddenly and went into the inn.

Nutzloser Dummkopf, he thought.

He raked one pile together, then another. Then he laid down the rake and walked over to where the telescope stood beside the terrace wall. No one had remembered to take it in when the storm broke, and its brass casing was filmed and tarnished with moisture. Getting a rag from the storeroom, Herr Knubel dried and polished it vigorously. When he had finished he cleaned the lenses with his handkerchief, bent to the eyepiece and began adjusting the sights.

A formless grayness flowed downward through the circular glass; then a blurred grayish-white; then a brilliant, almost blinding white. Very slowly he inched the telescope upward along the immense shining mass that rimmed the sky.

"They have not returned then?" a voice said behind him.

Herr Knubel turned and looked into the gaunt, weathered face of Christian Mehrwalder. His sharp brown eyes widened in surprise. "I did not see you on the road," he said.

371

"No, I came the back way. Through the fields." The guide's eyes were on the telescope. "They have not returned then?" he repeated.

Herr Knubel shook his head.

"Have you found them with the glass?"

"No, not yet."

Mehrwalder bent to the eyepiece. For perhaps two minutes he swung the telescope in long, slow arcs; then he straightened and shook his head. "There is too much glare," he said.

"In any case," said Herr Knubel, "they are probably already down at one of the huts."

The guide shrugged. "One hopes so."

"You mean it is bad up there, eh?"

"With such a storm? And on such a mountain?" Mehrwalder was silent a moment, and when he spoke again his voice had changed. "Yes, they are probably at one of the huts," he said. "One thing is sure: Andreas will have done what is best."

Herr Knubel nodded. Then suddenly he was staring at the guide, conscious for the first time of his nailed boots and ice ax and the rucksack on his shoulders.

"The message has come then?" he said.

The guide hesitated for a scarcely perceptible instant. "I have a message for Andreas—yes."

"What does it say?"

"I do not know what it says. Last night in the village my brother, who is with the railway, gave me a closed envelope and said, 'Here, take this to Benner. It is important—most important.' . . . So I am taking it up."

"Good," said Herr Knubel. "Good." He started to say something more, stopped himself abruptly and stood silently nodding. "Come," he said suddenly, taking the guide's arm. "We shall have a cup of coffee together, and then you will be on your way."

In the pantry they talked intermittently while they drank: about the damage the storm had done, the probable condition of the forest paths, how soon the climbers could get back to the inn. "You will find them at the Heilweg Hut," Herr Knubel declared confidently. "Mark my words—you will find them at the Heilweg. Or, at the very worst, at the Dornel, below the glacier."

But a while later, after Christian Mehrwalder had gone, he remained sitting at the pantry table, pulling meditatively at his nose.

Christian is worried about them, he thought. The storm was a bad one, and he is worried. What will he do if they are not at the Heilweg? Or at the Dornel? Or anywhere? What if he comes back alone? . . . Herr Knubel's thoughts raced ahead, a little wildly. . . . He comes back, and they are lost. He comes back, and they are all gone. There will be the alarm, the search party, the police, the questions. . . . He turned on himself in sudden anger. I suppose that is all you care about, he said. The police. What will happen to you. How about *them*, lying there frozen in the snow? Or crumpled and broken at the foot of a precipice? And then when they bring them down and they're lying under the blankets on the stretchers. . . . And Frau Benner . . . and the funerals . . . and the police . . . Herr Knubel almost jumped to his feet. No, he would not think about it. It was better not to think of any of it.

Looking up he saw Annamarie coming from the kitchen with a tray. "What is it you are doing now?" he asked irritably.

The girl stopped and stared at him. "I am bringing breakfast to—"

"Breakfast! It is after nine o'clock, do you know that, girl?—and you are still pottering around with breakfast!"

"But Madame Delambre—"

"Never mind Madame Delambre. Here—give me that tray. There is work to be done. Work, do you understand? Out on the terrace there is a terrible mess. Get the rake and put everything in neat piles along the driveway." Herr Knubel crossed to her and took the tray in his own hands. "I will take Madame Delambre her breakfast. Quick now! *Hinaus!*"

Annamarie's blank stare gave way to an expression of alarm; then, with a strangled giggle, she bolted for the door. Herr Knubel looked after her in disgust, turned and went through the dining-room into the foyer. He stopped, however, when he saw that the office door, on the far side of the foyer, was open and that Frau Knubel was at the desk inside. Retracing his steps to the pantry, he ascended the rear stairs, walked down the upper hallway and knocked at the farthermost door.

"*Entrez,*" said a woman's voice.

Astrid Delambre was reclining on the bed, knitting. Her loosened hair was spread in a golden aureole against the pillow, and she was wearing a bed-jacket that was the exact color of her deep-violet eyes. She answered Herr Knubel's good morning with a cool smile, put her knitting aside and took the breakfast tray on her lap.

"You have slept well, Madame?" Herr Knubel asked.

"Very well, thank you."

"The air of Kandermatt, it is excellent for sleep."

"I sleep well wherever I am. I do not have insomnia."

"You are very fortunate. It is a bad thing, insomnia."

"Yes, it is bad. My husband has it."

Madame Delambre poured her coffee and sipped it slowly. Herr Knubel cleared his throat.

"It will be only another day or two now," he said.

The cool violet eyes went up to him. "What will?" she asked.

"Before Monsieur Delambre and the others are back."

"Oh. They have climbed their mountain then?"

"Climbed it?" Herr Knubel could not keep the astonishment from his voice. "I am afraid that is too much to expect, madame. In such weather, and on such a mountain . . ."

"Unfortunately I do not know much about mountains."

"They are not good places in a storm." Herr Knubel shook his head slowly. Then abruptly his expression brightened. "But I am sure they were able to come down before it broke. They are at the huts now. Yes, I am certain of it—they are safe and sound at one of the huts." Madame Delambre sipped her coffee without comment. "And see—" he said, going to the window and raising the shade, "it is all clear now again. A perfect morning."

"Yes, it is very lovely."

"And there is no longer any need to worry."

"To worry?"

"About—about anything—"

"I am not worrying, Herr Knubel. I do not believe in worrying." The cool eyes were raised again. "Do you?"

"I? No, of course not. Certainly not, madame. Especially when there is—"

"No reason to?"

"Exactly."

"And even when there is," Madame Delambre went on, "it is a waste of time, don't you think? There are such an extraordinary number of things one can worry about once one has started. The

374

war, for instance. And money. And one's soul and one's health and one's complexion and one's husband." She paused and took a final sip of coffee. "And now, if you will be so good—"

Herr Knubel took the tray from her lap. "You wish nothing more, madame?" he asked.

"I think not." A slight smile touched the placid whiteness of her face. "Today I think I shall concentrate on worrying about my figure. . . . And on not dropping stitches," she added, taking up her knitting.

"I have often watched you knit. You do it very skillfully."

"Thank you."

"The sweater you are making—it is for Monsieur Delambre, no?"

"No, Monsieur Delambre does not like sweaters."

"Ah—for yourself then?"

"No, I seldom wear them either. It is simply—well—something to do, you know." Was it really a smile, Herr Knubel wondered, as she raised her eyes again—or was it mockery? "Everyone must have something to do, mustn't one, Herr Knubel?" she asked.

"Yes, of course. To be sure."

He crossed to the door, hesitated a moment and turned. The morning sunlight, shafting through the window, fell on the bookshelves, the paintings, the golden hair on the pillow

"Yes?" she asked.

"Is there anything else, madame?"

"No, nothing else, thank you."

Herr Knubel went out, closing the door.

Nicholas Radcliffe brewed himself a second cup of tea and turned down the blue flame of the Primus. Then, still holding the warm tin cup against his hands, he crossed to the tent-flap and pushed it open. Morning sunlight flooded in upon him, and he slitted his eyes against the glare.

On all sides of the tent the slope of the terrace lay buried under a sheath of new snow. Below, where the terrace levelled off above the rim of the lower precipice, the drifts rose in immense powdery billows and ended in a soft line of shining whiteness against the blue emptiness beyond; above, where the slope steepened, they climbed upward to the cliffs as smoothly as a tilted white sea. At the very crest of the slope the jagged crests of the great boulders

375

still showed—no longer gray, however, but a wet, glistening black. Then the cliffs themselves soared upward, tier upon tier, into shimmering distance. They were no longer gray, either, but mottled and streaked with snow, and the once-dark gash of the Funnel twisted up between them in an unbroken ribbon of sun-gleaming white.

For perhaps five minutes Radcliffe remained motionless, squinting upward. Then he turned back into the tent, took his binoculars from his rucksack and went outside again. Climbing a few yards through the snow to a slight bulge in the slope, he adjusted the glasses and swung them slowly over the frozen wilderness above him. . . . Nothing moved. . . . He lowered the glasses and listened; but there was no sound. The east face of the mountain rose above him in a white pillar of stillness.

Returning to the tent, he stood staring at the blankets and equipment and stroking his fingers gently along the gray stubble of his jaw. Then his gaze shifted to a small pile of stones in the corner—the fruits of his collecting tours along the base of the cliffs during the two days before the storm. Stooping, he picked up a stone at random and turned it slowly in his hand. Yes, hornblende, he thought. Hornblende, or, just possibly, metamorphosed diorite with a . . .

He tossed the stone back onto the pile.

Pick it up again, he thought. Pick it up. Take out your notebook and pencil. Get to work. . . . He stared down at the stone, but did not pick it up. . . . It's senseless, he thought. It's senseless and useless and hopeless. It was no go for you before, much less now. They're either all right or they're not, and there's nothing you can do. Nothing. . . .

Turning suddenly, he took his rucksack from its corner and filled it with a few articles that he selected from around the tent. Then he put on his outer clothing and snow-goggles, swung the pack onto his shoulders, took his ice ax from its corner, and went out again.

You must take it very slowly, he thought. You must not try to hurry.

But there was not even the possibility of hurrying in the deep drifts of the slope. The snow billowed up around him—to his knees, his thighs, his waist—until presently he was thrusting himself forward less by his legs than with his arms and the weight of his body. When, after ten minutes, he paused to take his bearings, the tent was only a few hundred yards behind him and the boulders and the precipice beyond seemed no nearer than before.

He rested briefly, leaning forward a little with his thighs pressed against the snow. Then he started off again. No faintest trace remained of their earlier route up the terrace, and each successive step required a fresh kick and shove into a blank white wave. As the slope steepened, however, the drifts became gradually less deep. At last they came only to a little above his knees, and, walking now rather than floundering, he was able to make somewhat faster progress than before. He plodded on for half an hour, rested, plodded on again. The angle of ascent was now growing steeper with each forward step, and the mid-morning sun streamed down on his head and shoulders. After a little while he paused, took off his wind-jacket, helmet and outer gloves and stowed them in the rucksack.

It is avalanche weather, he thought.

At his next stop he took out the binoculars and again moved them slowly up the face of the mountain. The base of the Funnel was close before him now, and the vast twisting cleft between the precipices seemed to rise not so much in front of him as directly above his head. But its very closeness, he knew, foreshortened it out of all true proportion, and its familiar features of color and shading, outline and texture were obliterated under a shroud of glittering white. His eyes searched for the first great bend. . . . Snow. . . . For the ledge where they had rested. . . . Snow. . . . For a recognizable landmark anywhere. . . . There was only snow. . . . He closed his eyes and listened, until the stillness became a roaring in his ears. Then he cupped his mouth with his hands and shouted.

Ridiculous, he thought.

He shouted again. . . .

And then he was trudging on again. He was climbing, zigzagging, threading his way along the crest of the slope and through the labyrinth of tumbled boulders beyond. He was watching the flaring walls that formed the base of the Funnel close slowly in on either side, until the sun was hidden and the sky was merely a long jagged streak between their converging rims. He was floundering through the last deep pocket between the boulders, pulling himself up to the flat top of the final boulder, staring up at the white chute of the Funnel proper that leapt away above him through the heart of the mountain rock.

Easy now, old man, he told himself. Very easy and steady now.

For a few minutes he stood perfectly still, waiting for the ache of fatigue to drain from his knees and thighs; then, raising an arm, he groped along the snow-wall above his head. The snow was soft, and his hand went through it to the wrist and touched rock. Finding a hold, he gripped it tightly and kicked at the snow below until he uncovered a ledge that would support his feet. Then he stepped up, clung, groped again, kicked again. The ledges of the lower Funnel, as he remembered from his previous ascent, were broad and well-flanged, and once he had found them and cleared away their cloak of snow, he was able to move with a fair degree of safety from one to the next. The constant probing and kicking, however, was exhausting work, and each time his arm moved up a miniature cascade of loosened snow poured down onto his face and shoulders. After twenty steps he had to pause for a rest; after ten more for another.

And now, as he reached up again, his searching hand could find neither hold nor shelf under the cloak of snow above. He moved it slowly to left and right; then, standing on tiptoe on his ledge, he stretched his arm up as far as it would go. A stream of white powder poured down on him, as before, but this time it did not stop after a moment or two. Suddenly the whole expanse of snow seemed to shudder, there was a muffled rumbling all around him, and an instant later the white wall above peeled off in its entirety from the underlying rock and toppled down upon him in a hissing torrent.

The impact knocked him from his feet and sent him spinning from the ledge. He groped out blindly, trying to stop his fall, first with his free right hand and then with the ice ax in his left. The prong of the ax scraped against rock and caught, and with a convulsive jerk he swung himself around so that he was gripping the haft with both hands. The ax held. His hands held. He clung flattened against the rock, while the avalanche stormed past him and shattered against the black boulders below.

When it had passed he climbed slowly back to the ledge on

378

which he had been standing. Sitting down on it, he rubbed the snow from his face and shoulders and drew in a dozen long breaths of the thin, cold air. Then his eyes went upward again: to the wall above, to the alternating stippled bands of rock and snow; to the knobs and shelves and crevices in the rock that had been uncovered by the avalanche. The nearest knob that seemed to offer a possible hand-hold was perhaps eight feet above his head and a little to the right. He got to his feet and reached for it, but he could not make it. He raised his ax and probed along its upper surface, but the smooth steel of the blade would not hold.

All right; he had to jump for it. If he was going to get so much as an inch farther up the Funnel he would have to jump for it.

He tightened the straps of his rucksack and fastened the ax in his belt. Then he stood quite still for another moment, measuring the distance with his eye.

"All right now," he said aloud.

He leaned forward a little, poised to jump. He crouched motionless, his eyes fixed on the knob of rock above, and felt the sweat cold on his neck and back and his boots like leaden weights on his feet and the ax like an iron bar hanging from his waist. The sound of his breathing seemed to come to him from very far away. The walls of the Funnel around him seemed to be undulating in slow gray-white waves.

He looked down and saw the boulders at the bottom of the Funnel a scant fifty feet below. Then he looked up again. At the knob . . . past the knob. . . . Beyond it were the white walls tapering away in an almost vertical pitch for a distance of perhaps a hundred feet. And beyond it, unseen but waiting, another pitch. And beyond that another and another; pitch after pitch, slick with verglas and choked with snow; the smooth slabs and shallow, holdless grooves; the bulging ribs and outthrust cornices; the cliff-faces and the buried pitons; the recess in the cliffs, the dome above, the arching walls. . . .

And now he was no longer standing, but sitting, crouched and motionless, on the ledge. He sat with his eyes closed and his head bent forward and resting on his ax, and he felt the long cool steel of the ax-blade against the beaded sweat of his forehead. The minutes crept past.

The miles and the years were creeping past. . . .

And it was the same again, Nicholas Radcliffe thought. Twenty years had passed, and it was the same again, it had come full circle again, and he was back where he had always been; in the place he had never left; hunched over his ice ax on a frozen mountainside —hollow, impotent and spent. In a moment now he would open his eyes. He would open them and stare down through the empty miles at the brown plains of Tibet, and then turn and stare upward at the forlorn slopes of rock and ice that still rose above him toward the summit of the world. He would climb again, stumble, fall, crawl, sit hunched and motionless again. And the mist would close in again.

Mallory . . . Mallory . . .

The mist faded. The voice faded. He opened his eyes and got slowly to his feet. For several minutes he stood gazing at the white wilderness that tiered into the sky above him.

We will fall back in good order, Radcliffe, the Colonel's voice said, very distinctly.

But, sir—

Those are the orders, old boy. That's the way it goes.

Yes, of course, he thought. That was the way it went. He had almost forgotten. . . . You fell back from Passchendaele. You fell back from Everest, from Geneva, from the White Tower. From every assault and every dream. You fell back to the previously prepared position, the fortress, the valley, the Garden of Rocks. In good order, of course. Always in good order. In the very best and most admirably executed retreating formation . . .

He was no longer conscious of fatigue as he clambered slowly down the Funnel wall and began the descent through the boulders. He was scarcely even conscious of it two hours later as he floundered down through the last deep powder-drifts of the slope and dropped his rucksack to the floor of the tent. Taking out his binoculars, he went outside again and remained there for a long while, staring up at the snow and the stillness. Then he returned to the tent, brewed a cup of tea and sat on his blanket-roll against the wall, sipping it slowly.

When he had finished his eyes went to the pile of stones in the corner. Getting up, he crossed over and squatted down beside them and took a notebook and stub of pencil from the breast pocket of his shirt.

Four thousand feet up the mountainside Andreas Benner worked his way slowly across the snow slope between the great cornice and the juncture of the east and southeast ridges. The drifts here were even deeper than on the lower terrace, and for most of the distance the guide had to push and kick through powdery billows that rose about him to his waist and armpits. When he left the tent the dawn had been the merest gray streak in the eastern sky. By the time he came out on the high promontory between the ridges the sun was already streaming, red and horizontal, from behind the hooded white shoulder of the Himmelshorn.

On the promontory he stopped for the first time and rested. The brown speck of the tent had long since disappeared above him, and now even the outline of the cornice was gone. Below, the Riesensteg, the two terraces and the glacier were still hidden by the ice-masses that overhung the precipices of the south face. There were only the two diverging ridges, the snow, the gleaming ice-walls, and far beyond them, unimaginably tiny and remote beneath an ocean of space and stillness, the dark green-brown ribbon that was the valley of Kandermatt.

Benner gazed down at the valley and rubbed his beard slowly with his mittened hand. Yes, there it had been bad too, he thought; when a storm came mostly from the west, as this one had, it was always bad in the valley. No snow, of course—October was too early for real snow down below, no matter what went on up above —but probably just about everything else in the dictionary of bad weather. Trees and fences down, mud everywhere, the topsoil washed away, the flocks scattered. It would be a man's work straightening things out again—Ilsa would not be able to do very much. Well, she would have to get along as best as she could until he got back. She was a guide's wife and had done it often enough before. The only difference was that all the other times he had come back with forty francs in his pocket for every day he had been away. . . .

That part of it was the war, of course. The verdammte war made everything different.

He rubbed his mittened hands together and shuffled his feet in the snow. There was no wind, and the sun was growing bigger and more golden with each moment that it climbed into the cloudless sky. But still his hands and feet were cold; it was senseless to deny it. Even with two pairs of mittens and three thicknesses of socks his hands and feet had been almost continuously cold ever since they had been on the mountain. Except when he was really climbing strenuously, of course; and then, where the coldness had been, he had begun to notice a slight stiffness and tightness of the joints that he had never experienced in the old days. The beginnings of arthritis, the doctor for the Patrol Corps had told him when he had examined him that previous winter. That was *Schwärmerei*, of course—arthritis was for the old ones. And still . . .

Still he was forty-five, Andreas Benner thought. Almost forty-six. And almost-forty-six was no longer so young an age for climbing out of season on a mountain like the Weissturm. His father had been—what was it?—not yet forty-two when he had clambered up those great white ridges for the last time and vanished from the sight of men. And even then Franz Benner had known that, win or lose, he was drawing near the end of his high-climbing days. "Another year or two," he had said before setting out, "and it will be you, my son, who will be the guide of the family. Perhaps, with God's grace, it will be granted that I climb at last to the summit of the Weissturm. If not, it will be granted to you, or your son, or your son's son. It does not matter, so long as it is a Benner."

No, it did not matter—except that he, Andreas Benner, did not have a son, but only four daughters who had married farmers and storekeepers. And if he had had one, he would not be climbing any Weissturms but marching up and down the frontier with a gun, like everyone else's.

He stood up, stamped in the snow a few times and began the descent of the southeast ridge. . . . It is not in the hands and feet that you are getting old, *Dummkopf*, he told himself, but in the head. There is a storm and the food is short and your *Herren* are scattered like lost goats all over the mountain—and you sit like an old grandfather in the snow and moon about your father, who is dead, and your son, whom you do not have. . . . His eye measured the height of the sun above the snow-peaks to the east. About eight o'clock, he estimated. He should reach the lower tent by eleven, if the snow that would now be covering the narrow part of the ridge had not yet begun to melt. If it *had* begun . . . he shrugged inwardly. Time enough for that when he got there.

The going was now considerably easier than before, for the snow on the exposed ridge was far less deep than on the adjoining slopes.

Slabs, boulders and all other landmarks, however, were buried beneath the white drifts, and every five or six paces Benner paused and squinted intently down along the frozen arc that curved into space below. Occasionally he would sound cautiously with his ax before taking the next step. At other times he selected his route simply by the contours and shading of the snow.

So far the snow was exactly as he had hoped it would be: deep enough to provide a footing over the ice-sheathed rock beneath, but not yet sufficiently thawed by the sun to be in danger of avalanching. Gradually, as the ridge widened and flattened, he held himself back less and less against the pull of gravity. Half striding and half glissading, he swung down the gleaming incline, while long feathers of spume streamed out behind his boots and lightly braking ax.

Then, with a jerk, boots and ax dug in. The ridge before him was narrowing again: from a ramp to a rib; and from a rib to a mere twisting ribbon. On their ascent the knife-edge had been a sharp line of black rocks, rising out of a sea of mist; but now, as he had expected, it was covered with snow, and on either side he could see the vertical mountain walls dropping away into blue gulfs of space. He leaned forward, probing with his ax, and took a tentative forward step. The soft powder gave for an inch or two under his boot, coagulated, and held. He took another step. It still held. And now, as he moved forward for the third time, he felt relief pouring in a sudden warm tide through his body. The knife-edge was passable. It would go.

Step by step, foot by foot, he picked his way along the white tightrope in the sky. From long training he did not even so much as glance to either side, but kept his eyes fixed unwaveringly on the snow beneath his feet, conscious of every ripple and furrow as it moved slowly into the line of his vision. He did not go down on all fours or to a straddling position, as they had done before, because he knew that the least lateral motion might displace the delicate balance of the crust. He merely put his left foot in front of his right, and then the right in front of the left. And at last he saw that the ribbon beneath them was widening. He was moving more quickly again. He was off the knife-edge and squatting, panting, in the drifts on the broad bulge of the ridge beyond.

Resting briefly, his gaze moved down along the twisting ramp ahead. Beneath the knife-edge the ridge descended more steeply than before, and for the first time now, craning forward, he could see the white-cloaked towers of the Riesensteg outlined against the valleys far below. His eyes travelled slowly across them—down and to the right a little—squinting against the distance and the glare. Then suddenly they found what they were searching for—a minute, scarcely distinguishable brown speck in the glittering ocean of the snow. There was no sign of life or movement. But the tent was there—unmistakably there. . . . And he is there too, Andreas Benner thought. Of course he is. Where else could he be? . . . He had had blankets, clothes and equipment, food for four days; and besides, the towers of the Riesensteg would have protected him from the worst battering of the storm. Delambre was in the tent, that was all. Sitting in the tent, waiting. . . .

Getting to his feet, he reached for his ax, which he had plunged into the snow beside him. But his stiff fingers would not grasp it. He rubbed and beat his hands together for a few seconds and tried again. This time the fingers bent, but still not enough, and, using his other hand, he forced them down until they were tight around the wood of the haft. Then he looked down again, took his bearings and continued the descent.

Yes, of course, he told himself: the *Franzose* is all right. And the others up above, they are all right too. . . . Or were they all right? . . . He should have made them come down with him—he knew that; no guide was ever supposed to leave his *Herren* on a mountain. And still, what else could he have done on such a mountain as this? And with such *Herren?* And the storm? . . . Do you know something? he thought suddenly. With this Hein you could have climbed to the top before the storm. He and you alone, travelling light—you could have done it. All those times he wanted to go on faster: you could have agreed, told the others to wait, and done the thing you have always wanted to do the most of anything in your life. . . . He could have, yes, but at the same time, he could not, because there was another, more important thing that he knew too, and that was that to climb the Weissturm in such a way was not to climb it at all. . . . And so he had not gone. And so the storm had come. And so . . .

And so, if you keep on like this, Andreas Benner thought angrily, you yourself will soon be getting as bad as the *Franzose!*

The ridge was falling away before him now in a succession of almost vertical pitches, and presently he descended from its crest and began making his way along the slopes immediately below. Here there was only a thin layer of snow, with ice beneath, and it soon became necessary for him to cut footholds with his ax. For perhaps half an hour he moved slowly and cautiously downward, his eyes on the incline before him and his mind concentrated on the techniques of his trade. Then, as the steepness lessened, he veered back and regained the ridge. The towers of the Riesensteg were much nearer now, and he descended toward them at a swift, easy pace.

A drunkard, he said to himself. He had thought he had had every kind there was in the twenty-five years he had been a guide; but never a drunkard before. . . . He had known there was something wrong from the beginning. Down there on the wasteland, when he had spoken with Herr Martin, he had known it and should have done something about it. When he saw the way the *Franzose* climbed. And how his eyes were. . . . He saw Delambre's eyes, dark, clouded, too restless and then too steady, staring up at the mountain that rose before them. The eyes of a drunkard—a silent and secret drunkard. . . . And yet—Benner's thoughts paused, groping in shadows—yet, had it been only that; only a drunkard and two bottles of brandy? Had it not been the mountain too? The mountain that was itself a drunkenness, a thirst, a torturing and consuming hunger. . . .

Now the Frenchman's dark eyes were gone, and in their place were two other eyes: deep-set, unwavering, as blue as the ice on the great slopes toward which they gazed. His father's. "He is like a drunkard," the old men in the village had said, shaking their heads. "The white devils of the mountain whisper to him in the night, and he is bewitched." But Franz Benner had paid no heed to them; nor to the other guides; nor to his wife. Holding Andreas' hand in one of his and pointing upward with the other, he had said in his deep, quiet voice: "Some day, when you are a man, we will go there. We will climb, my son—you and I together—and we will get to the top, or we will . . ."

The voice faded. The ice-blue eyes faded. Where they had been was the ridge and the sky and the wild, slanting miles of the snow. The towers of the Riesensteg were close beneath him now, no longer gaunt and black, but a frozen glittering white. He searched for the tent, but it was hidden behind them. He stopped, listening, but there was no sound.

Andreas Benner moved his mittened fingers vertically and then horizontally across his chest. "*Dein Wille geschehe,*" he said quietly, "*wie im Himmel, also auch auf der Erde. . . .*"

Paul Delambre lay with his eyes open, staring up into brown twilight. It was morning again, he thought. Deep into the night he had lain there in the yellow pool of the bed-lamp, reading the enchanted pages of Rimbaud's *Le Bateau Ivre,* and he must have fallen asleep while still reading, because he did not remember closing the book or putting out the light. He moved a hand searchingly over the blanket, then up to the left where the night table with the bed-lamp stood. His fingers scraped lightly along a surface that seemed to be made of canvas, and he withdrew them. Lying quietly again, he stared up at the sloping roof of the tent.

All you have to do is close your eyes, he thought. Simply close them—that is all, it is as easy as that—and it will be real again. . . . Yes. . . . There were the first rays of the sun streaming through the grillwork beyond the window. There was the clopping of the milkman's horse coming around the corner from the Avenue Kléber. "*Paul! Paul! Lève toi! Tu sera tard à l'école!*"

He listened until the last reverberations of the voice had faded away, and then raised himself on his elbows. It was quiet again, quieter and stiller than any stillness he had ever known. It is the snow, he thought. The snow on the roof. On the rocks. Everywhere. The snow falling soft and gleaming against the gray stone façades of the Rue Castellane.

He remained motionless, struggling with the images that thronged his brain. It had been that way for days now—ever since he had been alone in the tent. The present and the past, the mountain and the city, the storm and the stillness beyond the storm: all of them kept weaving in and out before him as if they were parts of some immense ravelling tapestry, now fading, now dissolving one into the other, now emerging again, until all sense of time and place had left him and he was drifting through a tortuous and endless labyrinth of fantasy. . . . *A la recherche du temps perdu,* he thought. . . . *A moins qu'il n'est pas perdu.* Except that it was not lost. Remembrance was as real as perception, the past as true as the present. Both were the truth. And neither was the truth.

If it is the truth you want, he said to himself, there is only one place that you have ever found it. . . .

He turned, looking for the old walnut chiffonier, but stopped himself suddenly and for a few moments remained quite still. Then he reached into the rucksack that had been his pillow, took a small steel mirror from one of its pockets and held it to his face. At first, in the faint light, he could just discern a wavering image of matted hair, dark staring eyes and sunken stubbled cheeks; but as he continued staring the image began to freeze into focus, and then, very slowly and subtly, as it had always happened, it had changed so that it was no longer the image of his own face at all, but the other image, the inwardness, the *thing*. He held the mirror motionless while it moved silently, almost imperceptibly toward him. And once again he felt the old familiar terror rising within him in a still, icy wave. . . .

He flung the mirror away and lay back in the dishevelled blankets. His body seemed suddenly to have become insubstantial and hollow again; but this time, deep within the hollowness, there was a remote, measured throbbing, as of a muffled pulse.

I am feverish, he thought.

And he was hungry. How long had it been since he had eaten, he wondered incuriously. Twenty-four hours? Thirty-six? The others had been gone since—when was it?—Thursday. And now it was . . . What difference did it make what day it was? If he was feverish he should lie still. If he was hungry he should eat. He turned and looked at the row of tins that stood along the canvas wall. Beans—tea—stew—biscuits. And the bottle of Courvoisier. Reaching for the bottle, he held it up before him and gazed at the inch or two of amber fluid that still remained in it. It is almost like the mirror, he thought; as still and lucent as the depths behind the mirror. He raised himself on one elbow and opened the bottle. "A notre grande victoire, Monsieur Ordway," he said aloud.

He held the bottle to his lips until it was empty. Then he lay back again and felt the brandy spreading down within him—harsh and burning at first, then soft and warm, finally with an exquisite slow tingling through the cold hollowness of his body. The pulse within the hollowness seemed to be beating more deeply, more strongly.

Yes, strength, he thought. That is what I must find in myself now. That is all that matters—here or anywhere. Not knowledge, not wisdom, not talent, not loving-kindness, not understanding, but only strength. Strength to stand up. To go on. To climb a mountain. To write a book. To fight a war. To-kill-and-not-be-killed. Blessed are the strong, O Lord of Hosts, for theirs is the Kingdom of Earth.

He closed his eyes again, slid back into the past again. He was at his desk in the little room above the Quai Voltaire; in the crimson and magenta garden in Naxos; sitting hand in hand with violet-eyed Astrid Varnholm on a silver Baltic beach. The miles and the years flowed past him in a gentle tide, and it seemed to him as if he were softly sinking into a deep warm pool. The realization came to him dimly that his bowels were emptying themselves into the blankets. *O le petit méchant*, a woman's voice was saying, *il a fait encore la saleté dans le lit.*

He lay waiting. He lay motionless with eyes closed and waited for the touch of the cool familiar hand. But it did not come. It would never come. So, *mon brave*, he said to himself, you are warm at last, eh? You have fouled your nest, but at least the foulness is warm. Warm and cozy and safe and right for sleep. He felt himself slipping gently down into sleep. He felt his body and brain being carried gently away on a soft wave of soundless laughter.

And then, very suddenly, he was sitting upright. His eyes were burning, and all his body was wet with sweat. With a tremendous effort, he pulled his legs toward him, pushed out with his arms, lurched to his knees. The hot stench of excrement rose up around him, enveloping him, and he thought he would fall. But he did not fall. Fumbling and jerking, he pulled at the blankets, dragged them across the canvas floor to the tent flap and pushed the flap open. Sun and snow exploded in his eyes in a white burst of light, but he kept crawling until he was through the opening and into the deep, billowing drift outside. Letting go of the blankets, he slipped down into its soft embrace.

For several minutes he lay perfectly still, his body panting and trembling, his mind drained and spent. Then very gradually he began to be aware of the coolness of the snow against his face and hands. Turning his head a little, he felt the warmth of the sunlight and lay watching the play of its hundred weaving colors upon his closed lids. When presently he opened his eyes all was whiteness again. He sat up and looked around him at the slanting miles of whiteness. The snow was no longer blinding, but bland and softly luminous, climbing wave on wave up the mountainside in immense and gentle purity. The deep throbbing was gone from his body. The sweat and the fever were gone. He remained sitting quietly for a little while, then got slowly to his feet.

There was the snow. There was the mountain and the sun. And that was all there was between the earth and sky, except for the opening of the tent that showed like a gaping wound in the drifts beside him and the crumpled blankets at his feet. The folds of the blankets were slimed with ordure that glistened darkly in the sunlight, and a thin exhalation of steam rose from them into the motionless air.

> Life, like a heap of many-colored dung,
> Stains the white radiance of eternity. . . .

He spoke the words aloud, in English. Shelley, he thought. Shelley revised and modernized. He smiled inwardly a little, pleased at the conceit.

He felt very calm now—almost happy. The burning and the throbbing had vanished, and where the hollowness had been inside of him there was, instead, a strange new lightness and serenity. . . . You know what you must do now, he thought. You have known all your life what it is that you must do, and now at last, for the first time, you have the strength to do it. . . . Bending, he began to scoop up handfuls of snow and throw them on the blankets. He continued doing this until the blankets were wholly covered and then patted down the snow so that no trace remained of what was hidden underneath. *Alors,* he said, straightening.

He turned his face to the white radiance.

He began to climb.

Moving slowly, but without strain or effort, he ascended through the soft drifts of the slope. When at last he stopped and looked back the tent was merely a minute brown speck among the white billows below; and when he looked for the second time it was gone altogether. Turning, he looked upward, his eyes searching for the towers of the Riesensteg. . . . The towers, he thought. The towers, then the ridge, then the upper slopes, then the shoulder. . . . But, staring into the distance now, he could find none of them. Above him, as below, there seemed to be only a sea of snow extending, featureless and boundless, into space.

It does not matter, he thought quietly. It does not matter at all.

He climbed on again. And now presently, watching the slow swing of his hands against the whiteness of the snow, he realized that he did not have his ice ax with him. He had forgotten his ax. He had forgotten his rope, rucksack, crampons, helmet, gloves. I must go back, he thought. I must stop and go back for them. But even as the thought came to him he smiled again, inwardly, for he knew that they did not matter either.

They did not matter, because now, for the first time since he had been on the mountain, he was climbing strongly and surely; now for the first time he was climbing without fear. What was it, he wondered musingly, that he had been afraid of before? He could not remember. He could not imagine. For he saw now that the stillness and emptiness that encompassed him were not hostile, but beneficent; that the mountain was not desolate and evil, but soft and kindly and gently gleaming. Stopping again, he picked up a shred of snow and held it in his palm. It lay there for a moment against the reddened flesh—pure, exquisite, a tiny shining scintilla of ice and fire. Then it melted; a single drop of water lay in his cupped palm. He raised his hand and touched it to his lips. And it was gone.

He seemed to be climbing faster now. He no longer felt the tug of the drifts at his feet and his body was gradually taking on an almost feathery lightness, until he felt that he was no longer climbing at all, but flying—flying swiftly and strongly and effortlessly across the white ocean of the snow. He watched the snow flowing past him, around him. Raising his eyes, he saw it flowing downward in great glittering waves from the mountaintop. Or was it upward?—he could not be sure. And then suddenly, in the next instant, he was sure. It was not height at which he was staring, but depth; not a mountain, but a gigantic mirror. Vast, soundless and overwhelming, the image behind the image was moving toward him out of the blue mirror of the sky.

He waited, and it came. It came with the cool whiteness of the snow, with the soft whiteness of a woman's body, with a searing, radiant whiteness of unimaginable purity. He reached his arms out and gathered it to him. He felt it against his body, his cheeks, his lips, his eyelids. He had it at last. He was part of it; one with it.

Chapter 21

There was the stillness. There was the sunlight and the snow. . . .

Standing on the lip of the cornice in the brightening dawn, they had watched Andreas Benner move slowly across the slopes below toward the meeting point of the east and southeast ridges. Gradually his figure became a blur, and then the blur became a speck, and then the speck disappeared and all that remained was a dark trail of bootprints slanting away across the drifts. When, a little later, the sun came up they saw a sudden tiny glint on the promontory between the ridges that might or might not have been Benner's ax. Then that too was gone. In all the frozen world around them only the sun moved, climbing inch by inch from the white horizon into the stainless emptiness of the sky.

The bright rays shone and glittered, but they did not warm. "It is even colder now than with the wind," Carla said.

Ordway nodded.

"It is a good thing," said Hein. "With a whole day of cold and no wind the snow will be all right for tomorrow."

Back in the tent they cleaned up, took off their stiffened boots and oiled them, and checked carefully through their equipment and remaining food supply. By the time they had finished it seemed to Ordway that most of the morning should have been gone, but his watch showed only half past nine, and when they went outside again the sun was still low above the ranges to the southeast.

"I am afraid it is going to take its time today," said Carla.

For the first time since the mist had closed in upon their lower camp three nights before, they were now able to see plainly everything that lay around them. It was a world of only two colors at which they looked—of the whiteness of mountains rising and falling into distance and the incredibly deep and lustrous blueness of the sky. Straight out before them, beyond the curling rim of the cornice, were the hooded summits of the other peaks of the range, many of them already below them, a few rising to their own level or even a little higher. To their right, as they faced outward, the south face of the Weissturm still climbed skyward in its seemingly endless vertical ascent. To the left and a little below was the snow-slope up which they had come and, beyond it, the diverging arms of the two great ridges plunging steeply away into space.

Turning, their eyes moved up the mountainside directly above them. The upper rim of their hollow, as they had noted when they first came to it, consisted of a low curving wall of outcropping rock, but the wall, like everything else, was now a gleaming wind-bevelled white. Beyond it was a snow-slope, similar to the one below, narrowing and steepening as it rose, until it ended, perhaps five hundred feet above, in a jagged, slanting skyline that marked the continuation of the combined east and southeast ridges. Then very abruptly, a little above and to the left of the slope, the ridge, too, ended. The precipices of the south face seemed suddenly to abandon their smooth upward flow and curve over toward it in a sweeping, violent lunge. They reached the ridge, sprang upward through it, obliterated it; and where the long, slanting crest had been there was, instead, the immense, squat bastion that formed what was known as the southern, or Kandermatt, shoulder of the mountain.

Ordway's gaze crept upward over the savage walls of rock and ice to the flat, snow-eaved platform of its summit and the sky beyond. "The final pyramid must start right behind it," he said.

Hein nodded. "Yes—first a long slope of snow; then the belt of rocks they call the Citadel; then the last slope and the top."

They stood staring again in silence.

"It looks unclimbable," Ordway said.

392

"The shoulder? No, from the slope or the ridge it will not go."

"Do you think we can work around to its far side?"

"Either we must try that," said Hein, "or we must find a way up through the cleft."

"The cleft?"

"The cliffs are split into two sections. Wait—I will show you." Hein went into the tent and returned carrying the binoculars. For a few moments he peered upward through them, then turned and handed them to Ordway. "Yes, you will see it now. Over to the right."

Adjusting the glasses to his eyes, Ordway could see at once that the German was correct. The walls of the shoulder, which had appeared before as an unbroken expanse of vertical rock, were actually divided into two separate masses—the main body of the shoulder to the left, and, on the right, a narrower, tapering tower that jutted out from it like the turret of a castle. Between them, splitting the rampart about halfway from top to base, was a thin, wedge-shaped sliver of sky.

"You see the narrow, projecting part?" said Hein. "That is called the Watchtower."

"And you think it may be possible to get up to the cleft?"

"From here one cannot tell. But if we cannot get around the shoulder on the other side it will be our only chance."

Ordway handed the binoculars to Carla and stood looking upward silently with squinted eyes. The sky, against the white waves that framed it, was now so intense a blue as to seem almost black, and the sun was a polished disc, burning with cold yellow fire at its core. The slope, the ridge and the immense promontory of the shoulder stood up against them, washed in a glittering, crystalline clarity. Never in his life, Martin Ordway thought, had he seen or believed it possible to see such sharpness of texture and outline, such stillness and purity of mass. And, as he watched now, the sharpness and clearness seemed moment by moment to be increasing, the stillness to be swelling, the slope and the ridge and the tower to be moving very slowly toward them out of frozen, blue-black space. The mountain was no longer a mountain at all, but an apparition, an image of light. It grew nearer, brighter, huger, hung quivering before him with an intensity that he could no longer bear—and in the next instant shattered. A shaft of yellow fire leapt from the sun to the snow, exploded into a blinding white, and struck down in a thousand splintering spears against his eyes. Covering them quickly with his hands, he turned away.

"It is better that we wear our glasses today," Hein said.

They got their sun-goggles from the rucksacks in the tent, put them on and came out into the hollow again. The mountainside still loomed above them in preternatural stillness and clarity, but the intolerable dazzling brightness was gone. The sky was darker and deeper than ever now, and the snow gleamed with an eerie greenish light.

"Which will be the best way to the shoulder?" Carla asked. "Straight up the slope or back to the ridge again?"

"I believe we will find the slope better," said Hein. "It gets steep higher up, but so does the ridge; and the ridge is much longer." He continued staring upward for a few moments; then he crossed the hollow, clambered over the wall of its upper rim and tested the drifts beyond with the toe of his boot.

"Better?" said Ordway.

"Yes, it is already better." The German returned to the tent, went inside briefly and came out carrying his ax and crampons. "I think I will look around a little," he said.

"Look around?"

"For the best way to the shoulder." Hein paused, turning, and suddenly Ordway knew that the gray eyes behind the goggles were smiling at him mockingly. "You need not worry, Herr Kapitän —I am not going to run away to the top."

Ordway started to speak, stopped himself, and said nothing.

"You would like to come along perhaps?" Hein suggested. "To make sure?"

"Thanks all the same"—Ordway was smiling back at him now —"but I think I'll stay here with Miss Dehn."

Hein nodded. "Yes, that is wiser," he said. "There is no need for both of us to go. And I will be back in an hour or two."

He climbed up over the wall again, floundered for a few paces in the deep drifts and came out on the thinner snow of the slope above. Ordway and Carla watched him work diagonally across it, to the right, until he disappeared from sight behind a white-cloaked outcropping of boulders. Then they went back into the tent and sat down.

394

"Are you sure?" Carla began—

"Of course I'm sure," he said.

"How?"

"There are a dozen reasons. It's too late in the day. The snow's still dangerous. He hasn't any food. . . . Besides, I don't think he would."

"You mean you trust him?"

"I don't know about trusting him. After you've knocked around a war for a while you do your trusting in God, and not too much of that. But I don't think Brother Hein is any more anxious to kill himself than the rest of us."

Carla shook her head slowly. "You do not know Germans," she said.

"Meaning that Germans *do* want to kill themselves?"

"I am not joking, Martin."

"That they have more courage then?"

"It is not a question of courage, but of—" she paused, searching for the words "—well, wanting things."

"And other people don't want things? Americans, for instance? Or Englishmen or Russians or Fiji Islanders?"

He smiled at her, but she did not smile back. "It is a different thing," she said, shaking her head again. "When there is something that a German really wants, he has his own special way of trying to get it."

It was a moment before Ordway spoke again.

"Hein will be back," he said.

"I am not so sure."

"Wait and see."

They lapsed into silence, and Carla took a rag from one of the rucksacks and began cleaning the Primus and cooking utensils. Ordway watched her for a while, then went outside and stood staring up and down the white slopes. He looked at his watch and it was not quite ten. He paced back and forth across the hollow, edged to the lip of the cornice and peered over, returned to the tent and adjusted the guy ropes, and went back inside.

"Hello," he said, smiling.

This time she smiled back at him. "Hello, Binks."

"Fancy seeing you here."

"Where else should I be on our honeymoon?"

He bent and kissed her nose, and then sat watching her again as she worked.

"Let me help," he said.

"No, I am almost finished."

"If you don't let me help I'm going to smoke."

"I don't mind if you smoke, so long as you don't cough."

Taking out his crumpled pack, he lit a cigarette, strangled a rising cough and watched the smoke curl aimlessly through the brown twilight. "God, it's quiet," he said.

Carla nodded. "When the snow is thick it is like no other time."

"Maybe we should make some noise."

"What do you suggest?"

"You could bang on the pots."

"No, I have a better idea. You can sing."

"Mairzy Doats?"

"Yes, of course. Mairzy Doats."

He began to sing, but his voice came out as a muffled croak, and halfway through the first verse he broke off, laughing.

"Go on," said Carla. "It is lovely."

"No—I've got the kind of voice that needs a tiled bathroom."

He tried to finish the verse by whistling, but all that came out between his cracked lips was a thin stream of condensed breath. He sat silently again, watching the cigarette smoke and listening to the stillness. When he looked at his watch it was twenty minutes past ten.

"He must be there by now," he said.

"Andreas?"

"Yes."

He put out his cigarette and sat looking at the canvas walls and listening to the stillness beyond the walls; and then Carla got up and went outside for a while and came back and they sat quietly, waiting; and then he must have dozed off, because presently the canvas walls were gone, and Carla and the stillness were gone, and in their place was the humming of engines and the dark oblongs of wings, and in the co-pilot's seat Ted Riggs was turning to look at him, only there was some mistake, something had gone wrong, because he realized gradually that it was not Ted's face at all, but Paul Delambre's. . . .

396

And then he was awake again and the Primus was going and Carla was bending over it with a pot of melting snow.

"You should rest," he said.

"I did, for a while."

"I mean really rest. Sleep."

"I tried, but I couldn't."

"You're too tired."

The girl shook her head. "No, it is not that. It is only—"

"Yes, I can tell. You're damned tired."

She did not answer him, but remained for a few moments bending over the bubbling pot. Then she came over and sat down close beside him. "Martin," she said—

"Yes, baby?"

"If Andreas—" She stopped. "When Andreas comes back and it is time to start for the top, I want you to promise me that you will go, even if—"

She stopped again.

"Even if what?"

"Even if I cannot."

He sat quietly looking at her, and when he spoke again his voice was very low and even. "We're going together," he said.

"I hope so, Martin. I hope so so very much. But in case I cannot—"

"Then I'm not going either."

"No. That is wrong. That is what you must not do."

"It's together or not at all," he said.

"No." With a quick gesture she placed her hand over his and held it. "Oh, can't you see, Martin? This is a thing you must do. With me or without me."

"Without you it's nothing."

"But you will not really be without me—that is the point. Even if I am too tired—too weak—I will still be there with you—inside you—part of you. We will still be climbing our White Tower together."

She turned abruptly away, and there was a silence.

"Promise me, Martin," she said.

"We'll talk about it later."

"Promise me."

"You'll be all right, I tell you. Get some sleep now, and you'll

397

be—" There was a faint sound outside the tent, and he broke off and sat bolt upright, listening. "It's Andreas—" he said.

It was not Andreas Benner, however, but Siegfried Hein, who presently came crawling in through the entrance sleeve. "Yes, the slope is better," he said, squatting down by the stove. "As I thought, it gets steeper higher up—under the ridge it is almost an ice wall. But that is good, because there is little snow."

"How far did you go?" Ordway asked.

"Almost halfway to the shoulder. Then I cut over to the lower part of the ridge, but the ridge is no good at all."

"What about the cleft?"

"I could not see it straight on, but I think it will go. It will not be easy. We will have to feel our way up very carefully. But it will go."

They ate their meagre lunch slowly and without appetite. The food stuck in Ordway's throat and the tea tasted of boiled snow, but he forced them down stubbornly and when he had finished felt a little warmer and less hollow. Presently Hein took off his boots, wrapped himself in a blanket and went to sleep, and after a while Carla did likewise. Ordway took out another cigarette and lighted it, began coughing almost immediately, and put it out. He sat watching the tent walls and the muffled forms of the sleepers. He lay down, dozed, woke again, sat up again. His watch showed one forty-five. Moving carefully so as not to disturb the others, he put on his goggles, helmet and outer gloves and crept from the tent.

There was the stillness. There was the sunlight and the snow. . . . The only thing that had changed was the position of the sun—no longer low above the eastern mountaintops but high in the blue void beyond the ranges to the south and west. Ordway stood gazing up at the slope, the ridge and the shoulder. Then he slowly crossed to the lower rim of the hollow, mounted to the edge of the ice cornice and looked down. And as he did so he saw that something else had changed too. The gulf of space beneath him, that earlier in the day had been as empty as the sky above, was empty no longer. The base of the mountain was gone. The glaciers and wastelands and boulder-slopes and remote valleys, all of them were gone—the whole earth was gone—and in their

398

place, spreading like an immense, billowing carpet between earth and mountaintops, was an unbroken sea of white clouds.

His eyes moved slowly over them: from the cliffs beneath into the distance; from horizon to horizon. Their upper surface, he estimated, was about three thousand feet below him, or at approximately the height of the upper Funnel; and although there must have been at least a breeze during the late morning to have brought them there, they were now utterly motionless. Indeed, they appeared less like clouds at all than like a field of snow. The mountaintops rose out of them as if from solid and eternal bases. The sun struck across the white miles, glittering and dazzling, out of the blue-black arch of the sky.

Ordway cleared a patch of snow from the cornice and sat watching. Nothing changed; nothing moved; and he did not move either. Presently he began counting the other peaks of the range, now curiously truncated and looking less like mountain summits than snowy, angular islands in a foaming sea. Nearest and highest was the Wunderhorn, and beyond it the Graf, the Gräfin, the Himmelshorn, the Dornelberg. His eyes travelled on, searching for the Rotalp and the Karlsberg, and then suddenly he realized that their crests were not high enough to pierce the clouds. They were not there. Nothing else was there. . . .

That's all there is, Marty, a voice said quietly beside him. *There isn't any more.*

He looked slowly around him. There were the tent, the ice axes standing in the snow, the mountain, the white clouds, the sky. And nothing else. No Ted, no Harry, no Bix. No plane, no plane-wing or nacelle. No garages rising or cathedrals toppling. No earth, no war, no bombburst, no blood, no death, no life. . . . Well, here you are, old boy, Martin Ordway thought. Out of it at last; above it at last; high on your mountain, sealed away, alone. Here you are where you wanted to be.

For a long while he sat staring out at the boundless glittering sterility. Then he got stiffly to his feet, moved to the far end of the cornice and peered intently downward at the white arc of the southeast ridge that curved away below into the floor of clouds.

Suddenly there was another voice beside him, and he turned again.

"You are an optimist, Herr Ordway," said Siegfried Hein.

Ordway did not answer.

"You do not really expect him back, do you?"

"Of course, I expect him." Ordway hesitated an instant. "Unless—"

"Unless something has gone wrong with Delambre?" The German shook his head slowly. "Take my word for it: our friend Benner will not be coming up again—no matter how it goes with Delambre."

"Nonsense. You don't for a minute think that he'd—"

"There are several things that I think, if you would like me to tell them to you. In the first place, he is a superstitious Catholic peasant and has no more intention of climbing this Sunday than last. In the second place, he is suffering from arthritis—you have noticed it yourself. And in the third—" Hein paused.

"Well?"

"He is afraid."

For a moment Ordway's eyes rested motionless on the German's face. "That's a contemptible thing to say," he said quietly.

"Contemptible?" Hein shrugged. "The truth can be unpleasant and painful, but it is never contemptible. . . . There are some things you should know about men as well as I, *Herr Kapitän*. On a mountain, in war, anywhere—it is the same. Each one has a point to which he can go, and no farther. It is not only a question of the legs, the lungs, the heart, or even the mind, but of the will—the *Geist*. You do not think your friend Radcliffe could not have lifted his feet another step, do you? Or Delambre? Or now Benner? If it were merely that, I assure you they would be beside us now. A battle, they say, is won by fire-power; but what makes the guns fire? A mountain is climbed by raising one foot above the other; but what makes the foot rise?"

Hein stopped, as if waiting for an answer, but Ordway did not speak.

"If Benner is not here by evening," the German went on—

"He'll be here."

"Perhaps. But in the event that he is not it might be wise for us to discuss what we plan to do."

He waited again, shrugged and turned away. For a few minutes he paced back and forth across the hollow, testing the surface of the snow. Then he went back into the tent.

Ordway remained motionless, staring down at the ridge. Then

very slowly his gaze went out again to the floor of clouds, the mountaintops and the sky. Nothing had changed. Nothing moved. Mile beyond mile, from horizon to horizon, the world above the world spread away under the frozen sunlight, transfixed in whiteness and stillness, more terrible in peace than in storm. . . .

And then, very softly, out of the stillness, another voice—or a sound. He turned quickly, but there was no one there. He waited, listening, with eyes closed. It's the wind, he thought.

But there was no wind.

He shook his head a few times, rubbed his hands together and shuffled his boots in the snow. Suddenly he realized that he was very cold. Getting to his feet, he descended from the cornice, crossed to the tent and crept in through the sleeve. Carla was still asleep, only the white crown of her helmet showing above the top of the blankets, and Hein was squatting against the wall kneading the frozen kinks from one of the ropes. Ordway sat down opposite him, took a second rope and began doing likewise. His watch showed two-thirty. When he looked again it was ten minutes of three.

The same gentle, numbing torpor that he had experienced during the storm began to creep through him again. He closed his eyes, and when he reopened them the sloping tent-walls seemed to have drawn in a little closer. . . . Our foxhole, he thought, almost smiling. Our little brown womb in the sky. . . . He dozed, and the stillness changed to a droning and the brown canvas to the long shapes of wings.

When he looked around him again Carla had still not moved, but Hein had finished with the rope and was rubbing the blade of his ax with a scrap of emery paper. He felt better now—his mind was sharper and clearer—but he was vaguely and uncomfortably aware that there was something he wanted, or needed. Presently he realized that it was a cigarette. He took out his pack and opened it, but it was empty. Removing his mittens, he searched in the pocket and then in his other pockets, at first slowly and methodically, but after a few moments more quickly and then still more quickly, until his stiff fingers were digging and probing with an almost panicky agitation. Suddenly he stopped and thought back. He had had five cigarettes the afternoon before and had smoked—how many? . . . Five. All of them. . . . But with at least two of them he had taken only a couple of puffs, began to cough and snuffed them out. Getting to his hands and knees, he crept along the wall, found a crumpled butt in the crevice between wall and groundcloth, brought it out and began to smooth it carefully in his fingers. Then he looked up and saw Hein's gray eyes watching him.

For a moment he did not move. Anger, hot and sudden, rose in him like a wave, but whether at the German or himself he did not know. Then, as suddenly as it had come, it passed. Creeping slowly along the wall, he found two other butts, crossed to the entrance-sleeve and threw the three out into the snow. When he returned to where he had been sitting Hein's head was again bent to his ax blade. The only sound in the tent was the thin scratching of emery paper against steel.

He sat silently with a blanket pulled up about his shoulders, and his glance moved over the canvas walls and the food and utensils and equipment and Carla's motionless figure and then back to Hein. He watched the firm, clean lines of his face and the concentration in his eyes and the strong hands moving swiftly and deftly along the bright surface of the axhead. . . . "What makes the guns fire?" the German had asked. "What makes the foot rise?" . . . And what, for that matter, made Hein's hands move? What made him climb this mountain and climb it so arrogantly and magnificently? What did he think, feel, want, love, fear? What made him tick?

Martin Ordway was suddenly aware of the fact that he did not know.

What did he know about him then? he asked himself, still watching him. Almost exactly nothing. They had been together for ten days now—climbed, eaten, slept, planned, suffered hardship and danger together—and yet, as far as any actual knowledge of each other was concerned, they were still as complete strangers as on that first afternoon when they had met on the meadow path below Radcliffe's chalet. Hein at least knew that he was a downed American flyer; he did not even know that much about Hein. He could have asked, of course. That night on the verandah of the inn, when the German had seen his dog tags and they had agreed to climb together—he could have asked then, and Hein would have had to answer. But he had not asked. It had not seemed to matter.

Now, however, for some reason of which he was not quite sure, it did matter. In the brown stillness of the tent on that frozen, desolate mountainside, the sort of man that Siegfried Hein was seemed suddenly to matter to him very much indeed.

He is a German, Martin Ordway thought. And what else? A Nazi. A Nazi, period. As an air force pilot you had never had much personal contact with the enemy, but everyone you knew, who had, said they were all the same. They were Nazis, period. The synthetic German *ersatz* men, period. You had heard it a hundred times, read it a hundred times. You saw it, felt it, believed it, or rather almost believed it, but never quite, never wholly, because somewhere deep within you there remained the stubborn and indestructible conviction that no man was ever anything period. He was a Nazi. He was a Communist or a Catholic or an American or an aviator or a bootlegger. He carried his label, and the label was useful and often valid. But behind and beyond it he was still an individual human being.

All right then—what were Hein's qualities as an individual, insofar as he had seen them? He had skill as a climber. He had endurance, determination, pride. . . . And he had courage. . . . Yes, give the devil his due. Give the enemy his due. He had courage. That was the trouble with courage, perhaps: too many men had it. The men in brown and the men in green; the men in the Marauders and the men in the Junkers; the men fighting each other with stones and clubs and axes and spears and swords and catapults and bowie-knives and flintlocks and Gatling guns and Bren guns and detonation bombs and fragmentation bombs and delayed-fuse bombs and butterfly bombs and V-1 and V-2 and V-1000. They all had had courage—did have it—would have it. It was a terrible thing to admit, perhaps, but after enough years of killing-and-not-being-killed you got a little tired of courage. There was so damned much courage in the world, and so damned little wisdom. . . .

He watched the man opposite him through half-closed eyes. He watched the strong face and the clear gray eyes and the deft hands polishing the ax that Siegfried Hein was using to climb the same mountain that he, Martin Ordway, was climbing. . . . You are enemies, he thought. And at the same time, you are not enemies. Not here, at least. Here you are two men trying to climb a mountain together; two men sitting in a tent in the white stillness. Why are we here, Hein? It's not an easy question to answer, perhaps; but try to tell me, and I shall try to tell you. I know you are a Nazi, 'but that does not satisfy me. I know you have skill, endurance, pride, courage, but that does not satisfy me either. Who are you, Hein? What are you? What makes you tick?"

"Hein—" he heard his voice say.

The German raised his head and looked at him, but the voice did not go on.

"Yes?" Hein said.

"Have you another piece of emery paper?" Ordway asked.

Hein reached into his rucksack and gave him a strip, and now the two men sat silently against the tent walls, polishing their ax-blades.

After a while Carla awoke. "What time is it, Martin?" she asked.

Ordway looked at his watch. "Twenty of five."

He waited until the hands were at the hour, then took the binoculars and crept from the tent. The sun was hidden behind the skyline of the south face—and the filtered light of early evening was already beginning to dim the blue-white glitter of the frozen miles. To the left and below, the shadow of the Weissturm lay in an immense, jagged cone upon the floor of clouds. Ascending to the top of the cornice, Ordway focussed the glasses and for a long time moved them slowly up and down along the great arc of the southeast ridge.

When he returned to the tent the Primus was lighted and Carla was preparing supper. She glanced up as he came in, but did not speak, and he put the binoculars away and sat down where he had been before. After a few minutes the canvas of the roof began slowly to change color, and he knew that the sun was gone.

He wrapped himself in a blanket again and must have closed his eyes, because when he looked up the supper was ready and Carla was handing him his plate and cup. He took a few mouthfuls, but had even more difficulty eating than at midday. The aching knot had returned to his throat, and his lips were so thick and cracked that he was barely able to open them around the spoon. He waited, ate another few mouthfuls, waited again. By the time he was finished it was almost dark.

Hein crept to the entrance, went out for a few minutes and came back again. "The snow is good," he said. "By daylight tomorrow it will be all right for any sort of climbing."

"We should be able to get down in three or four hours," said Carla.

"Down?" Hein paused, but the girl did not speak again. "I am talking about up, *Fräulein*."

Here it is, Martin Ordway thought. . . .

"No," he said.

There was another silence. For a few moments the German sat motionless in the dusk, his gray eyes on Ordway's face, and when he spoke again his voice was level and quiet. "You do not really believe that I am going to go down, do you, *Herr Kapitän*? That I am going to come so close to the top of the Weissturm—to the thing that I have wanted most of anything in my life—and then turn around and go down, beaten?"

"We have to go down," Ordway said.

"Have to?"

"You know that as well as I do. How about Andreas? How about Delambre?"

"I could have told you from the beginning that these others could not climb such a mountain as this."

"It's not a question now of whether or not they can climb it. It's that they're probably in trouble."

"Trouble?" Hein shrugged a little. "It is possible, but not likely. . . . Believe me, I am not being more indifferent than you, but only more sensible. What could have happened to Delambre? He was not hurt, not sick, but only drunk, and that would be over a few hours after we left. He had a tent, food, a stove, enough clothing. The only accident that could have happened was that the tent blew away in the storm. If it did, he is done—finished. We can do him no more good today than tomorrow, or tomorrow than next month. If it did not—and there is no reason why it should have—he is all right. As for our friend Benner: the weather and snow were both good when he started down this morning, and he is a man who knows the technicalities of climbing. Whatever 'troubles' he may be having, I can assure you they are not the sort about which you are thinking."

"In other words, you're implying that—"

"I am not implying anything, Herr Ordway. I am saying what I said before—that Benner will not come back, no matter how things are at the lower tent."

Ordway's hands were tight against his bent knees. He felt the flame of anger rising in him, as it had before, when Hein had sat watching him silently as he searched for cigarette butts. And a moment later, as before, he felt it flicker and die. He had neither the strength nor the will for anger. He started to speak, retched, and bent over in a paroxysm of coughing.

"We have already told Andreas," said Carla quietly, "that if he did not come back today we would go down in the morning."

Hein shook his head. "That is what *he* said."

"And we agreed."

"I did not agree, *Fräulein*."

There was silence again. Ordway controlled his coughing and sat for a few moments drawing in deep breaths of the thin, cold air.

"Look, Hein—" he said. His voice had a strangely muffled sound, and he spoke very slowly, as if selecting his words one by one. "We've come a long way on this mountain together. I think that by this time you know that I want to climb it as much as you do. Do you think it will be easy for Fräulein Dehn and me to turn back now? Do you think it's easy for us to come so close to this thing we've been wanting all our lives, and then lose it? But we've no choice, can't you see that? If we're beaten—all right, that's the way it is. At least it's better to be beaten than to . . ."

The strain of continued talking was too much for him and he fell into another fit of coughing. Hein waited until he was finished, then said evenly: "No, it is not better to be beaten. And this is one time, *Herr Kapitän*, when I do not intend to be beaten."

"You won't go down tomorrow, then?"

"No—I shall not go down tomorrow. Tomorrow I shall go to the top."

"Alone?"

"If need be, alone."

In the dim light Ordway could see the tight line of Hein's lips and the gray eyes steady on his face. Anger flickered in him again, flared up, burst suddenly into words.

"That's the German way, I suppose?"

"I had thought we had agreed not to become involved in nationalities on our mountain," Hein said, his voice still quiet. "But as long as you have brought them up—yes, perhaps it is the German way. We Germans, as your country seems to be finding out again to its surprise, do not like to be beaten. In war—on a mountain —anywhere. We are not going to be beaten, and *I* am not going to be beaten. And do you know why I am not? Do you know why it is I who am going alone to the top of the Weissturm, while the rest of you drop off one by one for this excuse or the other? It is for exactly that reason: because I am a German. Because I am climbing for Germany and am a part of Germany, and the rest of you are climbing for yourselves and are a part—"

"Of nothing," said Carla.

Hein looked at her curiously.

"I remember my Doktor Goebbels too, Herr Hein."

"But you do not agree, I gather?"

"No."

"That is regrettable—for a German."

"I am not a German. I am an Austrian."

"German—Austrian: it is the same thing now." Hein paused briefly. "And when you return to the Reich, *Fräulein*, may I suggest, for your own sake, that you leave behind you some of the ideas that you seem to have acquired from your American friend here?"

Ordway had half risen to his feet. "That's enough, Hein," he said.

"*Bitte?*"

"You heard me. That's enough."

"You are not foolish enough to think I am afraid of you—are you, Captain Ordway?"

Ordway's hands tightened into fists. He felt the anger swelling again, twisting in his stomach, filling his chest and throat. Then suddenly he was coughing again. He sat back again and bent over the blankets, hacking and retching, and Carla put her hand lightly over his and kept it there until he stopped.

"Don't, Martin," she said.

He nodded and looked at her in the darkness, and then he looked at Hein. The anger was gone again, and where it had been was a dull and hollow emptiness.

After a while Hein got up and went outside.

"Carla—" Ordway said.

"Yes, Martin?"

"What should I do?"

"You must do what you think right."

"That's a help."

"What else can I say?"

"What would you do?" he asked.

407

It was a moment before she answered. Then she said: "I would go down to the others."

"And let Hein go on alone?"

"Yes."

Presently Hein returned, lay down and wrapped himself in his blankets. Ordway looked at his watch, and it showed a few minutes past eight. . . . We must get this thing settled, he told himself. We must fight it out to a decision. . . . But he no longer seemed able to think. Thoughts became mere words, and then words became mere sound, and finally sound itself trailed away into stillness. It was pitch dark in the tent now. There was only stillness and darkness.

When he looked at his watch again it was almost nine. Carla had lain down also, and she and Hein were two lumpy, motionless shapes on either side of him. He spoke her name softly, but she did not answer, and after a little while he too pulled the blankets over him and closed his eyes.

He dozed and awakened, and it was ten-thirty. And the second time he awakened it was not quite twelve. He lay quietly with his hands clasped under his head, listening to the tiny metallic ticking of his watch in the stillness. Then he slept again, and the ticking swelled into the drone of planes, and the drone swelled to a roar, and the roar faded and was gone, and in its place was a faint, rhythmic sound, as if of footsteps—of distant footsteps, blurred and muffled in the snow—of the boots of climbers on the still, white slopes of the mountainside, far below. . . .

When he woke for the third time it was to the consciousness that he had slept longer and more deeply than before. And as he lay with eyes open in the darkness he became slowly and vaguely conscious of something else as well—of something that was in some way different about the tent; of something that had changed. He listened, but there was no sound. A few feet away he could see the huddled shape that was Carla, still motionless under her blankets. Turning, he looked at the other side of him, to where Hein slept, and for a moment lay peering through the darkness. Then he groped for his flashlight, raised it and snapped on the beam.

Hein was not there.

Chapter 22

He snapped off the beam and lay propped on his elbow in the darkness.

He's just gone out to relieve himself, he thought. For a few moments he lay still, waiting, while sleep drained like a thick, sluggish liquid out of his body and brain. The knot was still in his throat, drier and tighter than before, and there was a peculiar wooden feeling, or absence of feeling, in the lower part of his face. He put out his tongue and licked his lips, but there was no sensation. Fumbling under the blankets, he pulled the mitten from one hand and touched his lips with his fingers. They were thick and hard under the stubble, like the surface of a rough-barked tree. Rubbing them gently, he could feel their swollen tautness and the deep lines of their cracks and fissures. But with the lips themselves he could not feel the touch of the fingers.

He raised his arm in front of his face and looked at the dimly glowing dial of his watch. It was not quite four-fifteen. He waited until the hand lay directly over the minute mark; then he pushed down the blankets and sat up. Pulling on his helmet and the windbreaker he had been using as a pillow, he crept on hands and knees across the tent floor and out through the sleeve.

The night seemed almost to strike at him with its black brilliance of snow and stars. There was no wind, no cloud, no sound or movement of any kind. On the far side of the tent the white mountain wall plunged steeply away into space. In front of it, and above, it climbed in wave upon frozen wave toward the high wild glitter of the sky. Martin Ordway got to his feet and stood quite still. Directly before him were the trampled drifts of the hollow, with the ropes and rucksacks dark against the snow and the steel of crampons and axheads glinting faintly in the starlight. Beyond it were the two sets of footprints from the previous day: Benner's curving down toward the cleft in the ice cornice and Hein's cutting diagonally across the slope above. And beyond it, too, there was now a third trail of footprints, leading upward.

Slowly, almost one by one, Ordway's eyes followed the new steps in the snow. They led over the low wall that formed the upper rim of the hollow, climbed straight up the slope for a distance of perhaps fifty yards and disappeared briefly into a second hollow. Above this he could see them again, far smaller now but still black and clear against the glittering whiteness, cutting across the upper, steeper section of the slope toward the point where the east ridge merged into the base of the shoulder and the Watchtower. Along the white line of the ridge was only space and stillness. He strained his eyes through the darkness but could see no movement. He turned his head, listening, but could hear no sound.

His breath hung in the air before him like a thin gray rag. And now suddenly he became aware that the cold of the snow was penetrating through the woolen thicknesses of his socks. Turning, he crawled back again into the brown, stale gloom of the tent.

Carla had not moved. She lay on her side, deep in sleep, with the blankets pulled up high around her so that only her hair and the upper part of her face were exposed. He squatted down on his own blankets and sat for several minutes watching her. Twice he reached his hand out toward her shoulder, but each time he stopped himself before he touched her. . . . No, he thought. No. . . . He pressed his eyelids tight together and shook his head, trying to break out of the lethargy of weariness in which his mind was swimming. He sat motionless in the cold darkness, struggling to think.

Then suddenly, very quietly and quickly, he was making ready. He pulled on his outer socks and climbing boots, his half-numb fingers fumbling stiffly with the frozen rawhide laces. He took off his windbreaker, pulled on two additional sweaters over those he was already wearing, wrapped a muffler around his neck and put on the windbreaker again. Using his flashlight cautiously, he assembled the few other things he would need and stowed them in one of the small rucksacks. There were snow-goggles, an extra pair of mittens, the binoculars, a canteen, a knife, a bar of chocolate and a package of crackers. Finding the jar of windburn cream, he opened it and spread a thick layer of grease over his forehead, nose and lips.

You should eat something now, he thought. But he was not hungry; his body did not want food. What it wanted, he realized suddenly, was something hot to drink—a few gulps of sweet, steaming tea. It needed that now as a motor needs fuel. But there was no way to brew tea except on the Primus, and if he lit the Primus it would awaken Carla. Creeping from the tent again, he stood in the space before it, forced himself to eat two crackers and washed them down with water from the canteen. The water tasted partly of boiling and partly of snow, and it went down past his swollen lips and his dry, aching throat with the heavy coldness of liquid ice. His body began suddenly to shiver under its layers of wool and flannel.

He put the crackers and canteen back in the rucksack with the chocolate. Perhaps you should take along more food, he thought. But almost in the same instant he knew it would be pointless. For one day's climbing what he had was enough. And if he were not back at camp by nightfall, all the food from all the banquets of all the Roman emperors. . . .

The hell with that, he thought.

He picked up his crampons, some pitons and karabiners and a piton hammer from the stack of gear in the clearing and put them in the rucksack; then he took a coil of thin rappeling rope and looped it securely through the straps. An ordinary climbing rope, to be sure, would be a rather ironically useless burden to a solitary climber, but it was more than likely that a rappel line would be useful when he came down. . . . When. Or was it *if?* he thought, smiling thinly to himself.

Now he was ready. Or, rather, one more thing and he would be ready. Crawling back into the tent, he found a scrap of paper and pencil and sat down again on the blankets, flashlight in hand.

Hein gone for top, he wrote. *Going after. Back tonight. In case* —he hesitated a moment and rubbed out the last two words. *We* are climbing together. Remember that—together. I love you, Carla. M. He looked at his watch and wrote the time—4:45—at the top of the sheet. Then he laid it on the blankets, where she would see it when she woke, and weighted it with the pencil.

He did not go quite yet, however, but for a few moments sat in the brown darkness looking at the muffled figure of the sleeping girl. He was not thinking; he was not, in any clear and definable sense, even feeling. He was simply sitting there, simply looking at her, and his body and brain were one great aching hollowness of wanting and loving. Her head was half-turned from him now, almost hidden by the rough wool of the blankets, so that he could not see her face. But that, he knew now suddenly, was what he had to do; that was what he wanted now, urgently, desperately, more than he had ever wanted anything in his life before. Not to hold her in his arms. Not to kiss her or speak to her. Only, for one quick moment, to see her sleeping face. Crawling along the few feet of canvas wall to where she lay, he reached out toward the covering blankets; but in the same instant his knee nudged into something in the darkness and the Primus stove tilted over against a stack of food tins with a metallic clank. His body went rigid, and for a moment he stopped breathing. But Carla did not wake. Her body stirred slightly and she murmured a few blurred words; then she nestled down still deeper into the blankets, until only her hair was showing. Ordway groped for the stove, righted it and crept quickly to the tent flap.

Then the close, still sanctuary of the tent was gone. Carla was gone. Everything that had been was gone. There was only the snow and the stars and a mountain rising into space. He slung his rucksack and rope onto his shoulders, pulled on his inner and then his outer gloves and picked up his ax. Then he climbed over the low rock-wall that overhung the camp and started up the long snow-slope above. When, after ten or fifteen minutes, he turned and looked around him, the tent was no more than a tiny, scarcely distinguishable brown speck in the black and white immensity of the night.

He plodded on—up the slope, over the ice-glazed black rock, up the steeper slope beyond, toward the gleaming saw-edge of the east ridge. He did not look back again, but held his eyes downward at the snow. He watched the monotonous tramp of his boots, the

412

long swing and thrust of his ax, the dark chain of footprints flowing down the white mountainside into his line of vision. . . . Hein had been right again, he thought. The snow was tight and firm-packed, with no possibility of avalanching; and whereas Andreas, the previous morning, had floundered in soft drifts up to his thighs, his footprints were now biting no more than an inch or two into the glittering frozen crust.

His footprints?

He stopped again, suddenly, and stared up at the single track that climbed the long slope above him. Then he turned and stared at the single track that dropped away behind. . . . not his footprints. Hein's footprints. . . . For the first time he realized now that he had been following the German's steps, stride by stride, ever since he had left the tent. Turning again, his eyes travelled up the mountainside, and he stood motionless, waiting for the hot, bitter tide of anger to rise within him. But the anger did not come. He did not feel anger any more than he had felt it when he had first discovered that Hein was gone; any more than he had felt anger or fear or hope or any other recognizable emotion during those endless hours and days since the storm began. He felt the cold hollowness of his body and the dry, aching numbness of his throat and lips. He felt the cold blade of the axhead through the wool of his gloves and the cold crispness of the snow beneath his boots. And that was all he felt.

"The hell with it," he said aloud.

He began climbing again. The minutes slipped past. The mountainside slipped past. . . .

Presently he became aware that the slope had steepened and that the footprints before him were petering out into a glassy pitch of frozen snow. Pausing, he unslung his rucksack, took out his crampons and strapped them to his boots. With them he was able to continue straight upward for another hundred paces or so, but then the incline became still steeper and he was compelled to work his way upward in a series of long diagonal traverses. The snow underfoot grew harder and glassier, until it was no longer snow at all but solid blue-white ice, and he was held to the mountainside only by the thin, delicate bite of twenty-four steel prongs.

The ridge was close above him now, looming like a gigantic white parapet against the star-blazing night. To the right it fell away in a seemingly endless sweep of jagged spires and notches, disappearing at last into the blackness below. A little to the left, and now, he judged, no more than three hundred feet above him, it ended abruptly against the squat battlements of the Kandermatt shoulder. Staring up through the snow-glittering darkness, he could see the smooth convex flutings of the shoulder proper bulging outward into space and beyond it, the flat, ice-veined profile of the Watchtower; and he could see, too, that the binoculars had not lied. Both appeared hopeless from the ridge. The only possibility of getting by them would be either by skirting the tower on the far side, above the north face of the mountain, or by working through the cleft between tower and shoulder—if he could reach the cleft.

Well, he would find out soon enough. . . .

After another hundred zigzagging steps the angle of the slope had increased to the point where it was no longer a slope at all but a tilted, smooth-gleaming wall—too steep for even the steel grip of the crampons. He paused, looking about him for some sign of Hein's route, but apparently he had diverged from it since coming to the hard snow, for as far as he could see in either direction the mountainside rose blue-white and unbroken above him. Reversing his ax, he bent to the work of carving himself a stairway in the ice. Six blows and a step up, six more blows and another step. Ten steps diagonally to the left, ten more diagonally to the right. After the first fifty steps he rested, one foot in the topmost step and the other in the one below it, his body bent forward with head and arm resting on the curved blade of his ax. After another forty steps he rested again. His shoulders and chest, under their layers of flannel and wool, were dripping with sweat; the muscles of his arms and legs burned with fatigue, and his breath sucked up and down through his bone-dry throat in long shuddering gasps. Looking downward now between his spread legs, he no longer could see the white mountainside directly beneath him but only the blackness of space. He knew that if the angle of the wall steepened by so much as a degree or two he would be unable to hold himself to it any longer.

He hacked twenty steps and rested; twenty more and rested. Then he bent to the hacking again. The angle did not steepen, but remained the same. For another twenty, forty, sixty steps it

414

remained the same, while the ax-blade rose and fell and his aching legs forced his steel-shod boots upward from hold to hold. And then suddenly, blessedly, it was lessening. It was no longer ice, but snow again. He kicked at the snow with his boot, and it went in and held. Kicking slowly and firmly, he bore off for ten paces to the left, then for ten paces back to the right, then straight up. Step by step now the slope was easing off before him. It was almost gone now—almost level. It was level. He rounded the base of an outcropping gendarme, took a final step upward over a lip of jutting granite and sat down in the snow on the east ridge of the Weissturm.

For perhaps five minutes he sat quite still, his back propped against his rucksack and his legs stretched out straight before him in the snow. Gradually the dull ache in his arms and legs ebbed away, and the pounding of his heart and the straining of his lungs subsided; but the tight knot of pain was still throbbing and swelling in his throat, and his lips and the lower part of his face were numb. His mind felt numb too, almost as if it were muffled like his body in thick coverings of flannel and wool. He wanted to sink back against the soft, glinting snow—to lie there quietly—to sleep.

He shook his head, struggling to clear it, and rubbed his fingers through the stubble of his chin and jaw. Sensation returned slowly to the flesh beneath, at first softly tingling, then in sharp, burning waves, but his lips remained wooden and unfeeling beneath their thick sheath of grease. With a conscious effort he made himself turn and look upward along the ridge. He was, he saw at once, within twenty or thirty yards of its upper end, and the towering walls of the shoulder and Watchtower loomed in the darkness almost directly above his head. Their bases, however, were still hidden behind the intertwining humps and pinnacles of the ridge, and he could not yet tell if there would be a route around them or between them. Well, he would find out soon enough, he thought. . . . Yes, very soon now. . . . For, turning again and staring outward from the mountain, he saw now suddenly that the darkness was breaking.

In the eastern sky the stars seemed to be slowly, almost imperceptibly receding. The void beyond them was no longer black but sombre purple, and then no longer purple but a deep ashen gray. Leaning back against his rucksack, he watched, motionless, while the thin, cold ocean of the dawn flowed westward—across the paling firmament and the gulfs of the air and the spreading earth below. There was no mist, no wind, no motion or sound of any kind. Day, in this austere and lifeless world above the world, was being born out of the stillness of space and time.

Now the great rocks of the ridge about him emerged one by one from obscurity, their gray shapes leaning twisted and forlorn into the emptiness beyond. The mountainsides and valleys below emerged slowly, as if from beneath a dark, withdrawing sea, and in a great semicircle to the south and east the unnumbered peaks of the Alps seemed almost to be rising up, moment by moment, out of the earth. Incredibly remote and pure they appeared to Ordway, staring at them through the miles of the dawn. His eyes, straining, could just distinguish the gray desolation of their slopes, the soaring arcs of their ridges and rock-walls, the gleaming ribbons of their glaciers. As the minutes passed the last remaining shreds and wisps of darkness seeped from the sky. The mountains grew still clearer, still purer; now they seemed actually to be drawing nearer —a gigantic cosmic image shifting slowly and majestically into focus.

Another five minutes passed—perhaps ten. Then he got to his feet. The sweat had dried on his body and he felt suddenly cold and stiff. He stood for a little while scuffing his feet in the snow and beating his mittened hands together. Then he removed his crampons, stowed them in the rucksack and started off up the ridge.

In less than a hundred paces he was at the top. Rounding the last intervening gendarme, he came out onto a sort of small, flattened platform filled with snow-covered talus, and there, directly before him, was the wall of the shoulder soaring into the thin dawnlight. From the camp and the slope below, it had appeared unclimbable. And now, in that first instant that he stared at it face on, he knew that it was unclimbable. Rising first in a vertical face and then, as they climbed higher, in a beetling overhang, its smooth-ribbed, bulging columns presented scarcely a crack or rugosity to which an insect might have clung—much less a man. Along the southern edge, above the route which they had followed, it was also as they had surmised: smooth rock, an overhang and space.

All right. It was either the north face or the cleft. . . .

Picking his way slowly among the tumbled rocks and patches of snow, he followed the wall toward the far side of the ridge. He was now directly beneath the jutting turret of the Watchtower and perhaps a hundred feet below the point at which it forked off from the main body of the shoulder. At the farthermost edge of the ridge the wall curved out of sight over what he knew must be the north face of the mountain, but whether the ridge ended at the wall or followed it around in a negotiable slope or series of ledges he was not yet able to tell. A few more steps brought him to the very rim, and he peered down and around. The ridge proper, he saw now, ended at the very point at which he stood, but about five feet below a narrow, curving shelf bore off to the right, hugging the base of the tower. Lowering himself carefully, he followed it around. After perhaps twenty paces it dwindled away into the smooth rock-wall, but, peering down again, he saw that there was a second shelf leading onward another few feet below. He lowered himself again, crept forward again. The second shelf led to a third and the third to a fourth. Then the fourth shelf petered out like the others, and once again he came to the edge and looked down. There was no shelf beyond it. There was only the smooth rock-wall and gray depths of space and the dully gleaming thread of a twisting glacier seven thousand feet below.

He did not know how long he stood there, looking downward. Nor how long it took him to creep back over the four curving shelves to the crest of the ridge. Nor how long he remained squatting among the broken rocks and snow patches staring at the narrow, almost vertical chimney that zigzagged upward between the shoulder and the Watchtower to the cleft between them. When next he became aware of time he had risen to his feet again and was walking slowly toward the base of the chimney, and the level rays of the sun were glinting on the steel blade of his ice ax and the mica in the rocks. He stopped, tied the ax onto the webbing of his rucksack and took off his two pairs of mittens. Then, with slow and measured movements, he began to climb.

For the first fifty feet or so the chimney was little more than a deep crack in the granite wall, and he climbed partly by minute holds and ledges along its lip and partly by jamming his knees and elbows into it and pushing himself upward by main strength. Then it broadened to a width of about a yard, and he maneuvered his whole body into it. For a short stretch there were adequate holds, but this was followed by a longer stretch of almost marble smoothness, up which he had to hoist himself by the alternating thrust of back and feet against the two opposite walls. Soon the sweat was pouring from his body again; his heart leapt and pounded; and the knot of muscles in his right thigh that had bothered him four days before during the ascent of the Funnel, began to throb and twitch under the cramped pressure of his movements. He rested a moment, supported only by the traction of his back and left leg. Then he hoisted again, rested again, hoisted again. And at last, just as the last of his strength was ebbing, he came to a three-inch ledge in the wall on which he could hold himself in a standing position.

For two or three minutes he remained perfectly motionless, his torn hands spread flat against the wall above him, his face pressed against the cold smoothness of the rock. Then, when the pounding of his heart and the jerking of his thigh muscles had subsided a little, he craned his head back and looked upward again.

He had come more than two-thirds of the way up the chimney. The walls above him were no longer vertical, but sloped diagonally off to the right, and where they ended, not more than thirty feet above him now, he could see a bright wedge of sky that marked the beginning of the cleft. Only one formidable obstacle seemed to remain. At the very top of the chimney, bulging darkly against its walls, was a huge chockstone. To get up into the cleft beyond he would either have to squeeze his way between it and the inner wall of the chimney or work his way up over it on the outside.

He began climbing again and, encountering no difficulties, soon found himself crouched on two adequate footholds directly beneath the wedged boulder. For a few moments he remained there, motionless, his eyes moving over the rough bulge of granite above his head; then slowly and cautiously he worked his way toward the patch of daylight that showed between the chockstone and the inner wall. He found a hold for his right foot and pushed himself upward. He found another for his left and pushed again. Now his chest was pressed flat against the chockstone and his hands, stretched high above his head, were groping for another hold above. He found one, pulled, and, kicking with his feet against the chimney wall, inched himself upward until his head and the upper part of his shoulders were through the narrowest part of the opening. Then his rucksack jammed against the wall. He pulled and kicked, twisted and writhed, but the more he struggled the more tightly the pack became wedged. Precariously he lowered himself back to his original footholds and, loosening his ax and rope from the pack-straps, fastened them to his belt. Then he tried again. And failed again. He tried it with the rucksack slung sideways under one arm, and strapped to his chest, and held in his hand, and finally tied to one foot. But each time he worked upward to the same point only to find himself hopelessly wedged between the chockstone and the wall. Grimly, desperately, he continued the struggle, until there was no breath left in his body and it seemed to him that with his next movement his heart would explode against his ribs. Then for the last time he lowered himself to the holds below.

It was the outside of the chockstone or nothing.

For perhaps ten minutes he remained where he was, half standing and half crouching, while the breath and strength slowly returned to his body. Then he shifted his position slightly and stood staring up at the outer contour of the rock. Beginning at a point almost beside his shoulder, it rose vertically for a distance of some six feet, bulged outward from the chimney in a sort of rough, blunted nose, and then curved back in again above. The lower part would obviously be delicate and precarious going, but seemed to him not impossible, for the vertical stretch was banded by a few narrow, yet feasible, ledges and the nose appeared to be well fissured with cracks and holds. The backslope, above the nose, he could not see. If it were not too steep and had holds, or even cracks for a piton, it would probably be all right. If not . . .

He opened his rucksack, took out a piton and the piton-hammer and put them in the breast pocket of his windbreaker; then he stepped up and out onto the first ledge of the chockstone. For an instant, looking downward, he was aware of the east ridge twisting away below him, fragile and razor-thin now, with its sides sloping like steep white eaves into space. Then his face was to the rock; his toes, inside his boots, were curling against the two-inch ledge; his hands were groping upward. He found his hold and raised himself to the second ledge. He groped and raised himself once more.

Now he was well out on the nose, holding himself to the chockstone partly by minute hand and footholds and partly by the friction of his body against its rough, wrinkled surface. Looking upward, he saw that the outermost bulge of the rock was no more than a foot above the level of his eyes.

He shifted his feet slightly in their shallow holds and closed his left hand firmly over the knob of rock beneath it; then, with his right hand he let go his hold and groped upward again, above the bulge. There was only smooth stone. He moved his hand slowly to the right and left, as far·as it could reach, but still there was no hold. He stood on tiptoe on the ledge, pulled himself up off the ledge, and clung to the rough bulge of the rock with his left hand and the straddling pressure of his thighs. His chest and shoulders were damp with sweat again, and he felt a single cold drop trickle from his underarm and run down along his side. . . . And now, suddenly, as his right hand stretched upward to its fullest, straining limit, it touched a fissure in the rock above. It was only a crack—not a hold—not wide enough to grip even with the tips of his fingers. But it was wide enough for a piton. If he could manage to get his piton up there, and the hammer, and drive it home. . . .

He could not do it. Piton and hammer, in his breast pocket, were wedged tight against the bulge of the chockstone. His left hand was pressed against the knob of rock, supporting him—and now suddenly he realized that he could not bring his right arm down again without losing his balance. For a moment he clung motionless, spread-eagled on the snout of the boulder. Then he began to slip. He heard the faint, ominous scraping of his bootnails on the granite below, felt the upward pull of the rock on the front of his clothing and his left hand slowly losing its grip on the knob, as if the fingers were being pulled from it by some monstrous, invisible force. He clutched at the rock with his knees, pressed against it with his body, clawed at it with his hands. In a last instinctive and despairing effort his right hand strained upward once again: over the smooth stone—to the crack—along the crack . . . to the hard, smooth, unyielding object that protruded from the top of the crack. . . .

He had it now. He was pulling himself up, first with one hand, then with two. He was pulling himself up over the bulge of the chockstone. His head and shoulders were past it. His waist was past it. His knees were past it. He was lying sprawled in the cleft between the shoulder and the Watchtower, staring dully at the steel piton of Siegfried Hein's that rose slender and glinting from the fissure in the rock.

He was lying in the cleft, and the cleft was a gateway to the west. There was the north wall of the Weissturm, below him and to the right, falling away in precipice after precipice into a sea of space. There were the other peaks of the Kandermatt Range, lying flattened and remote beneath the blue miles, and beyond them, sprawling wildly into the distance, the crumpled, snow-choked wilderness of the Pennines and the Oberland. They were all there before him now, the great peaks and ranges of the heart of Europe, exactly as he had seen them on so many other unforgotten mornings beneath the trembling, tapering wings of Mitchell or Marauder. The solemn crags of Monte Rosa and the Mischabel; the jutting spires of the Matterhorn, Weisshorn, Finsteraarhorn; the Jungfrau, Eiger, Mönch, Schreckhorn; and, above and beyond them all, the immense dome of Mont Blanc arching white and glittering into the stainless sky. Between the ranges, deep and hidden, were the valleys and lakes and villages that were Switzerland. Beyond them, spreading still and mist-sheathed to the farthest horizon, were the blue, distant foothills that were France.

His eyes knew the familiar contours. His tongue knew the familiar names. But they were no more real to him now than the painted patterns of a canvas cyclorama on some remote and implausible stage.

He drew his handkerchief from his pocket and held it first around one and then the other of his torn and bleeding hands. He opened his mouth wide and sucked great draughts of the thin, freezing air into his burning lungs. His eyes slowly followed the trail of footprints that led down from the gateway of the cleft along a gentle snow-slope, dipped to a narrow saddle between the north and east faces of the mountain and disappeared up an equally gentle snow-slope at the base of the summit pyramid.

It is only a walk, he thought.

He leaned back against the rocks of the cleft, closing his eyes.

You should eat something, he thought.

He found a cracker in the rucksack and took a bite from it, but the dry flakes rasped like splinters in his throat, and after a moment he spat them out. Then he tried a sliver of chocolate, but it turned instantly into a thick, doughy pellet against his tongue. For a few minutes he sat bent forward, his forehead against his drawn-up knees, retching and coughing. Then he opened the canteen and took a sip of water. He did not feel the water at all in his mouth or throat, but only in his stomach, when it got there, lying cold and heavy as stone. A moment later he was retching again, coughing again.

He got up and closed the rucksack and slung it on his shoulders and wiped his hands again with the handkerchief and pulled on his inner gloves and then his outer gloves and picked up his ice ax.

"All right—let's go," he said.

He felt suddenly very strong and lightheaded and lighthearted, but when he tried to sing a snatch of song no sound came out from between his cracked lips, and when he turned to smile at Carla she was not there.

He followed the slope down, looking intently at the footprints in the snow before him. Not at the blue space on either side of him nor at the mountaintops below him nor at the mountaintop above, but only at the firm, even-spaced footprints in the snow. He followed them to the bottom of the slope, across the narrow bridgelike saddle and up the slope on the far side. When he reached the crest and turned to look back, the shoulder and the Watchtower and the cleft between were already far beneath him, a remote and insubstantial gray silhouette superimposed upon the blue-white depths beyond. He tried to sing again, but again no sound came out. And Carla was still . . .

He shook his head sharply. This is no good, he thought. No good at all.

He sat down on the frozen snow. This time he did not lie back or close his eyes or try to eat or drink, but merely sat quietly, drawing in slow, deep breaths, sucking the oxygen from the air into his lungs and blood and brain. When he stood up again he felt steadier. He pushed back the wristlet of his mitten and looked at his watch. It was half past eight. Holding the watch closer, he looked at the second hand circling its measured, unhurried way around the dial; then he held it to his ear, under the flap of his helmet, listening to its precise, metallic clicking. Yes, he felt steadier now. He felt very steady.

Turning, he stared up the mountainside. Directly beyond the crest on which he stood the snow flattened out into an almost level ramp for a distance of perhaps a hundred feet; then it climbed in another long slope to a second crest and, beyond that, to a third and a fourth. It was more like a sea than a mountain, he thought—a bright, sungleaming sea seen from the gunwale of a heeling boat, tilting in great frozen billows toward the sky. Beyond the fourth crest, which jutted out more steeply and boldly than the others, he could see only blue space. There might be more slopes, more crests, behind it—or there might be the walls of the Citadel. It could not be so very much farther now to the Citadel: about fifteen hundred feet, Andreas had said, from the shoulder to its base, and he was already standing a good three or four hundred above the shoulder. Suddenly he was aware that his heart had begun to pound again, but this time it was neither from exhaustion nor from fear.

He took the binoculars from the rucksack, raised them to his eyes and swept them slowly over the white waste above. A zig-zagging trail of footprints leapt into focus before him, and steep blue pitches of glare-ice and granulated drifts and hummocks of snow. But there was no human figure. Nothing moved. Lowering his glasses, he slung them by their strap around his neck; then he put on his rucksack again and started up the slope.

He put one foot in front of the other. He put one foot above the other. He kicked and stepped, kicked and stepped, in slow monotonous rhythm, and the humps and cracks and ripples of the snow crept slowly and monotonously past beneath his downturned eyes. From the crest of the second slope he could still see three crests above him. And at the crest of the third there were still three. Wave upon wave the frozen snow-masses rose above him, their reflected sunglare beating down upon him with a fierce white incandescent light.

On the fourth crest he stopped and put on his snow goggles. On the sixth—or perhaps it was the seventh—he stopped again and sat down to rest, his elbows propped on his knees and his forehead resting on the cold steel head of his ax. He was tired now —very tired. His feet felt like two enormous lumps of iron on the ends of his legs, and a deep, throbbing bone-ache was spreading in slow waves from his knees and thighs into every joint and cranny of his body. There is no hurry, he thought. No hurry at all. You can close your eyes and lie back in the snow a minute. For just a few minutes. . . .

He jerked himself to his feet. For a few moments he stood motionless, the upper part of his body swaying a little as he leaned for support on his ax. Then he began to climb again. He kicked, stepped, kicked, stepped. He put one foot in front of the other; one foot above the other. The white tilting billows of the mountain rolled down past him like a sea.

And as he climbed on—with the snow slipping by, and the yards and footprints and the minutes slipping by, and time and distance and the mountain and the sky all slipping silently by together—as he put his left boot before his right boot and then his right boot before his left boot, he became gradually aware that a curious thing had begun to happen to him. His body was numb now; it felt muffled and remote, scarcely any longer a part of him at all. But his mind and perceptions were growing clearer. Plodding step by step up the unending mountainside, it seemed to him as if the stainless clarity of that high, gleaming world were slowly and magically being distilled into his own brain and senses. The sky was a bluer blue than he had ever seen before, the snow a whiter white. The contours of the slope above no longer sprawled away in a confused and meaningless blur of distance, but rose up still and frozen before him in sharp-edged focus. Where before there had only been mass and height, only snow and sky, all was now substance and form, color and texture, detail upon minute detail, piled one upon the other, blending one into the other, separate from and yet a part of each other, infinitely complex and yet infinitely clear. He felt the steel of his ax through the two thicknesses of his mittens and the cold thin air against the sweat of his forehead and the tiny crunching contraction of each pinpoint of snow beneath the thick, nailed soles of his boots. He smelled the wool of his sweaters and the leather of boots and harness and his own man-smell and the fresh snow on the slope and the older snow beneath it and the ancient ice beneath them both. He saw the great lift of the snow, the structure and texture of a mountaintop of snow, and he saw too the smallness and closeness and secrecy of the snow, its humps and hollows and cracks and wind-ripples, the structure and texture of its flakes, its grains and molecules. He felt and smelled and saw these things not one after the other, but all at once, all together. He knew them all together. It was as if slowly, as he climbed, one veil after another were being withdrawn from between him and the apprehensible world, until all that had once been hidden was now revealed, all that had been secret was made known. He kicked and stepped, kicked and stepped. He moved slowly and steadily upward through the snow; through the white billows of the mountain; through the purity and stillness of time.

And then, presently, within the stillness . . .

He stopped and stood quite still. He stood leaning on his ice ax, his eyes narrowed, listening, but the only sounds were the faint soft crunch of snow beneath his boots and the measured rasping of his breath in his throat. His eyes moved slowly over the slope above; then he turned and stared down the slope below. There was only sky and sun and snow and the footprints in the snow. There was only silence and space.

And yet the illusion that he had heard a sound persisted; the illusion—if it was an illusion—that he was no longer alone. His mind went back to the night on the lower terrace when he and Radcliffe had sat listening to the distant humming of the wind; to the Englishman's description of the presence that filled the stillness on the frozen wastes of Everest. . . . *Mallory used to say it was ourselves. The selves we were trying to leave behind.* . . . He shook his head and closed his eyes, pressing the lids tightly against the balls. Opening them again, he did not look up or down the mountainside but moved his gaze slowly and deliberately from one close, tangible object to another: from the minute globules of snow on his boots to the smooth yellow wool of his mittens. He raised his arm, pushed back the wristlet of the mitten and looked at his watch.

The hands still pointed to half past eight.

He brought the watch closer to his goggled eyes, staring at the second hand that slanted motionless across the dial. He held it against his ear, under his helmet, and fumbled with the stem through the awkward thicknesses of his mittens. A sudden hollowness of panic filled him, and he twisted and jabbed at the stem and shook his arm violently; but the thing that was strapped to his wrist was merely an inert functionless rectangle of glass and steel. Dropping his arm to his side, he stood looking about him again at the snow and the sky. The sun was high over his left shoulder now: to the east—or was it the southeast?—or the south? He turned, circling slowly, but the sun seemed to follow him around. It seemed to be blazing down on him not from any one point in the sky, but from the whole sky, from the snow, from everywhere.

He stood still again, staring up the slope, listening again. There was no sound. Nothing moved. He began climbing again. And the sun and the silence climbed after him.

There was the snow and the footprints in the snow. There was the slope and the crest, and the next slope and the next crest, the slope and the crest beyond. There was the smooth, ice-veined wall of the Citadel rising sheer into the sky beyond the last crest. There was a ramp of snow curving around the wall to the right, and a sharp bend in the ramp, and the ramp narrowing and steepening, and beyond the ramp the summits of the Alps and the blue valleys that were Switzerland and the blue horizon that was France. There was Siegfried Hein standing beyond the next bend in the ramp and turning and looking at him, his eyes very gray and steady in his sun-blackened face.

Ordway stopped.

You must think clearly now, he thought. His eyes moved over the muffled figure, over the torn boots and the great jagged rents at the knees and elbows, and back to the burned, stubbled face and the gray eyes. You must think and talk very clearly now.

"You have changed your mind, I see," Hein said.

He nodded.

"A long, hard climb, is it not?"

"Yes."

"But you found the footprints and the piton helpful, perhaps?"

"Yes, I found them very helpful."

He could not feel his tongue or lips moving, and the words stuck like thick lumps in his throat. Suddenly he leaned against the rock-wall beside him, choking and coughing.

426

Hein watched him in silence. "You will excuse me if I go on now?" he said presently.

Ordway started to speak, choked again and stood crouched with his head against the rock. Then the paroxysm passed and he turned slowly back to the German.

"On?" he repeated thickly.

"To the top."

"I'm going to the top too."

Hein shrugged. "That is up to you, of course." His eyes were still fixed on Ordway's face. "Permit me to make a suggestion, however, *Herr Kapitän*. Do not waste your time trying to climb the rock."

Ordway's gaze moved slowly upward over the vertical ice-sheathed wall of the Citadel.

"It's the same all around?" he asked.

"Yes, it is the same all around. I have reconnoitred it for more than an hour and made a start in two or three places; but it is unclimbable. You will forgive me, perhaps, that I was not even able to hammer in a piton for our mutual convenience."

Ordway looked at him for a long moment in silence. Very steady now, he thought. Very clear and sure and steady . . .

"And this ledge?" he asked.

"Is the one possibility."

Ordway moved forward to a point a few feet beyond the German and peered around a protruding buttress in the rock-wall along the curving flange of the ramp. Only a short pitch of precipice remained above them—twenty vertical feet, perhaps, twenty-five at the most—with the ramp cutting diagonally upward across its face. It was far narrower and steeper than the section on which they stood—a mere ribbon of snow clinging to the mountainside. But it was there. It extended in an unbroken path to the top of the Citadel and ended in a broad, jutting platform of rock above.

Ordway turned back to Hein.

"It looks all right," he said.

"Yes, it does, doesn't it?"

"Let's go, then."

He took another step forward, but stopped suddenly when he saw that the other had not moved. For a moment the two men looked at each other in silence.

"I would not be quite so impatient if I were you, *Herr Kapitän*," said Hein quietly. "If, for example, you would take the trouble, as I did, to study the ledge ahead from various angles, you would perhaps notice something that will change your mind."

Ordway's eyes moved from Hein back to the ramp. He pressed himself in against the precipice wall and stared upward. Then he crouched and leaned outward. Digging his fingers and toes into the snow, he inched the upper part of his body out over the rim of the ledge until at last he could see what lay beyond and beneath it. And in that same instant he saw what Hein had meant. The section of the ramp on which they stood was, in effect, the slopping top of a bulge in the cliffs below, and the snow that covered it rested on a firm, if narrow, base of solid rock. But directly ahead, where the ramp steepened across the final pitch, the bulge no longer existed. The ribbon of snow that formed its surface was not a covering over rock beneath, but merely a cornice or unsupported platform, clinging of its own adhesiveness to the face of the precipice. Below it was no firm outthrust of the mountainside, but eight thousand feet of air.

Ordway stood up slowly.

"It wouldn't hold a man," he said.

Hein shook his head. "No, it would not hold a man."

"Then—"

He felt the gray eyes on his face again—the gray eyes, steady and mocking.

"Then if you will let me by, *Herr Kapitän*—" Hein moved past him for a step or two, stopped again and stood staring up along the ramp. "—I shall be starting now."

"But how can you? Which way?"

"You have heard of a hand traverse, perhaps?"

"Yes, but—" He broke off abruptly, his eyes following Hein's along the sheer face beyond. And now for the first time he saw that there was a crack in the smooth surface of the rock. Beginning not more than two yards ahead of where they stood, it slanted upward across the precipice, roughly parallel to the snow-ramp and about five feet above it, and ended where the ramp ended, at the base of the jutting platform above. It was a thin, hairline crack, far too narrow and shallow to hold a booted foot; but its lower lip

428

seemed to curl upward and outward just enough to support the grasp of a man's tightly curved fingers.

Ordway's eyes went back to Hein.

"It's at least forty feet," he said.

"Yes."

"And a thirty-degree angle."

"Yes."

"But you think you can make it?"

"Yes, I think I can make it."

There was another silence between them. Ordway looked once again at the thin, slanting crack and the ribbon of snow beneath it and the gulf of space beyond. Then he quietly unslung his rope from his shoulder.

"All right," he said.

Hein looked at him without speaking.

"Shall we go?" asked Ordway.

The German shook his head slowly. "I am going alone," he said.

"We're going together."

"No. Whether you try to follow me or not is your own affair, although having seen your attempts at climbing I would advise most strongly against it. But I am afraid I have finished with dragging you and your companions to the top of the Weissturm."

Ordway stood straight and still, his palms flattened against the rock behind him. For a moment the only sound was the deep rasping of his breath in his throat.

"I am not asking you to help me," he said quietly.

"No? What then?"

"I'm suggesting that we help each other."

"You are under the impression then that I need your help?"

"As much as I need yours." Ordway held out the rope. "Here. Tie it on."

Hein did not move.

"Tie it on, I say!"

He heard his own voice, tiny and hoarse and straining in the silence of snow and sky. He saw the gray walls of the Citadel and the white glint of a slope above the eaves. He felt the tautness of his body, the straining of his lungs, the wild pounding of his heart.

"We've come this far together, Hein," he said. "Let's finish it together. . . ."

429

The German stared at him silently for a moment. The eyes in the blackened, bearded, ice-crusted face were now no longer mocking, but as cold and hard and bleak as stone. "No," he said, his voice low and even, "we will not finish it together. I will finish it alone, and you will not finish it at all. And shall I tell you why that is the way it will be, Captain Ordway? It is because I am strong and you are weak. It is because I have the courage and the skill and the will to do it, and you have not. It is because I am a German climbing for Germany, and you are not climbing for anything, but only running away."

Ordway did not speak. He did not move. He stood there, as immobile and frozen as the mountain wall behind him, the coil of rope in his extended hand.

What happened then remained in his memory afterward not as remembered reality but as the blurred images and sensations of a half-apprehended dream. There was the sudden great surge of anger rising within him; an anger such as he had never felt in his life before; an engulfing and consuming tide that was more than anger, deeper and colder and more bitter than anger. There was Hein standing in front of him, Hein turning away again and moving slowly up the ramp. There was the wild, shaken, despairing instant in which he was about to hurl himself forward upon him. . . . But he did not hurl himself forward. He still neither spoke nor moved. . . . And now, as he stood watching, Siegfried Hein approached the lower end of the unsupported snow-ramp, studied the slanting crack in the rock above, and, grasping its lower lip with the fingers of both hands, swung himself out onto the face of the precipice.

With slow, measured movements the German pulled himself across and upward, his head and shoulders held close in against the line of the crack, his feet dragging without pressure along the surface of the snow below. His right hand slid forward, gripped and pulled. Then his body moved after it as the left hand slipped forward too. He reached, gripped, pulled, reached again. After each five or six swings he rested a moment, with his hands close together in the crack and his chin resting on its outcurving lip. Then he moved on again. Presently he was halfway to the rock platform above. Perhaps a minute later he was two-thirds of the way. And still he moved on, steadily and silently. The only movement in that enormous stillness of snow and air was the slow, rhythmic motion of his hands and body. The only sound was the faint scraping of his clothing against the wall of rock.

And then suddenly, startlingly, there was another sound. . . .

With a sharp, dry crack the lip of the crevice to which Hein was clinging broke away from under his hands. For a terrible, timeless instant Ordway heard the scratch of his bootnails against the rock and saw his fingers clawing at the wall. Then he was no longer clinging to the wall at all but standing on the unsupported snow-ramp below. The snow trembled, seemed for a moment to be slowly buckling under his weight . . . and held.

Then there was silence again. Hein did not move. Nothing moved.

"Can you get back on the wall?" Ordway called.

The German did not answer. For a few moments he remained frozen where he stood; then very slowly and cautiously, without moving his feet, he raised his arms and groped upward to the right along the rock-wall. Apparently, however, he could find no hold. Lowering his arms, he stood staring down at the snow, and Ordway could see that he was carefully shifting his weight and advancing one foot, inch by inch, in front of the other. He took one step, then a second. But he never took the third. For in the next instant the snow directly in front of him disappeared. It did not seem to break away or to fall. It was just soundlessly and magically no longer there. In the spot where Hein had been about to set his foot there was now revealed the blue sea of air that washed the eight-thousand-foot north face of the Weissturm.

Ordway shut his eyes, but only for a second, and when he opened them Hein was still miraculously there.

"Don't move!" he heard his voice calling. "Don't move an inch!"

And at the same moment he realized that, without having thought it or willed it, he himself had begun to move; that he had unslung his pack and dropped his ax and rope; that he was edging toward the snow-ramp, grasping the crack above it with bare hands, swinging himself out onto the precipice beyond. . . .

He kept his face to the mountainside and his eyes on the gray rock creeping past them. He reached, gripped, pulled, reached again. He clung motionless to the lip of the crack, counted ten and swung on again. When at last he turned and looked ahead he

431

was no more than ten or twelve feet from the point where Hein stood. When he turned for the second time he was almost within arm's reach of him.

Directly ahead of him now was the section of the crack from which the lip had broken away in Hein's grasp. Slanting diagonally upward above the German's head, it was now no more than the merest fold in the vertical rock, shorn clean of all protuberances or roughnesses on which a hand or finger could secure a grip. It was not a long section—a yard across perhaps, four feet at the most —and beyond it the crack was deep and flanged again, cutting upward in its final stretch to the summit of the rock-wall and the jutting platform above. But the point at which the lip began was still a foot or more beyond Hein's grasp, and between him and its granite safety was the jagged hole in the snow-ramp and blue depths of space. Ordway's eyes moved back to Hein and from Hein to the point in the lower section of the crack to which he himself was clinging. Here, too, there was a distance of perhaps a foot between the German's farthest possible grasp and the nearest projection of the lip. But there was one difference. On the far side there was only one man's reach to bridge the gap, and on this side there were two.

"The crack's strong enough here to hold the two of us," Ordway said quietly. "I'm going to reach out my hand. Don't move until you're sure you have a grip on it. When I pull, jump."

He shifted his left hand to the securest grip he could find and jammed his elbow deep into the crack. Then he swivelled slowly around and extended his right hand until it was within two feet of Hein's shoulders.

"Take it," he said.

Hein did not move.

"Take it!"

But even as he spoke he knew now, with sudden and absolute certainty, that Siegfried Hein was not going to take his hand. The German stood, motionless and silent, looking at him, and Ordway looked back at him across the intervening yard of space and the arc of his extended arm. He saw the square-lined, blackened face and the tight, rigid flesh of the cheeks and jawline. He saw the snowflecked stubble of the beard and the greased, frozen crack of the thin lips and the minute glistening beads of sweat that coursed

432

slowly down through the grease and stubble and flecks of snow. He saw the bleak-gray unmoving eyes and the bleakness behind the eyes. And in the same instant it seemed to him that he was seeing everything that was behind the eyes. For one flashing, time-less instant on that forlorn and timeless mountainside he looked into a man's eyes, and everything that the man was was there. He saw it all now, naked and manifest before him: the frustration and bitterness and contumacy; the fear and the pride and the bottom-less sterility of pride; the despairing lonely hunger of the unloving and unloved; the will to conquer and the will to die. . . .

He saw it all. And then he saw the face turning from him, Hein turning away from him, advancing one foot slowly in front of the other, reaching out with both arms toward the upper section of the crack that slanted upward toward the platform at the summit of the cliff. He saw him stop and crouch, motionless. He saw him leap toward the rock-wall, hit it, grasp it, cling to it, claw at it, slip from it, fall slowly backward from it onto the snow-ramp. Hein did not seem to hit the snow. He simply disappeared through it, soundlessly. In the same instant the ramp itself was gone. Then there was only silence and stillness again, and the mountain wall curving downward, and a few puffs and shreds of spindrift wreath-ing gently in the windless air.

Martin Ordway hung from the crack and stared dully at the wall of rock from which the snow had broken away. The ramp was gone, and in its place was space—but not only space. For along the line where the concealing snow had joined the mountainside there was now revealed a narrow but solid flange of granite, banding the smooth face of the Citadel. He lowered himself to it, edged along it, grasped the lip of the crack on the far side, pulled himself for-ward and upward. . . .

He was lying face down, and the rock was pressing cold and smooth against his forehead and cheeks and lips. Then he was ly-ing face up and the rock was an island in the sky. He closed his eyes and opened them again and lay staring upward at the blue cone of space. He lay quietly listening to the deep, familiar hum-ming.

Suddenly he sat up.

"Ted," he said. "Harry—Bix—"

433

He sat for a little while without moving, then slowly looked around him. He looked down the rock-wall to the slanting crack and along the crack to where the snow-ramp had been and along where the snow-ramp had been to the end of the solid, rock-based part of the ramp, where he and Hein had stood. There were footprints in the sloping snow. There was his ax leaning against the rock and the rope and the rucksack and a glove on the snow beside it.

I'll have to get them, he thought.

But he could not get them.

And do you know why you can't get them, he thought quietly. You can't get them because they're gone. The ax and the rope and the rucksack and the gloves are gone. And Ted is gone. And Harry and Bix are gone. And the *Spirit of Perth Amboy* is gone. And Carla and Andreas and Radcliffe and Delambre are gone. And Hein is gone. They're all gone now, and you're not going to get them back. They're all gone now, and you're alone.

His eyes moved along the mountainside, down the mountainside, out from the mountainside. They stared down through the blue miles at the ranges and valleys and plains of Europe.

"Panoram!" he said aloud.

He laughed. Or, rather, he thought he was going to laugh; but the laughter caught in a thick knot in his throat and he sat with his head bent forward against his knees, coughing and retching. . . . I should drink some water, he thought. . . . He groped behind him for the rucksack; turned himself slowly in a complete circle, searching for the rucksack. Suddenly he was laughing again. And then coughing again. When the coughing stopped he reached out to the drift beside the rock platform, scooped a handful of snow and put it in his mouth. He could neither taste it nor feel it. He tried to swallow it, coughed again and spat it out. Lying back on the rock, he closed his eyes.

If this is the end of you, he thought, for God's sake get it over with. . . .

But it was not the end.

He opened his eyes again, and there was the platform and the precipice. There was space, and beneath space the earth, and above space the sky. There was the gentle white line of a snow-ridge rising above him, and a second white line sloping in toward it from

434

the right, and a third white line sloping in from the left. There was a point in the sky where the three lines met.

And that was the end.

He raised himself slowly to a sitting position and then slowly to his feet. It must be getting late, he thought. He raised his left arm and held it steady with his right and looked at his watch. The hands pointed to half past eight. Dropping his arms, he raised his head and turned, staring at the sun; but the sun seemed to turn with him, whirling and circling, and then the sky and the white slope above him and the rock beneath his feet were circling too, and he was falling and trying to support himself on his ax, but there was no ax, and he was still falling, and then suddenly there was the platform rushing up and hitting him in the knees and thighs and chest and face and the dull stab of a rough surface against his cheekbone and the thin sound of his goggles splintering on the rock.

For a few moments he lay where he had fallen. Then he sat up again; stood up again. Standing with his feet spread well apart, he took off his goggles, looked at them and threw them away. A trickle of blood was running down from somewhere on his face onto the front of his windbreaker, but his eyes, apparently, were all right. He could still see the rock and the snow and the sky. He could still see the white ridge before him climbing gently into the sky.

There is a mountain to climb, Martin Ordway thought.

His head felt clearer now. His senses were clearer. Rock, snow, mountainside and mountaintop all seemed to be shifting slowly into a brighter, sharper focus around him—seemed to be emerging slowly from behind the veils of space into immense and preternatural clarity. The minutes slipped past as he stood motionless, watching and listening. And then time itself seemed to stop. No sound or motion stained the frozen hemispheres of earth and sky, and the white ridge rose up before him into the heart of a pure and gleaming stillness.

It is only another few hundred feet, he thought.

He began to climb.

He stepped from the rock platform onto the snow. He leaned forward, steadying himself against the slope with his hand, and took another step, and then another, and then fell forward against the slope. He pushed up with his hands, got to his knees, then to his feet, and climbed on again. Opening his mouth wide, he drew in three long breaths with each step. Then he fell again. He lay on the snow-slope with his head on his arms and listened to the sound of his breathing. He lay with his eyes closed and his face pressed to the cold whiteness of the mountain and listened to the sound of the wind.

And yet . . . he was standing again now; he was staring again up the slopes. . . . And yet there was no wind. No slightest movement of air touched his face or hands or clothing. No breath or stirring touched the crystalline stillness of the snow. . . . It is below, he thought. It is the wind of the valley that you hear; the wind of earth. It is moving slowly and softly along the walls of houses in the valleys. It is creeping through the sweet green grass of the pastures, rustling in the treetops of the slanting forests, brushing across the gray scree-slopes, fingering through the gorges. It is a million trickles of moving air in a million crevices of rock; a thousand streams of air pouring through a thousand clefts and notches and couloirs; a hundred rivers of air flowing up a hundred passes and glaciers; a single and immense ocean of air rising along the buttresses and ice-walls, the precipices and ridges. It is scouring the twisted black rocks of the Riesensteg, swooping along the forlorn knife-edge of the ridge above, moaning through the guy-ropes of the tent in the hollow, raising its wild crest of spume on the snowfields below the Watchtower. It is no longer merely a wind now, but a wave, a tide, an enormous rising sea. It has risen past the Watchtower now, past the shoulder and the upper snow-slopes. It is roaring up the gray walls of the Citadel, always higher, stronger, nearer. . . .

He leaned forward again and lay against the snow, listening to the deep rasp of his breathing and the pounding of his heart.

It is only a few hundred feet, he thought.

He climbed on through the stillness above the wind. The angles of the ridge steepened, and he took ten steps and stopped, another five and stopped. Then the ridge was no longer covered with snow but with hard, tilted verglas, and he cut away from it across the face of the slope toward the ridge on his right. Here there was snow again. The gleaming white powder drifted up over his boots, over his knees, over his thighs. He stopped, resting his body against the drifts, fell forward, struggled to his feet again, stumbled on again. He came out onto the second ridge and clung with bootnail and fingertip to its smooth shingles of ice.

Looking up, he saw the gentle white line of the ridge rising above him, and the second white line sloping in toward it from the right, and the third white line sloping in from the left. His eyes moved slowly upward along their converging arcs—and in the next instant he saw nothing. The mountaintop struck suddenly down at him with an intolerable, blinding whiteness of sun and snow. He groped for his goggles, but could not find them; covered his eyes with his hands; closed his eyes; pressed his eyes and hands and body against the smooth coldness of the ice. When he looked upward again the mountain was a prism. The white fire was gone, and in its place was red fire, blue fire, green fire, yellow fire, streaming in long quivering lances into his eyes.

It is only a few hundred feet, he thought.

He lurched forward again. He kicked and hacked and clawed and stumbled, and the bright lances broke and shattered against him. Then they were one lance again—a sword, a shaft—a burning white incandescence that beat down against his eyes and into the channels of his brain. He climbed with his head bent forward and his eyes closed to slits, watching the remote blurred outlines of his boots moving slowly, one after the other, against the snow. He saw the boots stop, move on again, stop again.

And he looked up again.

The blinding glare was gone. The prism and the lances were gone, and the sun seemed to hang, withdrawn and shrunken, behind the depthless layers of sky. The snow of the slope rose up before him in cold and leprous whiteness. The mountaintop crouched, hooded, against the emptiness of space.

He stood without moving, almost without breathing. He felt coldness and emptiness closing in about him like a sea and a cold empty torpor rising in a slow tide through his body and mind. He felt the last of the tiny deep fire that was within him flickering and fading and seeping numbly away into the monstrous, encompassing nothingness of snow and sky. . . . So this is the end, Martin Ordway thought. This is the dome of the temple, the crest of the flight. This is the soldier's victory, the lover's consummation. This is the top of the mountain. . . .

He felt his eyes closing, his body relaxing. In another moment he would be sinking down into cool white depths of emptiness. But the moment did not come. He did not sink down. His fingers were clawing at the snow again. His feet were thrusting slowly forward again. No, it was not the top—it was not the end. . . .

It is only another few hundred feet, he thought.

He moved upward through emptiness, and the emptiness was a deathly white and then a streaming prism and then a vast blazing whiteness and then emptiness again. He moved upward through stillness, and at first there was only stillness, and then there was the wind again. . . . He stopped and listened and the sound of the wind drew nearer. Or perhaps it was not the wind, but something that was in and behind the wind. As he waited now, motionless and straining, the sound rose and swelled until it filled his ears and throbbed in the bones of his skull. It was not loud, but low, persistent, pervading; very far away and far below, but approaching ever nearer and nearer. Yes, he thought, it is the sound of the wind. But he knew, too, that it was the sound of something else as well; of the deep droning of a plane's engines, perhaps; of the distant roar of burning cities; of the thunder of guns and the tread of boots; the slow, measured, unending tread of boots along shattered roads and across gutted fields—through the towns, villages, meadows, forests—up the valleys, up the glaciers, up the rock-walls and ice-walls—up the mountains and the ranges into the still, white emptiness—always closer and closer, always stronger and stronger—beneath him, behind him, beside him. . . .

You are a part of nothing, a voice said very distinctly at his elbow—and you are running away.

Martin Ordway stopped and stood quite still.

"No," he said.

What are you doing then?

"I am climbing a mountain."

Why?

"Because it is there, of course," he said, smiling a little.

He turned and looked around him, and the voice was gone, and there was only whiteness and emptiness. But in the whiteness he could see again; and in the emptiness he was no longer alone.

"Take my hand, Carla," he said quietly. "Take it, Ted—Harry—Bix. Have you the rope, Andreas? Tie it on. Tie it on, Nick. Tie

438

it on, Paul. . . . *Tie it on, Hein.* . . . We're all on the rope now, do you understand that? We're all on it together. We're going to the top together."

He turned back to the slope and looked upward. And presently they were moving upward. The mountainside—or was it the airstrip?—sank away beneath them, the white ribbon of the ridge unrolled, and the mountaintop moved slowly toward them out of the blue depths of the sky. He heard the wind—or was it the right-hand engine?—humming below them: deeply and wildly at first and then more and more faintly. But he only smiled. There was no going back now. Nothing could stop them now. . . . And then, presently, the wind was gone entirely and there was only stillness. There was only stillness and space and themselves moving through it, swift and strong and sure: above the valleys and the wastelands, over the charred fields and burning cities, through the sunlight and the snowlight, up the glaciers and the ice-walls, up the ridges and the precipices, toward the gentle white crest that rose into the sky above them—toward the heart of an immense and shining peace. . . .

The sun was sloping away toward the ranges in the west as Andreas Benner clambered up onto the rock platform above the Citadel. Here he rested for a few minutes, and then, very slowly, he followed the wandering footprints upward across the white slopes above. Three hundred feet below the summit of the White Tower he stopped and knelt beside the sprawled figure that lay motionless before him in the snow.

439

Chapter 23

. . . At first there was only sound: the stillness, and the drone of planes through the stillness, and the drone merging into the murmur of a voice, and the voice fading back into the drone. Then there was the whiteness again. There were the sky and the three converging lines in the sky and the long lances of red and blue and orange and the exploding prism. A white blade of pain struck down, searing, into his eyes, and he ground the heels of his hands against the closed lids.

"Try not to rub them too much, Herr Martin," said Andreas Benner's voice.

"What's happened, Andreas?"

"It is the snow-blindness. You were not wearing your goggles."

"I broke them."

"*Ja*, I know."

The white pain danced and stabbed behind his lids. He opened them, but the blank whiteness was still there.

"Do not worry about it," Benner's voice said. "It is painful, but it does not last long. A day or two at most. Sometimes only a few hours."

There was silence again, and through the silence the pain and the faint droning. . . . "Careful now," the voice came to him, "there is a little steep place right here."

He could not only hear now, but also feel a little. He felt an arm locked strong and tight around his own, and the movement of his legs, and the snow yielding and contracting softly under the soles of his boots.

They were climbing down.

He put his right foot in front of his left, his left in front of his right. He turned to one side and then the other with the firm pressure of the arm that held him. And then presently they were no longer climbing, but standing still, and Benner's voice was saying, "Sit down now, Herr Martin—we will rest a little here."

He sat down, and there was smooth, bare stone under his hands. "Here?" he asked.

"It is a little sheltered place, under the Citadel."

Ordway sat with his elbows on his knees and his hands cupped over his eyes. There was the whiteness and the pain. And then suddenly, through them, a thing far deeper and sharper and more monstrous than pain. . . .

"Andreas—" he said.

"Ja, Herr Martin?"

"Hein's gone."

"I know."

"He fell."

"You will tell me about it later," Benner said.

"No, now."

"Later is better. You must save your strength now."

Ordway began to speak, stopped himself and sat silently for a few moments. "All right—later," he said.

Later. . . . All at once he thought he was going to laugh. But he did not laugh. "I'm sorry, Andreas," he said quietly. "Oh God, I'm so sorry."

The guide did not speak, and in the stillness Ordway could hear him fumbling with his pack. Presently he felt him crouching close beside him, and a canteen was being put into his hands.

"I can't," he said.

"You must, Herr Martin."

He raised the canteen to his lips but could not feel it until the rim of the neck struck against his teeth. Taking a half-mouthful of the cold tea, he held it a moment and then swallowed. He gagged, but succeeded in controlling the gagging, and the tea went down.

"Now one more," said Benner.

He half-filled his mouth again; waited and swallowed again.

Benner took the canteen, and he could hear him screwing on the cap and putting it away.

"Andreas—" he said.

"*Ja?*"

"How did you find me?"

"You were lying there in the snow. I could already see you when I came up over the top of the Citadel."

"How—" Ordway hesitated. "How far did I have to go?" he asked.

"About three hundred feet."

"And you? You went on to—?"

"No, Herr Martin."

"You should have," Ordway said bitterly. "You should have—you should have. . . ."

The guide did not speak. There was stillness and whiteness and pain, and then, suddenly and wildly, another thought. Another image.

"Andreas—"

"You should not talk so much, Herr Martin. You must save your strength."

"Carla . . . Fräulein Dehn . . . Where is she?"

"She is at the upper tent. She wanted to come after you with me, but I would not let her."

"And she's all right?"

"*Ja.*"

Ordway's hand reached out, groped for Benner's arm, and gripped it. "You're telling me the truth, Andreas?" he asked, very quietly and evenly. "She *is* all right?"

"*Ja*, Herr Martin—" The guide hesitated for a scarcely perceptible instant. "When you come back she will be all right."

The minutes passed in silence. Five; perhaps ten. . . .

"You can go on now?" the guide asked.

"Yes, I can go on."

"*Also*—"

Ordway rose, stumbled, put out his hand, and Benner caught it. Then there was Benner's arm tight and firm under his own again. There was the snow under his boots, the snow falling away before them, the white pain stabbing at his eyes, the next step and the next, and the next hundred and the next . . . and then suddenly

442

the bright blades ripped at him so that he thought he would cry out in agony, and he stopped and stood bent over with his face buried in his hands.

"We will rest again a little," said Andreas Benner.

This time it was snow on which they sat, and Ordway knew it was on the open slope above the shoulder, and after the worst of the pain had passed he opened his eyes and tried to see around him.

"It is a mean thing the snow-blindness," the guide said.

"It's not quite so bad any more. I think I'm beginning to see a little."

"No, it is still too soon for you to see."

"But I can, I tell you." Ordway pointed up into the shimmering whiteness. "Look, I can tell. There's the sun."

"You will be all right, but it is still too soon."

"But it's the sun. There. Straight before us."

"There is no sun, Herr Martin," Benner said quietly. "It is eleven o'clock at night."

The whiteness throbbed, slashed down at him, ebbed again. There were the red and blue and orange lances, and then darkness, and then flickering whiteness again. Ordway sat motionless with his eyes closed and his head in his hands.

"Sunday night," he said dully.

"*Ja*, Sunday night."

"I've fixed you up fine, haven't I, Andreas? Even to the Sunday." For an instant it seemed to him again that he was going to laugh. "I've fixed everybody up fine. . . ."

The guide did not answer, and they sat silently, waiting.

"Let us go on now," said Benner presently.

There was the snow again, and the next step, and the next hundred steps, and the slope falling endlessly away before them. The whiteness still danced and glittered in the sockets of Ordway's eyes, but the pain was not so intense now as before—or if it was, he was too tired to feel it. For he was becoming tired now, he realized dimly, as he had never been tired before in his life. An immense, opaque veil of numbness was settling over him, gently sheathing the pain, the motion of his legs, his body, his brain. They sat down again, and he slept. Then they were descending again, and he was still sleeping, and they were moving onward and

443

downward through the dark, deep channels of a dream. It seemed to him that he was no longer walking at all, but simply floating through space, supported on Andreas Benner's arm. He wished that Benner would take the arm away and let him sink down, sleeping, into the soft sweet coolness of the snow. . . .

Through the dream there came the droning of engines and, through the droning, a voice. A mittened hand was rubbing and slapping his cheeks, and a moment later there was the taste of cold tea in his mouth and throat.

"Yes, Andreas?" he murmured.

"We are at the shoulder, Herr Martin." The voice came from very far away. "You remember—the cleft between the shoulder and the Watchtower? It is steep for a little way, and we must rope down."

He nodded, and the voice went on—talking, explaining. He felt a second rope being passed over his shoulder and under his crotch. The distant voice grew suddenly louder and clearer. "You are listening to me, Herr Martin?"

"Yes, Andreas."

"We will rappel now. I have put the rope around you, and you must hold it with your hands—so—and let yourself down. If you can do it yourself it will be easier, but do not worry if you cannot. I have the second rope around your chest, and there is a good belay point here for me to let you down. You understand?"

"Yes, I understand."

"Also—"

He felt two hands turning him around and pushing him slowly backward. He felt the ground slant sharply away beneath his feet and leaned back against the pull of the ropes. And then the ground was gone, and there was a sudden sharp pain in his groin like the pain of a jerking parachute harness, and his feet were dangling, and he was hanging in air. He gripped the double strand of the rappel rope with both hands and let it out slowly. After a moment, however, it began to vibrate and slipped from his hands. He groped for it, found it, fumbled, lost it again, and began to fall. He could feel the cry rising inside him, but in the next instant it was cut off as if by a knife, as the second rope went tight about his chest. He was hanging motionless again, slowly descending again, supported only by the noose under his armpits, choking and suffocating.

444

Then the pain was gone, and in its place was the numbness again, and through the numbness a gentle descending and revolving. He was spinning in space now, floating and soaring, the earth gone, lost and forgotten. . . . And then suddenly, incredibly, there again. . . . There was something under his feet; rock and snow under his feet. He was standing with his face pressed to a cold stone wall, listening dully to the scraping, clinking sounds that seemed to be drawing nearer and nearer through the white darkness above him.

"Ted?" he said. "Harry? Bix?"

There were fingers fumbling at the iron band that bound his ribs. "*Also*," a voice murmured, "the rest is easy."

He awoke to darkness and pain.

"Carla?" he said.

"Yes, Martin."

He reached out his hand and after a moment felt hers, cool and firm in his palm.

"It's chapped," he said.

She did not answer, but he could hear her moving above him, and although he could not feel it he knew that she had kissed him on the lips. He lay silently for a while, holding her hand. Then he spoke her name again.

"Yes, Martin?"

"My eyes—there's something there."

"They are compresses. They are cold now, and I am going to change them."

"No—don't go away."

"No one is going away, silly. I am going three feet across the tent to heat some water."

He heard the sounds of her moving about, followed by the familiar low humming of the Primus. Then presently there was another, different sound, as if of creaking canvas, and he was aware of a second presence in the tent.

"Andreas?" he said.

"*Ja*, Herr Martin."

"You're all right, Andreas?"

"*Ja*, I am all right. Your eyes, do they feel better now?"

"A little."

"They will feel much better with the new compresses," Carla said. Coming back to him, she lifted the old pads from his lids, and he opened his eyes.

"Can you see anything?"

"No."

"It is still too soon," Benner said.

Carla put on the fresh compresses, and he felt the damp cotton pressing warm and soothing against his throbbing lids. "And now you are going to eat something," she said.

"I can't."

"Oh yes you can. And you are going to. And then you are going to sleep again."

He heard the hum of the Primus again and the sound of Carla and Benner moving about; then there was an arm under his shoulders, raising them a little, and a trickle of hot broth into his mouth. He tried to swallow, gagged and vomited, and the arm beneath him let him gently down. He lay quietly for a few minutes, feeling Carla's cool hand move over his cheeks and forehead; then the arm raised him again and there was broth in his mouth again. This time he swallowed and kept it down. When he lay back in the blankets once more the pain darted in white streaks through his eyeballs, but he felt a little stronger than before, and his mind was a little clearer.

"Hein's gone," he said suddenly.

"Yes, Martin, we know."

"It was up on the other side of the Citadel. I'd caught up with him there, and he was—"

"Yes, you have told us."

"I told you? When?"

"When you were awake before. Don't you remember?"

His mind went back, groping, into darkness. But there was only darkness. There were Hein's face and the gray eyes and the clawing hands and the dissolving snow—and then the white, blinding darkness. . . .

"Andreas—" he said

"Ja, Herr Martin."

"You found me in the snow."

"Ja—above the Citadel."

"When?"

446

"About five in the evening."

"You climbed all day then—and back all night. And before that you had come up here from the . . ."

He stopped suddenly, remembering.

"Delambre," he said. "How about Delambre?"

It was a moment before Benner answered. "He is all right, Herr Martin," he said quietly.

"He's at the lower tent?"

"*Ja*, at the lower tent."

"And now you are going to sleep again," said Carla.

"No."

"Yes."

"Give me your hand then."

The voices were gone now, and in their place was the low droning of the engines. There was Carla's hand in his. There was the pain and the whiteness and the numbness and the darkness. . . .

For the first time since he had come back to Kandermatt he slept and did not dream. When he awakened, Carla was still beside him, and presently there was the hum of the Primus again, and fresh compresses and more broth and a few spoonfuls of stew. Then he lay back in the blankets, found Carla's hand again, slept again.

The next time he awoke it was to a vague consciousness that something was different from before, but it was not until he turned his head a little and one of the compresses slipped from his eyes that he realized what it was. The blackness and the whiteness were gone, and in their place was the brown canvas of the tent walls. He could see the shadowy figures of Carla and Benner sitting on their blankets close beside him.

"It is better now?" Carla said.

"Yes."

"And the pain?"

"That's better too."

He took off the other compress and lay quietly looking around him. The stabbing white flame that had tortured his eyes had subsided to a dull ache, but feeling had returned to the lower part of his face, and his lips and throat felt as if they were on fire. He shook his head a little, trying to clear it. Then, propping himself

447

on his elbow, he looked at his watch, but the phosphorescent dial was only a yellowish blur in the darkness.

"It must be almost morning," he said.

"It is evening, Herr Martin," said Benner.

"Evening?"

"Ja—almost nine o'clock."

Ordway raised himself slowly to a sitting position, and a long moment passed before he spoke. "You mean I've—"

"Ja, you have been sleeping all day."

Ordway started to speak again, stopped, and sat silently watching Carla as she rummaged in one of the rucksacks and brought out the jar of windburn cream. Creeping to his side, she opened it and rubbed the thick grease gently over his lips, nose and cheeks. Then she went to the Primus, lighted it and set a pot of water with a can of stew in it over the flame.

"Carla—" he said.

"Yes?"

"Don't bother, please."

"Since when is boiling water a bother? And besides, you must eat all you can to get some strength for the morning."

"The morning?"

"We must start down tomorrow, Herr Martin," said Benner. "It would be better if we could wait for another day, so that you would be stronger, but there is not enough food left, and if another storm should come—" He broke off, shrugging.

"I can make it," Ordway said.

"Also, the message we have been expected may have come by now."

"The message?"

"From Interlaken."

Ordway stared at him uncomprehendingly.

"You remember, I told you I had arranged with Christian Mehrwalder that if the message came while we were on the mountain he would come up a way and try to signal to us. The last few days, of course, we have been too high to see anything from the huts or glacier, but it is—how long?—two weeks tomorrow since I was in Interlaken, and it is very possible the message has come."

Ordway nodded. "Yes," he said vaguely. "Yes—of course."

"The way I have figured it then is that tomorrow we go from

448

here down to the lower terrace, where Herr Radcliffe is. The next day we go on to the glacier and down the glacier to the *Dornel-hütte*, and the day after—that is Thursday—to the Heilweg and the valley. That will mean hard going for you, of course, but it is best now you get down as soon as possible, and also that I make my report on Herr Hein and Herr Delambre."

"Delambre . . . ?"

Benner did not speak, and for a few moments the only sound in the tent was the faint humming of the Primus. "What about Delambre?" Ordway asked very quietly.

"I did not want to tell you before, Herr Martin. He is lost."

"Lost?"

"Dead."

There was another, longer silence.

"Go on," said Ordway.

"On the morning I went down—you remember?—the snow was still deep and soft, and I did not get there until after twelve. Herr Delambre was not in the tent, and outside there was a line of fresh footprints leading away from it. They did not go up through the Riesensteg or down to the terrace, but across the slopes farther on, under the ridge. I followed them for ten, perhaps fifteen minutes, and then, looking ahead, I saw what had happened on the slope. There had been an avalanche. And the footprints stopped."

"You didn't find him?"

"No. I looked for three hours, four hours, but the snow was too deep. When I came back to the tent it was already too late to start up the ridge, so I spent the night there and came up in the morning."

"And kept right on going—after Hein and me."

"*Ja*, Herr Martin."

The Primus hummed, and the water in the pot began to boil. Ordway stared into the blue flame for a few moments, then shifted himself slowly forward onto his hands and knees and crept toward the entrance of the tent.

"You should lie still and rest, Martin," Carla said.

"I'll be right back," he told her.

"And your food is almost ready."

"I'll be back in a minute."

Outside there was the snow and the night. Crossing to one of

449

the empty packboards that lay in the hollow, he squatted down on it and sat looking up at the mountainside above him. The hollow rose to the slopes, the slopes to the ridge, the ridge to the shoulder, the shoulder, to the stars. There were no clouds, no wisp of wind. The glory of the night struck down in a million tiny darts of pain into his aching eyes.

He closed them and bent his head into his hands, and when he looked up again Carla was there.

"Don't, Martin," she said.

He did not speak, and after a moment she sat down beside him and took his hand in hers.

"Don't, Martin, my lover . . ."

For a little while he sat motionless, staring up at the mountain and the darkness. Then he turned and buried his raw, burning face in the warm softness of her breast.

And now the mountainside was flowing up past them like a slow white river, from the valleys into the sky. There was the lip of the ice-cornice curling above them. There were the snow-slopes and the promontory between the ridges, and the southeast ridge falling away before them, and the smooth, ice-slicked slabs, and the sharp ribbon of the knife-edge. There were the hooded towers of the Riesensteg moving gently toward them out of blue-white space below.

It was not quite half-past-five when they started out, and for the first hour in the paling dawnlight Ordway's eyes did not bother him at all. Soon after they reached the ridge, however, the sun came up, and in an instant the world around him dissolved into a blinding, stabbing whiteness. Even with Andreas Benner's goggles, which the guide now insisted on his using, the light shimmered and flashed against his eyeballs in a steadily swelling tide of pain. He walked with his head bent and his eyes narrowed to the merest slits, so that all he could see was the patch of snow or rock directly before him and the slow, monotonous shuffle of his boots.

The order of their descent was Carla first, himself second and Benner in the last position, from which he could best manipulate the rope and protect them on the steeper stretches by hitches and belays. At intervals they paused briefly, and the girl and the guide called back and forth from either side of him, discussing which

450

route she should follow. Now and then Carla waited for him and told him which way he should turn or where to place his feet, and on the more difficult sections, such as the slabs and the knife-edge, Benner moved up close behind him and held the rope taut a mere foot or two behind his back. He neither asked for their help nor protested when it was given. Except for the throbbing pain in his eyes, his whole body, and his mind as well, were wrapped in a deep caul of lethargy and numbness. The tiredness in his bones, the voices of the others, the rock and snow and sky around him were blurred and remote behind it: as blurred and remote as Hein—as Delambre—as the lost and receding mountaintop.

There was the next step and the next step and the next. There was the patch of snow before him and his boot moving forward onto it and the gentle jerking of the rope around his waist. . . .

And then there was the Riesensteg, the gnarled towers, the tent in the hollow. They sat in the tent and ate a little and rested and looked silently through the brown twilight at the dishevelled blankets, the utensils and climbing gear, the unopened food-tins, the two empty brandy bottles. When they were ready to go Benner took down the poles, wrapped everything neatly in the canvas and wedged the bundle into a cleft between two outcropping rocks. "We cannot carry it," he said.

No, they could not carry it.

Through the glittering midday they worked their way down the slopes to the ramp of the upper terrace; across the ramp to the mouth of the Funnel; down the boulder-choked slant of the mouth to the sheer walls of the precipices below. Here their descent was no longer a matter of walking, or even clambering, but of roping down, one after another, from one ledge, cleft or vantage point to the next. As before, Carla went first, Ordway second and Benner last; and as on the rappel down the shoulder two nights before, the guide belayed Ordway with a second rope against the possibility of his losing his grip. But this time he did not lose it. He roped down ten times—fifteen—twenty times. Then he lost track. Sometimes it took them several minutes to locate a knob or boss to serve as a rappel point, and sometimes they had to search carefully for a landing place on the smooth walls below; but each time, in the end, they found what they were looking for, and each rappel brought them another fifty or sixty feet down the immense granite face of the mountainside.

They rested on the curving dome-like ledge where Radcliffe had turned back and Ordway and Carla had sat waiting for Benner. . . . (How long ago had that been? he wondered. . . . Five days —a week—ten days? . . . He could not remember.) . . . They swung down under the dome into the recess; down from the recess over the slabs; past the slabs and the overhangs and the pitons; past the walls and clefts and ledges, and more walls, more clefts, more ledges. There was the Funnel slowly narrowing and biting deeper and ever deeper into the cliffs, until the sky was only a thin blue strip at their backs. There was the faint sound of trickling water, and the wet rocks, and the melting snow on the rocks, and the snow on the boulders below, and the boulders coming nearer and nearer, and the boulders under their feet. There was the base of the Funnel receding behind them, and the sun slanting away toward the west, and the white slope of the terrace, and the brown dot on the slope. There was Nicholas Radcliffe coming toward them, wringing their hands, talking, embracing them . . . and then suddenly stopping and looking around them and past them, his bright blue eyes going slowly sombre and cold.

It was twilight. Then dark.

Ordway awoke and lay with his eyes closed listening to the hum of the Primus and the low voices of the others. There was Benner's voice, and then Radcliffe's, and then Carla's. And then Hein's and Delambre's.

There was darkness again. Dreams again. . . .

The message from Interlaken had come. Christian Mehrwalder had ascended the glacier and lower ridge and delivered it to Radcliffe on the second day after the storm, and the next morning, as they huddled about the Primus drinking their tea, Benner read it to Ordway.

Arrangements made for Friday afternoon, 10/21, it said. Detailed instructions to follow.

Ordway said nothing.

"That is all?" Carla asked.

The guide nodded. "It is a lucky thing, Herr Martin," he said. "We have timed it just right. Today is Wednesday and we will

452

reach the *Dornelhütte*, and tomorrow night—Thursday—we will be at the *Gasthof*. . . . *Ja*, it is a lucky thing."

Ordway nodded, but still did not speak, and they finished their breakfast in silence.

"How are the eyes, old boy?" Radcliffe asked him, as they moved about stowing their gear.

"Better, thanks," he said.

The Englishman watched him curiously for a few moments. "I don't seem to have much of a load here. How's to my taking a bit of yours?"

"No thanks—I can manage."

"You really shouldn't try too much, you know."

"I hardly notice it," Ordway said.

And it was true. As they cut across the snow-slope of the terrace toward the southeast ridge, he was as unaware of the fifty pounds on his back as of the ax in his hand, the rope at his waist, the voices of the others, the brightening morning. Even when the sun came up and stabbed again into his eyes, he was scarcely conscious of the by now familiar burning pain. The minutes and the hours flowed past. The slope, the ridge, the lower slopes, the icefall, the glacier swung slowly up out of the gulfs of space like gray-white images on an enormous screen.

They stopped to rest at the head of the icefall. And again at its foot. They crossed the *Bergschrund* without difficulty on a newly-formed snowbridge, but the crevasses in the glacier beyond had been choked and hidden by the fresh fall, and their progress became laborious and slow. Benner was in the lead now, with Ordway second, Carla third and Radcliffe last, and through the long hours of the afternoon they barely crept downward, while the guide probed and sounded, detoured and zigzagged his course through the treacherous honeycomb of ice. The sun disappeared as the rock spurs that hemmed them narrowed and twisted, shone down on them again as the glacier straightened, and disappeared for good in the graying light of early evening.

And still Ordway trudged on, his eyes bent to the snow before him and the slow, rhythmic tread of his boots. When the others stopped, he stopped. When they rested, he rested. When they went on, he went on. He was no more conscious than when they had started of the weight of his pack, or of tiredness, or of pain;

and it was not even with a sense of relief that he at last saw the moraine and the saddle and the brown dot of the Dornel Hut moving slowly toward them through the gathering darkness. He could with equal ease have kept on trudging through the night or dropped in the snow where he stood.

There were the hut and the humming Primus and the blankets. There was the darkness again and then morning again. There were the saddle and the boulders and the scree-slopes and the gray miles of the wasteland. Shreds and patches of snow still checkered the plateau, but there were no great drifts or billows such as covered the higher mountainsides, and even after the sun rose he was able to look ahead and about him without pain. As the path dipped and twisted and climbed and dipped again the serried peaks of the Kandermatt range shouldered one by one into the sky above them, and his eyes moved slowly over the familiar shapes of the Karlsberg and the Rotalp, the Graf and the Gräfin, the Dornelberg and the Himmelshorn. There was only one direction in which they did not turn. Backward. He had not looked back once through all the hours and all the days since they had left the tent in the hollow above the ice-cornice.

They stopped for lunch beside one of the foaming streams that tumbled down over the rocks from the glacier to the Blausee. And as they made ready to go on again Benner paused thoughtfully and turned to him. "There is something I have been thinking about, Herr Martin," he said. "It is perhaps better that you do not go all the way to the valley this evening."

"I can make it," said Ordway.

"It is not that. But it is safer, I think, if you are not too long at the Gasthof before it is time for you to go."

"Safer?"

"In a small place like Kandermatt it is a hard thing to keep a secret. One cannot tell what stories have got about in the two weeks we have been away. Then also—" Benner paused briefly —"also I must at once turn in to the authorities a report of the —accidents; and there is no knowing who will be around asking questions."

"But I should be there for that, shouldn't I?"

"For the report? No—that is not necessary."

454

"Don't forget, Andreas, it's I who—"

"It is not necessary," the guide repeated. "Do not go on thinking and thinking about them, Herr Martin. We cannot help them now." He paused again, but Ordway was silent, his eyes bent to the churning stream. "No, it is better now that we do the sensible thing. Herr Radcliffe and I will go down tonight and make the reports and arrangements. Then you will come down in the morning, and everything will be in order, and in a few hours off you will go."

Still Ordway did not answer.

"It's the best way, old boy," Radcliffe said quietly.

Ordway raised his head and looked from one to the other of them. Then his eyes moved to Carla and away again.

"As you say," he murmured.

They crossed the stream and then a second one, and after a while a third, which was the stream in which Delambre had slipped and fallen. They passed the bend in the path where Hein had shot the hare. And as midday merged into afternoon and afternoon softened into early evening, they wound down the gray slopes toward the dark cobalt gleam of the Blausee, skirted the little lake by its western shore and trudged up through the boulders beyond toward the gorge between the Karlsberg and the Himmelshorn. Ahead of him, presently, Ordway saw a familiarly shaped flat rock —the rock on which he had sat that first afternoon when he and Carla had walked up to the Heilweg, staring up at the White Tower across the forlorn miles of the wasteland. He slowed his pace as he passed it, but he did not stop or turn. They entered the gorge, threaded it, and emerged on the far side, and there below them was the green hollow and the hut and the silver brook and the fat marmot eyeing them curiously from his rock.

They brewed tea and ate some crackers and marmalade, and when they were finished the hut was filled with dusk.

"Come," said Benner, rising. He and Radcliffe slung on their packs and picked up their axes; then he turned back to Ordway. "If you leave here at ten o'clock, Herr Martin, that will bring you to the upper bridge across the Aarn about noon. I will come out and meet you there, in case there are any difficulties or new arrangements."

Ordway started to speak, stopped, and merely nodded. The

guide's eyes went to Carla. "You are staying, *Fräulein?*" he asked.

Carla looked at Ordway. "Do you want me to, Martin?"

"Yes," he said. "Please stay."

Benner and Radcliffe went out, and he sat with his eyes on the floor, listening to the sound of their footsteps receding on the rocks. Suddenly he jumped to his feet, crossed to the door and threw it open. Standing on the steps outside, he half raised his arm and seemed about to call after them. But he did not call. For a little while he stood silently watching their retreating figures; then he turned back into the hut, closed the door and rejoined Carla at the table.

"Well, here we are again," he said.

"Yes, Martin, here we are."

They took a few things from the rucksack and changed from their heavy boots to rope-soled espadrilles. Then they collected several armfuls of juniper and furze for the fireplace, washed in the stream, and prepared and ate their supper. When they went outside again it was almost dark. For a long time they sat silently on the soft bank of moss, watching the night climb the still slopes around them, and the lights come on, one by one, in the valley below.

"The Blue Hour—" Carla said.

Ordway did not speak, and after a few minutes she moved her hand a little so that it rested lightly on his. The marmot left its place on the flat boulder, came cautiously down to the stream to drink, and disappeared. The stars brightened very slowly over the Burggen ridges, to the west.

"Martin—" she said.

"Yes?"

"Talk to me."

"What's there to talk about?"

"About what you are thinking."

He turned and looked at her and seemed about to speak and turned away again.

"Delambre's dead," he said.

"Yes."

"Hein's dead."

"Yes."

"And Old Nick is washed up. And Andreas will never climb a

456

high mountain again." He paused a moment. "And do you know why?" he asked. "Because of me."

"That isn't true, Martin."

"Yes, it's true. And do you know what else is true? If it weren't for luck and Andreas' strength and guts, he and you and all of us would be dead too—and I'd have done it." Carla's hand tightened on his, and she seemed about to speak; but he went on talking, quietly and tonelessly. "And all for what? To climb a mountain. . . . And why climb a mountain? . . . Yes, that's the point, isn't it? Why? . . . You put one foot in front of the other. You drop one bomb after another. You climb or you fight or you build or you hope or you love, and it's all the same. At the end there's a blue X. At the end there's—nothing."

"You are quite certain you believe that?"

He did not answer.

"And that you are not just being sorry for yourself?"

"All right, I'm sorry for myself," he said. "I'm sorry for you and Andreas and Nick and Delambre and Hein. I'm sorry for three boys I used to know called Ted Riggs and Harry Wasniewicz and Jack Bixler. I'm sorry for everybody in the goddamned world."

He turned away, and they were silent again, watching the valley and the night. Presently Carla got up and went into the hut, and when she came out she was carrying two sweaters. "It is colder than on the way up," she said.

He nodded. "And there's a mist forming in the valley."

"Yes, I was noticing it before. Along the center there, above the Aarn." Her eyes moved up to the white ridges and the stars. "I think the weather is going to change tomorrow."

They put on the sweaters and sat side by side again in the still darkness.

"Carla—" he said.

"Yes?"

"More than anything else there's one thing I'm sorry for."

"Stop thinking about them."

"This isn't about them. It's about you. . . . That morning when I left you alone there in the tent; when I went off for the top without your knowing it—"

Carla shook her head slowly. "No, you are wrong," she said.

"Wrong?"

"I knew you were going, Martin."

Ordway looked at her in astonishment. "You knew? You were awake, you mean?"

"No, I was not awake when you went. But the night before—I knew then. Hein made it that way. He made a—well—a war out of it. And when I saw that he was going I knew that you would go too—either with him or after him."

"And you didn't even—"

"Try to stop you? No."

"Why not?"

"Because I wanted you to go. . . . Because you *had* to go." She paused, and he could feel her eyes watching him, gray and steady in the darkness. "Just as you had to try to climb the White Tower from the first day you came back to Kandermatt. Just as you have to leave Kandermatt tomorrow. . . ."

Ordway did not speak.

"Martin—"

"Yes?"

"That is what you have been thinking about, isn't it? That is what you were going to talk to Andreas about when you went to the door and almost called after him."

He hesitated. "I don't know," he said.

"Yes you do. And I do too. . . . You were going to tell him that you were not going, weren't you?"

"Yes."

"Why didn't you, then?"

"I couldn't."

"Of course you couldn't."

He looked at her, and her eyes held his for an instant, and then he looked away again.

"I've got to go back, Carla," he said.

"Of course you do. You've known it all along."

"All along? Yes, in a way—I suppose so." He paused, and when he spoke again it was in a voice so low that she could barely hear him. "And yet the strange thing is that I've realized it, fully and clearly, only since we started down the mountain. Since Hein and Delambre died. Since we tried and failed and came down to—" He hesitated and stopped.

"To go on trying."

458

Ordway closed his eyes. "Yes, I suppose so," he said. "To go back. To go on."

"Because you must."

He did not answer.

"And because you want to."

"Want to?" He reopened his eyes, and a bitter smile flickered for an instant on his lips.

"Yes—want to. You may not feel it now. You may not know it now. But it is true—and it is the important thing. That in your heart you do want to."

"And you?" he asked. "Doesn't it make any difference to you?"

"You know it does."

"But you don't want me to stay?"

"No."

"Why not?"

"Because of yourself—the kind of man you are. And also because—"

"Yes?"

A long moment passed before the girl spoke again. "Because I am not going to stay either," she said quietly.

Ordway stared at her. Then slowly his hand moved out and took her arm and held it tight. "What do you mean?" he asked. "What are you going to do?"

"I am going back to Austria, Martin."

"To Austria?"

"Yes."

"But—but you can't . . ."

"Yes, I can. It will not be easy, perhaps, but if I really want to and really try to I shall find a way. There are my friends in St. Gallen who will help me, and certain others still at home—"

"But Stefan. And the Nazis. You don't think they've forgotten what you did? They'll find you, and God knows what they'll do to you."

"No, they will not find me. Not if I am careful. It will probably be wiser if I do not go to Vienna—at least at first. Or to Linz either. But there are plenty of other places in Austria, and plenty of Austrians who are not Nazis."

"But where—how—" He groped, fumbling. "What would you do there?"

"What millions of men and women in Europe have been doing for five long years. Help where I can. Do what little I am able to end this thing sooner. It cannot last so much longer now. How long? Six months, perhaps. A year. But there is still so much to do before it is over . . . and so much more after."

As she spoke he had swung her slowly around, so that now she was facing him, half sitting and half kneeling. His hands, gripping her shoulders, pulled her toward him, and his eyes were dark and burning on her face.

"No," he said. "No!"

"I cannot stay in Kandermatt any longer, Martin."

"Come with me, then."

"That is impossible, and you know it."

"Nothing's impossible if you want it enough. If it matters enough."

He held her, tight and rigid, his fingers digging into the flesh of her shoulders.

"You are hurting me, Martin," she said gently.

He held her for another moment; then his grip relaxed slowly, and he let her go. She sat staring down into the distant valley, and when presently she spoke again it was without turning to look at him.

"No," she said, "it is a lovely dream—that we could go somewhere together. But it is only a dream, and you know it as well as I." He tried to interrupt, but she put her hand on his and continued in the same quiet tone: "You cannot come to Austria, and I cannot come where you are going. The people who are helping you would not help me. Even if they would, there is scarcely a chance of their getting me across the French border. And even if there were—what then? I would be interned; put into a camp somewhere as an enemy alien. They would not let me be with you. They would not even let me help in some way or do anything. It would be worse than Kandermatt; purposeless, hopeless. . . ."

She stopped and turned and looked at him, but he was sitting motionless beside her with his eyes on the ground. "Martin—" she said.

He did not answer.

"Martin."

He raised his head and looked at her.

"You know that what I am saying is true."

"I'm going to lose you again," he said.

"Yes, you are. You are going to lose me again, and we are going to lose each other again, because that is the way the world is. But the war will not last forever. Almost forever, maybe—sometimes it will seem like forever—but not forever. And at least we will be losing each other the right way, so that, when it is over and we have found each other again, there will be something left to find."

"Finding each other." His voice was a low, bitter whisper. "It sounds easy, doesn't it?"

"No, it does not sound easy. But for us, strangely enough, it will be."

"How? Where?"

"Where we found each other the first time. And the second."

There was a long silence between them. Ordway's eyes moved slowly downward across the little hollow to the boulders below and from the boulders to the long bands of starlit rock, and from the rock to the slanting forests and the pastures and the remote lights on the valley floor. Half the lights they had seen before were gone now, and the rest showed yellow and dim through the thickening ground-mist. On the opposite slope of the valley he could see the whitish billows of vapor creeping slowly upward against the dark backdrop of the trees.

"I don't understand," he said quietly.

"Yes you do, Martin."

"When did you decide all this?"

"While we were on the mountain. While we were climbing, waiting, talking."

"After the—accidents?"

"After them; before them; I don't know. It was not a question of deciding, really, but simply of finding the strength to do what I have known all along I should do. Ever since I came to Kandermatt; since I ran away . . ."

Ordway turned again and looked at her, but did not speak.

"Martin—" she said presently.

"Yes?"

"Why did we want to climb the White Tower? Why have we always wanted to climb it?"

"I don't know," he said.

461

"Yes, you do. Think back. Remember."

He smiled a little. "Because it's there, I suppose."

"Of course—just as old Nick used to tell us—because it is there. . . . And why have you fought so long in this war? And why are you going back now to fight it again? And why am I going? For the same reason. Because it is there. . . . Oh, can't you see, Martin?—that is the whole answer, the whole meaning. *Because things are there.* A mountain, a war, an idea, a song, a friend, everything. Because they are part of us and we are part of them.

"Do you think I do not know how you feel now?" she went on. "Do you think I do not feel the same myself? It is heartbreaking, what has happened on our mountain and what is going to happen to us tomorrow. It is heartbreaking what happens day after day in the world. . . . All right, our hearts are broken. They are broken, but they go on beating. They go on hoping and wanting and caring. . . . That is what I know now, Martin—what I have learned on our White Tower. And you know it as well as I, because it is you and our loving each other that have taught it to me. The terrible mistake is to pretend that we have no hearts; that we no longer hope nor want nor care. That is what I did for four long years, but I am not going to do it again, and you are not going to do it either.

"Tomorrow you are going back into the war. And in a few days, in some way, I shall go back too. Not because we are forced to; not because we are beaten; but because it matters to us. And when it is over we will come back here, to each other, to our valley and our mountain—yes, we will, Martin, we will, I know it, because that also matters—" Her voice broke suddenly, and her head dropped slowly forward until it rested on his chest. "We matter. . . ."

There was the stillness and the darkness and the whitish mist creeping up through the darkness along the valley walls below. There was the hut and the darkness and the smell of juniper and the dry straw of the mattresses and the firelight slowly flickering into darkness against the sloping shingles of the roof. There was only darkness. A man and a woman in the darkness.

He awoke in the night and went quietly to the door and opened it. The valley and the lights of the valley were gone, and the mountainside below fell away into a deep well of mist. But the sky was still clear, the stars still bright and sharp, and the rock and ice and snow above them tiered away, blue-white and gleaming, into the miles of the night. Turning presently, his eyes moved slowly upward: along the glaciers and snow-slopes and scree-slopes —up the buttresses and ridges and precipices—past the summits of the Karlsberg and the Rotalp—past the Graf and the Gräfin and the Himmelshorn—past the Dornelberg and the Wunderhorn —farther and farther, higher and higher. . . .

"It is still there," Carla's voice said quietly in the darkness behind him.

"Yes—it's still there."

He turned and closed the door.

"Martin—" she said.

"Yes?"

"I am still here too."

Chapter 24

H e sat on the bed in the little room in the *Gasthof* and looked at the yellow-flowered wallpaper and the iron bedstead and the porcelain bowl and pitcher on the washstand and the window with its tied-back white net curtains. Beyond the window were the branches of a tree, and beyond the branches mist.

On the chair in the corner was the same clothing he had found there when he had first awakened in that same room, three weeks before. There was no sign of his own flying clothes, but on the bedspread beside him was a neat little pile of articles that had been taken from them: a comb, a flattened pack of cigarettes, a few French coins and bills, his army identification papers, his silver captain's bars. Picking up the bars, he sat turning them slowly between his fingers.

There was a knock on the door, and Herr Knubel came in.

"You are feeling all right now?" he asked.

"Yes, I'm all right."

"The snow-blindness, it is not bothering you any more?"

"Not right now. I don't know how it will be in the sun, though."

"Sometimes it takes a few days, of course. But at least you will not have to worry about the sun today." Herr Knubel pulled vigorously at his nose, and his sharp eyes moved quickly about the room. "You have everything necessary, yes? It is impossible, of course, that you wear your own clothing—that will stay here.

These other things that you have used before, they will do again."

"But Madame—"

"It is perfectly agreeable to Madame Delambre that you wear them."

Ordway started to speak, stopped himself, and sat silently looking at the worsted trousers, tan sweater and maroon sport shirt with the embroidered P. D. on the pocket that lay spread on the chair in the corner.

Herr Knubel had pulled a big gold watch from his vest. "It is now ten past three," he announced briskly. "A car will be here in twenty minutes, and you will be in the village in time for the afternoon train at four. From Kandermatt to Interlaken is two hours and a quarter. There another car will meet you and take you on to the place where you are going. The plane will take off as soon as it is dark."

Ordway came back to him from his thoughts. "The plane?" he repeated.

"Yes, that is how it has been arranged."

"But I'd expected—"

The innkeeper shrugged. "Sometimes it is by train or truck or bicycle or even on foot. Sometimes it is by plane. The plane is best, of course, when it can be arranged."

"But how can they—" He broke off again. The hell with it, he thought. Do what you're told to do and never mind the questions.

"Yes, of course," he said. "It sounds fine."

Herr Knubel looked around the room and pulled at his nose again. "Just leave your climbing clothes here and we will take care of them later," he said. "Is there perhaps something else I can do for you?"

"Thanks—I don't think so."

"And I shall expect you downstairs in fifteen minutes, yes?"

"I'll be there," said Ordway.

When the innkeeper had gone he undressed quickly, washed and combed his hair; then he stood looking at his reflection in the wall mirror above the washstand. His first impression was that he was seeing a figure in mask and gloves. The flesh of his chest, shoulders and arms was a smooth, almost startling, white, but the whiteness ended in abrupt lines at the wrists and neck and beyond

465

the lines his face and hands were burned to a deep reddish-brown. The face was thinner than it had been, too, and the contours of its bones showed clearly under the skin of cheeks and jaw. His nose was roughened and peeling, his lips cracked and gray. His eyes, deep-socketed and with fine white lines radiating from the corners, were curiously blurred and lustreless, and as he leaned closer to the mirror he saw that the pupils had shrunk to the merest black motes.

Well, at least the pain was gone, he thought.

For an instant he felt the impulse to laugh. Then he turned away, dressed quickly in the clothes that were waiting for him and put his handful of possessions in one pocket. He glanced at his watch. It was twenty past three. He crossed to the door, turned and looked around the room. Had he forgotten anything? No, there was nothing to forget. There was only the yellow-flowered wall paper, the white iron bed, the washstand and chairs, the long wavering crack in the ceiling that looked like the Channel coast of France. . . . This isn't the way you should leave here, he thought. By a door, a flight of stairs, a car, a train, a plane. You should leave the same way you came. You should lie down on the bed and sleep. Sleep and dream again. Awake and dream again. . . . He went out, closing the door behind him.

He walked down the hall to the stair landing, but did not go down the stairs. Instead, he continued along the hall to a door at the far end, stopped in front of it for a moment and knocked.

"Entrez," said a woman's voice.

He opened the door and entered the Delambres' room. Paintings and rows of books gleamed around him on the walls. Astrid Delambre lay on the chaise by the window, knitting.

"I—I hope you don't mind," he said hesitantly in French.

Madame Delambre put her yarn and needles carefully on her lap and looked at him with placid violet eyes. She was wearing a negligee of crimson silk that heightened the whiteness of her arms and throat, and the golden coils of her hair glowed richly in the gray, fog-filtered light.

She shook her head slowly, without speaking.

"I'm leaving now," Ordway said. "I wanted to say good-bye—and thank you."

"Thank me? For what, monsieur?"

466

"For these, for one thing." He looked down at the clothes he was wearing.

"It is nothing. He would have wanted you to have them."

There was a brief silence.

"I also want you to know how terribly—" he fumbled for the word "—faché—" He stopped, looking past her at the window. It was bad enough to be fatuous in English, he thought grimly. Now he had to be fatuous in French.

"I can't tell you what I feel, madame," he said.

The woman looked at him with her cool violet eyes. "There is no need for you to," she said quietly. "I know what you are think-ing—that you are in a way responsible for what has happened. But you are wrong. You are not responsible. Believe me when I say that."

"It is kind of you."

"I am not speaking kindness. I am speaking the truth."

"Still, if it hadn't been for me—"

"If it had not been for you, Captain Ordway?" Astrid Delambre shrugged her white shoulders. "If it had not been for so many things. I have been his wife for eight years, and always it has been the same. What it was he wanted, what it was he needed, I do not know. I do not think that he knew himself. But always he was reaching for it, searching for it: in his books and pictures; in cities and islands and oceans; in the war; in cognac; in his own mind; in my body. . . . And now, finally, in you and this great white mountain of yours."

"He was a brilliant and remarkable man."

"Brilliant? Remarkable? Perhaps. But most of all he was an unhappy man—a weak, lonely, unhappy man. No, do not blame yourself for what happened, monsieur. It is better this way."

She turned her head a little and sat staring at the window and the fog beyond. "What is the use in talking about it?" she said quietly.

There was another silence.

"And you?" Ordway asked.

"I?"

"You will stay here in Kandermatt?"

"For a few days. There is a possibility, I suppose, that there will be some sort of investigation, and in any case Herr Knubel says there will be certain formalities with the authorities. Afterwards—" she shrugged again— "I have not yet decided where I shall go. Zurich, perhaps. Or Vienna. Or Madrid. It does not greatly matter. As a Swedish subject, you see, I am freer than most."

"You have—everything you need, then?"

"Money, you mean? Oh yes, monsieur—my husband was a wealthy man. The Germans have taken much, of course, and the lawyers and tax-collectors and the rest will take more; but there will be enough remaining, I am sure, and my wants are quite simple." She paused, and for an instant in the uncertain light it almost seemed to him that her violet eyes were smiling at him. "It is good of you," she said, "but you must not worry about me, really. I promise you that I shall get along."

Ordway nodded, and his eyes moved slowly from her face to the rich golden coils of her hair, and from her hair to the white flesh of her throat and shoulders and the lush silk-sheathed contours of her body. He started to speak, but stopped himself, because he realized suddenly that there was nothing to say. And there was nothing to say because she had spoken the simple truth. Yes, he thought, a little wryly, a little bitterly: she would get along. Come hell or high water, war or revolution, Armageddon or the Day of Judgment—as long as there were Empire chaises and Lanvin negligees and Chanel No. 5 and lonely woman-hungry men on the face of the earth, the Astrid Delambres of the world would get by.

He crossed to her and took her hand.

"You are a very intelligent woman," he said.

She shook her head. "Merely a practical woman."

"Good-bye."

"Good-bye, mon capitaine." The cool violet eyes seemed to be smiling again. "I hope that some day you reach the top of your White Tower."

She took the knitting from her lap, and he turned away. As he closed the door behind him he could hear the soft clicking of her needles in the quiet room.

In the hall outside he stopped and looked at his watch. It was twenty-five past three. Continuing down the hall, he came to the stairs and began descending them; but halfway down he stopped again. For a long moment he stood still, staring down at the deep, discolored gouge which his hand had touched on the smooth bannister railing.

No, his mind said. Don't think about her. Think about her later. Later, later, later, his mind said. . . .

But in the same instant his thoughts ripped like a savage blade through the numbness that enveloped him. Yes, that's fine, he told himself. Fine and dandy. There's only one small trouble with it, and that is that there isn't any later. Later is now . . . and you might as well start thinking about her right now, because she's all you're damn well going to be thinking about through the days and the nights and the months and the years.

It can't last forever, she had said. Germany was cracking, crumbling. . . . Sure. But after Germany there was still the Japs. After Germany they'd send you to New Guinea or Luzon or Kunming or Myitkyina or the lovely primeval and well-bulldozed island of Whachimacalla. No, the war wasn't going to last forever, but it was going to give a pretty damn good imitation before it was through. The Five Years' War. The Seven Years' War. The Hundred Years' War. The dirty rotten bloody sonofabitching war.

Carla, Carla, Carla, he thought. . . .

He stood motionless with his hand on the bannister railing, and the knuckles showed white through the cracked red flesh. He closed his eyes and fought back the slow, hot tide that seemed suddenly to be rising within him, choking him, blinding him. Never mind the Pagliacci, he thought savagely. Never mind the Hamlet. There's a war to fight—understand? There's a train to catch, a car to be ready for, a flight of stairs to go down.

He went down the stairs and entered the lounge.

Radcliffe was sitting in a corner of the couch, one long leg crooked over the other, reading the *Illustrierte Zeitung*. Andreas Benner, in a blue serge suit, sat massively upright on a chair nearby, both feet on the floor, both hands on his knees. On the far side of the room, near the curtained French windows, stood Carla. She was wearing a dark-green, formally tailored skirt and jacket and high-heeled shoes, and on the floor near her feet stood two small cream-colored suitcases.

Ordway stopped, staring at her.

"I am going down with you," she said, smiling a little.

"Down?"

"To where you get the plane. Andreas says it will be all right. Then I will go on to Lucerne and St. Gallen."

"You're leaving—for good, then?"

"There is no point in my staying here longer. With only one guest Frau Knubel will not need me. By tomorrow afternoon I can be with the people I know in St. Gallen, and they can begin making the arrangements." She came toward him across the room. "It is the most sensible thing, don't you think?"

He nodded. "Yes, of course. Yes—"

But he scarcely heard his own words. As she came toward him he stood quite still, looking at her: at the soft curling copper of her hair; at her face, brown and smiling above the whiteness of her shirtwaist, at her trim green suit, her long slim legs, the black high-heeled pumps. You've never seen her in high heels before, he thought.

It's not the end yet—not quite yet—he thought. . . .

Radcliffe unfolded his long legs and laid the *Illustrierte Zeitung* on the table. There was the sound of wheels on the gravel of the driveway outside.

There was the bare hardwood floor of the foyer and the dining-room beyond it and the wide plate-glass window and mist. There was the verandah and more mist and an old Chevrolet sedan and a thin man with a red, drooping moustache at the wheel. There was Andreas Benner putting Carla's bags on the rear seat and Frau Knubel telling him to put them somewhere else, and then Frau Knubel crying and Herr Knubel tugging at his nose and Anna-marie peering from the foyer window and giggling.

"I can't tell you," Ordway began—

All right, he couldn't tell them.

"Good-bye," he said.

"Finish off the blighters," said Radcliffe.

"Don't worry."

"And soon."

"Yes, soon."

"You are coming to the station with us, *Herr Doktor?*" Benner asked.

"No, I think not," said Radcliffe. "No use crowding things. And besides"—a smile touched the tired blue of his eyes—"Mrs. Meach

470

is baking fresh scones for tea this afternoon and has issued specific orders that I report for duty at five o'clock sharp."

Carla put her arms around him. "Wait for us," she said.

"Yes."

"And practice your scales every day."

"Yes."

"And the next time we sit on the verandah steps together you will play Debussy's *Fantôches* without a single mistake."

"Never can tell," said Radcliffe.

And now there was Benner in the front seat beside the driver, and himself in the rear seat beside Carla, and the mist condensing into crooked gray rivulets on the car windows, and the three mist-blurred figures on the verandah steps, waving. The car ground across the gravelled terrace and onto the dirt road that twisted steeply down the knoll. The figures disappeared. The verandah and the terrace disappeared. The pointed white gables disappeared. When he turned from the window Carla was sitting very still and erect on the seat beside him, staring at the back of the driver's neck.

They reached the bottom of the knoll, crossed the narrow wooden bridge and gained speed along the level valley road.

"When we are at the station," said Benner, turning his head, "I will buy the tickets and make any other necessary arrangements. Also, when we are on the train, Herr Martin, I think it will be wiser if you do not speak in English."

Ordway nodded.

"Just a precaution, you understand. There is really nothing for you to worry about."

"I'm not worrying," Ordway said.

The empty fields rolled by them, dark green and gleaming with moisture. A black-and-white dog limping along the roadside stopped and barked as they went by. A little farther on they passed a boy on a bicycle and beyond him two or three farmers' carts, loaded with hay. Then, in quick succession, there were barnyards, farmhouses, a cobbled street, the village. The neat dormered houses were identically the same as when Martin Ordway had last seen them, twelve years before; but only a few scattered villagers were about, and the shop windows, once filled with boots, ropes, cuckoo

471

clocks, woodcarvings and great mounds of chocolate, were either gapingly empty or shuttered tight.

"The young ones are in the army," said Benner, "and the old ones on the farms. Besides, without the *Turisten* . . ."

Ordway's eyes moved over the few passers-by, searching out Christian Mehrwalder, Peter Zürneisen or one of the Kronig brothers; but he could not find anyone he knew. Presently the car crossed the square, under the beech trees, and stopped in front of the rust-colored frame station. The driver lifted out Carla's bags, shook hands expressionlessly, first with Carla and then with Ordway. "*Glückliche Reise,*" he said to each of them. Then he got back in the car and drove away.

They waited outside while Benner went into the ticket office. "It is five minutes of four," he said when he returned. "We can go aboard now."

The train, standing on the single track beside a rickety wooden platform, consisted only of two third-class coaches and a baggage car. Entering the forward coach, they sat down on the straight-backed wooden benches, Ordway and Carla next to the window, facing each other, and Benner on the aisle, next to Carla. There were perhaps twenty other persons in the car, all of them farm people except for a solitary trooper of the canton police who was lounging, half-asleep, on a bench at the far end of the car.

"Do not bother about him," Benner said in German, "and he will not bother about you. But remember not to speak in English."

A few more farmers entered the car, stowed their baskets and hampers and sat down. A conductor came down the aisle and disappeared into the rear coach. Then the train started. The rickety platform slid slowly past, and at its further end a rectangular green-lettered sign reading: KANDERMATT. The mist clung in gray beads to the windows. Beneath them the wheels clacked dully against the rails.

The train wound down the narrow valley of the Aarn. For perhaps two-thirds of the time its path lay through the green meadows, close beside the river; then, at intervals, the valley walls shouldered in above it, and it plunged through long tunnels, tooting wildly in the darkness. Every ten or fifteen minutes it stopped, creaking, at a village station, and some of the passengers got off and others got on. Then it clacked on again. For a while the mist lifted, revealing a patch of blue sky and the glint of snowfields high up on a mountainside. Then it closed in once more. A thin rain began to fall.

Benner dozed, his arms folded on his chest and his brown face relaxed into a hundred heavy creases. Carla, who had been sitting motionlessly looking out the window, turned, and her eyes met Ordway's.

"Carla," he said.

She put her finger to her lips.

" 'Carla' isn't English," he said in German.

She smiled.

"It's Esperanto. Like 'Mairzy Doats.' "

Her smile deepened. For another moment their eyes held each other. Then they broke away.

Carla, he said again, in his mind. . . . Carla, Carla. . . . What else was there to say, he thought. What in God's name was there to say—in English, German, Esperanto, Tagalog, Sanskrit? Nothing: that's what there was. Nothing to say. Nothing to do.

She was staring through the window again, and he sat looking at her—at the line of her throat and the gleaming of her hair and the soft brownness of her skin—until he could bear looking no longer and turned away. His eyes moved slowly down the aisle of the coach, past the farmers and the farmers' wives and the baskets and the hampers, and rested on the policeman on the bench at the far end.

You know damn well what you can do, he thought. You can stand up right now and walk down the aisle and tap the Law on the shoulder and introduce yourself as Captain-Martin-Ordway-at-your-service-suh of the U. S. Army Air Forces. You can get yourself pinched, that's what you can do. You can get yourself interned and spend the rest of the war in one of those picturebook resort-hotels of theirs, catching up on your food and sleep, brushing up on your skiing and maybe even learning to yodel. And Carla will live in the village just down the hill from the hotel—and they'll let her come up to see you every day—and they'll let you go down to see her every night—and you'll ski together, and laugh together, and be together. . . .

Yes, of course, he thought. That's all you have to do. Stand up. Walk down the aisle. It's as simple as that.

473

As impossible as that.

It had stopped raining, and the mist seemed to be lifting a little. The valley was slowly opening out into a plain. The train stopped at still another village, larger than those before, and the trooper and several more farmers got out. Then it bore off to the east, along the shore of a large, slate-colored lake.

Benner opened his eyes and peered from the window. "Die Thuner See," he said. After a few minutes he stood up stiffly and lifted Carla's bags from the rack.

Then they were on a station platform again. They were standing silently and inconspicuously against the station wall beside the baggage room, and Benner was talking with the man who had driven up beside them in another old Chevrolet sedan. They were in the car, with Benner in the front seat beside the driver and himself and Carla and Carla's bags in the rear. The lights of Interlaken were fading away behind them in the mist-filled dusk.

He listened to the tires humming on the wet tarmac of the road. He listened to the soft ticking of the watch on his wrist. . . . You can talk now, he thought. You can talk in English or German or Esperanto or any damn language you want. . . . Only you didn't talk. You didn't talk, because there was nothing to say. Because your watch was ticking too loudly on your wrist.

He turned and watched Carla's face, softly outlined against the window and the dusk beyond. Look at her, he thought. Look at her sitting there, quiet and lovely—as calm and quiet and lovely as if we were driving out to a Saturday night dance at a country club. No bellyaching. No listening to watches. Just sitting there, taking it. And you're the one that's going to the country club, compared to where she's going. You're going back to the greatest air force of the greatest nation in the world. You're going back to a job, friends, silver bars, decent food, decent people, strength, hope, victory. . . . And she? . . . Nowhere—that's where she's going. Hell—that's where. To bombed cities and broken lives. To a furtive hole-in-the-wall rat-race in the shadow of the jailer and the hangman. To defeat. To despair. To an alien, evil, hopeless world that will be all the more dangerous and terrible for her because it was once home.

All right, he said to himself—that's how it is. And if she can take it you'd damn well better learn how to take it too. Turning away

474

again, he looked out the window on his side of the car. There were only a few farmhouses, wet fields, twilight, mist. We must be getting near the country club, he thought.

He felt very calm now—very cool and drained and empty, like an engine that had gone dead or a well that had gone dry. The car swung off the tarmac onto a dirt road, and now there were trees on either side of them. He reached out and took Carla's hand and held it in his own.

All right, he thought—this is the way it is. War is the way it is —good-bye is the way it is—wanting-and-not-getting is the way it is. What you're trying to say is that the world is a stinking place. You're damn right it's a stinking place. But the crazy thing about it is that it's a fine place too. A world with Carla in it is a fine place. A world with Andreas and old Nick in it is a fine place. A world with Shakespeare and Beethoven and Abraham Lincoln and the Manhattan skyline and Long Island Sound in the summer sun and hot-coffee-in-the-morning and home-runs-with-the-bases-full and the Grimbacks' garage and the White Tower in it—that is a fine place too, and worth fighting for and dying for.

. . . And living for. . . .

You believed that. You had always believed it and you always would. But sometimes you get tired. Sometimes you forgot. . . .

That was the big thing, of course. Not to get tired. Not to forget. It was the one real thing your life thus far had taught you —the one great truth that rose up like a gigantic pillar out of the lies and evil and corruption of the earth. To want and to seek— never the one without the other—that is the Law. It's not where you seek that matters: in the roaring of a plane's engine; in a blue-print on a drafting table; in the eyes of a girl beside you; on a mountaintop rising white and shining into the sky. It's not finding that matters, because you never will. The thing you are looking for is nameless and boundless. You will never find it, never possess it. But it exists. It is real. It is the stuff your very life is made of. It is there. . . .

He held Carla's hand lightly in his own. He turned and looked at her, and she smiled at him. The car slowed and stopped.

There was a grove of trees and a low shed-like structure and beyond the shed and the trees an open field. A man came out of the shed and approached the car, and Benner got out, and the two

475

spoke together briefly. Then the man came over and shook hands with Ordway.

"It will be only a few minutes," he said.

Ordway and Carla got out of the car and stood under the trees outside the shed while Benner and the man went inside. Beyond the interlacing branches the dark gray of the sky was deepening quickly into blackness.

"The fog is not too bad now," Carla said.

"No," said Ordway. "It's not too bad."

After about ten minutes Benner and the man reappeared, and the latter stopped for an instant, squinting at the sky.

"All right, now," he said.

They came out from under the trees onto the field, and there before them was an expanse of smooth grass, and beyond the grass more trees, and against the trees, in the far corner of the field, the dark outline of a plane. As they walked toward it their shoes made a soft sucking sound in the wet turf.

"The pilot is a good one," the man said.

Ordway nodded.

"He has flown much before and knows how these things are done. It is not likely that he will be able to take you to one of your own army fields, but it will at least be among friendly people. You must of course allow him to use his own judgment in all matters."

"Of course."

They had approached close to the plane now, and Ordway saw that it was a light open-cockpit two-seater, of a design unfamiliar to him but not unlike a Stinson trainer or a Piper Cub. The single engine was idling in a soft drone.

"You will find a helmet, glasses and jacket on the seat," the man said.

The shoulders and helmeted head of the pilot showed in the forward cockpit. He raised a gloved hand in greeting as they came up to the plane, but did not speak. They stopped, and there was a short silence, and Ordway looked at the man beside him.

The man nodded.

"I hardly know how to—"

The other made a deprecating gesture. "It is nothing. Some can

476

do one thing, some another." He shook hands briefly. "*Glückliche Reise, Herr Kapitän.*"

Ordway turned to Benner. In the darkness he could just see the square brown face, the short gingery moustache, the blue eyes. He felt the pressure of a thick hard hand against his own.

I don't know how to tell you either, Andreas, he thought. . . .

"Watch that arthritis," he said.

"*Ja, Herr Martin.*"

"And keep your boots oiled."

"*Ja.*"

"Because next time—"

"*Ja,* next time—"

The hand was gone. The brown, seamed face was gone. There was only the dark damp-glistening grass and the long wing of the plane and the soft humming of the plane's engine. There was only a girl standing, slender and still, beside him.

Quick now, he thought.

He turned without speaking, and Carla did not speak either. Then he bent and kissed her. He kissed her and drew her close and held her close, and she was there—her eyes, her mouth, her hair, her body were there—softness and brightness were there—and the snow and the wind and the sunlight were there—and yesterday and today and tomorrow and all of time and all of wanting and all of living, they were all there—everything-there-was was there.

Because next time, he thought—

Because next time . . .

And now Carla was gone too. Everything was gone. There was only the swelling drone, the trembling wing, the cool hissing tide of the slipstream as he clambered into the cockpit. He was putting on the jacket and helmet that were on the seat. The pilot's goggled face was turned toward him, and then away again. The black oblong of the wing was moving slowly against the grass; a little less slowly against the grass; faster and faster against the grass. Beyond it there were three figures in the darkness . . . one figure in the darkness . . . darkness.

In the darkness he felt the plane take off, climb, bank, climb again. He felt the still earth wheeling away beneath and heard the moaning of the air against the wing struts and the humming of the engine. The humming seemed to him to be growing deeper, louder. . . . It can't be, his mind told him. It's only a single light cruiser engine, a sixty-horsepower job at most. . . . No, it couldn't be. But it was. As he sat now in the trembling cockpit, his body motionless and his eyes closed, the sound of it beat back upon him like a great wave, deepening and swelling, until the steel thunder of its roaring seemed to fill his very bones and blood and brain.

She is gone, he thought. They are all gone. Carla, Andreas, Radcliffe, Delambre, Hein. The inn, the Aarn, the forests, the huts. The glaciers, the ice-walls, the rock-walls, the ridges. The still white shape tiering pure and shining above them into the sky. Everyone and everything was gone—gone, vanished and dissolved behind the ranges and the miles and the years. He had lost them. He had never had them. They had never been. In a moment now he would open his eyes again and begin his life again where he had left it off. He would reach out his hand and take the wheel, and they would be coming in, swift and black and roaring, over the great lake of orange fire. . . . Ready, Ted? Ready, Harry? Ready, Bix?

He opened his eyes. He looked downward.

Beneath them, half-visible through the veils of mist, the earth slipped past—black, featureless and still. Before them, beyond the helmeted head of the pilot and the blurred whirl of the propeller, there were only darkness and gray banks of vapor streaming away, depth upon depth, into the miles of the night. His eyes moved upward. Darkness. . . . To the right. Darkness. . . . To the left. . . . He turned and sat staring into the darkness; at the nothingness that filled the darkness; at the nothingness beyond the darkness; at the thing that, as he stared, seemed very slowly to be taking shape before him out of the nothingness and the night. . . . And yes, he thought suddenly: yes, it is the same again. The mist parting, the darkness thinning, the gleaming and the whiteness behind them. Ted—Harry—Bix! Here we are again. It's the end again. The end and the beginning. . . . In another moment now darkness would close in. The plane would shudder, lurch, begin to fall. . . .

But the plane did not fall. The darkness did not close in. Moment by moment the white gleaming brightened. Moment by moment the night and the mist thinned, and the thing that they

478

had hidden emerged from the emptiness beyond. Martin Ordway sat motionless. The roaring of the engine filled his ears, but he did not hear it. The tides of the wind passed over him, but he did not feel them. . . . For now, before his straining eyes, a range of mountains seemed to be rising like a great white wave out of the miles and the night. A range of mountains, and at its core, immense and alone, a single, unforgettable shape. . . .

It is an illusion, he thought. A trick of your eyes, or of the mist.

But it was not illusion. The mist swirled over it, but it did not vanish. The night encompassed it, but it did not fade. Vast, still and immutable, the White Tower rose out of the darkness of the earth into the darkness of the sky. It was a fact. It existed.

It was there.

He turned away. Before him now were only the helmeted head of the pilot and the faintly glowing dials of the instrument panel. The little plane bored westward through the night.

had hidden emerged from the emptiness beyond. Martin Ordway sat motionless. The roaring of the engine filled his ears, but he did not hear it. The tides of the wind passed over him, but he did not feel them. . . . For now, below his straining eyes, a range of mountains seemed to be rising like a great white wave out of the miles and the night. A range of mountains, and at its core, immense and alone, a single, unforgettable shape. . . .

It is an illusion, he thought. A trick of your eyes, or of the mist. But it was not illusion. The mist swirled over it, but it did not vanish. The night encompassed it, but it did not fade. Vast, still and inimitable, the White Tower rose out of the darkness of the earth into the darkness of the sky. It was a fact; it existed. It was there.

He turned away. Before him now were only the helmeted head of the pilot and the faintly glowing dials of the instrument panel. The little plane bored westward through the night.